Praise for
Susan Crandall

DISCARD

Promises To Keep

"FOUR STARS! Crandall once again tells a heartwarming story of the Boudreau family."

—*Romantic Times BOOKclub Magazine*

"Touching, well-written."

—FreshFiction.com

"An appealing heroine . . . [an] unexpected plot twist . . . engaging and entertaining."

—The Romance Reader.com

"Heartw . . . Crandall deftly takes up where she left off in *Th* . . .

—Booklist

"Another . . . story by Susan Crandall."

—RomanceReviewsMag.com

"This is one book you will want to keep to read repeatedly."

—MyShelf.com

more . . .

On Blue Falls Pond

BOOKS BY SUSAN CRANDALL

On Blue Falls Pond

Promises to Keep

Magnolia Sky

The Road Home

Back Roads

On Blue Falls Pond

SUSAN CRANDALL

Warner Forever and logo are registered trademarks of Time Warner Book Group, Inc.

Cover design by Diane Luger
Cover illustration by Alan Ayers
Typography by Ron Zinn
Book design by Stratford Publishing Services

Warner Books

Time Warner Book Group
1271 Avenue of the Americas
New York, NY 10020
Visit our Web site at www.twbookmark.com

Printed in the United States of America

First Paperback Printing: January 2006

10 9 8 7 6 5 4 3 2 1

*In loving memory of my dad, Vic Zinn,
who, as a youth, scorned school and still managed to
hold passion for books.*

Acknowledgments

THROUGHOUT MY EXTENSIVE research into macular degeneration, autism, and service dogs, I came to know and respect a whole new world. I'd like to thank all those who shared their experiences and expertise with me as I wrote this book. As always, any errors or variances for fictitious purposes are my own.

I appreciate the patience of those in the MD Forum who answered my countless questions about coping with macular degeneration, especially Dan Brown, Jan Hancock, and Kathy Grant.

Thanks to my friends at NINC Link who shared their knowledge about autism and its treatments: Jeane Weston, Kelly McClymer, and Sabrina Jefferies.

My greatest understanding came from discussing the reality of raising a child with autism with their loving parents. Thanks to Janna Bullough and Joanne Markis for all their stories and insight. I stand in awe of these families.

Thanks to Dr. Mona Gitter for helping me with my research on service dogs (and for being such a great vet for all of my critters!).

And, as always, thanks to Indy WITTS, the greatest support and critique group in the universe: Alicia, Brenda, Garthia, Pam, and Sherry. And to Karen White, who has been with me since the beginning.

Prologue

❀

Granny Tula insisted with all of her Jesus-loving heart that God's hand was in everything. She held the deep conviction that, although it might not be readily seen, there was a divine reason for all that transpired in His earthly kingdom; even the terrible derailment of Glory's life. But Glory Harrison didn't possess her grandmother's unwavering faith. Glory had spent the past eighteen months on the run and had never once seen a glimmer of God's hand in any of it.

Tragedy, a dark and unexpected assailant, had robbed her of her home, her husband, and her unborn child. Drowning in grief, Glory had fled Tennessee. Small towns could be a comfort during times of disaster and misery—but they could also hold your heart forever in that place of loss. The piteous looks and well-meant platitudes were going to do just that, keep her heart a bloody mess that would never heal.

Granny had never understood Glory's need to leave. Luckily, Granny did not hold that incomprehensible need against her. She might not understand Glory's choice, but kin was kin—and that meant she would hold on to you no matter how far from the hollow you roamed. More than once, Gran had said, this family tree was oak, not poplar; and its roots went deep into the bedrock of eastern Tennessee soil. She lived her life by a simple rule: In the face of adversity you raised your chin, stiffened your back, held on to your faith, and marched forward on the very path that had become littered with your broken dreams. Certainly, Granny had trod on the splinters of her own life often enough. But Glory had not been able to force her feet to crush the fragile remains of who she used to be. So she left it all behind and tried to reinvent herself.

Unfortunately, new Glory bore the same heavy sadness as old Glory, just in different climates. It had become clear that no matter how far she ran, the pain, deep and cold and fathomless, would follow her like a shadow. Sooner or later, she realized, you have to either accustom yourself to its presence or stay forever hiding in the dark.

The time was fast coming to step into the light.

Chapter One

❀

GLORY'S KEY STUCK in the old lock on her apartment door, refusing to turn; refusing to slide back out. She gritted her teeth, gripped the doorknob, and shook until the door rattled on its hinges, fully aware that her response was overreaction in the extreme. This lock had recently become an unwelcome symbol of her life: stymied in a dull and disconnected present, unable to move toward her future. She knew it was wrong, this hiding, this pretense of living. But she'd buried herself here and couldn't find a way to claw back out.

Taking a deep breath, she tried to use more delicate force against the lock. Her nerves had been raw and on edge all day long. Her job at the veterinary clinic normally had a soothing effect upon her, allowing her to focus on something outside her own aching hollowness. But today she couldn't shake a nagging feeling that something was wrong. It was an insidious awareness that she just couldn't quell. Maybe it was simply her own growing understanding that she was running from the inescapable. But it seemed heavier than that; she was anxious to get inside and call Granny, just to ease her mind that the feeling had nothing to do with her.

For all of her life, Glory had had an inexplicable connection to her grandmother. Time and again she'd call and Gran would say, "I was just about to call you." Glory didn't share that mysterious connection with anyone else. When she was young, Granny would wink and lean close, saying they came from a long line of spooky women. Back then it had made Glory think of witches and spells. But now she understood; there were some people who were knit more tightly together than just by family genetics.

The telephone began to ring inside the apartment.

Glory jiggled the key with renewed vigor. Finally, on the telephone's fourth ring, the key turned, and she hurried inside.

"Hello," she said breathlessly as she snatched up the phone.

"Glory, darlin', are you all right?"

Granny's slow Tennessee drawl immediately soothed Glory's nerves.

"Fine, I was just coming in and had trouble with the lock." She pushed her hair away from her face. "You've been on my mind today, Gran. How are you?"

There was a half-beat pause that set the back of Glory's neck to tingling before Granny said, "Fine. Busy. Had Charlie's boys here for the weekend."

"All of them?" Glory's cousin Charlie was getting a divorce and had taken to foisting his five little hellions off on Granny when it was "his weekend." It really burned Glory, his taking advantage like that. Granny was seventy-three, and five boys under the age of thirteen was just too much.

" 'Course. We had a great time. Hiked back to the falls. They can't get enough swimming. Travis caught hisself a snake."

Glory closed her eyes and drew a breath. The very idea of Granny alone with five rambunctious little boys—swimming, no less—a two-mile hike from help made her stomach turn. Blue Falls could have a wicked pull at the base.

"Everyone all right?" Glory tempered her question; Granny's feathers got ruffled if you treated her like an old person—overprotection was a sin not to be forgiven. Any allusion to aged infirmity quickly drew pursed lips and narrowed eyes.

" 'Course. Them boys all swim like fish."

"Charlie shouldn't expect you to take the boys all of the time." *Careful, don't make it sound like it's because of her age.* "They need to spend time with their father."

Granny made a scoffing sound. "Keeps me young. It's only a couple of times a month. Charlie sees 'em plenty."

Glory sat on the rest of her argument; she'd be wasting her breath. After a tiny pause too short for thought, she said, "I'm thinking about moving again." Even as the words tumbled out, she surprised herself. She'd been skirting around the idea for a few weeks now, but didn't have any solid plan laid out.

A knowing *hmmm* came over the line. "Where?"

"I don't know yet. I can't imagine staying in St. Paul through winter. The snow was fun for a while—but the thought of a whole winter here makes me depressed."

She heard Granny take a deep breath on the other end of the line. It was a telltale sign of trouble.

"What? Is something wrong?" Glory couldn't keep an edge of fear from her voice. She'd known something was happening.

"Not wrong. It's just . . . I had a little episode with my eye—"

"Why didn't you call me?" Glory's heart leaped into her throat. Her all-day foreboding now honed in on its source.

"I just told you."

"So have you seen a doctor? What happened? Is someone there with you?"

"Calm down. I'm fine enough. I saw the doctor this mornin'. He said it should clear up this time."

"This time? Have you had other episodes?" A few years ago Granny had been diagnosed with macular degeneration, a disease that would most likely rob her of her central vision, altering her life immeasurably. But so far Granny had been lucky. This was the first time Glory had heard a hint of a problem.

"It was a tiny broken vein. He wants to see me again next week."

Glory forced herself to ask, "Can you see?"

"Right eye's fine."

"But the left?"

"Eh." Glory could see her grandmother dismissing it with the lift of a sharp-boned shoulder.

"So the condition is getting worse."

"Not necessarily. But, darlin', you know it's just a matter of time. I been luckier than most. Time's come to take note."

Glory couldn't swallow; emotion had closed off her throat.

"I was wondering . . . could you . . . could you come home?" Granny rushed on, "Not permanent. I just want to see your face clear one more time."

This was the first time in Glory's memory that Tula Baker had asked *anything* of another human being. A cold sweat covered Glory from head to foot. "I'm on my way."

Twelve hours later, Glory had her car packed with her few belongings and was headed south. She barely noticed the miles and the hours passing as she wrestled with emotions that were quickly becoming a two-headed monster. It certainly wasn't difficult leaving St. Paul; she'd been inching closer to that decision every day. For the past eighteen months she'd thought of herself as "trying on" different places, like one would search for a new winter coat. She'd left Dawson with the firm conviction that there was a place out there that would act as a balm, a salve to her soul; and she could bask in it like a healing Caribbean sun. But the climates changed, population fluctuated, and Glory still felt as if she were an empty vessel, insides echoing her barren life like a bass drum. East, West, cities, small towns, suburbia . . . nothing brought peace.

No, leaving Minnesota was easy—but the very thought of returning to Tennessee brought beads of sweat to her upper lip and a sickness deep in her belly. What if Granny's sight didn't return? What if this truly was the beginning of the end of her independence? Glory's heart ached for lost time and uncertain futures. A part of her could barely force herself to press the accelerator for the dread of seeing her hometown again; yet another part of her could not reach her grandmother's wiry embrace fast enough.

Before she knew it, she was a mere handful of miles from the Tennessee state line, less than two hours from Dawson. Her grandmother lived a few miles beyond that, deep in Cold Spring Hollow, nestled in the verdant, misty foot of the Smoky Mountains.

The rolling lay of the land in Kentucky seemed to be priming Glory for that inevitable moment when she would cross into the lush hill country that had nurtured her for her first twenty-six years. As her car chewed up the rapidly decreasing miles, she assured herself that there would not be a great crashing wall of memory that would overcome her at the state line. Months of therapy had suggested perhaps there would be no memories— ever.

Still, Glory doubted the professionals' opinions. True, she had no "memory" of that night. But she did possess an indefinable sense of gut-deep terror when she turned her mind toward trying to recall. Which told her those memories were there, lying in the darkness, waiting to swallow her whole.

Could she face Dawson and all she had lost there? Could she actually *live* there again? If Granny needed her, of course she would. Still . . . one day at a time. First thing was to get home and assess the situation.

She rolled down the driver's-side window. The roar of the wind at seventy filled her head. She glanced at the graceful rise and fall of the green pastures beside the interstate. She drew deep breaths, as if to lessen the shock by easing herself home, by reacquainting her senses gradually to the sights and smells of hill country.

As a child, Glory had loved visiting the wild of the deep hollow where Granny Tula had lived since the day she was born. Life in the hollow was hard, but straightforward—understandable. People of her grandmother's ilk had no time or patience for dwelling on the superficial. They accepted whatever life handed them with a nod of stoicism and another step toward their future.

Hillbillies. That's what her in-laws called folks like Tula Baker. Of course, they would never say anything like that directly about Granny—but the thought was there, burning brightly behind their sophisticated old-money eyes. What they had never understood was that neither Glory nor her grandmother would have been insulted by the term. Glory's mother, Clarice, on the other hand, would have been mortified. Clarice, the youngest of Tula Baker's seven children, had struggled to separate herself from the hollow and all it implied.

As Glory watched the terrain grow rougher and the woodlands become increasingly dense, she didn't feel the tide of panic that she'd anticipated.

I'm going to make it. The thought grew stronger with each breath that drew in the mingling of horse manure, damp earth and fresh grass. *I'm going to make it. . . .*

The instant she saw the large sign that said WELCOME TO TENNESSEE Glory's lungs seized. All of her mental preparation disappeared on the wind rushing by the open window.

Suddenly light-headed, she pulled onto the emergency lane of the interstate. As soon as her car stopped moving, she put it in park, fearing that she might pass out and start rolling again.

The car rocked, sucked back toward the racing traffic when an eighteen-wheeler whizzed by going eighty. Miraculously, the truck was gone in no more than a blur and a shudder, and Glory's four tires remained stuck to the paved shoulder out of harm's way.

She concentrated on her hands gripping the steering wheel—hands that could no more deny her heritage than her green eyes and thick, auburn hair. Sturdy, big-boned hands that somehow remained unsoftened by the cultured life she'd led. Hands that reminded her of Granny Tula's. That thought gave her strength.

After a few minutes, the cold sweat evaporated, the trembling in her limbs subsided, and her head cleared. She put the car in drive and rejoined the breakneck pace of traffic headed south.

Eric Wilson left the fire station in the middle of his shift— something he would have taken any of his firefighters to task for. But he was chief, and as such frequently had business away from the firehouse. No one questioned when he got into his department-owned Explorer and drove away.

But this was far from official business. This was personal—very personal. He and his ex-wife, Jill, shared amicable custody of their nearly three-year-old son, Scott. But Scott's increasing problems were something that the two of them were currently butting heads over. In Eric's estimation, Jill was in denial, plain and simple. And lately, it seemed she was doing as much as she could to prove Scott was just like any other boy. Part of that strategy was *not* hovering by the telephone worrying if today was going to be the day for trouble.

Whenever he mentioned the idea that she should get a cell phone, she took the opportunity to remind him that she couldn't afford one. Which was a load of bull. She worked as a medical secretary and made decent money—comparable to Eric's fire department salary. It was more convenient for Jill to be unavailable—especially on Wednesdays, her day off.

This was the third time since the summer session began five weeks ago that the preschool had called Eric at work because they couldn't locate her. It had been a familiar message; Scott was having a "behavior problem," causing such disruption that the teachers requested he be taken home. Jill had responded to a similar call on at least four occasions.

The staff at the church-housed preschool were sympathetic and had made every effort to help assimilate him into classroom activities; but, they repeatedly explained, they had to consider the other twelve children in the class.

As Eric pulled into the rear parking lot of the Methodist church, his stomach felt as pocked and broken as the ancient asphalt. Weeds of frustration sprouted through the numerous cracks, filling his middle with something poisonous to all of his hopes for his son. This summer preschool program was intended for children who were going to need extra time and attention to catch up; children who would benefit from not having an interruption in the development of their social skills by a long summer break. Even so, it seemed Scott was on a rapid backslide. Eric couldn't help the feeling of terror that had begun to build deep in his heart, as if he were locked high in a tower watching his son drown in the moat outside his window—close enough to witness yet helpless to save him.

For a long moment, he sat in the car, staring toward the forested mountains shrouded in their ever-present blue mist. In a way, Scott's mind was concealed from him just like the detailed contour of those mountains. He wished with all of his soul that he could divine the right course to lead his son out of the mysterious fog. The local doctors had varying opinions; from developmental delay (a catchall phrase, he'd decided), to mild autism, to he'll-grow-out-of-it, to it's-too-early-to-tell.

Eric was willing to do whatever it took to help his son—if only there was a definite answer as to what that was.

He slammed the steering wheel with the heel of his hand. Then he took a deep breath and tried to exhale his frustration. He would need all of the calm he could muster to deal with what awaited inside.

When he entered the hall that led to the basement classroom, he could hear Scott crying—screaming. A feeling of blind helplessness *whooshed* over him like a backdraft in a fire. He quickened his pace.

With his hand on the doorknob, he paused, heartsick as he looked through the narrow glass window beside the door. His son stood stiffly in the corner, blue paint streaked through his blond hair and on his face. Mrs. Parks, one of the teachers, knelt beside him, talking softly. Eric saw her hands on her knees; Scott really didn't like anyone other than his parents to touch him.

Scott ignored his teacher, his little body rigid with frustration. It was a picture Eric had seen before. Still, it grabbed his gut and twisted with brutal ferocity every time.

When he went into the room and knelt beside his son, there was no reaction of joy, no sense of salvation, no throwing himself into Eric's arms with relief. Scott's cries continued unabated.

Was this behavior an offshoot of the divorce, as Jill insisted? It seemed implausible, as he and Jill hadn't lived together since Scott was ten months old. Still, that nagging of conscience couldn't be silenced.

Mrs. Parks, a woman whose patience continually astounded Eric, said, "I'm sorry. I didn't know what else to do but call you." She pursed her lips thoughtfully and looked back at Scott. "I think he wanted the caps put back on the finger paints. Although I can't say for sure." In her hand she held a wet paper towel. She handed it to Eric and got up and walked away. "Maybe he'll let you wipe his hands."

Eric took the towel. Scott had become increasingly obsessed with closing things—cabinets, windows, doors, containers—with an unnatural intensity. Anything that he wasn't allowed to close sent him into an inconsolable tantrum, as if his entire world had been shaken off its foundation.

Jill's mother said the child was overindulged, spoiled because his divorced parents were vying for his love. Jill's family *did not* divorce. At first Eric had bought into the theory. But he'd been careful, watched to make sure they weren't acquiescing to Scott's every demand.

"Okay, buddy, can I wipe your hands?" Eric asked, holding out the towel.

Scott's cries didn't escalate; Eric took that as permission. He got the worst of the blue off his son's hands, then scooped him up in his arms and carried him, still stiff and crying, out of the classroom.

Scott wiggled and squirmed, but Eric managed to get him strapped in his car seat. By the time he was finished, Eric had almost as much blue paint smeared on him as Scott did. Before he climbed into the driver's seat, Eric tried to call Jill again. No answer.

Eric then called the station. When the dispatcher picked up, he said, "Donna, I'm going to have to take the rest of the afternoon off; I had to pick Scott up at school, he's . . . sick."

Eric hadn't discussed his son's possible condition with anyone. It was still too new, too baffling. How could he explain something that was currently such a mystery to his own mind?

Donna made a tiny noise of understanding. "No problem," she said, with overkill on lightheartedness. "Hope he feels better soon."

Eric realized he hadn't been fooling anyone.

By the time Jill called forty minutes later, Scott was sitting quietly on the floor of Eric's living room, playing with his current favorite toy, a plastic pirate ship.

"What happened?" she asked. "I went to pick him up, and they said you'd taken him home early."

"More of the same. A tantrum that wouldn't stop." Eric rubbed his eyes with his forefinger and thumb.

"You would think a preschool teacher could handle a two-year-old tantrum without calling parents."

"Jill"—he took a deep breath—"you know it's more than that. Dr. Martin—"

"Stop! What if *Dr. Martin* is wrong? Dr. Templeton saw nothing out of the ordinary in Scott. Why do you insist upon thinking the worst?" Thankfully, she caught herself before she pushed them into their normal angry confrontation on the subject. Her voice became pleading. "Eric, I don't want him to be labeled. If they treat him like he's disabled, he's *going to be* disabled. He's just slow to mature. Lots of kids are. He's just a baby! A friend of Angela's said she knew a boy who didn't talk until he was four and he's making A's and B's in school and gets along with everyone. And Stephanie's daughter has tantrums all of the time. A few more weeks in school and—"

"And what?" Sometimes Eric felt he was fighting the battle for his son on two fronts—against both an as-yet-unnamed developmental disorder and Scott's mother's refusal to face facts. "They'll probably ask us not to bring him back. We need to find a better solution for him. It's not just the fact that he's not talking. He doesn't interact with the other kids. Maybe he needs more structure, like Dr. Martin said."

"And Dr. Olfson said it's too early to be sure. None of the experts can even agree! And you want him locked up in an institution!"

"Stop overreacting. You know that's not what I meant." He closed his eyes and willed his anger to subside. "We need to find a better way to help him learn, help him cope."

She sighed heavily. "Let's give this school a couple more months. Please. Then we'll decide."

"I just feel that time is slipping away. The sooner we start, the better his chances."

"I *do not* want this whole town talking about Scott as if he's retarded. He's not."

"Of course he's not! But he's going to need more help."

"Maybe. Maybe not. I won't take the risk for nothing. I agreed to send him to school over the summer, isn't that enough for now?"

"All right." It was all Eric could do to keep from arguing. It was going to take time to get Jill turned around. "We'll leave things as they are for a few more weeks. But I think it's time to start at least looking for options."

She let it drop, apparently satisfied with her temporary victory. "Since tomorrow is your day, why don't you just keep Scottie tonight? I have a ton of things to get done. It'd really help me out. I'll just pick him up out at Tula's on Friday after work."

This was yet another tool in Jill's arsenal of denial—spend less time with Scott so she didn't have to see what was becoming progressively more obvious.

"Sure. Do you want to say hi to him before I hang up?" Eric spoke to his son every day on the phone, regardless of the empty silence on the other end of the line.

"Sure."

After holding the phone next to Scott's ear for a moment while Jill held a one-sided conversation, Eric got back on the line. "I'll tell Tula you'll be there at five-thirty on Friday."

"Okay. You boys have fun." She hung up.

You boys have fun. As if he and Scott were going to a baseball game and sharing hot dogs and popcorn. Would Jill ever be convinced their son wasn't like other children?

Eric hung up the phone and stretched out on the floor next to Scott. He'd taken to only setting out one activity at a time for Scott and keeping the background noise to a minimum, as Dr. Martin had suggested. It did seem that Scott was less agitated.

There was still blue paint in Scott's hair. Eric decided to leave that until bath time—which would develop into a battle of its own; Scott didn't like to be taken away from whatever he was doing. Changing activities seemed to trigger more than just normal two-year-old frustration.

For now, Eric tried some of the repetitive exercises he'd read about, just to see if it seemed to make a connection. Dr. Martin said sometimes these children needed to find alternative ways of communication—it was just a matter of searching and working with repetition until you found the right one.

As Eric worked with Scott, the light in the room turned orange with sunset. Scott's pudgy toddler fingers spun the pirate boat in tireless circles. With a lump in his throat, Eric wondered if he would ever understand what was going on inside his son's mind.

Jill sat in her living room, listening to the insects drone outside the open window. Absently, she twirled a strand of hair around her index finger. The sun was low, and shadows were gathering darkness in the corners of the room, but she didn't move to turn on a light. Instead she waited for the gloom to completely encompass her. It wasn't often she held herself still long enough to allow her thoughts to overtake her. Her life was stressed beyond belief with working and taking care of a baby alone.

Up until a few weeks ago, she hadn't been alone—not totally. Although even her mother didn't know it, Jason had been more or less a live-in since spring. He'd insisted on keeping his place—for appearances he'd said.

She still couldn't believe the jerk had dumped her. She'd left her husband for him—not that anyone knew that. She'd been careful while she was married, and equally careful after. That had been Eric's price for a quick and uncontested divorce—that she not see Jason publicly until after the divorce was final. He'd said he was keeping quiet for Scott's sake. And it probably was. Eric was a conscientious father.

Even as clean as the divorce had been, Mother had been appalled. Landrys didn't divorce—especially not what Mother called "good husband material" like Eric Wilson. Luckily, Mother didn't know the full story about Jason, or Jill would never hear the end of it.

She had hoped living together would bring Jason closer to commitment. But the entire thing had skidded in the wrong direction. The fewer complications for them to be together, the less interested he became.

Well, she thought with a sigh, that was over. She wouldn't think of Jason anymore.

She shifted on the couch, drawing her feet up under her and grabbing a pillow to hold over her midsection. That's right, she'd waste no more time and energy on Jason. Her baby was her whole world now. Why did Eric keep insisting there was something wrong with him? Lots of children developed more slowly—lots of very *intelligent* children. She would not let Scott be the kid who was stared at, the one other children made fun of. She simply wouldn't allow it. She would do whatever it took to ensure his place in this world was not one of ridicule and hurt.

She closed her eyes and briefly, ever so briefly, wished things were as they had been during those first months after Scott had been born—when she and Eric had marveled at his tiny perfection and she had felt safe.

* * *

It was sunset as Glory wound her way into Cold Spring Hollow. She'd driven twenty-five miles out of her way to avoid passing through Dawson; approaching the road to the hollow from the north instead of the west. It was foolish, but she somehow felt she'd be better fortified to face the town after spending the night with Granny.

In the shadows of the wooded hollow it was dark enough that her headlights came on. Glory slowed for a hairpin curve. After the road straightened back out, she saw three deer standing nearly close enough to reach out and touch. They held their bodies poised for flight, their dark eyes wide and their ears twitching. But they remained in place, studying her as closely as she studied them.

She felt a peculiar kinship to them, with their wary eyes and nervous posture. She imagined she had a similar air about her at the moment.

The narrow gravel road that led to Granny's house cut off to the right. Glory made the turn and felt more settled already. Normally, Granny would be on her porch with a cup of tea about now, impervious to the swarming mosquitoes as she sat on her beloved swing.

Before Glory's grandfather died, he and Granny used to sit on the porch every evening, at least for a short while, even in the winter. Glory remembered spending the night, lying in her bed and listening to their quiet voices drift up to her bedroom window. There was something about listening to them, to Granny's soft laugh and Pap's gruff chuckle, that soaked contentment deep into Glory's bones.

Granny's house came into sight. Glory's heart skittered through a beat when she saw it sitting dark and silent under the canopy of trees. It looked deserted.

Finally, in the deep shadow of the L-shaped front porch, Glory saw movement of the swing and drew a breath of relief.

By the time she'd put the car in park and gotten out, Granny had moved to the top of the front steps, leaving the swing to jiggle a jerky dance after her departure.

She stood there, her silhouette in the twilight tall and wiry, looking as strong as the ancient willow down by the old millpond.

Glory got out of the car quickly and ran up the steps. She paused on the tread before the top. The instant she opened her mouth to say hello, the tears that she'd thought were spent spilled forth.

Granny opened her arms and pulled Glory's head against her chest. "It's all right, darlin', you're safe in the Holler now. You're home."

As Glory cried in the comfort of her grandmother's arms, she knew coming home was going to be even more painful than she'd imagined.

Chapter Two

❧

WHEN GLORY WOKE early the next morning, she studied the lavender floral wallpaper in the bedroom. She'd awakened in this room countless times over the years, and nothing in it had changed as long as she could remember. Andrew—she tried to think of her husband without the shadow of sadness—had always called Granny's decor "early Cracker Barrel." But Glory liked the homeyness of it, the fact that Granny's possessions had memories attached.

The dresser still held a collection of tiny ceramic animal figurines from Granny's childhood. The mirror on the wall above was streaked with gray where time had worn away the silvering on the back. There was a watermelon-size brown water spot on the ceiling paper in one corner. Pap had fixed the roof twelve years ago, but Granny said the paper had plenty of life left in it, that people should have their eyes closed when lying on the bed, anyhow.

There wasn't a clock in the room, and Glory had left her watch in the bathroom after her shower last night. It was early; the sun had yet to send its bright shafts of light over the hills and into the little cove that cradled Granny's house. Birds twittered, coaxing the new day.

The quiet noises of morning in the hollow wrapped her in warm contentment. She stretched and wished this moment of peace could extend beyond these sheltered walls, that it could endure the battering of reality beyond her bedroom door.

Then she heard hushed voices downstairs. Sliding from the bed, she went to the window and moved the lace curtains enough to peek out. A white SUV that appeared pale purple-gray in the early light and had an emergency light bar on the top sat in front of the house.

She dashed out the door of her bedroom and down the stairs. The voices came from the kitchen. She was at a dead run when she burst through the door.

Her bare feet skidded to a stop on the linoleum when she saw Granny sitting at the table drinking coffee with a man in a blue shirt who was just turning toward the sound of her panicked footsteps.

"You're all right!" Glory said, the adrenaline draining from her muscles, leaving her legs feeling like jelly.

"Right as rain, darlin'." Granny's eyes smiled over her blue willow cup as she sipped coffee. "You look a bit peaked, though."

"I thought you were sick . . . or hurt. . . ." Glory's gaze cut to the man sitting at the table with Granny, looking at him fully for the first time. Her mouth went dry.

Granny said, "You remember Eric Wilson." Her words sounded as if they came from somewhere in the depths of a cavern.

Suddenly, Glory smelled smoke—the sharp, biting combination of burning wood, plastic, and human hair. It made her stomach lurch, her eyes sting, and strangled her breath.

Eric stood in what appeared to Glory as slow motion and extended his hand. "Hello, Glory." His voice seemed to be resonating, slow and muffled, from underwater.

She stood there stone mute, pulling at the bottom of the T-shirt she'd slept in, trying to draw air into her suddenly starved lungs.

Still sounding deep in a cavern, Granny cleared her throat; Glory recognized the gentle prod into politeness, but could no more respond than she could erase the impressions that flashed in an incoherent parade through her mind.

Darkness. Rain on her face. Flashing red lights. The cold ground under her back. The blurred image of a fireman leaning close and ripping his breathing apparatus away. The sound of his shouting her name.

She blinked, and the fireman's face came into clear focus: Eric Wilson. But he wasn't in her mind; he was standing right in front of her—and moving quickly in her direction.

His hands were on her arms, big and warm and secure, as she felt her knees begin to give way.

He held her erect as she stared at him, her memory-evoked emotion battling the flesh-and-blood man. With numb lips she said, "It was you."

"Let's get you in a chair," he said, as he moved her with the confidence of a trained rescuer in the direction of the seat he'd just vacated.

Granny was on her feet, hovering close as Glory sat down. "Good lands, girl, are you all right?"

Before Glory could answer, Granny was at the sink getting her a glass of water. When she placed it in Glory's hands, the liquid in the glass shook like it was in a paint mixer.

She took a tentative sip, more to buy time than to quench thirst.

Eric knelt in front of her, concern in his whiskey-colored eyes—just like . . .

"It was you," she said again, her words not much more than an exhaled breath.

"What was me?" he asked gently.

Glory felt Granny's bony hand fall on her shoulder and squeeze slightly.

"You brought me out of the house . . . the fire." She could hardly believe four therapists hadn't budged a single image from her memory, yet one glance at Eric Wilson's face had catapulted something right to the forefront of her mind.

Eric cast a worried glance at Granny. Then he said quietly, reverently, as if he suddenly saw the magnitude of what was happening to her, "Yes."

Glory locked gazes with him, trying to budge another memory loose.

None came.

After a moment, she began to feel reconnected to her surroundings. "I didn't remember that until just now. I haven't been able to remember. . . ."

His gaze remained upon her, making her feel the need to retreat. He said, "I'm sorry."

It was a phrase she'd heard a thousand times since the fire. But this time it ignited a fury in her that she couldn't quell—a fury born of months living with an aching void that reached to the center of her soul, a fury reignited by the horrible memory that had just assailed her.

Her voice was cold when she said, "Sometimes I am too. Sometimes I wish you hadn't done it."

"Glory!" Granny's sharp, shocked tone cut through the emotional haze that swaddled Glory's brain.

Eric didn't appear surprised—or shocked—by her words. He stood slowly, but didn't move away from her.

Granny said, "That's the hurt talking." Then she said to Eric, "She just come back last night. It'll take some time for her to sort her feelings out."

Glory worked to free herself from the grip of anger. She kept her gaze safely on the floor at her feet, and said, "Yes, that's right. I shouldn't have said that. I do appreciate you risking your life to save our—mine."

When she forced herself to look at him again, she saw an edgy look in his eye that surprised her.

Well, I was pretty damned rude.

He shifted his weight, and said, "I'd better get going." Then he moved to the corner of the room and knelt.

For the first time, Glory saw a small boy sitting in the corner. He held his fingers in front of his face, closely examining a string from Granny's throw rug. The child's unwavering focus on the string seemed unnatural—especially since Eric was kneeling right in front of him.

"Scott, Daddy's going to work now."

The toddler continued to examine the string.

"Scott." Eric put his hand under the boy's chin and raised it, gently forcing him to look up. "Daddy's going to work. I'll be back to pick you up this evening."

He kissed the top of the boy's head, got up, and said good-bye to Granny.

Glory stopped him halfway to the door. "You aren't leaving him here, are you?"

He turned with a furrowed brow, and said, "Yeah. Is there a problem?"

Glory's gaze cut to Granny and back to Eric. "Well, yes. Granny's sight . . . you can't expect her to watch a toddler."

"I told you, Glory, I can still see fine. I always watch Scott on Thursdays and Friday afternoons." There was a snap of fire in her voice and a flash in her eye that clearly broadcast Glory's transgression.

"Of course." Glory tried to brush away the crackling annoyance in the air. "I'll be here to lend a hand today anyway."

Eric lingered in the doorway.

"Go on, now. You'll be late," Granny said.

Eric cast one last look toward his son, then nodded and left.

Glory sat watching the space in the doorway he'd just vacated. Instead of this unexpected breakthrough in her memory fostering anticipation for healing, an icy fear settled in her chest.

"So you remembered something." It was a statement, not a question that Granny uttered as she sat back down at the table across from Glory.

Glory gave her head a slight shake. "Not much really. Just that I remember seeing his face." How could she explain the cascade of emotions that ripped through her in that split second?

As she thought of Eric's face again, she tried to grasp at something just beyond her flash of memory, lurking in the rainy shadows of that night. She'd sensed it before, when the terror scratched at the back of her brain in therapy sessions. But now she was met with the same blank wall as always. Maybe that flash generated by the surprise of seeing Eric was all she'd ever get.

"After . . . he came to check on you, you know."

"What?" Glory's gaze snapped to Granny's face. "Eric Wilson? When?"

"While you was in the hospital. Ever' day."

Glory's brow knotted. She remembered the stay in the hospital—every excruciating detail. "You must be mistaken. I never saw him."

"No, you didn't. Not after that first time . . . the night of the fire. He came into the emergency room and you . . . well, you were upset."

Try as she might, Glory didn't remember anything more of that night. Even the smells and sensations that had momentarily been so vivid and immediate that they robbed her of her strength were dulled until she could almost pretend the whole glimpse of memory hadn't happened.

But her knees were still rubbery and her body drained. And she could still feel the security of Eric's grip as he'd guided her to this chair. It *had* happened.

Granny's words sank in. "Oh, God, what did I say to him?" Had she screamed and ranted and laid blame on the man who'd saved her? In those first days, Glory was now ashamed to admit, she had blamed the doctors for not saving her baby. Had that grief-fueled fury spilled over to the firefighter who'd saved her too?

For the briefest second, Granny's lips pursed. "You weren't in your right mind, ever'body knew that."

Glory's gaze followed Granny's as she glanced over at the little boy who had not moved one inch from where he was sitting ten minutes ago.

Granny said, "That's Eric's way; he didn't want to take the chance of upsetting you again. So he'd stop by regular on his way home from work to check with me or your mama." She seemed to measure her words before she went on. "He came to the funeral. Stayed at the back of the crowd, out of your sight. 'Course he and Andrew played football together in school, so he had every right to be there. But he kept to hisself, so's not to make it harder on you."

Andrew's funeral. Although it had been just under two years ago, it was as if trying to recall a movie she'd seen so long ago that the details had run together, the cast had become indistinguishable, and the plot become tangled with every other movie she'd ever seen. Eric Wilson could have been standing two feet in front of her that day, and she wouldn't have seen him. She'd floated through the endless hours of calling and the funeral on a silken gray cloud of disconnection—thanks to the little pills her mother had fed her at regular intervals. Pills not prescribed by Glory's own doctor, but by her mother's new husband, Karl Gustafson, M.D.

Clarice, Glory's mother, had landed the doctor not long after she'd sold her mobile home and transplanted herself to Florida. It was a move she'd been talking about for years—the final step that would forever eradicate the shadow of the hollow that tainted her in Dawson. As Glory had grown up, her mother had spoken of Florida as if it were a magical place where she could realize her full potential without people's preformed notions holding her back—Glory thought maybe it was the influence of all the Disney World commercials. Nonetheless, Clarice had finally made the move, and her dreams *had* come true.

It had been with some relief that Glory had dropped her mother and Karl at the Knoxville airport two days after the funeral. Although Karl had to get back, Clarice had offered to remain in Dawson as long as Glory needed her. But Glory wanted nothing more than to be left alone with her grief. The last thing she needed was her mother hovering, examining each tear and every mood swing, assessing what drug Karl might prescribe to make it go away. Glory had wanted to wrap herself in her pain, feel every nuance of it, not blot it out in a pharmacological haze. She felt that she'd earned the right to retreat into her own suffering—at least for a while.

Apparently she'd closed her eyes to more than her mother's good intentions. The man to whom she owed her life had been relegated to hiding in the shadows.

"I had no idea," Glory finally said.

"He didn't want no gratitude, said he was doing his job."

Glory knew that Eric and Andrew had known one another; they'd graduated from Dawson High together, five years ahead of her. But it seemed like a strained friendship in the few instances that she'd been present when they'd run into one another, as if hostility rippled beneath the sportsman's camaraderie, as if they had been enemies forced into alliance. Once she'd asked Andrew about it. He'd told her it was her imagination. But she saw bitterness in his eyes and couldn't help but think something had transpired between the two men that set them at hidden odds.

Glory shook off those thoughts, not wanting to delve any deeper into the murky past just now. She turned her gaze back to the little boy, just briefly; she didn't like the twinge of jealousy she felt when she looked at those chubby cheeks blushing with pink health.

"How's your eye this morning?"

"Cain't even tell anything was wrong."

"When do you go back to the doctor?"

"Monday. But I don't see the need. It's doin' just what Dr. Blanton said; I'm seein' again. Nothin' he can do anyhow. No sense in paying him just to peek in there with his little light."

Glory had no intention of letting Granny miss that appointment. But she decided to fight that battle later. She had three days until Monday. "Do you really think it's a good idea to continue to babysit? What if you have an episode while he's here? How will you handle a two-year-old if you can't see?"

"Seems foolish to give up afore I have to. Why, I could just sit here for years, doing nothin', waitin' to go blind. That'd be a sin. Changes will come in God's time."

"But, Gran, a toddler? And you're all the way out here—"

"I got a phone and can call if something happens. Dr. Blanton says it's not likely that my sight will just"—she snapped her fingers—"go like that. The bleeding was a fluke." She went over and picked up the boy. "Besides, Scott and me, we're partners. Ain't we, big fella?" She kissed his cheek with her pale, papery lips.

The boy blinked, but showed no other response.

Curiosity overcame her reluctance, and Glory asked, "Is he okay? I mean . . . he's so quiet."

Granny settled him back on the blanket on the floor and set a plastic pirate ship in front of him. He reached out and began turning the toy in slow circles.

Glory looked away.

"Depends on which of his folks you ask. Jill says he's just shy and slow to talk. Eric thinks there's something wrong. They been doctoring a lot lately." Granny caressed the top of Scott's blond head. Then she sat back down. "From the looks of your car, you're plannin' on a long visit."

Glory had brought in a single small bag last night. It had been dark enough that Granny hadn't seen that her car was packed to the roof; pillows and blankets piled on top of TV, stereo, and computer until they were pressed solid against the backseat windows, looking ready to spring out the instant a door was opened.

Time to tread carefully. If Granny thought Glory was planning on hanging around Dawson because she thought Gran needed her, she would pack Glory back in her car and have her headed north before sunset.

"I'm in transition," Glory said breezily.

Granny raised a gray brow.

"St. Paul wasn't working out. I'm not sure where I'm going next." Glory decided to leave it as broad and ambiguous as she could possibly get away with.

After a deep breath, Granny said, "You made your decision to leave here. I cain't say I understand it, but I won't be havin' you change it for me. I just needed a day . . . that's all."

Glory didn't say anything. Instead she concentrated on the shafts of early morning sun that broke through the kitchen window, the hypnotic dance of dust motes. She heard the sound of the toy boat spinning in endless circles. Suddenly she felt just like that boat, spinning, spinning, and going nowhere. As if she were caught in a whirlpool that pulled her deeper the harder she struggled. What would happen if she just stopped struggling? Would she be sucked into a cold blackness and never be able to resurface?

Staying in Tennessee would be like sitting in the eye of the vortex. She felt sure her strength would fail, and the whirlpool would win. But if she left here again, where would she go? Arizona maybe. Someplace where the heat and the blazing sun could bake the cold desperation out of her bones. She hadn't been west yet. Would the vast differences in landscape cradle her? Did she need a more pronounced differentiation from the lush green of Tennessee? Perhaps beige upon tan, sand and stone, brittle vegetation and prickly cactus would make the difference.

But how could she leave Granny again—knowing that at any time, her sight might fail? Glory had plenty of cousins . . . but none she would trust to care for Granny. They'd put her in a home, or bicker about whose turn it was to take her to the grocery store; they'd make her feel like an invalid. And for a woman like Tula Baker, that would be the cruelest fate of all.

She took Granny's square, knobby hand in hers. "One day at a time, Gran. Today, let's pick raspberries."

As Eric drove the curving road out of the hollow, he realized he was gripping the wheel with brutal force. Wisps of fog reached across the road in places, like fingers of the past trying to force him to stumble. But he couldn't stumble; there was too much at risk. Glory's return to Dawson was certainly an unexpected turn of events. He'd just begun to feel secure in thinking his questions were going to remain safely buried with Andrew Harrison.

Why was it that every bad turn his own life had taken pivoted around Andrew Harrison?

Eric remembered the flash of terror that momentarily sparked in Glory's eyes; how she looked like a fearful child standing there in her oversized T-shirt with Scooby-Doo on the front. He hoped with all of his heart that Glory's memory of that night remained a blank canvas. He told himself it was to prevent her further pain . . . but the coward in him recognized it for the desperate wish of self-preservation that it was.

Chapter Three

❀

GLORY WAS SKEPTICAL when Granny insisted that Scott could walk all the way to the raspberry patch. It wasn't a long hike, but with those stubby legs, he'd be taking four steps for their every one.

"Scottie and me walk most every afternoon," Granny said as she packed the last of the junk they were having to haul for the little guy into a quilted tote.

Glory's eyes lingered on the bag. Since Pap died, Granny had been supplementing her social security income by selling her quiltwork. For years folks had encouraged her to do it, but Granny had always insisted that her quilts were just to be shared with family and friends—that's why she enjoyed it so much. Every newlywed couple, each new grandchild and great-grandchild received a quilt lovingly made by Granny. But necessity had won out, and Granny now sold quilted place mats, tote bags, and bed coverlets in touristy places around Gatlinburg.

The bag riding on Granny's shoulder as they left the house was one of Glory's favorite patterns, done in colors that reminded her of the hills in October.

Before Granny stepped out the door, she put on her ancient sunglasses with lenses the size of headlights. They made her look like a praying mantis, all long, skinny arms and legs and giant eyes.

They would be walking through the woods the entire way; there should be plenty of shade. Glory must have given Granny an odd look, because Granny said, "Been wearing them outdoors lately even on cloudy days. Just more comfortable."

Glory paused, contemplating the significance of this revelation. It hadn't hit home until this very moment that if Granny's sight deteriorated to the point that she couldn't quilt, how would she make ends meet? That just added another stone in the "reasons to stay in Dawson" basket.

"Awww, stop lookin' like that. It don't mean my eyes are worse. Let's get goin'." She led the way down the back steps.

Glory followed along behind Granny and Scott, leaving plenty of space between her and the toddler.

Surprisingly, Scott walked along at a reasonable pace, clinging not to Granny's hand but to the tail of the baby quilt she had draped over her arm. That quilt was definitely Gran's work. Had Scott rated up there with Granny's own grandchildren, or had his parents purchased it? For some reason, the answer mattered to Glory.

"That quilt, it's beautiful . . . is it Scott's?" She tried to sound offhand.

"His favorite. Sleeps with it all the time."

"Gosh, it looks pretty new to have been dragged around by a baby for a couple of years." She was almost ashamed of herself.

"He's only had it 'bout six months."

Glory let go of the fishing line. The answer obviously wasn't going to come without a direct question, and she wasn't quite ready to resort to that yet. She felt petty enough already.

The trail was fairly even, well-worn with only slight rises and dips. Scott didn't once ask to be carried, just trudged along in silence, neither asking questions, nor pointing in curiosity, nor looking beyond the path immediately in front of his feet.

Halfway to the meadow, a narrow, fast-moving stream cut across the path, tumbling around a cluster of smooth gray rocks. Granny shifted the tote and reeled in the blanket, as if to pick up the toddler. For a moment, Glory stood motionless. Then she stepped up.

"I've got him." She grasped Scott under the arms and held his sturdy body away from hers. Then she stepped carefully from the dry top of one rock to the other. Immediately when she reached the other side, she set him back on his own little feet. Then she shoved her hands in her pockets. It was no more personal than lugging a bag of potatoes over the obstacle.

When Granny joined her on the far side, she gave Glory an odd look, slightly puzzled yet slightly reproachful.

Again, Glory felt almost ashamed of herself. What kind of woman was she that she was so resistant to physical contact with this little boy?

She turned away from the question, fearing what she'd see inside herself. She walked on ahead, leaving Granny to set Scott up with his quilt once again.

The raspberry bramble was probably within two hundred yards of Granny's house, yet felt as isolated as Blue

Falls Pond. It sat on the edge of a small clearing, a patch of brilliant sunlight in the green gloaming that covered most of the hollow. Here there was nothing but the still heat of the afternoon and the rustle of foraging squirrels.

Glory blinked against the brightness as she stepped into the clearing. Even with Granny wearing sunglasses, Glory noticed that Granny paused behind her and waited for her eyes to adjust before leaving the shadowy trail.

Immediately the heat of the sun mixed with the heavy humidity, making Glory pluck her T-shirt away from where it clung to her chest. A butterfly flitted in front of her, black wings glistening in the sun, bright blue tail shining like a beacon. She felt Scott's presence by her leg and wondered if his brown eyes—Eric's eyes, she realized—followed the flighty course of the butterfly too. She didn't glance down to see.

"Whew!" Granny fanned herself. "Hot one. Let's put Scott in the shade over here."

She spread a blanket under a tall yellow buckeye tree near the thicket. Then she pulled out his toy ship.

Scott soberly walked over and plopped down. Beads of perspiration dotted his forehead.

"Maybe we should give him a drink," Glory said.

Granny smiled, rummaged in the canvas tote, and brought out a Sippy Cup. She poured water from a bottle into it and handed it to the boy. Then she lifted the bottle toward Glory. "How about you?"

Glory took a long drink, then gave it back to Granny.

When she looked down at Scott again, he was moving the boat in the same tedious circles as he had earlier in the day. He still hadn't said a word.

"Alrighty. Let's get to pickin'." Granny handed Glory a small galvanized bucket. "I'm thinkin' cobbler."

Glory grinned and nodded. Berry cobbler and ice cream. The remembered taste sprang onto her tongue. At least once every year during berry season, she and Granny would pick berries and make a cobbler. Then when Pap came home from work, the three of them would eat the entire thing while it was still warm, melting the ice cream into a pool of creamy sweetness. It was always Glory's favorite day of the summer.

She moved closer to the berry bushes with her mouth watering. Her first few attempts to pluck berries were marred by sharp stinging scratches from the thorns, but soon she remembered her technique and fared better. Granny was picking four feet away with her back to Scott.

Glory gave frequent sideways glances in their direction.

Every two- and three-year-old she'd ever been around had been out of one thing and into the next, little whirling dervishes. She'd seen mothers exhaust themselves at a park trying to keep their children from eating sand, chasing squirrels into the street, and climbing to dangerous heights.

Again she looked at Granny, who was picking berries with her mouth pursed in concentration. Glory bit her lip, considering.

Granny had always been so vigilant—covering outlets, locking doors, using wire ties on the cabinet under the sink that held the cleaning supplies—when her cousins' children had been babies. Maybe age had begun to impair her judgment; her seemingly careless nature with this boy finally prickled too much.

"Aren't you afraid he'll slip away, get lost out here?" If he ran into the underbrush, he'd be awfully hard to find. There were rock ledges, steep slopes, a dozen streams for drowning, and poisonous plants aplenty here.

Granny cast a quick and casual glance over her shoulder at Scott. "Nah. Once he starts with that boat, he'll keep at it until you take it away from him."

Glory could hardly argue the point; there he sat, not even looking at the squirrels as they became braver and grew gradually closer. "Odd." She was surprised when she realized she'd said it out loud.

Granny sighed. "Reckon it is. He didn't used to be so . . . so focused."

"He seems, I don't know, disconnected. Like he doesn't really care what's going on around him."

"Just try to take the boat away. He'll throw a hissy that'd wake the dead."

Glory couldn't imagine this silent, impassive child reacting that strongly to anything. She went back to her berry picking but kept a sharp ear out for the patter of tiny Nikes making for the woods. All she heard was the steady friction of that boat on the blanket.

Once the buckets were filled, they both sat on the edge of Scott's blanket to cool off before walking home. Just as Granny had predicted, Scott had stayed in one place, turning his boat the entire time they picked. He didn't stop when they joined him.

Glory lay on her back, watching a bushy-tailed squirrel jump from branch to branch overhead, chittering loudly.

Granny's gaze followed hers. "Buckeyes from this tree make a right fine paste."

Glory's gaze shifted to her grandmother.

"Pa used to make all of our school paste," Granny said. "Didn't know you could buy it at a store 'til I was ten."

Glory closed her eyes and thought of the jars of white paste with the flat plastic spreader built right into the lid that she'd used in grade school. Paste was cheap. That single statement brought into sharp focus just how poor Granny's family had been. The kind of poor that even Clarice could never imagine.

But Granny never spoke of being poor, of doing without. Her stories of childhood were all about adventures she and her brothers had had in the hollow. How once they'd actually roamed so far that they'd been lost overnight and her father had whipped the boys for endangering their little sister, when in reality it had been Tula that had led the way. Of the wounded baby bird she'd found in the yard that she'd nursed back to health; of the barn cat's litter of kittens Tula had taken into Dawson to find homes, then visited on a regular basis to make sure they were being treated well—a feline protection agency of one; of Fourth of July parades and watermelon-eating contests. Never of threadbare, outgrown coats or winters without enough coal for the furnace.

Granny had what couldn't be bought; she was happy in her own skin, with whatever life gave her.

A bee buzzed nearby. Glory opened one eye to see if it was too near Scott.

Granny said, "You tell your mama you were coming back here?"

Glory shook her head. She really couldn't explain *why* she hadn't called her mother in Florida. Since Glory had left Dawson, she'd been avoiding speaking to her mother as much as possible. Clarice was like a counterpoint to

Granny; chased by her own unhappiness and insecurity for years. It was suddenly startling to realize that Glory herself had fallen into a similar mind-set—but at least Glory had just cause. Her mother had lived with a chip on her shoulder most of her life. From grade school on, the driving force inside Clarice Baker had been to divorce herself from the hollow.

The first step in that transition had happened the weekend after high school graduation when she had married Glory's father, Jimmy Johnston, a town boy in her class whose parents both held respectable jobs with the telephone company and had a nice new ranch-style house on the outskirts of Dawson. But Clarice soon discovered that her new husband had no intention of following in his parents' footsteps by finding a job that offered security and a pension, and buying a nice house on a quiet Dawson street. Jimmy loved dirt-track racing as much as he loved anything in his life. Clarice had settled for a mobile home on a city lot and a husband gone every weekend. But at least it was out of the hollow.

When Glory was four, her dad had been killed in a motorcycle accident. The thing Glory remembered most about him was the smell of Goop, the hand cleanser he used after working on engines.

After he died, his parents, Glory's other grandparents, retired and moved to Florida. Clarice had gone to work at the bank as a teller. She was trapped in the mobile home, but she spent her salary proving to the town that she and her daughter were respectable—Girl Scouts, ballet lessons, and brand-name clothes for Glory; manicured nails and bridge club for herself. She had encouraged Glory to run for student government and try out for cheerleader.

Clarice was fifteen times more excited when she made both than Glory had been.

The icing on Clarice's cake had been Glory's marriage to Andrew Harrison, son of the most prominent family in Dawson. But even in that moment, the hollow had reached out and laid a hand on her shoulder. At the garden wedding reception, Glory had been standing beside her mother when they overheard someone say through the meticulously manicured boxwood hedge, "She seems like a nice enough young woman, especially considering where her people come from." Glory had had to grasp her mother's wrist to keep her from reaching through the hedge and grabbing the woman by the throat.

Clarice had moved to Florida the next month.

When Glory left Dawson after the fire, her mother had been insistent that she come to stay with her. After all, Florida had saved Clarice from her world of slight and unhappiness; surely it would do the same for Glory.

But Glory had needed to be alone, not coddled in a way that reminded her every day of her loss. She'd struck out first for Asheville, then to a small town in Ohio, then to Kansas City, and finally St. Paul.

She had yet to forget her loss.

On their way back from berry picking, they took a fork in the trail that took them past a plain white clapboard church with a row of clear-glass-paned windows lining either side. In the churchyard stood an old iron fence that surrounded the graveyard where Bakers and Prathers (Granny had been a Prather before she married Pap) had buried their dead since long before the Civil War. From here they would follow the gravel road the rest of the way to Granny's house.

It had never struck Glory before how limited the geographic scope of Granny's life had been. She'd been born on a farm not three miles from where she now lived. She'd gone to school a mile from that farm in a building that housed first through twelfth grades—before the days of consolidation. She and Pap had been married in this church, her seven children had been baptized here. And she'd buried her parents, three siblings, a husband, and one child in this graveyard.

Carrying the tote and berry pails, Glory walked just ahead of Granny and Scott as they passed the front of the church.

Granny said, "I believe I'll stop for a minute."

Glory turned around. Granny was standing beside the cemetery fence. "Okay," Glory said, and started toward the gate.

"You and Scott go on ahead. I have some things to discuss with your granddad."

Glory didn't know which alarmed her more, being alone with Scott or her grandmother thinking she could converse with the dead.

It must have shown on her face because Granny was quick to add, "I ain't crazy. It's what keeps troubles from weighing you down—sharing them with someone. Always did run things past Sam." She winked at Glory. "Now he can't disagree with my conclusions."

"We'll just wait here." Glory cast a furtive look at Scott, who was in the end sniffles of the tantrum Granny had accurately predicted when they put the boat away. They hadn't been able to leave the meadow for ten minutes after; he howled, stiff-legged, reacting to Granny's soothing touches as if they were hot pokers against his skin. Getting him moving back toward home had been an exercise in patience. But Granny had done it, one hard-fought step at a time. Now he was moving along fairly well. Glory wondered why Gran insisted on upsetting the apple cart.

Granny seemed to be sizing up the distance from Pap's headstone and the path, as if gauging whether Glory would be able to overhear. Finally, she said, "All right."

Glory and Scott stood at the front of the little church as Granny walked over to Pap's grave. Glory continued to hear Scott's quivering breaths and sniffles, but didn't dare do or say anything for fear she'd set him off again.

Granny laid her hand on Pap's headstone, keeping her back to the gate. Glory saw Granny's hands gesture and her head move as she spoke, as if she were sitting across the table from him.

After a few minutes, Granny returned, a look of serene composure on her face. Glory hadn't thought of Granny as tense, but there was a definite change in her as she stepped out of the cemetery.

Glory had not returned to Andrew's grave since the funeral. After seeing Granny's renewed calm, Glory wondered if a visit to his graveside would offer a new perspective on her own life.

Instead of calm rising from that thought, dread crept over her skin like a damp humid night in August.

Scott was taking a nap on a quilt on the floor of Granny's living room. The afternoon temperature had continued to climb, and Granny's house didn't have air-conditioning;

the floor was the coolest place. And for some unthinkable reason, Granny had decided to fry chicken for dinner.

"Really, Gran, let's just do tuna salad or something," Glory said, then leaned against the kitchen counter and took a long swig of sweet tea. She hadn't realized until now how much she'd missed sweet tea while living up north. She rested the dewy cold glass against the side of her neck and welcomed the shiver it gave her.

"I won't have your first dinner back home come from a can." Granny turned from the stove to deliver one of her "don't argue with me" looks. The entire end of her nose was a flour blotch—definitely counteracting the bad-ass look she was trying to deliver.

Glory's heart nearly burst with love. Tula Baker was probably the only woman in this century who would fry chicken in ninety-degree heat just because her grand-daughter had come home. Laughing, Glory stepped closer and wiped the spot from Gran's nose. "In that case, what can I do to help?"

Granny took a swipe at her nose, as if shooing a both-ersome fly, replacing the flour Glory had just brushed away. "Go out and pick the ripe tomatoes from the garden." Then, as Glory headed for the door, Granny added, "You do remember how to tell a ripe 'un?"

Glory shoved her hands on her hips. "No need to get nasty just 'cause I'm tidy and you can't keep the flour off your face. I hear some of the best cooks are slobs in the kitchen—have to have people like me to clean up after them."

Granny dipped her fingers in the flour and flipped them at Glory, who ducked the puff of white and ran out the door giggling.

She muttered as she entered the garden, "Do I remember how to tell a ripe tomato? Really."

She could feel taut red skin under her fingertips just thinking about it. Twenty years of working with Granny in the garden had left her with the touch for things ripe. That oddly phrased thought made her giggle to herself. The laughter started somewhere beneath her breastbone and bubbled right up through her lips. The late-afternoon sun was warm on her head, she smelled dinner cooking through the open kitchen window, and her toes dug into the warm, rich earth beneath her feet. She would never have guessed she'd feel this good ever again, especially in Tennessee.

"Never heard a woman laugh like that at tomatoes." A man's voice came from behind her. "They must have a great stand-up routine."

After this morning Eric hesitated saying anything to Glory at all, had nearly bypassed her, taking the opportunity to bundle Scott out of the house while she was occupied outside. But she looked so childlike crouched in the garden, and her laugh had sounded so light that he hadn't been able to help himself.

Glory turned her head, her smile steady, her auburn hair tossed over her shoulder, fiery in the sunlight. It was a relief that her smile remained when she looked at him. She was beautiful in a way he hadn't noticed this morning. They had each been too unprepared for the other, too unsteady in the moment of surprise.

He crossed his arms over his chest. "Me, I've always found cucumbers have the best one-liners." *That's it, keep the mood light.* He wanted to prolong that delightful sparkle in her eye.

She straightened up, lifting the basketful of tomatoes with her. "Then it's obvious that you're not very familiar with Granny's tomatoes. A couple of them have actually appeared in Vegas." She started in his direction. "Of course, the span of their careers is limited by the availability of good, reliable refrigeration."

At that he chuckled, as much in relief as at her joke. He needed Tula. He didn't want to have to avoid this place because of Glory. And in this moment, he felt just the opposite might happen.

As she stepped out of the garden, he put his hand out to take the laden basket. It looked as if she'd hand it over, then she hesitated and pulled it close to her waist. She glanced down at the ground, and when she looked back at him all of the laughter had faded from her eyes.

She said, "I owe you an apology . . . actually, two."

He started to wave her comment away, then paused. "Why two?"

"First, for my little scene this morning. I don't know why—"

"Hey, you were caught off guard." He lifted a shoulder. "Plus you were already running on adrenaline when you flew into the kitchen. Actually, it's nice to see someone worry about Tula. She's always doing for everyone else."

"Yes, she is." Glory paused. "And as long as we're on the subject"—she glanced at the back door of the house—"and Gran's out of earshot, I really think you should reconsider having her sit for Scott. I don't know how much she's told you about her condition—"

Dread gripped his chest. "Condition? She's ill? Is that why you're back?"

"Her eyesight. She has macul—"

"Oh, that." He blew out a breath. "You had me scared there for a minute. Of course she's told me about her 'condition,' but you'd better not let *her* hear you call it that."

"Granny downplays the seriousness of it. But—"

"I've done my research. I know full well there might come a time when she has to bow to . . . limitations. We've talked about it. She's assured me that she'll let me know if it becomes a problem."

Glory barked out a sharp cackle. "You don't really think she'll ever admit it, do you?"

He looked at her, tensed with annoyance. "Yes," he said stiffly. "I do. She would never risk Scott's safety by keeping him if she wasn't fit."

She didn't reply, just stood there looking at him like he didn't have a brain in his head.

"What was the other one?" he said gruffly, more challenge in his voice than he'd intended.

She blinked her incredibly green eyes and appeared confused.

"The other apology. You said you owed me two." He hated sounding like an ass. Uncertainly about Scott's future was making him jump to the offensive much too quickly when it came to people questioning his parenting.

"Never mind." She stepped around him. "I've reconsidered."

He waited a few seconds before he followed her to the house. His previous concern that there might be some attraction between him and Glory to complicate his already complicated situation was blown completely out of the water. It seemed they were destined for a bumpy road every time they were within shouting distance of one another.

As he walked across the lawn, he wondered just how long she was planning on staying.

Hesitating at the screen door to the kitchen, he watched her washing the tomatoes in the sink. Her jerky movements told him just how aggravated she was. He himself felt like he had grasshoppers in his stomach. The reality was, Glory's presence in town could present a lot more trouble than awkward social interchanges.

"'Evenin' Eric," Tula called. She hadn't turned from the stove to look at him, how had she known he was here?

He pulled open the screen and stepped inside. "'Evenin', Tula."

Tula did turn to look at him then. "Somethin' wrong?"

He shook his head.

"Go on, then, beer's in the fridge like always. Supper'll be a bit yet."

Eric saw Glory's shoulders tense. Then she looked at Tula with her jaw set in clear irritation.

Tula grinned. "Eric and Scott always have supper with me on Thursdays."

"Oh." Glory wiped her hands on a dish towel.

Eric took in her skittering less-than-enthusiastic glance in his direction. He cleared his throat and didn't make a move toward his routine beer. "I thought maybe I'd just take Scott on home tonight—Glory being home and all." Glory's pale shock of this morning might be gone, but that last look had told him he still wasn't welcome across the supper table.

"Don't talk foolish," Tula said in her take-no-prisoners voice. "Get Glory a beer too; she looks like she could use one."

Glory said, "I don't need a beer."

Eric pulled one out of the fridge and opened it. He took a long swig, keeping Glory in his sight over the bottle. She licked her lips, looking at the cold bottle like a starved urchin peering in a bakery window.

Tula flipped chicken in the sizzling oil with one hand and pointed to the refrigerator with the other. "She always was the most contrary child ever born. Give her a beer. And you two go out and sit on the porch where it ain't so hot. Scott'll nap for at least 'nother half hour. I'll call you when supper's on."

Eric got the beer, opened it, and handed it to Glory, who snatched it away from his grasp.

"Seems I got that contrary streak honest," she mumbled as she headed toward the front porch.

He followed behind, wondering what on earth they were going to talk about for thirty minutes. At the rate he'd been going, he'd have her so worked up she'd need to breathe into a paper bag by the time Tula called them back inside.

Eric perched himself on the porch railing. Glory sat on the swing and began pushing herself back and forth with one foot, her other leg tucked beneath her. Contrary to her earlier dismissal of the beer, she quickly consumed over half the bottle.

After several minutes, just when Eric thought maybe they'd actually pass the time until dinner in silence, Glory said, "Does your wife work late on Thursdays or something?" She didn't look at him, instead concentrated on fingering the fraying label on her beer bottle.

He took a swig of his own before he answered. "No. We're divorced. I have Scott on Thursday nights."

"Oh."

Something confrontational lurked in that single word, as if she now saw through his diabolical plan.

"What?"

She lifted a shoulder, still not looking at him.

"There's obviously something you want to say to me. Spit it out," he said.

She let go of a long breath. "I just don't like to see Granny's good and giving nature taken advantage of." Then she raised her eyes and looked square at him for the first time since she'd left him in the garden.

He ground his teeth together to keep from letting loose his frustration. She couldn't know his situation. She obviously didn't know the arrangement he had with Tula—and how Tula had come to depend upon it as much as he did. Maybe Tula, in her pride, didn't want Glory to know.

He got up and walked down the porch steps without saying anything.

Chapter Four

❀

GLORY RETURNED TO the kitchen before Gran came out to call them for dinner. She didn't want to have to explain why Eric wasn't still on the porch with her. She paused in the kitchen doorway. Granny was mashing potatoes and humming a country tune. Her movements were sure and steady; she certainly didn't appear like a woman with any visual impairment. Maybe she wasn't covering up a worsening condition as Glory had feared.

That thought brought about a serious—and surprising—case of mixed emotions. The last thing she wanted was for Gran to lose her sight. Glory had come home reluctantly but with the full intention of staying if Granny needed her. Dawson was a hotbed of pain, but she'd face it for Granny. But if Gran really was fine and wanted Glory out from underfoot . . . where would she go?

As she rolled these questions in her mind she realized that, beginning with Granny's call, this was the first time in months that Glory had felt a sense of purpose. If Granny didn't *need* her . . .

She grabbed on to the positives, pushing away the unexpected hint of panic that teased the edges of her senses. She told herself she would be glad to get out of Tennessee without venturing inside the Dawson town limits; without having to pass where her house used to stand, where her life used to be. However, the mere thought of leaving the security of Granny's warm home left her with a chunk of ice in her stomach.

Just then Granny looked over her shoulder. "Oh, I didn't hear you come in. Where's Eric?"

Glory avoided answering that question. "I came in to help. I'll set the table." She moved toward the cabinet that held Granny's Blue Willow Ware.

"Let's eat out on the picnic table. It's too dang hot in here." Granny dabbed the perspiration on her forehead with a paper towel. "There's a cloth in the pantry there . . . got roosters on it."

"I thought Pap made you get rid of that one." Glory's grandfather had always hated that tablecloth; said it was impossible for him to eat chicken—which was his favorite—with those roosters staring at him with their accusing eyes. Said it gave him the whim-whams. The last time Glory remembered Granny using it, Pap had gotten up with a huff and taken his plate to eat on the front porch—even though it had been the middle of February.

Granny chuckled. "Wasn't that the most ridiculous thing, a grown man run off from his own table by pichures of chickens." She shook her head. "And Sam raised on a farm like he was!"

Glory smiled at the memory as she retrieved the tablecloth. Then she carried it and a stack of plates into the backyard. As she descended the back steps, she saw Eric rummaging around in his Explorer. He was leaning far inside the passenger door. She caught herself staring and quickly looked away; he had what Granny would call a "fine backside." And Glory felt extraordinarily rude in noticing.

A slight breeze began to move, bringing relief from both the closeness of the air and the burning of Glory's cheeks—even though she tried to deny that they were burning. She busied herself with readying the table and lighting the citronella candles, even though the light breeze held promise of keeping early-evening mosquitoes at bay. Just as she unfurled the tablecloth, the wind kicked up a notch, flipping the far end of the cloth back on itself. Before she got her end situated and moved to the other side, Eric was there, spreading the cloth evenly over the table. She took the plates and set them at the corners to hold it in place, which left her standing beside Eric.

Neither of them said a word. Glory sensed a standoff of sorts. He didn't move away. His nearness somehow changed the air around her; she could actually "feel" him without touching at all. She fought the urge to step away, to shake that sensation off her skin.

Well, one of us has to say something. "Thank you," she said flatly, without looking at him.

"No problem," he replied in an equally distant tone. Then he finally moved, picking up the small black cardboard box he'd set on the picnic table bench.

Glory stood in place until she heard the screen door swing closed. "Guess I really ruffled his feathers," she muttered. But she wasn't sorry. He had asked her to speak her mind, and she had. She hadn't been hateful about it; she'd simply stated her case. It seemed that every divorced dad in the county counted on Granny to take care of their kids. Cousin Charlie and his brood were bad enough.

She returned to the house but stopped on the stoop just outside the kitchen door. She held her breath as she looked through the screen.

Eric and Granny stood face-to-face, and he was handing the black box to her. Granny opened it and looked inside, then put a hand on her chest and looked up at him. The gratitude and excitement Glory saw in her grandmother's eyes squeezed her heart, making it ache with love.

Then, without a word, Granny shook her head and pushed the box back toward him.

He laughed then, taking Granny's wrists in his hands. He kissed her on the forehead before he reached inside the box and pulled out a pair of black-framed sunglasses and settled them on her nose. Glory recognized them as expensive Oakleys—a sharp contrast to the old, cheapie sunglasses Granny had worn to the raspberry bramble today.

Finally, manners gained the upper hand and Glory stopped acting like a peeping Tom, opening the screen door and stepping inside the hot kitchen.

Granny turned and tilted her nose haughtily. "Do I look like a movie star?"

Glory smiled. "Very glamorous."

"Eric says they'll be better for my eyes."

Glory glanced at Eric; his gaze skittered away.

Granny said, "They're polar lenses."

"Polarized," Glory offered.

"That's what I said." Then Granny lowered her voice. "I'm sure they were costly. Much too costly." She cast a reproachful look toward Eric.

"I told you, Tula, I got a deal," Eric said dismissively, then quickly headed toward the living room. "I'd better wake sleepyhead or I'll never get him to bed tonight."

"He's always 'getting deals' for me," Granny confided quietly when he was out of the room. "Got plenty of troubles of his own, don't know why he frets 'bout me." She sighed as if the answer to that particular mystery would forever elude her. Then she brightened and turned her head from side to side for Glory to inspect. "See how they curve 'round? Keeps the light out of the corners."

"I'm sure they'll be a big improvement." And for some reason the fact that Eric was the one to think of it rankled just a bit. *That's because it makes you feel like a heel for your remarks on the porch.*

She shook off the thought and started to fill glasses with ice, while Granny took up the chicken.

Eric paused and looked at his sleeping son. Scott lay on Tula's living room floor. He was on his back, with his arms thrown over his head, the end of the quilt Tula had made for him clutched tightly in one chubby fist. Scott had had a name for that quilt, "bink," but it had been weeks since Eric had heard him use it. Eric's heart felt as if a steel band were tightening around it. If it hadn't happened so often in the past weeks, he might have thought he was having a heart attack. But now he knew it was a symptom of love—and fear—not disease.

Up until recently, Eric had been a stranger to fear.

Scott's cheeks were pink from the heat, the curve of his face still gently rounded with baby fat. In moments like these Eric could almost fool himself into believing Scott was just like any other toddler. And he was tempted to bury himself in that belief, just as Jill had done. But there was too much at stake to dwell in the comfortable land of make-believe.

Long naps were becoming rare. In fact, Scott's sleep patterns had been increasingly erratic—another sign, according to all of the books Eric had been reading on autism. He closed his eyes and drew in a breath. God, he was beginning to hate that word, as if it alone were responsible for robbing him of his son.

He sighed, trying to loosen the knot in his gut. It wouldn't do at all if he couldn't eat the dinner Tula had roasted herself in the kitchen preparing. He closed his eyes. Three deep breaths. Three long exhalations. Deep breath. Exhale. His heart began to feel less constricted; he willed his stomach to follow suit.

When he opened his eyes again, Glory was standing in the doorway, arms crossed over her chest, watching. The expression in her eyes was unreadable.

Without a word, she turned and went back into the kitchen.

Tula wore her new sunglasses as they ate dinner at the picnic table; it did Eric's heart good to see his gift so appreciated. But then, Tula appreciated everything, even the smallest, seemingly insignificant nuances of life.

When Eric's own parents had moved to Gatlinburg several years ago, Tula had taken Eric into her heart, just as if he'd been one of her own grandchildren. She'd accepted Scott when Eric and Jill had been desperate—all of their other babysitters, with the exception of Jill's mother, Gail, had refused to deal with Scott's disruptive and erratic behavior. And even Grandma Gail, after Eric had offered to match her part-time wage at the Dixie Bee

Flower Shop, admitted that she couldn't cope with Scott more than two days a week. So, as far as Eric was concerned, Tula deserved far more than he was able to give.

She would have rocketed into orbit if she knew what he'd paid for those sunglasses. But he'd done his research; those were the best option for Tula's problem. Truth be told, he'd have paid twice as much to ease her discomfort. He didn't want to contemplate what might happen if Tula's eyesight did begin to fail—and not only because of Scott.

Eric immersed himself in appreciating the moment. Scott was being relatively cooperative, Tula was beaming in her sunglasses, the food was excellent and the weather agreeable. The only fly in the ointment was Glory's distant reserve. And that actually had benefits of its own. No small talk, no unpleasant subjects.

Tula had made Scott the only food he was currently eating: a peanut butter and banana sandwich, white bread, crust trimmed, cut into four perfect triangles. It was served on a paper napkin, not a plate. The napkin had to be square with the edge of the table. His Sippy Cup of milk positioned just off the upper-right-hand corner of the napkin. Any variation of this resulted in refusal to eat and a crying fit that took an hour to abate.

Since the divorce, Eric's life had been a steady, monotonous grind of work and worry—and Scott wasn't the only cause for the latter. Eric really looked forward to Thursday nights with Tula. He glanced at Glory over his iced tea glass. Her reappearance was forcing him to think about things he'd kicked under the bed eighteen months ago. Things his conscience would rather not reexamine.

Trying to sound offhand, he asked, "So, Glory, are you back here for good?" He took another bite of fried chicken to emphasize the casual nature of the question.

Glory's gaze cut to Tula. "Yes."

The look the two women exchanged—even with Tula wearing sunglasses—made Eric suddenly feel as if he were balancing on a beehive.

Tula huffed. "Glory's got the notion in her head that I shouldn't live alone." Her lips pressed together the way she did when she was particularly peeved. "I shouldn't have call—"

"I was coming home anyway." Although the retort was quick, the tone in Glory's voice was less than convincing.

"Bullhonkey! Don't think you can fool me, missy. You had no ideas a'tall about comin' back here 'til I called you." Tula was bristling now. "I won't have it. I'm fine. And if the day comes that I ain't—I won't be having you come home and babysit me!"

Glory's back visibly stiffened. She drew herself up for the fight, just the way he'd seen Tula do more times than he could count.

"I told you that I'd been thinking about leaving St. Paul. The winter—"

"Had nothin' to do with you comin' back here. You explained it all to me afore you left—you cain't live here now." She paused and appeared to rein in her temper. "I was just scairt is all. Jumped the gun; shoulda waited. Ever'thing is fine; my eyes ain't no worse than before."

Eric shifted uncomfortably. He didn't need to worry about Glory thinking his question held ulterior motives with all of this going on. Still, he felt responsible for the confrontation. He chanced a comment. "I've been reading up on MD; Tula could get along fine indefinitely. It might not progress."

The fiery look Glory shot him could have melted a hole in plastic. Lucky for him he was made of steel. He said, "I'm just saying there's no need to get worked up over this right now."

"And I'm saying that's *not* why I came back," Glory directed more toward him than Tula. "I'm here because it's time to come home."

Time to come home? The haunted look in Glory's eyes and her nervous posture said otherwise.

And Eric was afraid he just might know why.

Eric shot further holes in Glory's assumption that he was taking advantage of her grandmother when he got up from the table and started doing the dishes. He settled Scott in the kitchen with his plastic ship and filled the sink with water; Granny didn't own a dishwasher.

Glory was further astounded when Granny made herself a cup of tea, leaving the dirty kitchen to Eric.

She paused and smiled at Glory. "It's our way; I cook, he scrubs."

After a moment, Glory said, "Since I didn't cook, guess I clean too."

"Reckon that's fair. Eric could use the help. He doesn't get another beer until he's finished, and it's hotter 'n blazes in here." She took her cup and headed toward her front porch swing. "Got to hurry or I'll miss the fireflies comin' up out of the grass."

"You two have quite the routine." Glory was slightly ashamed of the jealous edge in her voice. Luckily, Granny didn't seem to notice and kept going. But, out of the corner of her eye, Glory caught Eric pause as he scraped chicken bones into the trash and look at her.

She ignored him, pulling a ponytail holder from her pocket and tying her hair up off her neck. Without another word to him, she shuttled the rest of the dirty dishes in from the backyard.

By the time she was folding the tablecloth, he had a stack of dishes ready to be dried. She picked up a towel. "You do pretty good work for a man."

He looked at her and raised a brow. "A *fire*man. Lots of downtime at the station." He tilted his head from side to side as he listed, "We cook. We clean. We polish."

She completed his unfinished accounting. "You rescue cats from trees. Clean up toxic spills. Administer lifesaving measures at accident scenes." She paused, then added softly, "Carry women out of burning buildings."

At that his hands stilled in the water, but he didn't look at her again. "All in a day's work," he said, with what sounded like forced lightheartedness.

"Was it?"

"Was it what?" Now he turned to face her, his eyes holding her motionless as her heart raced.

"Just another day at work?" She bit her lip but held his gaze, unsure why she was pursuing this at all. Maybe it had something to do with the odd way he had looked at her as she and Granny had argued over her returning to Dawson. It hadn't been pity in his gaze—she'd seen enough of that to identify easily. He seemed to be . . . speculating. She couldn't shake the notion that something was on his mind. "I mean, in a town this size, stuff like that doesn't happen every day."

He simply looked at her with an unreadable expression for a long moment—long enough that she thought he wasn't going to answer. And as she looked into his eyes, eyes the shade of fine aged bourbon, she felt herself leaning slightly toward him, as if coaxing his response. Suddenly she *needed* to know. Had the destruction of her life been just another day on the job? It seemed impossible the same event that was so significant in her life could be ordinary to others who had been drawn into it.

Finally, he said, "No. That night still haunts me."

His admission snatched Glory's breath away. Not only by what he said, but by the way he said it. It was as if he too suffered nightmares and dark hours filled with doubt.

Just as she overcame her surprise and opened her mouth to ask why, he closed the subject by returning his focus to the dishwater. "You'd better get busy with that towel. You're way behind."

Chapter Five

✿

FRIDAY MORNING GLORY was awake before the sun but lingered in bed, contemplating how she wanted to attack the day. Suddenly she realized that was the way she had begun to think of each and every day, as if she were embarking on a carefully planned military maneuver. Instead of outflanking an enemy, she worked to avoid anything that reminded her of what she had lost.

She was analyzing that realization when she heard a car roll to a stop in front of the house. She glanced at the clock. It wasn't even six-thirty yet. A short time later she heard the kitchen door open and close, then Eric's unmistakable voice speaking to her grandmother. There was something infinitely comforting about the timbre of his voice as it sifted through the floor and echoed through the ductwork.

There was another thing she was going to have to deal with, she thought. Eric. They had been friendly acquaintances before she left Dawson. But now every time she looked at him, it was impossible to separate him from the night of the fire. And it was definitely going to be difficult to arrange her daily battle plan in a way that their paths didn't cross.

Now that she'd come home, she was going to have to revise her thinking. She couldn't avoid everything that provoked feelings of loss. She was going to have to find a way to face the town with an eye toward the future.

Well, she didn't have to start this morning. She curled deep into her covers, pulling them over her head.

She chastised herself for behaving like a reluctant child. Still, she didn't get out of bed until she heard the back door open and close and Eric's car start.

To avoid the appearance that she had just been waiting to hear him leave, she took a long shower and got dressed before she went downstairs. When she entered the kitchen, Granny was reading to Scott. She sat on the floor across from him, not holding him in her lap as she'd done with Glory and all of the other grandchildren.

Scott didn't seem to be paying any attention to her as she changed the pitch of her voice to imitate the different characters and gestured with her hands to show a bird's flight.

She looked up. "'Mornin', Glory."

Pap had always said that to Glory at every opportunity, always with a chuckle. After he died, Granny had taken up the greeting.

"'Morning, Gran." Glory helped herself to coffee and toast, skirting widely around the little boy. Again she thought there must be something fundamentally wrong with her. Before the fire, she would have been on the floor herself, playing with *any* young child. Children and animals—she'd never been able to resist either one. But for some reason she felt as if she and this boy were two negatively charged particles, the very force of their being insisting upon not occupying the same space.

"What do you think the three of us should do today?" Granny asked brightly. "Scott normally goes to school on Friday mornings, but he's got today off."

Glory shot a glance at the little boy over the rim of her coffee mug and mentally scrambled for an out. "Actually"—she set the mug down and fiddled with her coffee spoon—"I thought I'd drive into town today."

Granny looked surprised. "Why not wait 'til tomorrow, and I'll go, too. I got some shopping to do."

"Make me a list; I'll be glad to pick things up for you."

After a pause, Granny said, "You sure you want to go alone?" Her tone was filled with unformed questions: *What if you panic like you did when you saw Eric? What if you REMEMBER?*

"Yes . . . I think I am." And she was surprised to realize it was the truth. Perhaps it was because if she did fall into a million pieces, she could sit alone in her car until it passed and not have to worry about the reaction of those who would be spectators. After her reaction to Eric that first moment, she knew she didn't want to have witnesses to what could very well be so much worse.

Granny laid down the book and came to sit at the table. She grasped Glory's hands. "I'd feel better if I was with you."

"I'll be all right, Gran." She squeezed Granny's hands. "I probably won't even go . . . there. Not yet anyway." *Maybe not ever.*

"I don't like it." She got up and grabbed a pencil and paper from next to the phone. "Here's Eric's number. He'll be at the firehouse—close by. Promise me you'll call him if you—"

"I'll be fine. It's been a long time—"

"*Promise* me!" She held the slip of paper so tightly it trembled in her hand.

"Okay." Glory had never seen Granny so adamant. "Okay, I promise."

Tula watched Glory's Volvo disappear around the curve in the lane. A lump of worry sat in the pit of her stomach. There was so much that Glory hadn't faced. So much in her past that she'd hidden away from herself. So much talk after she left—talk Glory knew nothing about. People called her "the rich widow," not knowing anything about how Andrew had left her with nothing. And when she up and left town, it had been like pouring gasoline on a fire.

The talk had died down quite a while back. But the memories of those who thrive on gossip are quick to recall. What if today, while Glory was alone and unsuspecting, somebody said something hurtful?

Tula was no fool. She knew she couldn't keep Glory hidden in the hollow forever. But she didn't want Glory to face awful truths alone.

This morning there wouldn't be anyone to catch her when she stumbled—unless she called Eric.

Please, Jesus, let her call Eric if things go bad.

Tula sighed and turned away from the window. Maybe it would have been better if Glory hadn't come back at all.

Thunder rumbled in the distance, heralding a break in a long string of sweltering days. Eric closed his office door. Storms usually meant lightning strikes and car accidents, maybe even a flash flood. It looked as though a busy day loomed ahead for the department. If he was going to have an uninterrupted hour, this would be it.

Hands on his hips, he circled his desk, staring at the file folder lying between his untouched coffee and a stack of mail that needed his attention. It had been over a year and a half since he'd opened this particular file. He should leave well enough alone.

He inched closer, then paused, staring at the folder as if it were a wild animal and he was prey. No quick movements, no posture of fear, or it'd all be over.

Slowly he reached out and settled the fingertips of one hand on the folder, but went no further. There was no sensible reason to open it. He'd run a by-the-book investigation. The report was complete. The state fire marshal had signed off on it. End of story.

The tab read: 11632 LAUREL CREEK ROAD. It sounded like an idyllic place for a newlywed couple to build their storybook cottage. And that's what Andrew and Glory Harrison's house had appeared to be, something from a fairy tale—of course, it was the updated, *Southern Living* version of happily-ever-after, spacious and new, nearer castle than cottage. It had been tucked into the fold of a wooded hillside. In Eric's mind's eye he could still see it: a white-painted Carolina house, with steeply pitched gables, forest green shutters, and a deep verandah with red geraniums in huge pots flanking the front door. A brick drive led to a quaint carriage house garage in the rear.

Jill had lusted after the Harrisons' house, had asked Eric to drive past every time they were on that side of town. Which was probably why he could recall it so vividly now; that, and the fact that those drive-bys often led to a point of contention. Jill had always taken notes and clipped magazine articles, planning on how they would build *their* new house.

As far as Eric had been concerned, the 1920s crafts-style bungalow they owned (without a gargantuan mortgage), set on quiet, tree-lined Montgomery Avenue, left nothing to be desired. It had a big fenced yard. It had hardwood floors. It had character.

Jill had said it had other people's dirt.

Instead of the old adage: location, location, location, Jill's motto had been: new, new, new. That had been part of their undoing, Jill's overriding desire to have the best, her worry over everyone else's opinion of her house, her car, her clothes. He'd never been able to figure out where her insecurity had come from, but it had loomed larger with each passing day of their marriage. She had refused to quit work after Scott was born, as they'd originally agreed— and not because she was a career-minded woman, but because she'd wanted that house more than she wanted anything in her life.

Eric closed his eyes and forced Jill away from his thoughts. Best to keep focused on one bothersome issue at a time.

He drew again on the memory of the Harrisons' house. *Idyllic*; nothing described it better. Only the discreet sign noting the security company that guarded the house had marred the image of peaceful perfection.

But the storybook cottage had turned into a house of horrors. And Eric couldn't ignore his suspicion that it had begun to transform long before the night of the fire. He recalled one day in particular:

It was Eric's first day back on duty after Scott's birth. Jill called with a list of things for him to pick up at the drugstore on his way home. It was only late afternoon, four-thirty or so, when he pulled into the Walgreens at the edge of town.

He didn't waste time with a cart; he figured he could handle the five items easily enough. Anxious to get home after eight long hours of separation from his newborn son, he dashed up and down the aisles, looking for unfamiliar things like Desitin, nursing pads, baby wipes, newborn diapers, and sanitary napkins. He was down to the last item. He juggled the load in his arms and ventured into the uncharted territory of the Feminine Hygiene aisle. There he stopped dead in his tracks.

What appeared to be several thousand varieties lined a multitude of shelves. Hundreds of combinations of shapes and sizes, fragrances and various "duty" ratings stretched endlessly before him.

Feeling as out of place as he had when he'd accompanied Jill to the obstetrician and been the only male in the crowded waiting room, he glanced up and down the aisle. He was alone.

Scanning the labels quickly, nothing jumped out and said "obvious choice." So he stepped closer and began to read more carefully. He leaned forward and the box holding the tube of Desitin tumbled off his stack. When he stooped to pick it up, the nursing pads bounced onto the floor. He picked them up, and while he was down there, decided to read the packages on the bottom shelf.

"You look about as comfortable as a cat in a car wash." A soft, teasing voice came from behind him.

He looked over his shoulder, his cheeks warming with embarrassment—which was ridiculous after all of the things he'd been through with Jill in the past few weeks.

Glory Harrison stood there with a smile on her face. Not an "I'm laughing at you" smile, but a sympathetic "I can get you out of this" smile.

"Out of my depth," he admitted.

"Did she say what brand?" Glory asked matter-of-factly.

He stood up, managing to keep his load from toppling to the floor. "She did . . . and I can't remember. It seemed easy enough when she told me."

She stepped around him and quickly selected a package and handed it to him. "This should be middle-of-the-road enough to get her by."

As he took the package from her, he noticed she wasn't looking at him, but at the baby items in his arms. There was something like yearning in her eyes.

He said, "Um, well, thank—"

"There you are!" Andrew interrupted as he strode down the aisle toward them. The look on his face was not one of cordial greeting. He stopped beside Glory and gave Eric a curt nod.

"Andrew." They could hardly pretend they didn't know one another, as much as Eric wished they could. They'd been friends in high school—before everything changed. But no one knew of those changes except Eric and Andrew. He said, "Glory helped me out of a jam. Sorry to hold her up."

Andrew grasped Glory by the elbow and said, "We're going to be late." He propelled her toward the front of the store.

"Congratulations," she called over her shoulder.

He must have looked puzzled.

"On the new baby," she added.

"Thanks," he said, his eyes focused on the grip Andrew had on her arm.

Andrew leaned close to her ear and said something. Glory cast her husband an affronted look. Then she tried to pull her arm away, but Andrew must have tightened his grip as he propelled her more quickly out of the store.

Outside of Eric's office, the wind suddenly kicked up, whipping a tree branch across the window, startling him back to the present. If only he'd had the gift of foresight, he could have read the significance of that encounter. But he'd been a harried new father with much more than Andrew Harrison on his mind.

He ran his hands through his hair. "Maybe I'm way off base," he muttered to himself.

But he'd ignored his instincts after that fire, taking what was before him at face value. And he'd been able to put it out of his mind . . . until Glory showed up.

He sat down at his desk and opened the file. As the gloom gathered outside, he reread the facts he'd recorded eighteen months ago.

Glory entered the town limits with none of the dramatic reaction she'd experienced two days ago when she'd crossed into Tennessee. She credited Granny for that; time with her grandmother had stabilized her, just as she'd known it would.

Of course, Glory had carefully avoided Laurel Creek Road. *That* she wasn't ready for.

The gray clouds boiled overhead, fueled by the summer heat. The wind rose, sending dust skittering across the street and the occasional breeze-filled Wal-Mart bag sailing by. It would have been much smarter to stay home, or at least wait out the storm.

But home had hazards of its own. She didn't want to spend the entire day examining her unwarranted aversion to an innocent little boy.

She cruised slowly up and down the streets in the six-block area that was downtown Dawson. As much as she felt that she herself had changed, it seemed odd to see that the town had remained much the same as the day she'd driven away.

Dawson was off the well-beaten tourist path, so it hadn't experienced the proliferation of gift and trinket shops, motels and pancake houses, condos and time shares that catered to those passing through to the Great Smoky Mountains National Park. And even though she'd run from the place, Glory was suddenly glad of its constancy. Having lived in several places, she could see it so clearly; urban people, in their quest for a rural experience, had brought with them all of the congestion and growth of suburbia—the very thing they were running from. Dawson remained an island of independence. The town council had debated for years over the advisability of attracting tourism.

Granny had often said that if the tourists came in—she was getting out. Glory had thought it tough talk; after all, Granny had lived in Cold Springs Hollow her entire life. But the reality was, if there was a steady stream of hikers parking on the road and parading back to Blue Falls Pond, the hollow wouldn't be the same.

She prayed for Granny's sake it wouldn't come to that. She couldn't see Granny living anywhere else on God's green earth. Granny—who might someday have trouble seeing the rainbow in the spray at Blue Falls, who might very soon have a hole in her sight that would affect so much of what she loved.

As Glory drove the streets thinking of Granny's visual clock ticking away, she passed the Dixie Bee Flower Shop and got an idea. She parked the car and went inside.

No one was at the counter, so she browsed the displays as she waited. Plenty of grandkids came to Granny with fistfuls of wildflowers, but a real flower delivery... Glory couldn't recall Granny getting a single one. Gran's own garden was filled with day lilies and snapdragons, so those wouldn't do. It had to be special.

Roses? Everyone sent roses. She wanted something that said, Tula Baker.

"May I help you?"

Glory had been so deep in thought, the voice startled her. She turned from a refrigerator case and looked at the woman behind the counter. She recognized Mrs. Landry, Jill Wilson's mother and Scott's grandmother. Mrs. Landry was an older version of her daughters—willowy, fair, classic wholesome beauty. Jill's younger sister Jennifer had been in Glory's class—prom queen as a matter of fact.

"I'm looking for something original, for a home delivery." Glory wasn't really ready for a trip down memory lane; with any luck at all, Mrs. Landry wouldn't remember her.

There was a chilly edge to the woman's smile. Glory attributed it to the fact that Mrs. Landry had come from up north and always held herself slightly apart, as if she'd had a more *refined* upbringing. "Planter or cut flowers?"

"Flowers," Glory said. "Something simple and . . . strong."

"Let's see." Mrs. Landry stepped around the counter to the cooler. Leaning close to the glass, she said, "We have bird-of-paradise, here."

"I don't think that's quite right." Glory had never liked those orange-headed, long-beaked bird-looking flowers; they gave her the creeps.

Mrs. Landry said, "Let me think . . . strong . . ." She tapped her chin with one well-manicured finger. "Gladiolus? We have several colors."

Glory shook her head. "Reminds me of funerals."

Mrs. Landry's gaze sharpened. "Well, you certainly have had enough of those." Before Glory could react, Mrs. Landry went on, "This is a happy occasion then?"

Was it happy . . . sending Granny flowers because this time next year she might not be able to see them?

Glory simply nodded, still a little taken aback by Mrs. Landry's funeral comment.

Then Mrs. Landry opened the cooler door, shifted a bucket filled with Asian lilies, and Glory saw exactly what she was looking for.

"There! Those in the back corner."

Mrs. Landry smiled at her as if Glory were an apt pupil. "Excellent choice. White calla lilies. Very regal." She reached for them. "Would you like greenery, or perhaps another type of flower, to fill out the bouquet?"

Glory considered for an instant. The thick-stalked, pure white funnel-shaped flowers needed to stand on their own. Anything else would dilute the effect. "No. Just the callas—maybe fifteen of them? In a plain, tall thick-glass vase."

"It will be beautiful. Your taste is to be commended. Most people around here want roses or carnations. This will be on the expensive side." She paused. "But I suppose price is no object."

"It's for someone very special." Even as she said it, she doubted that was what Mrs. Landry had meant.

While Glory filled out the note card, Mrs. Landry wrote up the order.

"To whom and where would you like this delivered?"

Glory nearly let a chirp of laughter slip; she'd bet money that Mrs. Landry was the only person in Dawson to use the word "whom." "They're for Tula Baker."

"Cold Springs Hollow Road?"

"Yes, ma'am."

Glory gave the woman her credit card and concluded the sale. As Mrs. Landry handed the card back, her countenance shifted. Glory recognized the look immediately. She'd seen it on every face she passed in Dawson after the fire; a peculiar blend of pity, curiosity, and relief that they were not in Glory's shoes.

"I'm so sorry for your loss." She paused and shook her head slightly. "It was a terrible thing. Andrew was a wonderful young man. His mother still hasn't recovered."

I haven't quite gotten over it myself.

Glory concentrated on tucking her credit card back in her wallet. She'd forgotten that Mrs. Landry and Andrew's mother, Ovella, played bridge together. When she looked up, Mrs. Landry was still staring at her.

Mrs. Landry's voice was low, confidential, when she said, "Ovella said they decided it was the furnace?"

"Yes." Glory assured herself that every initial encounter was bound to bring up the subject of the fire, but after people got used to her being here again, it would die down. And surprisingly, Mrs. Landry's questions weren't breeding panic but irritation. Maybe she was stronger after two days with Gran.

After a pause, as if Mrs. Landry was weighing her allegiances, she said, "Odd, to have a furnace fire like that in a house only a few years old." She pursed her lips. "Ovella just couldn't believe it." A challenge seemed to lurk in the woman's voice.

Glory said nothing, just put her wallet in her purse and picked up her car keys. "Thank you for your help." She turned to leave.

That seemed to shake Mrs. Landry out of her rare breach of polite aloofness; her curious mood concealed if not quelled. "These should be there by early afternoon."

"That's good. Thank you." As Glory left the store, she could feel Mrs. Landry's probing stare on her back.

Tula tried to hold her fretting at bay by doing some quilting, but the morning was too dark. Even with all of the lights on, the fine details of the work were obscured. Eric had ordered her one of those round hobby lights, mounted on a rotating arm with the magnifier right in the center, but it hadn't come yet.

She had put a lot of hope in that light. Sometimes it scared her to think what she'd do if it didn't help. But her mama had always said, *If you was born to be shot, you'll never drown.* Tula got up and straightened her back. No need to worry over fate; if the light didn't help, she'd trust Jesus to guide her in figuring out something else.

She said to Scott, "Come on now. We'd best get our walk in early. Gonna rain."

The little boy didn't appear to hear her.

She knelt before him and put her hand under his chin, like Eric always did. With gentle pressure, she raised Scott's gaze to meet her own. "Walk," she said cheerily.

He pulled his chin away and went back to circling his boat. It was getting harder and harder to get him to stop what he was doing and move to something else. But Eric had said it was important not to let him remain doing one thing all day long. So Tula gathered her patience and her resolve and took away the boat.

The squealing cry that followed was no surprise. She put her hands under Scott's arms and set him on his feet.

He continued to scream, his knees now rigid with fury.

She took his little hand and pulled lightly toward the door. "It's a fine mornin' for a walk. Let's go see if we can find us a squirrel." She continued telling him all of the things they might see outside, just as she would to any of her own great-grandchildren, steeling her heart against his pitiful tears.

They reached the door more by stumble-and-drag than walk. Eric had explained to her what needed to be done to help Scott, yet never pushed her to fight these battles; said he was just grateful that she would care for him. But Tula Baker never in her life backed down from a challenge, so she forged ahead, one hard-won step at a time, repeating over and over in her mind: *The right thing ain't always the easy thing.*

Once they were out on the back steps, she stopped for a moment; it seemed only human to let the boy have a minute to adjust.

Scott crumpled to the concrete, burying his face in his hands.

After a minute, she picked him up and set him on his feet again. "Let's go." With a little pressure, he took a step forward. Then another. Then, eventually, another.

Ten minutes later, Tula had him moving along pretty well. His cries had reduced to shuddering breaths and sniffles. She pointed out the bumble bee humming around the cone flowers and the garter snake that slithered into the grass beside the road. She wasn't sure if he paid any attention, but it seemed only right to keep talking.

They reached the cemetery, and Tula led him through the gate. "We'll just take a minute for Pap."

Scott sat on a short, boxy granite stone next to Sam's grave and watched the movement of the grass in the increasing wind as she spoke to her husband.

"'Member I told you Glory'd come home? Well, Sam," she sighed, "now I got me a real problem. She says she's staying—and I know she prob'ly should, but not 'cause she thinks I need her. She'll never find her way if'n that's the way of it. There's things I want to talk to her about, but just seein' how she was when she saw Eric t'other day—I told you 'bout that—I'm thinkin' maybe bringin' it up might make her worse, not better.

"I don't think she remembers certain . . . things 'bout Andrew. It's like she's locked all of the bad up in a closet and can only see the good she lost.

"Oh, I know," she continued, as if he'd commented. "I know a person sometimes should do just that. But with Glory . . . I don't think she'll heal without opening up that closet and takin' a long look inside."

She paused a moment. "You're right; you was always the patient one. I should sleep on it afore I do anything hasty. I'll know when the time is right."

Thunder rumbled, and the wind gave a gust. Tula patted the top of Sam's gravestone. "Thanks for listenin'. I do sorely miss you."

Then she turned to Scott. "We'd best get goin'." She looked at the dark gray clouds as they tumbled across the sky and thanked God for holding off the storm until she'd come to Sam. "It looks lik'n it's gonna be a real toad strangler."

"I'm so glad you could meet me for lunch," Gail Landry said to her daughter after they ordered chicken salad sandwiches at Arlene's Tea Room—the only decent place for lunch in this town.

"You made it sound like there was something important you needed to talk about. You're not going to bail on sitting for Scottie, are you?" Jill said.

"What makes you think that?" Gail wondered just when her daughter had grown so perceptive. Gail *had* been trying to think of a way to back out of her two days a week with Scott.

"You're not exactly hiding the fact that you're finding him . . . taxing."

"Well, it is quite a lot. When he was a baby, he slept, and I could just bundle him up and take him wherever I needed to go." She shook her head; Scott wasn't the reason for this invitation to lunch. "But no, I'm not 'bailing' on you." *Not yet anyway.* "I just thought it'd be nice if we had lunch together once in a while."

Jill lifted a brow. Gail thought sitting across from her daughter was sometimes like looking at a photograph of her younger self. Where did the years go?

The waitress arrived with their lunch. Gail waited until she'd moved away from the table before she said, "You'll never guess who's back in town."

"Who?" Jill didn't sound overly interested.

"Glory Harrison." Then the thought occurred to her. "I wonder if Ovella knows."

"I'm sure she does." Again, Jill wasn't drawn in.

"Funny she didn't say anything about it at bridge last night."

Jill shrugged and took a sip of water.

"Maybe it was too painful," Gail offered. "This has to dredge all that up again for her." Then she asked, "Did Eric ever say anything to you about that fire?"

"No, Mother. And you know if he had, I couldn't tell you anything. Next time we have lunch, we should ask Jennifer, too." Jill seemed awfully quick to change the subject. "I'm sure she could use a break from the twins."

"That's a good idea; even though Greg is there every night to help her. It's just so much easier with two parents."

"Scott *has* two parents, Mother."

"Yes, yes, I know. Eric is a wonderful father—"

Jill held up a hand. "I don't want to ruin a perfectly good lunch with this conversation. You've made yourself abundantly clear already."

Gail forked into her chicken salad. "I just worry."

"Really, Mother, I'm fine. Scott's fine. You don't need to worry."

Gail knew the conversation was over. But there had to be some way to get her daughter to see reason.

* * *

By midafternoon, Glory felt she had the worst behind her. She'd run into old high school girlfriends when she stopped to pick up a sandwich from Arlene's Tea Room, an overly fussy establishment with great chicken salad sandwiches and a ton of clutter that Arlene called Victorian charm.

Glory realized as she'd spoken with girls who'd advanced into womanhood that she hadn't had much contact with most of them since graduation and her marriage to Andrew—which happened in the same month. Still, they all wanted to talk about the fire—compassionately, of course. But there was a bright curiosity burning in all of their eyes, as if hoping to get a crumb of inside scoop. It made Glory more than a little uncomfortable. When she'd left Dawson, everyone had been so sympathetic. Now there was a hard edge to their interest, one that felt . . . well, voyeuristic.

After that depressing encounter, she'd driven past the old house trailer where she'd grown up. The day had turned itself over completely to a wave of thunderstorms and heavy rainfall. It cast an even more dismal pall on the sight. What had been tidy and well maintained while Glory and her mother had lived there had deteriorated greatly. A rusty Chevy Citation was parked in the overgrown grass in the front yard. It looked like it hadn't moved since the grass greened and began to grow in the spring—maybe long before that. The screens on the windows of the trailer were torn and the body of a waterlogged headless doll lay sprawled on the rusting metal steps to the front door.

She'd driven on, resolved to get as much unpleasantness out of the way as she could. She stopped at the bank that held the homeowners insurance money from the fire—which she'd refused to touch—to register a change of address. Doing that had made her start thinking of all of the things she'd been neglecting. She'd intended to donate the full amount to a charity, but hadn't really applied herself to researching and selecting which one.

And throughout the afternoon, Mrs. Landry's last comment nagged and nibbled at the edges of her consciousness. Had Ovella said something to the woman insinuating that the fire report was wrong? Or was that just Mrs. Landry's way of fishing for more information? Certainly, Ovella had never made such allusions to Glory.

After one quick stop at the Shop-n-Save for a few groceries, Glory headed back toward the hollow. She glanced at the piece of paper with Eric's phone number lying on the seat. It pleased her that she'd navigated her way though the emotions of her first encounter with Dawson without falling apart and having to have him rescue her . . . again. She'd always hated weak women, never been one to swoon and be catered to.

The trip left her flooded with emotion, both warmly nostalgic and deeply mournful. She realized she didn't feel she belonged here any more than she'd felt she belonged anywhere else since the fire. Maybe this was going to be the way of things for the rest of her life. Maybe she was looking for something that would never be; she was destined to drift and never fit anywhere.

One small storm had passed earlier in the day, but the heavy, humid air said there was more to come. Shortly after she left town, it let loose. She flipped on the radio to listen for tornado warnings.

The weather got progressively worse as she drove out of town. The wind-driven rain came in pelting waves, the water sheeting across the pavement and running swiftly downhill, filling the narrow ditch beside the road. She drove carefully, mindful of her speed, knowing she was no longer used to navigating these twisting mountain roads.

She turned off the highway and started up the road to Cold Springs Hollow. Turning her wipers on full speed, she was still having difficulty seeing clearly.

Suddenly, a tree limb crashed onto the pavement in front of her as she entered a hairpin turn. She slammed on the brakes. Her car swerved into a skid, heading straight off the curve. She gripped the steering wheel tighter, mashing the brake pedal harder.

Let it off! You can't steer. Let the brake off!

But her adrenaline-infused body refused to listen. Her leg remained rigid, the brake pedal pushed hard against the floor.

The back end of the car swung wildly to the right.

There was a sickening moment when her tires left the earth completely. It seemed to last forever, her car hanging suspended over the steep slope. The roar of the racing engine echoed in her ears.

My God, this is it. This is how I'm going to die.

Then the nose of the car tilted downward. The last thing she registered was the sound of breaking branches as she slammed into a tree.

Chapter Six

❀

As ERIC DROVE slowly back toward town, he was very glad he'd insisted on picking Scott up himself. Jill was an okay driver, but the storm was the worst he'd seen in a very long time, coming in wave after wave of wind, rain, and lightning. In a couple of places the water edged out of the shallow drainage ditch and washed across the road in a muddy stream. Already the creeks were moving fast enough to be a problem for those who weren't aware of the deceptive power of water. The wind lashed the trees, sending small broken branches and leaves slapping and ticking against his windshield and the side of his car.

He frequently checked Scott in the backseat, worried needlessly that the child was afraid of the storm. Scott was snug in his car seat, slowly turning a small ball in his hands, his gaze fixed on the moving pattern of colors.

There was a curve in the road where the water normally sluiced over it in heavy rains. Eric slowed as he approached. Which turned out to be a very good thing. In the lane going the opposite direction on the outside of the curve there was a four-foot-wide, three-foot-long washout. The asphalt and the underlying roadbed were tumbling down the mountain in large, muddy chunks.

After getting out to inspect the safety of the right-hand lane, he was able to drive past, hugging the inside of the curve, undergrowth scraping along the passenger side of the Explorer. Once clear of the hole, he got on his radio and called the sheriff's dispatch. "We've got a six-foot washout in Cold Springs Hollow Road, eastbound side, about a mile from the highway. You'll want to get some barricades up."

"Right. What about the westbound?"

"This road's barely wide enough for two cars as it is, I wouldn't trust it with the way it's coming down."

"Hold on a second, let me tell the sheriff."

In a minute the dispatcher was back. "We'll send the road crew out to barricade at the highway. Deputy Martin is off duty and lives in the hollow. We'll see if we can get him to take care of it from that end."

"I'll hang here until it's secured. Let me know when those barricades are up."

"Will do."

There wasn't much traffic out here, the road went deep into the hollow and ended there. But it only took one unsuspecting driver to become a statistic. He thought of Glory. Tula had said she'd gone into town and wasn't home yet. He hoped she had the good sense not to try until the storm passed.

Less than a quarter mile farther was a dirt fire road that took off on the right. Eric pulled off the main road and parked. Deep rivulets had already been etched down the length of the fire road, depositing a large amount of mud in the culvert where the drainage ditch passed under it. That sinkhole was bound to get much, much larger.

He would try to locate Glory when he got back to town. No way was she going to make it back to Tula's tonight.

"Daddy has to get out of the car for a minute," he said as he turned to look at Scott.

Scott continued to stare at the little ball. That was another thing that worried Eric; his son didn't seem to have any sense of abandonment or danger. Where most children cry when left alone in a car, Scott was oblivious—unless you tried to take away the object of his attention.

Eric reached back and patted Scott's shin. "Love you, baby." The words were little more than a whisper around the lump that had gathered in his throat.

He shrugged on a department rain slicker and got out to place warning flares on the road. The instant he stepped out of the car, the wind ripped the hood from his head and tore at the hem of his raincoat. He squinted against the driving rain, managing to get the flares placed, but he might as well not have bothered with the slicker. He was soaked to his boxers.

He considered running back up the way he'd come and putting flares out there too, but he couldn't do that and still keep Scott in sight. Again he assured himself that of the few folks who drove this road, they should all have the sense to stay home or go easy.

He walked a few yards closer to the hole for another look. Another foot of asphalt had collapsed. If he'd been a few minutes later, he'd have been spending the night at Tula's. He could think of worse things—a stormy night with Tula as company sure beat the hell out of sitting around his place waiting for the electricity to go out. And it would. It always did.

When he got back into the car, Scott was still sitting as passively as he had been when Eric had gotten out. Cell phones didn't work in the hollow, so he radioed his own dispatcher and had her call Jill to tell her he'd be late and not to worry.

Then he waited.

Downtime was never a good thing when he had something nagging his mind. And the Harrison fire report sure as hell qualified as nagging.

He recalled the details of the fire from a professional perspective: The 911 call had come in at 3:50 A.M. from a neighbor who was up with a sick child. As the Harrison house had been situated on a wooded five acres, that neighbor was nearly a quarter mile away. When the department had arrived on scene, half of the house had been fully involved.

As fate would have it, Eric had been on his once-monthly night rotation. He had been the one to go on search and rescue while the remainder of his firefighters battled the blaze. He'd located Glory first, near the back door. The far end of the house, where the bedrooms and Andrew were, had been too hot to enter. Later, when it was safe to go in, Andrew's body was discovered in bed.

Eric's ensuing investigation had revealed that there had been no battery in the carbon monoxide detector. The smoke detector's battery backup had been intact.

Both Glory and Andrew had suffered from carbon monoxide poisoning. *Nothing surprising there.*

Burn patterns indicated that the fire had started in the area of the furnace—the *two-year-old* furnace; it had been replaced under warranty. A malfunction in a furnace that age was surprising—not impossible, but definitely unusual.

Eric had calculated that the fire had begun sometime around three a.m. *Arson hour.*

Glory, the only living witness, couldn't remember anything about the hours prior to the fire.

All of these things were common enough in an accidental fire. But when lumped all together, they should make an investigator look more closely.

And he had, looked, that is; making every effort to ignore his personal suspicion that there were too many coincidences. He had to conduct his investigation without prejudice. There had been no damning evidence that would have held up a ruling of arson.

Still, he knew Andrew—and history often repeated itself. Eric's own knowledge might be the missing link to arson—the unsubstantiated missing link. But his gut had told him that something had been very wrong behind the closed doors of that storybook cottage.

Years ago, while he and Andrew had been teammates in high school, he'd seen things in Andrew's personality that more than gave him pause. The guy was perfect on the outside, yet Eric suspected something darker lurked beneath that perfection. Andrew had dated Jill's cousin, Meghan, for a while. Jill's aunt had been thrilled, always said how she couldn't have picked out a nicer boyfriend for her daughter. But months into the relationship, Meghan had dumped him for no apparent reason. Jill had seen bruises on Meghan's upper arms. She never admitted Andrew had given them to her . . . still.

Maybe the guy had changed by the time he married Glory. Or maybe not.

After looking at all of the evidence in the Harrison fire, Eric had ruled as logic dictated. A faulty gas line on the furnace. Accidental fire. Even after going over the report again today, he couldn't point to anything to contradict that finding. And yet—

His radio interrupted his thoughts. "Chief Wilson?"

"Yes, dispatch, go ahead."

"Sheriff's Office says the barricade's up on Cold Springs Hollow Road."

"Thanks. Tell them I'm leaving my flares on the road up here."

"Right."

He started the Explorer, and said to Scott, "Bet you're ready for your supper, big guy. Won't be long now." He pulled back onto the blacktop and headed toward the highway, windshield wipers thudding back and forth on high. Lightning flashed, followed quickly by a crash of thunder that said it had been very close. Eric's grip on the steering wheel tightened.

He approached the last hairpin curve with relief, creeping along at a speed that made his grandpa look like Mario Andretti. He'd be very glad to be back on the main highway with two wide, paved lanes and better runoff ditches.

As he navigated around a small limb in the sharp curve, he saw something dark on the left side of the road. At first he thought a deer had been hit, then he saw that the figure beside the road was human. He got a bit closer and recognized Glory sitting in the pouring rain. She wasn't moving, just letting the rain pelt her.

He stopped the car. "Daddy'll be right back," he said to Scott as he jumped out.

"Glory! What happened?"

She looked at him, her movements sluggish, her eyes unfocused and blinking against the rain. Slowly she raised a hand and pointed down the embankment beside the road.

He looked over the edge. Her car was smashed against a thick-trunked pine; he couldn't believe she'd gotten out and scaled all of the way back up by herself. She had to be injured.

He went down on one knee and put his hands on either side of her face, checking her pupils. Her lower lip was split and bleeding. She had a raw place on the side of her cheek from the airbag. He ran his hands over her head, feeling for lumps. He felt the alignment of the bones in her neck. And she sat mute while he did it.

"Glory." He lifted her chin so she had to look at him. "Glory. Does anything hurt? Do you have pain?"

She shook her head, blinked, then nodded.

An earsplitting crack rent the air at the same time as a flash blinded him. He jumped. She didn't. The smell of ozone burned his nose.

She started to shiver, her teeth chattering.

"I'm going to help you up." He moved beside her and put an arm around her, then hoisted her to her feet. "Slow. Nice and easy. Let's test and see if you can walk."

She put one shaky foot in front of the other, until they made it to the car. He sat her in the passenger seat and buckled her seat belt for her. He was leaning close when she grabbed his arm. He looked into her eyes, which were now focused and afraid.

"It's okay." He touched her cheek, brushing the wet hair away from her face. "You're okay. I'm going to take you back into town and have the ER check you out."

"No!" The fear in her eyes was edged out by raw panic. "No! No ER." Her fingers dug deeply into his arm.

"Glory," he said softly, "we have to make sure you aren't hurt. I wouldn't be doing my job—"

"Please, Eric." Her green eyes beseeched him, her plea pitiful in its intensity. "Please. I'm all right. Don't leave me there again."

Again. He'd left her there the night of the fire, and she'd miscarried her baby. When she'd first seen him two days ago she'd been terrified by memories brought on by his face.

He didn't want to see her frightened any more.

"I won't leave you. But you might have a concussion."

"I don't." Her fingers dug deeper.

He knelt on the running board and forced her to look him in the eyes. Water was running down the back of his neck, but he ignored it. "It'll be all right." He touched her cheek. "I'll stay with you the entire time. It'll only take a few minutes."

Her eyes closed briefly, and she swallowed hard.

He took that as acquiescence and got back in the car and headed toward town.

Jill listened to the rain pelt the house. She paced in front of the living room window, rarely taking her gaze from the street out front. Eric should have been back by now, even with the washout in the road.

That road into Cold Springs Hollow could be treacherous in a storm. What if there had been another washout or a mudslide, and Eric hadn't been able to stop? What if a tree fell on the car?

She had just about given herself a sour stomach when she saw him pull up. Breathing a sigh of relief, she hurried and opened the front door.

Eric left the car running with the windshield wipers beating back and forth when he got out and pulled Scott from the backseat. There was someone else in the car. The rain was so heavy, Jill couldn't even make out if it was a man or a woman.

He ran up the front steps with his department slicker thrown over Scott's head. When she looked at Eric's rain-soaked face, Jill suddenly realized she was as worried over Eric's safety as she had been Scott's.

Reaching out to take her son, she said to Eric, "You're soaked! You should come in and dry off; have something hot to drink."

Eric swiped his wet hair off his forehead. "Can't. Glory Harrison's in the car."

"Oh?"

"Bye, Scottie." He kissed Scott's cheek. "Bye, Jill." He hurried down the steps without responding to her questioning tone.

She stood there for a few seconds after his Explorer had disappeared down the street. Glory Harrison. What was Glory Harrison doing with Eric?

As she got Scott settled for his dinner, she couldn't get Glory out of her head. Mother's question about Eric's fire inquiry earlier today took on new light. Jill recalled that there *had* been something about that investigation that had been different. Eric had been so preoccupied, almost troubled, for weeks after. Jill had written it off as dealing with Andrew's death. But maybe, just maybe, there was more to it. Suddenly she wished she'd paid more attention.

When Eric got back in the car, he looked at Glory and wondered how in the hell she had managed to get out of her wrecked car and climb out of that ravine. She was a strong woman, just like her grandmother.

He drove directly to the hospital, not opening the topic for discussion again. When they stopped at the emergency door, Glory didn't protest. In fact, she looked more pale and tremulous than she had minutes ago.

When they got inside, he was glad that being fire chief had its perks. The nursing staff just about tripped over their own feet to accommodate them.

Glory was seen immediately by the ER physician, who checked her pupils, palpated her collarbone and legs, then ordered X-rays of her skull and her right knee. When the nurse started to wheel her away, Glory reached out and grabbed Eric's hand. She didn't complain or whine; she just stared straight ahead and held on tight. The fear was still there, making her body rigid and her breathing rapid. When he looked at the hand he held, he could see that her knuckles were white. For the fifth time since they'd been in the ER, he noticed her free hand move to her abdomen; he didn't think it was physical pain that prompted it.

He said with as much reassurance as he could, "I told you I wouldn't leave you, and I won't."

The young nurse cast a sardonic look toward him, but didn't say whatever was obviously on the tip of her tongue. Eric gave her a curt nod, and they were on their way.

Once in radiology, the technician laid a gentle hand on Eric's arm. "I'm sorry, you'll have to wait outside."

He felt a tremor in Glory's hand. "I'm staying with her."

"I don't have to explain to *you*, Chief, why we have this rule, do I?" she asked.

"A little scatter radiation won't hurt me."

"No, Eric, you should wait outside," Glory said. "I'll be all right."

"Let's get this done," he said to the technician. "We're wasting your time. I'm not leaving."

The technician reached behind a corner and pulled out a large gray apron. "Then put this on." She slammed it into Eric's chest. Then she put on her nice voice again and instructed Glory how to position herself for the X-ray.

Eric shifted his shoulders. The lead apron weighed a ton, but he kept ahold of Glory's hand.

Within thirty minutes the doctor announced there were no broken bones. He feared a slight concussion and said he'd like to admit her overnight.

The wild fear Eric had seen when he'd first mentioned the hospital to Glory sprang back into her eyes. "No." She shook her head in a jerky twitch. "I won't stay."

"You need to be monitored," the doctor said. "Awakened every two hours."

The color that had just begun to return to Glory's face drained away. She began to hyperventilate.

"I'll make sure she's awakened," Eric said. "She won't be alone."

The doctor looked unhappy. "I suppose, with your training . . . She'll need to sign a release—"

"No problem," Glory cut him off, as if anxious to be gone.

She signed the papers, then Eric stepped out while she got dressed.

The rain was still pouring when they left the hospital. After he started the engine, he paused to look at her. Her eyes were closed; her head was against the headrest.

She didn't open her eyes when she said, "I'm sorry I was such a pain in the ass."

She looked cold and shaken, scraped and bruised, her auburn hair still dark with rain. And he'd never in his life felt so compelled to take a woman in his arms and comfort her. He stopped his hand just short of caressing her cheek, balled it into a fist, and rested it on the console. "You had reason. Besides, I've seen worse."

Her eyes remained closed, but her lips curved in a slight smile. "Thank you."

He took a deep breath, then said, "There's no way to get you back to Tula's tonight." He let the statement hang there. He realized a moment later that he was waiting to gauge her response. As they sat there in his car with the storm crashing around them, both chafing in wet clothes, her lip swollen and a nasty bruise growing steadily darker on her cheek, he wondered if she felt the same pull of connection as he did.

Or maybe he was just so lonely that he was grasping at straws.

When she opened her eyes and looked at him but didn't respond to his statement, he added, "The road's washed out; it's impassable." The wind buffeted the car, rocking it on its wheels as if to emphasize his declaration.

"Oh." She looked intently at him with those moss-green eyes. She licked her injured lip, then touched it lightly with her fingers. "I . . . I don't really have any-where else to go. Most of my family lives in the hollow." Then she brightened as if just remembering. "Is the Hide-away Motel still in business?"

He barked out an unexpected laugh. "Yeah—and no way am I leaving you there." The Hideaway had been cited for more fire code violations and health department infractions than he could count. It spent most of its time with its "cabins" empty, save for the occasional desperate two-hour adulterous tryst. "It's not safe. Besides, some-one needs to wake you every two hours."

"I'm sure it'll be fine. I can set the alarm."

"Which you won't hear if you're actually unconscious and not sleeping. Nope." He took a breath and said what he'd been thinking since he picked her up off the road. "You're coming home with me."

She shook her head. "I couldn't—"

"Listen, it's my house or stay in the hospital. You can choose. But I'm not leaving you alone tonight." Then he added, "Tula would never forgive me."

Putting it in that context seemed to relax the tension in her face. "Okay. Your house."

It was nearly full dark when Eric parked at the curb in front of his rented duplex. It was one of the few old houses in town actually built as a duplex, not chopped up later. It was two stories, divided vertically in half down the middle, each half the mirror image of the other. It had nearly as much character as his old house, but late at night when he was alone its hardwood floors and high ceilings seemed to echo loneliness instead of charm.

The two units of the duplex shared a large concrete-floored front porch. His next-door neighbor, an elderly woman who'd lived there alone since her divorce in the 1970s (a very depressing thought each time Eric compared the similarities in their situations), had every light blazing, giving an unwelcoming contrast to his darkened windows.

The thunder and lightning seemed to be taking a break, but the rain was relentless.

"I'll run in and get an umbrella, then come back and get you," he said with a hand on the car door.

She laughed, a surprisingly sparkling sweet noise considering her condition. It made him glad he wasn't going to be spending this stormy evening alone. "You've got to be kidding!" She touched a still-shaky hand to her hair. "I sat out there on the side of that road in a downpour for who knows how long before you picked me up. I don't think I can get any wetter."

He tipped his head in acknowledgment. "Wait for me before you get out. Your legs might not be too steady."

By the time he'd run around the car, she had her door open and both feet in six inches of rushing water in the street's gutter. When he reached for her, she said, "I'm fine! Go on." Then she tried to take a step, and her knee buckled.

He reached out and put an arm around her waist and half carried her up his front steps. He didn't let go when he put his key in the lock and opened the door.

The light switches were the old push-button type—push in the top button for lights on, bottom button for off; not anything you could flip with your elbow as you entered a room with your hands full. He carefully guided

Glory to his couch and sat her down, then turned on a lamp.

"I'm surprised the electricity's still on," he said.

The lights immediately flickered, went off for a half a second, then came back on.

Glory hummed the theme from *The Twilight Zone*.

He laughed, glad again for her company; then immediately feeling selfish since she was here only because she'd wrecked her car and gotten hurt in the process.

He said, "Before I get you in a hot shower—" The look on her face cut his words off. "I didn't mean that the way it sounded."

"I know."

He knelt in front of her and instinctively reached for her knee before he realized they weren't at an accident scene, it was his living room; he should ask before he touched. He looked up at her. "May I? Not that I don't trust the doctor, but . . ."

She nodded and the newly born trust he saw in her eyes gave him pause.

"Um, it can wait until after you have these wet clothes off. Do you think you can stand alone in the shower?"

She raised a brow.

Every time he opened his mouth he just dug himself deeper. "I knew I should have insisted on admitting you to the hospital."

"Aw, come on, isn't it a good sign that I've still got a sense of humor?" she said. Then she added dutifully, "I can stand in the shower."

"Good. You shower, then you can put on a pair of my sweats. I can check and ice that knee better then. And I'll get some ointment for your lip."

The bathroom with the shower was on the second floor. He held her upper arm as they walked to the stairs. She stopped at the bottom and looked up, as if she were about to scale a sheer cliff. With a deep breath, she took the first tread. He kept a firm arm around her waist and the other hand on her upper arm next to him. She took another deep breath before she faced the second. She was one tough cookie. She'd probably collapse from pain before she admitted it was too much.

Before she took that step, he lifted her into his arms and started climbing.

"Stop! I'm too heavy," she protested.

"If we want to get you in that shower before you seize up completely, this is the way you're going. Besides," he said lightly, "I'm a fireman, remember. Carrying damsels in distress is all part of the job."

He didn't set her down until they reached the bathroom. Then he left her long enough to retrieve the sweats. As he set them on the toilet, he said, "I'll call Tula while you're in the shower and tell her you're here and safe."

"Don't tell her about the accident! She'll worry if she can't see I'm all right with her own eyes."

He nodded and stepped out of the bathroom. "Be sure and check yourself in the mirror for bruises . . . we might want to ice them after your shower. And take a couple of Tylenol from the medicine cabinet before you get in." He paused. "And don't lock the door."

After giving him a look that was either amusement or suspicion, she nodded.

He saw her take one hobbling step toward the shower to turn on the water just before he latched the door behind him.

He shucked off his own clothes and slipped into a fresh pair of jeans and a T-shirt that he'd grabbed when he got the sweats. Then he sat down on the floor in the hallway just outside the bathroom door. He picked up his cell phone and called Tula.

Glory realized she was getting stiffer by the minute. She pulled her shirt over her head and winced at the pain in her chest and shoulders. Not sharp broken-bone pain, but long-lasting somebody-took-a-ball-bat-to-my-muscles pain.

Once she had her clothes off, she did as Eric had suggested and checked herself in the mirror. Seeing the purpling bruise across her shoulder and chest where the seat belt had caught seemed to make it hurt worse. She leaned closer to the mirror and ran a finger across her split lower lip. It was already swollen to twice its normal size. Then she noticed her fingernails. They had mud caked underneath from her scrabbling up the embankment to the road.

After taking complete inventory, she decided Andrew had been right about the Volvo; considering the impact, she was in surprisingly good shape.

This was an old bathroom, with a pedestal sink and a tub/shower combination. The shower curtain surrounded three sides. She sat on the edge of the deep tub and swung both feet over. The last thing she wanted was to lose her balance, fall, and have Eric rushing in.

There was a peculiar attraction that she felt for him, not exactly sexual, more emotional. Maybe it was because he'd saved her life, maybe it was because—contrary to her first impression—he was showing himself to be so considerate of her grandmother. She guessed it didn't really matter, no reason to analyze it.

For a long while, she stood under the pelting spray of the hot shower, stretching her neck muscles, rotating her shoulders to loosen them. Then she closed her eyes and was assaulted by the image of the giant pine tree hurtling toward the windshield of her car. A sense of vertigo, of the world falling out from beneath her feet, grabbed her. Nausea came in waves. She decided she'd better keep her eyes open.

Once the nausea and light-headedness began to dissipate, she got busy with the soap, scrubbing her fingernails until the cuticles were raw but finally grime-free. Then she reached for the shampoo and found it to be a manly brand without conditioner. It would take her hours to get the tangles out of her hair.

She had worked up a nice lather when the lights flickered.

They came back on steadily for a few seconds. Then a loud crack sounded very near the house, and the lights winked out with an air of finality.

She stood motionless, waiting. No lights.

Then she heard Eric knock loudly on the door. "Glory! Are you all right in there?"

Having the lights out was much like closing her eyes, she felt dizzy and disoriented. "Fine." She had tried to yell, but her voice only squeaked.

"You don't sound fine." She heard the doorknob rattle. "I'm opening the door and setting a flashlight in there."

Dim light shone on the other side of the shower curtain, and Glory could breathe again.

The door didn't close. "Glory?"

"I'm okay."

"You've been in there a long time . . ." He let the statement hang.

"I'll be out in a minute." When the door still didn't close she added, "I'm fine, really."

The door closed quietly, but she didn't hear him walk away.

When she stepped out of the tub, her knees felt even more rubbery than before the shower. She sat on the edge of the tub to dry off. As she picked up the gray sweats, Glory realized the only underwear she had was still soaking wet; she slipped into the sweats without. The neck hung wide on her shoulders and the sleeves covered her hands. The pants rode low on her hips and sagged over her feet, but thanks to the drawstring she could keep them on.

She picked up the flashlight and opened the bathroom door. When lightning flashed, she nearly jumped out of her skin to see Eric standing just outside the flashlight's beam. He'd changed his clothes too and was barefoot.

He put a hand out and grabbed her arm, as if he thought she was going to collapse. "Let's get you lying down." He took the flashlight from her. "You'll have to use my room; I only have one bed. I'll sleep on the sofa tonight."

"Did you get in touch with Gran?" she asked as they made their way slowly down the hall.

"Yes. I told her that I ran into you and told you about the sinkhole and that you're staying at my house tonight. She's relieved you won't be driving home in the storm."

Glory was impressed that he'd been able to keep the fact that she'd wrecked her car from Granny and still managed to tell the truth. It said something for his integrity. She said, "I hope she's all right. If the power's out here . . ."

"Tula's used to power outages. I helped her get her flashlight and camp lanterns ready before I left. And her house is pretty protected from the wind by the lay of the land. She'll be fine."

They entered a bedroom at the front of the house. The only stick of furniture in it was a queen-size bed. It wasn't made.

"Sorry. Wasn't expecting company," he said, as he hastily handed her the flashlight. He straightened out the sheets, then gathered up the pillows and piled them against the headboard. "There."

Glory got on the bed, sitting against the pillows. She flinched as she moved her right knee.

"I want a look at that knee for myself."

She pulled the loose sweats up her leg.

He said, "Shine the light on it for me."

He examined her knee with sure, gentle hands. And for some reason she felt more assured after his exam than she did after the doctor's quick once-over.

"I'll go get some ice." He stood and looked down at her. "But I'm going to need to take the flashlight." Then he looked rather sheepish. "I don't own a candle."

She smiled, glad to have his hands occupied with something other than her bare skin for the moment. "Because they're a fire hazard?" she asked. "Or because you're too manly to burn candles?"

He smiled back, and in the reflective glow from the flashlight she saw that he had a set of shallow dimples on either side of his mouth. He said, "Both." As he walked out of the bedroom taking the light with him, he added,

"Don't move. I have a camping lantern in the basement I'll bring up."

As Glory waited in the pitch-darkness, dizziness returned. Then her eyes gradually adjusted to the dark and she could see the outline of the doorway and the window—enough to settle a bit of the disorientation. By the time Eric came back, her stomach had stopped pitching and her light-headedness had lessened.

Eric set the lantern on the floor. "You should elevate that knee." He set the ice bag down and slid one of the toss pillows he'd brought from the downstairs sofa under Glory's knee. Then he put the ice on her leg and secured it by tying a towel around it. "There. Did you take the Tylenol?"

"Yes." Glory put a hand on her head and remembered that she hadn't combed her wet hair yet. "Crap. I didn't bring my purse out of the car with me."

"No one is going on that road tonight. It'll be safe."

"Oh, I wasn't really thinking about that," she admitted, surprised when she realized her vanity was more of a concern than the security of her credit cards. "I don't have a comb." She lifted the tangled ends of her hair and wrinkled her nose.

"No problem." He left the room again. When he returned he handed her a comb.

"Thanks."

He stood there beside the bed for a minute, his hands stuffed in his jeans pockets, looking as if he wasn't sure what to do with himself. It was the first time Glory had seen him at a loss. She lifted her arm to start working the tangles out of her hair. A quick stabbing pain shot through her shoulder.

She must have winced, because Eric's hand was on hers in an instant.

"Here," he said. "You shouldn't strain your shoulder any more." He took the comb from her. "Scoot over."

She inched toward the middle of the bed, and he sat down.

"I'm afraid I've never done this before, so tell me if I'm pulling too hard," he said as he started to comb her hair.

She nearly objected, feeling horribly out of place here in his bed with him so close, doing something that felt so personal. But if those tangles dried in her hair, she'd probably have to cut them out. She sat stiffly as he put the comb to work.

He began at the crown of her head, and the comb immediately stuck and pulled.

"It works better if you start at the bottom and work your way up a little at a time," she said woodenly, trying to keep herself disconnected from the intimacy of this act.

His fingers brushed the base of her neck when he picked up a handful of hair. She gave an involuntary shiver.

"Cold?" His voice was low, as if in the muted light he was afraid to speak too loudly.

"N—" She couldn't get her own vocal cords to produce more than a whisper. She cleared her throat. "No."

He combed gently through the tangles at the ends, then worked his way toward the top of her head, section by section. In the silence, Glory concentrated on the sound of the rain pelting against the windows, but soon became too aware of the sound of his breathing right behind her.

She needed to say something, but the only thing on her mind was unease and embarrassment. It humiliated her to no end that she was continually being "rescued" by this man. And now, here he was saddled with her for the night—thrown out of his own bed. "I'm sorry," she said.

His hands paused in their work. He said, with laughter in his voice, "Ah, you're finally going to give me that other apology—the one you refused me when you got your knickers in a twist the other day."

He sounded so smug that she turned her head to confront him, all thoughts of apology now gone. The comb caught in her hair and pulled fiercely. She took it from his hand and shook it in his face. "I did *not* get my knickers in a twist. I just reconsidered . . . as I am now." She paused. "And, FYI, that wasn't what I was going to say."

He finger-combed her hair, gently lifting it and letting it fall as he did. "What were you going to say?"

"I'm sorry to interrupt your evening," she said stiffly.

He burst out laughing. "My, my, aren't we formal."

She turned to look at him again, the strain in her sore muscles complaining as she did. "You're stuck with me because of the storm . . . I should have let you leave me at the hospital. It was selfish of me and—I'm sorry."

His gaze held hers and for a long time, she thought he wasn't going to say anything. *How much more awkward could things get?*

"To tell you the truth, I'm glad for the company." He said it so seriously that she thought he might just be as lonely as she'd been feeling lately.

After a moment, she handed him the comb. "Then finish my hair."

He chuckled. "Yes, ma'am."

Once her hair was tangle-free, he gave her the ointment to put on her lip.

"Your movements are getting stiff," he said as he put the cap back on the tube. "Let me massage your shoulders a bit."

She gave him a wary eye.

"It's not a come-on. I'd put you on a heating pad if we had power."

The instant he set his hands on her shoulders, it felt so good that she wanted to cry.

The lantern had grown steadily dimmer over the past few minutes. It finally gave out. Even the lightning had passed, so they were plunged into darkness entirely. Glory tensed, waiting for the vertigo to return.

"What's wrong?"

"I've just been so dizzy when I can't see."

"Not uncommon after an accident like yours. I don't have another battery." He started to get up. "Maybe there'll be enough juice left in the flashlight—"

She put a hand on his wrist. "No. Just stay with me." She paused. "When you're touching me, it's not so bad."

He sighed and moved his hands down her upper arms, pulling her against his chest as he leaned back against the headboard.

"When the power comes back on I'll feed you," he said.

She moaned. "I really couldn't eat anything."

When he exhaled she felt his breath on the top of her head. "All right, then. Try to sleep."

She lay quietly for a few minutes, her back against his chest, riding on the rise and fall of his breathing. Maybe it was the sense of intimacy brought on by being so close in the dark that loosened her tongue when she said, "The other day, in the garden at Granny's. I was going to apologize for behaving so abominably when you came to the hospital the night of the fire. You were kind and considerate, and I was—"

"In shock," he finished for her. "There's no need for an apology."

Granny had said he had come every day, but never tried to see her face-to-face again. "Do you follow all of the people you rescue to the hospital?"

"To be perfectly honest, there haven't been that many. We've been lucky in Dawson."

She gauged that evasive answer, then found herself unable to contain her curiosity. Perhaps she was grasping at something that wasn't there. "But I'm not the only one to go to the hospital. There must have been accidents . . ."

He drew a deep breath. "No, Glory, I don't normally go to the hospital."

She nearly pressed further, but wasn't sure she was ready to know more than that, not tonight while she was feeling the security of his body next to hers, not while she was in his bed.

Chapter Seven

❧

"GLORY." THE VOICE called from a great distance yet brushed her ear as if a breath away.

"Glory." A hand grasped her shoulder. "You need to wake up."

She drew in a breath that told her she'd been drooling in her sleep and struggled to lift her eyelids. She shifted slightly, and said, "'Kay." Her eyes drifted closed.

"You have to wake up. Come on, just for a couple of minutes."

This time she roused herself to her surroundings. She blinked and breathed deeply, trying to make sense of where she was. Eric's bed.

The rest of her world shifted into place. It was storming. She'd wrecked her car. Her head throbbed. Every inch of her ached like a kicked puppy.

She wished she was back asleep.

The night beyond the window remained inky black; the streetlights were still out. The wind sounded like a beast battering against the glass.

When Eric spoke again, she felt the reverberation of his voice against her back. "How's your head?" He rested his hand gently on her crown.

"Oh, my gosh." She sat up so quickly the bed momentarily felt like the deck of a pitching ship. "I've been squashing you against the headboard! I'm sorry." He'd been trapped in a half-sitting position for hours while she'd leaned against his chest as she slept.

"Don't apologize." There was something just a little haunting in his quiet voice—some hint that said perhaps it hadn't been a hardship.

She looked at him curiously for a moment. It was difficult to make out the finer nuances of his expression in the darkness.

She couldn't deny there was something about him that drew her to him. But he was a rescuer by both nature and profession; she shouldn't take his concern as personal interest. The cold truth was: The very reason she was tempted to reveal her inner self to him was the same reason she held back—they had shared one terrible, tragic night, and it bound them together in a tangible, yet inexplicable way. Was there any way for them to connect without that bridge of tragedy?

She decided not to respond to *the tone*. "Has it been two hours already?"

"Four." He pushed himself up straighter and rubbed his neck. "You don't remember me waking you two hours ago?"

"No. Does that mean I have a concussion?"

"It means you were exhausted."

"And you served as my mattress all this time?"

"I like to think of myself as a human heating pad."

She cringed. "I can't believe I was so out; you should have just thrown me off and gotten up."

"I tried . . . once."

"Oh, God." She covered her eyes in shame. "What did I do?"

"Let's just say there was whimpering," he said lightly; she could make out a grin on his face. Before she could say anything else, he changed the subject. "Are you starving?"

She shook her head. "Stomach's still a little rocky. But you should go ahead and eat. What time is it?"

He lifted his wrist to look at the glowing hands of his watch. "Just a little after one."

"I'm so—"

He put a finger on her lips. "Don't. Don't apologize. I wanted to be with you."

There it was again, that tone that shot an odd concoction of longing and unease through her veins.

Then he said, as one would to a child, "I did promise, after all."

Had she imagined that earlier lacing of intimacy in his voice?

She said, "Thank you. Now I release you from bondage. Go feed yourself."

He rose from the bed, then stood there for a moment. "Do you think you can get back to sleep? Maybe I should bring you a couple more Tylenol before I go downstairs."

"I need to go to the bathroom anyway. Go on, I'll be fine."

"Wait a minute." He left the room. Glory heard his feet go down the stairs and return quickly. "Here's the flashlight. I can find my way around in the dark." He flipped it on.

She reached out and took it from him as she slid off the bed. "Thanks."

He hesitated. "Just call me if you need anything . . . or if you get dizzy again. I'll be on the couch."

She nodded.

He took one step toward the door, then stopped. "If you—"

"I'm fine. Go and get something to eat. You might have to carry me back down those stairs tomorrow; you're going to need your strength."

He chuckled, but stuck by her side all the way to the bathroom.

As she put her hand on the doorknob and began to ease the door closed, she said, "I'm not wobbly at all." It was a lie of course, but the man needed to eat—and sleep without being crushed. "You don't have to wait."

"All right." He started to walk back down the hall.

She stuck her head back out into the hall. "Eric."

He turned to look at her over his shoulder.

"It's really stupid for you to sleep on the couch. Your bed is big enough for both of us; I promise to keep to myself and not mash you."

He smiled. "Thanks." He held her gaze for a moment. "I'd better take the couch. I'll be back up to wake you in two hours."

She closed the door, unsure if she was relieved or disappointed.

Eric heard the mantel clock strike two-fifteen. In that dark hour, while the storm wreaked havoc outside, one fact became glaringly clear: That clock was the only constant in his life. It had been in his parents' home for as long as he could remember; up until he and Jill had moved into the little house on Montgomery Avenue and his mother had given it to them as a housewarming gift. It was one of the few possessions he'd retained after the divorce.

He lay on the couch with his arms crossed over his chest and his gaze fixed on the ceiling as he listened to the unrelenting wind. The hollow and desolate sound made him think: *That's what it's like inside me.* He could almost visualize the cold, whirling current contained inside his own chest, picking up the occasional bit of emotional debris and lifting it, flaunting it before his heart so he couldn't pretend it wasn't there.

The sound of the wind drew him deeper into self-examination than he cared to venture. Recently he'd been feeling like a man trying to bail out a sinking boat with a teaspoon. Scott seemed to be receding farther away each day. He was going to become as lost to Eric as Glory's baby was to her if he didn't do something soon. And he wasn't any closer to getting Jill to admit there was a serious problem than he had been two months ago.

Tula was in danger of losing her sight and, as selfish as it was, he couldn't deny his biggest fear was that she wouldn't be able to help care for Scott. Even as Eric thought this, he realized he'd grown to count on Tula for more than just child care; her pragmatic attitude and emotional support had helped him through many a dark day.

And now . . . Glory. He'd been able to put his professional questions behind him, but now that she was back, so were his questions—and not all of them *were* professional. He was attracted to her (if he were completely honest with himself, he would have to admit he probably always had been on some level). He'd always liked her humor and admired her giving manner. Had their paths been different earlier in their lives . . . aw, well, no sense in committing energy to such thoughts. That was then and this was now, and neither of them was in any way ready for a new relationship.

Still, the nonprofessional questions continued to present themselves. Just how scarred was she? Had her trauma all been caused by the fire and her subsequent losses? Or was there more—were his suspicions of Andrew's possessiveness and emotional control anywhere near the truth? And what extremes might that have driven her to?

He rubbed his forehead trying to wipe away his racing thoughts, but he could not get his mind to shut off.

He turned onto his side and was just grabbing a pillow to block out the sound of the wind when he heard a loud thud from overhead. He was vaulting up the stairs before he drew another breath. As he reached the top, he heard Glory crying.

He nearly tripped over her in the dark as he rushed into the room. She was crawling across the bedroom floor, sobbing with fear.

"Glory?" He knelt down and grasped her shoulders.

"I have to get out!" she cried frantically. "The door . . . out!" She tried to break away.

He touched her face. "Glory, you're safe."

She inhaled deeply. "Smoke!" She wrenched free with surprising strength and was scrabbling across the floor before he could catch her. A long thin whine of fear continued as she searched for the way out.

"There's no fire," he said firmly. He glanced around for the flashlight, but didn't see it. "Stop!" He was afraid she'd hurt herself thrashing around in the dark—he wasn't even certain that she was awake.

She thudded against the open door, slamming it into the wall.

The stairs . . .

Unable to get a good grip on her, he threw his body over hers and held her pinned to the floor.

She writhed beneath him. Her whimpers erupting into a feral scream of panic. She clawed at him to free herself.

"There's no fire. Glory!" he yelled.

She stopped screaming.

"You're safe, Glory. I'm here," he said against her ear, and she stopped struggling against him. "You're safe."

Her breath was coming in gulps and spasms.

Eric slid his arms around her and rolled onto his back, taking her with him. She burrowed her face in his shoulder and cried. It was the cry of loss, of grief, not panic. He wanted to take away her pain, but all he could do was hold her and let her weep.

After several minutes, she stilled, and her breathing evened out. She swallowed convulsively, then said in a trembling voice, "I was dreaming."

He squeezed her more tightly. "Do you have that dream often?" Had her nights been haunted like this since the fire?

She took a deep, shuddering breath. "No."

"Was it a memory, do you think?"

"I suppose it could have been . . . I . . . I don't know what really happened."

"Do you want to?" he asked carefully.

It was a few moments before she answered. "Not knowing is horrible—but I'm almost afraid remembering would be so much more horrible. If I remember, how will I ever get it out of my head?"

"Do you know anything at all?"

She shook her head against his shoulder. "The last thing I remember was the day before."

"What happened the day before?"

"Nothing out of the ordinary." Even as she said it, he could hear the uncertainty in her voice.

"You didn't . . ." He wasn't sure he should press, but he had his own questions about that night. "You didn't hear anything after . . . from the report, or newspapers?"

"Granny said it was the furnace; that's all I know. Everyone wanted to talk about it. And sometimes they looked at me like . . . I don't know . . . like they did Mrs. Cooksey after the authorities took her kids away." She licked her lips. "That's why I had to leave. I just couldn't stand it day after day."

Eric could imagine the looks—he'd heard the rumors. They'd been wide and varied, but mostly boiled down to the improbability of Glory's escaping and her rich husband dying. When Glory took off, it only made things worse. Of course, Eric had had his own questions; was it grief that had driven her away . . . or guilt?

"Do you want me to tell you what I know about it?" His heart accelerated slightly at this suggestion. Could he prod her into remembering?

She grabbed a fistful of his T-shirt.

If she said no, he would leave it alone. But if she needed to know—and he was convinced a person couldn't heal without knowing, Glory didn't seem in any way over the trauma—he might be able to help her. He ignored the little voice that said she might not be better off, but he would have answers. The question was, did he really want them?

"Okay."

He decided a clinical description would be easier for her to bear than his personal accounting of that night, of his own surprisingly emotional response to finding her inside a burning building and to the stillbirth of her baby.

"The alarm sounded at 3:50. The pumper arrived on scene at 4:03." The details were fresh because he'd just reread them. "Both you and Andrew suffered carbon monoxide poisoning. Even in small amounts, it causes confusion. That's why when you awakened you couldn't find your way out—"

Her head jerked up off his shoulder. "I was trying to get out?" She sounded truly surprised.

"I believe so. I found you near the back door. Andrew was in bed."

She didn't say anything for a long while, but she did settle her head back on his shoulder. Her body felt as if it were vibrating with tension, like the high-strung, rapid vacillations of a tuning fork. He kept his arm around her, not moving, feeling that somehow gathering comfort without having to look at him, wrapped in the anonymity of the dark, made it easier for her to hear.

He went on, "The investigation led to a faulty gas line in the furnace. The carbon monoxide detector didn't have a battery."

Her head came up again. "That's impossible. Andrew was a fanatic about things like that, especially with the— the baby coming. He made me sell my old car and buy that Volvo." She shook her head. "You're mistaken."

Eric didn't want to get into an argument with her over it right now. She needed to rest. "Well, it appears the Volvo did its job—you walked away."

Technically he was right, she thought; she had been able to walk, or at least crawl uphill, away from the wrecked Volvo. She had not, however, walked away from that fire. She'd been hauled out on Eric's shoulder, then plopped on the wet ground.

Suddenly that moment became crystal clear. But she felt none of the panic she had when Eric had triggered her first glimpse into the past. Rain had fallen on her face. He had told her she was safe; just as he had a few minutes ago. Then he had lingered over her even after the paramedics went to work—*because I wouldn't let go of his hand*!

"I remember!" she said as she sat up quickly enough to make her head spin.

Eric sat up, too, and took her hand. "You do?" he asked quietly.

She lifted their joined hands. "I wouldn't let you go."

"That's right."

"Then why did I freak out when you came into the emergency room?"

He brought his other hand to hold hers between both of his. "Because by the time I came to the ER—" He stopped.

"What?" She leaned closer, prompting. "What, Eric?"

His hands tightened around hers. "You'd lost the baby."

Those words struck her like a fist in the chest. For a second she had trouble drawing a breath. "I shouldn't still be such a mess," she half squeaked. She struggled to find her voice; she was not going to cry again.

Eric didn't rush in with platitudes or empty assurances. He simply sat in the silence and held her hand.

After a moment she asked, "I shouldn't, should I? Is there something *wrong* with me?" She remembered that in the hospital she'd lain in the bed, a cold stone in her middle, unable to stop crying. Everything was gone . . . empty womb, empty arms, empty heart.

It now came as a bit of a shock to realize that after all of these months, that same emptiness, in all of its intensity, still clung to her. She hadn't made a damn bit of progress.

Eric said, with a force that said he spoke from the soul, "It would be a terrible thing to lose a child . . . I don't think I'd be in any better shape if something happened to Scott."

"But everyone tells me that I didn't even *know* my daughter, I shouldn't be missing her so much. Everyone seems to think I should act like she never was. I don't know how many times I heard, 'Better to lose a baby six months into a pregnancy than after you'd taken it home.' I suppose that much must be true. I'm sure it would have been harder—but to act like she *never existed* . . ." She shook her head and said the words with all of the passionate incredulity she felt. "I just can't."

Removing one of his hands from hers, he touched her cheek. "Have these 'everyones' been through what you've been through?"

She drew a deep breath and let it out slowly. "I try not to think about her, but it'll hit me at the oddest times. Not just the logical milestones—you know, she'd be six months old now, or this would have been her first Christmas. But when I see the first hint of color in the trees in the fall, I wondered if the little girl she would have been would have liked to be tossed into a pile of raked leaves.

When I drink a cup of hot chocolate I wonder, would she have liked hers with marshmallows or without? When I imagine what she would look like . . ."

Eric reached a hand behind her neck and pulled her forehead against his. "Maybe you expect too much of yourself. Maybe you tried to forget before you allowed yourself to grieve."

The glaring truth in that simple statement shifted something inside her. She *had* focused on forgetting, almost from the start. She'd even refused to hear the details of the fire report. It had seemed the only way to survive. Maybe she'd gone about it entirely backward. It seemed safer not to think about it, especially since her memory of the day preceding the fire never came back to her. Perhaps she needed those memories to be able to move on.

However, there was something dark bundled up with those memories, something frightening, something she instinctively knew she didn't want to see. Perhaps that's why the therapy hadn't worked—she hadn't really wanted it to.

Now she feared that if she could open those floodgates, she might not like what churned out with the overflow.

The sun was shining the next morning. Its heat caused a mist to rise off the saturated ground, lending an otherworldly aspect to the dawn. Glory sat across the kitchen table from Eric, daylight accenting her darkening bruises.

He caught himself more than once just before he reached out to brush her hair away from her forehead and gently caress her injuries. There was something about her that drew upon his protective nature in a way that far exceeded what he should be doing for a woman who, in reality, was little more than an acquaintance. Her spending the night in his house was testament to that. He wanted to know her better, to understand her emotional pain. Not that he had anything to offer her. He was feeling rather emotionally bankrupt at the moment. And certainly her own plate was full. What a lot of good it would do her if he managed to draw her closer; she didn't need all of his baggage too.

Fortunately, the electricity was back on, and he was at least able to provide her with a cup of coffee.

For several minutes, they both skirted any topic of substance, commenting on the clear sky and the robust flavor of the coffee.

Was she running again? Had their conversations during the storm spooked her? Things had come out in the dark that he doubted she'd ever said aloud. And, he had to admit, he was as reluctant as she to open subjects that might be too difficult to face in the light of day.

As she set down her coffee, Glory said, "I've got to get back to Granny's."

"It'll be days before Cold Springs Hollow Road is passable. The washout was big, and it stormed for hours after I saw it."

"Just take me as far as the washout, and I'll walk from there," she said.

"You can barely hobble."

"I'm just stiff. I'll be better once I move around a bit."

He'd already called the station, telling Donna he'd be late. He thought he'd get Glory settled for the day before he went in. He suddenly realized he had been happily thinking in terms of her being trapped at his house for a couple of days. "You can't walk all that way. I suppose I could carry you . . ." He winked, and she tossed a wadded napkin at him.

"Very funny." She glanced over her shoulder, out the window to the bright, steamy morning. "I don't want Granny to worry."

"Why would she worry? She knows you're with me. You can call her anytime."

"What are the chances of her phone still working?"

He couldn't deny that had to be slim to none—considering the strength and duration of last night's storm. He'd been surprised the lines were still up when he'd called last evening.

Before he could respond, she went on, "What if she had trouble in the storm? I can't just leave her out there alone." There was genuine worry in her eyes.

"Charlie's just down the road." He felt a little like a child arguing to get his selfish way.

"*Pffft.* Charlie. Might as well count on a six-year-old." She rolled her eyes. Then that green gaze fixed on him for the briefest moment before she concentrated on wiping a drip off her coffee mug. "Eric, I'm going home. You can help me, or I'll figure out a way myself."

"Now you're hurting my feelings," he said. "Don't like my hospitality?"

She shot him a mocking look. "Oh, yes, that's it. I was treated to the only bed in the house, and you made yourself miserable for my benefit. I *cannot* suffer this kind of treatment another night."

"I wasn't."

Confusion crossed her face. "You weren't what?"

"Miserable . . . you said I made myself miserable."

She hid her expression under lowered lashes and took a long sip of coffee.

He searched for a way to explain that wouldn't scare her off or make her look at him with pity. "It was . . . comforting . . . to have someone here last night."

Her gaze snapped back to his face, her eyes questioning, but she didn't say anything.

He said, "It can get pretty boring alone when the lights go out."

"You heroes," she said glibly, "always deflecting a compliment." Leaning forward in her chair, she added, "But really, I have to get back to the hollow. That's why I'm here, for Granny."

"All right," he said. "I've got an idea. But if I decide getting around the washout is too dangerous, you're stuck with me for another day or two. No more talk of walking miles on your own—and no arguing."

"Deal."

There was a glint in her eye that told him it was a deal only if it went her way. But he'd fight that battle if and when it presented itself.

Twenty minutes later, Glory was pressed against his back as they took his normally garaged motorcycle up the winding road into the hollow. He felt her turn and look at the spot where her car had gone off the road. They'd called the towing service before they left his house. There was no reason to stop and let her look at how precariously her car had been hanging on the side of the mountain.

He couldn't deny his disappointment when he saw that most of the inside lane at the washout remained intact. After getting off and inspecting it, he took the bike as far to the left as he possibly could, skirting the hole with plenty of room to spare. As he picked up speed again, the wind blew away his pleasant fantasy of having another person in his house when he returned home after work.

He stopped in front of Tula's. Glory got off and removed her helmet.

"Thank you . . . for everything." She handed the helmet to him.

As he was fastening it onto the rear seat, Tula came out on the porch.

"Good gracious, Glory! Don't you know those things are dangerous?" She pointed to the motorcycle.

When Glory turned around, Tula gasped. "What on God's green earth happened to you?"

Glory walked to her grandmother and linked an arm through hers. "I'll tell you over breakfast. It's a long story."

Tula's lips were pressed together in disapproval. "I suppose you know this story," she said to Eric.

"Yes, ma'am."

"And you knew it last night when you called me?"

"Yes, ma'am."

"Maybe you'd better come in here, too."

"Sorry, Tula. I'm late for work." He started the bike before she could say anything else. As he drove off, he realized just how sorry he was; he'd have liked nothing better than to have lingered over breakfast with those two women—even if Tula was scolding.

Late that evening, after Glory had soothed her sore muscles in a hot shower, Granny insisted on rubbing her back, shoulders, and knee with an ointment that smelled like a combination of old lard and camphor. Glory subjected herself without complaint as atonement for keeping her accident a secret the night before. She twisted her hair on top of her head, unsure what Granny's concoction would do to it.

Granny's hands were surprisingly strong as they massaged her shoulders. "Now by mornin' you should be feelin' much better." She finally put the cap back on the jar. The smell lingered—as it probably would long after Glory's next shower.

"Thanks, Gran."

Granny sat down on the bed next to Glory. "I didn't thank you proper for them flowers. Nice as they are, you shouldn't have spent your money on something like that. You need to think about your future."

Glory took her hand—for such strength there certainly wasn't a lot of substance; it felt thin and bony. "I just wanted you to know how much I love you."

With a squeeze of her hand, Granny said, "That's nice. Next time just tell me. It'll be a lot cheaper."

Glory laughed and gave her a fierce hug. "You're one of a kind."

"That's what Pap used to say—but it didn't sound so flatterin' when he said it." She leaned back, and her face grew more serious. "I don't want you wastin' your money on me." Her back stiffened, ready for battle. "I still wish you'd contested that will. You had a right."

This was an old argument, one Glory had been surprised had waited so long to bubble to the surface. Andrew's parents had been the beneficiaries of his will and, thanks to a change months before the fire, his life insurance. Glory hadn't had the fortitude to face the legal fight—plus there was a part of her that didn't want to contemplate what had prompted Andrew to do such a thing. There were things about her relationship with Andrew that she felt were best left buried in the murky past.

Unbeknownst to Glory, all of their assets had been solely in Andrew's name, with the exception of her car and the house. Once the mortgage had been paid off, there hadn't been a lot left from the homeowner's insurance settlement. But that didn't matter to Glory. She hadn't been able to consider touching the money. It felt . . . tainted. It was in the bank, waiting for her to decide which charity would receive it.

"Granny, I really don't want to argue about this. I didn't contest the will. I never worked after we were married. I didn't earn that money. Andrew always said it was his job to take care of me. Most of it was in a trust that Andrew inherited from his grandparents with a stipulation to pass to a blood relative anyhow. And the life insurance . . . I don't want it."

"If it was Andrew's job to take care of you, why didn't he provide if somethin' happened to him?"

"He was young and healthy. He didn't plan on dying. I'm sure once the baby came, he would have changed the beneficiary."

Granny looked doubtful, then said, "Nobody plans on dyin'. You did your part in that marriage." Her gaze hardened. "More'n your part, I'd say. Even the law sees that. If you'd divorced, you'd have got half. You're left a widow, and you get nothing? It just ain't right." She softened. "I just don't want to see you without a place. You need a home."

Glory doubted she'd ever feel at home anywhere again, but instead of saying so, she smiled and said, "I thought I was home."

Granny chuckled. "Oh, darlin', I love havin' you here, but one woman in a house is enough. You'll soon get tired of me. I'm used to living alone and you'll be wantin' your own place."

"I thought I might be a help. You can't drive at night anymore. And with your sight—"

"Don't talk foolish. I ain't goin' *blind*. I got an *impairment*. Livin' alone might take some adjusting, but I won't need a nurse. You got your own life."

"Oh, Gran, that's just it . . . I don't."

Granny patted her hand. "Then you'll have to find yourself one."

Glory flushed with shame; Granny's vow for independence actually *disappointed* her. She realized that at some point since Gran's call to Minnesota, she'd begun to cling to Granny's "impairment" as a direction for her own life.

Chapter Eight

❧

As GLORY LAY in bed the next morning trying to figure out how she could be missing a man she barely knew, thinking herself sinful for the covetous way she recalled pressing herself against Eric's muscular back on the motorcycle, there was a swift rap on her bedroom door. Granny's voice called, "Time for church."

Glory paused in midbreath. Excuses or truth? She could claim herself too sore from the accident, or she could face Granny's disapproval straight on. As much as she leaned toward the former, she realized that was just putting off the inevitable.

She called through the still-closed door, "You go on, Gran. I'm not going." The last thing she wanted was dozens of curious eyes on her.

The door opened a crack. "I reckoned you were hurt worse than you let on."

"It's not that. I'm just a little sore. I . . . I don't go to church anymore."

Immediately the door swung fully open. Granny stood there with a frown on her face and her fists on her skinny hips. "What do you mean, you don't go to church? Since when?"

"Since I left here."

"Dear Lord. No wonder you're such a mess. A person can't bear all of their troubles alone. You got to ask for help."

Glory turned on her side and pulled the sheet up to her ear. "Please, Gran, I don't want to argue about this. I'm not going."

"Suit yourself." She took one step toward the hall, then paused. "The Lord has a way of healing—you're making a big mistake."

"It's not the first one."

Glory heard Granny come back into the room. Her steps were soft and her hand gentle when she laid it on Glory's shoulder. "Sometimes the mistakes that hurt the most are the ones you refuse to look at afterward."

Glory twisted to look over her shoulder. "What do you mean?"

Granny looked at her as if she were a dull-witted child and patted her gently. "I think you need to take a good clear look at the past afore it lets you go on to your future."

"Now that sounds just as multilayered as a Bible verse."

"That's the good thing about a Bible verse—makes you think." She bent down and kissed Glory's forehead. "You just go on ignoring the help being handed to you, and a day'll come you won't want to get out of bed a'tall."

As Granny left the room, Glory called, "I don't need help." What she didn't say was that she'd been to that place already, where each day is too much of a burden to face, where the hours hiding in bed slide night into day and back again. The only way to avoid going back there was to turn her back on the past.

Which was going to be very hard to do as long as she stayed in Dawson.

After Granny left for church, her words buzzed around inside Glory's head like a droning insect. *Ask for help . . . Clear look at the past . . . the past . . . the past . . . Ask for help . . .*

She didn't want to capture them and hold them still long enough to examine any truth they might carry. And the only way Glory had ever been able to shut off her mind was to push her body. So she climbed out of bed, pulled on a pair of shorts, T-shirt, and tennis shoes, put her hair up in a ponytail, took three of Granny's generic over-the-counter pain relievers, filled a bottle with water, and went out the front door.

She stretched her sore shoulders and back before she descended the steps. She had intended to go out for a fast-paced walk, but as she looked out on the vast greenness surrounding Granny's house, she decided on a longer hike; it was going to take a lot of physical activity to drown out Granny's words.

After running back inside and dashing off a quick note to explain her absence and switching to hiking boots, she headed off on the path she and Granny had taken when they went to the raspberry bramble.

When she reached the little white church, she paused. It sat on a narrow road that stopped at the church and graveyard. Beyond this point, she would follow a path through the woods. The entrance to the trail was just beyond the vehicles parked across the end of the road.

There were a dozen or so cars and pickups in the crushed-stone parking lot. Of course, Granny's wasn't among them; she'd walked to church nearly every Sunday of her life. It surprised Glory that, after all of her years away from this church, she recognized so many of the vehicles: there was Blackwell's Ford crew-cab truck parked in the shade at the end of the road. BJ, Mr. Blackwell's brown-and-white bird dog, sat panting in the bed—Mr. Blackwell couldn't get in that truck without BJ jumping in the back, so the dog went everywhere with him. Next to that truck was an eighties-era Ford station wagon with imitation wood grain on the sides. Glory recognized it as belonging to Denzelle Hibbard; her husband had died of cancer right after he bought that car, leaving her with very little insurance and six young children. And surprisingly, next to Mrs. Hibbard's car was cousin Charlie's old gray-and-red Suburban.

Charlie had always been more interested in Saturday night hell-raising than Sunday morning worship. Granny must have stayed after him until he relented—the woman could be like water on stone, slowly, carefully wearing away any resistance to what she deemed right. When Glory had gone to church with Gran, there had been very few Sundays when Charlie made an appearance on the inside of those walls. And on the few occasions he'd been coerced into coming—say, a family baptism or Easter holiday—he'd propped himself in the back pew and fought a losing battle to keep his bloodshot eyes open. It had been Glory's job to sit next to him and keep him from snoring.

Glory's mother had stopped going to their church in town after Glory's father died. Granny had worried for Glory's eternal soul; so for nearly as long as she could remember, Glory had gone to church with Granny. It was a habit that lasted until Glory had married Andrew. After that, she joined the Harrison family at the stately United Methodist church at the corner of Commerce and Abigail Streets, the same church in which she'd been married.

Glory remembered being a new bride sitting next to her husband in the fifth row on the right-hand side of the sanctuary, the Harrison pew. She had missed the robust sincerity of Granny's little church, where heartfelt "Amens" occasionally rose in agreement to the sermon, instead of only at the appropriately programmed times in the orderly Methodist service.

That first Sunday, Andrew had leaned close to her ear and whispered, "Quite a bit different from the snake handlers and faith healers out in the hollow, eh?"

He'd made Granny's wholesome little church seem like something to be ashamed of, as if the members were the equivalent of some bizarre cult. It shamed Glory to this day that she'd just smiled and let it go instead of setting him right.

As she stood in the hot parking lot, there was a hitch in Glory's chest. *That was always the way I dealt with Andrew—avoiding confrontation, convincing myself that there was no reason to argue over the little, insignificant things.*

Why did that thought, coming as fresh as the new day, bring with it a feeling of revelation?

A smattering of goose bumps covered her arms in spite of the powerful sun in which she stood. There was more to that memory, but it was hiding around a sharp corner.

Instead of forcing herself to look around that corner, Glory stared at the church, thinking of sitting next to

Granny. On hot mornings like this one, Glory remembered making little fans out of the offering envelopes.

As always in the summer, the front door at the top of the wooden steps was open, and the windows were raised in hope of a breeze. A chorus of voices suddenly rose in praise and tumbled out the openings. For a long moment, Glory stood listening, letting the memories of childhood simplicity soothe her. She closed her eyes and tilted her face to the sun.

She nearly jumped out of her skin when a voice said, "I figured you'd be inside."

She spun around and saw Eric Wilson walking toward her from an old stump at the edge of the woods beside the entrance to the cemetery. She felt a wash of guilt at being caught in the parking lot swaying to the hymn, just as if she'd been trying to take something that wasn't hers or peeping in someone's window.

"What are you doing here?" she asked.

"Tula's phone is still out. It'll be at least Tuesday before the road is open again. I rode the bike up here to see how you are—and if you two need anything." He lifted a shoulder as he said it, as if it were no big deal. Then he said, "So, why aren't you?"

Her mind was still trying to absorb his presence. "Why aren't I what?" she asked, trying not to sound like an idiot.

"Inside. Can't imagine Tula letting you miss church."

"I suppose I could ask you why you're not in church yourself." She crossed her arms over her chest—the best defense is always a good offense.

"Never been a churchgoer. I like to let the wind carry my prayers from my motorcycle."

"Sounds like an excuse you've made up so you can ride it on Sunday mornings."

He gave her a crooked smile. "Might be. But you shouldn't knock it until you've tried it. It's very therapeutic."

Glory remembered the exhilarating feel of cruising along, her arms wrapped around Eric's waist—and didn't think that thrill had anything to do with the motorcycle.

Before she gathered herself for another glib comment, he narrowed his eyes and asked, "Why are you here, if you're not going in?"

"Just passing by. I'm going on a hike."

"Ah. Good to know you're not wearing those shoes to church," he said with a chuckle as he eyed her scuffed boots. Then he said, "Where are you going?"

She hesitated. "Nowhere in particular."

He bored a hole in her with his eyes. That hesitation had been her mistake, now he was suspicious. "You know you should always let someone know where you are—in case of . . . an emergency."

She had to keep in mind, Eric's job was saving people from such emergencies. He wasn't very likely to give up and wave her on with a smile. "I'm going to Blue Falls Pond."

"Alone?" He looked disapproving.

"Done it a hundred times," she said confidently.

"Not two days after you drove your car off the mountain."

"I'm fine."

He took another step closer and fixed his gaze on the bruise on her cheek. "I'll bet the one from the shoulder harness is ten times worse."

"Luckily I walk with my feet and legs."

His gaze traveled to her bare knee.

"See, your doctoring did the trick," she said, trying to lighten the feel of his gaze on her. "No swelling at all." She flexed the joint to demonstrate its agility.

"It's purple," he said flatly. He locked gazes with her again, and she felt like there was a little hiccup stuck in her chest. The sun glinted off the gold in his brown hair, and the pupils of his golden brown eyes were little more than pinpoints. He wore a white T-shirt that nearly sparkled in the sun. The odd question of who did his laundry crossed her mind; luckily, she stopped it before it fell out of her mouth.

She took a little step away from him and said, "Best thing for soreness is to keep it moving."

"Not two miles on a 10 percent upgrade."

"It's not all up; there are lots of dips and curves along the way."

He didn't look any less disapproving.

"Hey, Granny just did it last week," she said lightly. "Even banged-up I should be able to handle it."

"I bet Tula wasn't alone. Besides, what if something happens? You could get back there and discover you're not nearly as fit as you think."

She added, "Will you feel better if I promise to rest every half mile?"

"I'd feel better if you didn't go."

"Don't make me feel guilty. I really *need* to go." How could she explain the healing power that place had for her? Granny had taken her there for the first time the summer after her dad had died. The sparkle of the waterfall, the feeling of absolute isolation, the soothing sound of rushing water had all combined to give the place an air of magic to her five-year-old senses. That magic had never faded for Glory as she'd grown older and other childhood treasures—like Santa and rainbows and the belief that your parents knew everything—lost their luster.

Eric stood there for a long moment in silence. His gaze seemed to be taking her measure, calculating the odds of talking her out of her madness. He then glanced back at his motorcycle, which was parked in the shade beside the stump where he'd been sitting. His gaze then traveled to the church. "Tula know you're going?"

"I left a note."

The sideways you're-gonna-be-in-such-trouble look he gave her said he knew just how Tula was going to react to that. Then he sighed and said, "Guess I'll come along, then. Tula finds out I let you go alone and she'll give me a real ass-chewing."

Company on this hike was the last thing she wanted. The fewer people around Blue Falls Pond the better. She didn't want to share. She didn't want the magic to be worn away by hundreds of pairs of hiking boots and buried under picnic litter. True, Eric was just one person; but one could lead to two, two to four, and it wouldn't stop until Blue Falls Pond was on all of the maps and trail guides. But she couldn't see any way of preventing him from coming.

"You don't have water," she said, in a last-ditch effort to discourage him.

"Wrong." He walked over to the motorcycle and retrieved a liter bottle and held it up to her as he returned.

"All right, then." She turned and started toward the path. "If you can't keep up, you're on your own."

He laughed and followed her into the shadowy woods.

* * *

Tula put on her new sunglasses, then descended the church steps, pausing to thank Pastor Roberts for the inspiring service.

Her grandson Charlie was waiting for her at the bottom of the steps.

She greeted him with a smile. "Glad to see you this morning, Charlie."

He blinked his bloodshot eyes. "Glad, but not surprised," he said, with an appropriate amount of respect.

Tula reached up and patted his cheek. "I gave you a choice."

Charlie was nothing more than an overgrown boy, in both spirit and appearance. He'd kept the handsome looks that had fallen upon him at birth; he'd bewitched women from the moment he drew his first breath. He had a wide smile and eyes so bright blue that even when he was a child she'd seen grown women catch their breath as they looked into them. Of course, these things contributed significantly to his immaturity; women just fell for him, they either wanted to mother him or capture his heart. And Charlie was a charmer; the boy could talk the dogs off a meat wagon.

She supposed she'd been as taken with him as anyone else she wouldn't have given him more leeway than was right.

While he'd been married to Crystal, he'd seemed a bit more settled . . . at least for a while. 'Course they'd married at nineteen, with their firstborn arriving some five months later. Since the divorce, Charlie had been acting like a kite without a tail, dipping and jerking in useless circles, unable to steady himself. Tula was worried that before long he was going to crash into the ground and not be able to get airborne again. That was why she never refused when he asked if his boys could spend time with her on his weekends; what kind of example would he be setting for five growing boys?

Last week, she'd begun to make . . . suggestions. Charlie had had his time to mourn his marriage. He was past thirty. He had five young'uns who needed to learn how to grow into men. It was time for Charlie to straighten up.

Tula said, "I'm proud to see you've made the right decision."

Charlie leaned down and kissed her cheek. "With you asking, Granny, how could I refuse?" Then he glanced across the parking lot to where Jenni Camp, who worked at the Blue Ridge Bar, stood waiting beside his Suburban.

Tula figured Jenni was both the reason for the bloodshot eyes and the fact that he made it to church on time.

He said, "Can we give you a ride home?"

Tula shook her head. "I got a stop to make. Y'all go on."

He gave her a quick one-armed hug and started toward Jenni. "I'll give you a call later this week," he said with a smile. "We can plan for next weekend."

She just nodded and waved him on. One step at a time. She'd gotten him to church. The next step would take a little more planning—there were young'uns' feelings at stake.

She watched Jenni's eyes light up as Charlie walked toward her. That boy was just too doggone handsome for his own good. She shook her head and crossed the parking lot, crushed stone sharp through her thin-soled church shoes.

As she did every Sunday after services, she made her way toward the gate at the side of the church that led to the cemetery. She stopped and gave Blackwell's bird dog a good scratch behind his ear as she passed their truck. She noticed when she looked at him dead on, his eyes looked like they weren't lined up right. 'Course it wasn't BJ's eyes that were wrong, it was her own.

Please, Lord, just a little more time . . . Least 'til Glory's sorted out.

Few people lingered around in the heat. They'd rather get in their cars and turn on air conditioners or roll windows down and create a breeze of their own on the shady mountain road. That suited Tula fine. She preferred being alone with Sam. All too often some well-meaning friend wanted to join her in the cemetery—likely worried she'd become overwhelmed with grief if left on her own.

But her visits with Sam always brought gladness. They gave her a sense of connection, of support, of reassurance that he was with her in spirit until the day the Lord called her home, and they could once again be together.

As she moved through the cemetery, along the same path she'd traveled at least once a week for the past ten years, she stubbed her toe on the uneven ground. She hadn't seen the little rise in the grass that caught her, and she stumbled forward a couple of steps before she regained her balance.

Normally Tula Baker would be the first to break into laughter over her own near spill; she was notorious for her inability to hold in her mirth over a fall, hers or anyone else's. As long as there was no blood and no broken bones, laughter exploded from her without a thought. Used to make Sam so dang mad; accused her of being unfeeling. People could be hurt, he'd say. But it wasn't that she didn't care; she just couldn't help herself when she saw legs sprawling this way and that or arms pinwheeling in the air.

But this time no laughter sprang forth. Her heart sped up and her mouth went dry. It shook her confidence enough that she waited several seconds before she took another step, glancing to see if anyone had seen her. Years ago, when she'd first found out about her condition, everyone had been so overly cautious, treating her like a robin's egg, offering to do this and that for her. She'd been months convincing them she was no different than she'd ever been. One look at something like this whoopdie-do would set the worry warts and the Nosey Nellies into a tizzy again.

Luckily, the only witness appeared to be BJ the bird dog.

After a moment to settle her nerves, she moved with renewed care toward Sam's headstone. She laid her hand on the warm granite.

"Hello, Pap. It's Sunday again. Weeks're going by blindin' fast." She sighed softly and waited—waited for the familiar feeling that he was listening. After a moment, it came. "I'm havin' the devil's own time keeping my nose out of Glory's business." She patted the stone thoughtfully.

"I know we reared our young'uns to make up their own minds and clean up their own messes if things ended poorly. The grandbabies should do the same. But this just feels too . . . *big* to let go racin' down the road like it is.

"I'm worried that afore long I won't be able to fool Glory into thinking my eyes ain't no worse. Once that happens . . . well, she'll be staying here for the wrong reasons. Cain't have it." Tula shook her head slowly and contemplated for a moment. "There's a big dark hole in the middle of that girl. She's kept herself running so fast you'd think she'd hear the wind whistlin' through it. But she cain't see it. And if she don't see it, it ain't ever gonna get filled."

Tula knelt beside the stone, her knees complaining. She pulled away the long sprigs of grass that the church superintendent left at the monument's base when he zipped around the cemetery with his power mower. Honest to goodness, nobody had any pride in their work anymore. She decided not to grumble to Sam about it, though; he'd heard it enough.

In the heat, her face was breaking out in a fine sheen of sweat. The Oakleys slid down her nose, and she pushed them back up with an index finger to the bridge. "Eric got me these new sunglasses." She paused in her grass pulling and looked at the granite stone. "Who'd a' thought I'd have sunglasses worth more than two weeks' groceries? But, I gotta admit, they do help."

She busied her hands again. "Now there's another problem . . . Eric. I'm afraid my eyes won't hold out long enough to get his boy through whatever is ailing him. Eric says it might be something that he won't ever get over." She bit her lip to keep it from quivering with frustration. "Ahh, criminy, I don't want to complain—really I don't. You of all people know I ain't a complainer. I know I've been luckier than most—it's just . . . well, right when ever'body needs me, things are going to pot."

She pulled a dandelion and tossed it toward the woods. After brushing the dirt off her fingers, she braced one hand on the headstone and got to her feet.

"You're mighty quiet today, Pap." So often the answers to her questions and the solutions to her problems fell softly on her consciousness as she talked things over with Sam. But today there was no gentle realization, no whisper of resolution.

Apparently, Sam was as perplexed as she was.

Chapter Nine

❀

Glory kept up an unrelenting pace—and it was nearly killing her. Almost two years of walking on flat ground had taken a surprising toll on her conditioning. Had she been alone, she might just have reconsidered and turned around. But she wasn't. So she gritted her teeth and forced her quivering legs to carry her over the increasing incline of the narrow trail, batting laurel branches and lush ferns out of her way, never pausing to look back and see if Eric was following.

Of course, she knew he was; she heard his quick, assured footfalls and his irritatingly unlabored breathing behind her.

They were nearing a place where it would take both hands and feet to scrabble over a jumble of tumbled boulders. Glory wasn't looking forward to the challenge.

Eric called, "Why don't we take a breather."

Glory's mouth overrode her tired muscles. "I don't need a breather," she said as she trudged forward with sweat trickling down her spine.

"I do," he said. "I didn't dress for an all-out assault on the mountain in this heat."

She pulled up and looked over her shoulder at him. She

didn't see a red-faced, sweat-drenched, ready-to-drop hiker; she saw a fine specimen of a firefighter who was barely perspiring in spite of the fact that he wore full-length jeans with his white T-shirt. He needed a breather about as much as she needed a jock strap.

"Guess you're out of luck then," she said, cursing the waste of breath. "I warned you that I'd leave you if you couldn't keep up." She would have laughed out loud at the absurdity of that statement, but she didn't have the wind for laughter. Without pausing, she found her first hand-hold on the rock. "See you at the falls."

She heaved herself up and prayed her sweaty hands wouldn't slip and her protesting muscles would hold out. It wasn't a difficult or long climb, not much higher than the top of her head. A couple of handholds and stepping in the right place and she'd be over. Granny had just done it with Charlie's boys, for heaven's sake. But Glory was sore and out of shape and short of breath; smarting off to Eric had wasted precious oxygen.

She was ready to shift her weight over the top when a small rock shifted beneath her foot. She made a grab at a woody shrub to pull herself the rest of the way up, but managed to grab the only dead branch on the damned thing. It snapped, and she pitched backward, belatedly realizing that she'd have been better off not to have tried to continue her forward movement by grabbing the bush and just given some ground and steadied herself instead.

The breaking branch acted like a catapult, and she lost all contact with the rocks. She was in a free fall.

The next thing she felt was Eric's arms wrapped around her. But she kept falling—now *they* were falling. As he landed between her and the stony ground, she heard the air leave his lungs in a huff.

For a second she held very still, hoping she hadn't killed him. When she heard him take a groaning breath, she stayed where she was, frozen by embarrassment and stubborn pride.

She'd just about gathered her dignity enough to get up and face him when he started to shake. At first she thought he had been hurt. But then he broke into a belly laugh that shook her as she lay on top of him.

She rolled off quickly and jerked herself to her feet. "Since you think it's so funny, I won't apologize for squashing you this time."

He was laughing so hard that he rolled onto his side trying to catch his breath. His pristine, blindingly white T-shirt was no longer. Ground-in mountain dirt covered the back from shoulder to waist.

He gasped out, "You . . . you . . . looked . . . I . . . like . . ." Laughter gobbled up his breath.

"What?" she demanded as she looked down at him.

He shook his head and waved her off, as if it was too much effort to explain around his guffaws. Breathlessly, he squeaked out, "Never mind."

"You might as well tell me. I'll get it out of you eventually." She fought the smile that threatened to break her stern countenance. She could only imagine what she'd looked like as she'd taken to the air.

He rolled onto his back again and wiped the tears from his cheeks. "A g-giant fl-flying squirrel." He chuckled again. "You were launched off there with your arms and legs flung out like you thought you might fly." He held up his hands, fingers splayed, and whipped them through the air.

She could just see it. She'd felt as if she'd been an insect flicked from the end of a long stick, must have looked that way too. Her own laughter joined his. "You're lucky you didn't see my face." She made a comical re-creation: wide, shocked eyes with raised brows and lips gaping with surprise and fright around clenched teeth.

He covered his eyes and turned his head away. "No. No. Don't show me! It's too horrible for a mortal man to witness."

With laughter bubbling inside her like soda and vinegar, she pulled his hands away and mimed right in his face.

"Aargh!" He grabbed her and pulled her face against his chest so she couldn't torment him anymore.

His T-shirt still smelled of laundry detergent.

He said with a rumble of laughter, "Now that image is gonna stick with me, and I'll never have the courage to catch another falling woman." Then he groaned and added in a serious tone, "I'll have to leave the department. You've ended my career."

His humor made it easier on her pride. She pulled her head free and sat up, her hand lingering on the center of his chest. "Well, serves you right. I did want to come alone."

He rested his hand on his chest over hers. She liked the solid way his heartbeat felt under her palm, the way his chest vibrated with suppressed laughter.

Shaking his head, he said, "I'd rather face the loss of my career than Tula Baker after I allowed her granddaughter to collapse alone in the wilderness."

Glory cocked her head and pressed her lips together as if considering. Reluctantly, she pulled her hand away from his. "Can't say that I blame you." She got to her feet, offering a hand to pull him up.

Once standing, he swiped the dust from his bare elbows.

"Here, turn around," Glory said. She brushed the worst of the dirt off his back. There was a scrape on his left elbow where the blood was gathering just under the skin. She cringed. "Does that hurt?"

"What?" He lifted the arm she was touching and glanced at his elbow. "Didn't even notice it."

Glory said, with an incredulous shake of the head, "*Heroes.*"

He ignored her, stepped past, and started to climb the rocks. Having learned her lesson, she let him lead. Once at the top, he motioned for her to follow. She did, carefully. When she was ready to lever her weight over the ledge, he reached down and grabbed her hand with one of his and her forearm with his other, lifting her easily to stand beside him.

He gave her a cocky look and said, "That's probably how Tula does it . . . asks for a little help when she needs it."

Glory shot him a dubious look. "And I thought you knew my grandmother." She pushed past him and continued upward toward Blue Falls.

The little scene at the first rock climb had sufficiently broken her pride, at least temporarily. Even though the next climb was easier, she let Eric take the lead.

As they rounded the last curve and entered the draw, although Blue Falls was still out of sight, Glory could hear the shimmering whisper of the water. It struck her senses like a fair tropical breeze might soothe a freezing woman. She halted in midstep, closed her eyes, and let it wash over her.

"Something wrong?" Eric asked from behind.

She drew in a deep breath that smelled of clean water and lush vegetation. "This is the first thing that's seemed right since I got back."

He took another step, until he was standing right at her back.

"Hear it?" she whispered.

He held himself still for a long moment. "The falls?" he asked quietly.

A relaxed smile came to her face. "The magic."

His hand came to rest on her shoulder. His voice was very close to her ear when he whispered, "Now I understand why you wanted to come alone."

She opened her eyes and turned to face him, surprised. She didn't have words to explain what this place meant to her, but apparently she didn't need them with Eric. He knew, understood fully; she could see it in the depths of his eyes.

For a long moment, she stood there, listening to the distant falls, looking into his eyes and she felt . . . calm. For the first time in nearly two years, she felt calm. It startled her to realize it. She didn't know which was more disturbing—the fact that he evoked such a feeling, or that she had gone this long and fooled herself into thinking her insides were no longer a buzzing knot of tension.

His hand left her shoulder and cupped her cheek. "Do you want me to wait here for you?"

Tenderness washed over her. For all of her initial resentment at his intrusion, it suddenly seemed right that he be here. She shook her head. "Somehow, I think you need this place as much as I do."

The muscles in his throat worked, as if he was choking down his own emotions. His gaze held hers as he leaned closer and his hand left her cheek and slid behind her neck.

He's going to kiss me. Her breath caught in her chest as she realized how much she wanted him to.

At the last second, as she readied her lips to meet his, he dipped his head to the side and brushed the lightest of kisses on her cheek, near the corner of her mouth. Then he rested his forehead against hers and closed his eyes. His whispered "Thank you" was barely audible.

Glory took his hand and led him toward her sacred place, to the healing magic of Blue Falls Pond.

The dew of the mists reached her just before the falls came into view. Glory was tempted to close her eyes and have Eric lead her the last few yards, so she could be standing beside the rippling pond when her gaze first fell on the waterfall. But she kept walking.

When the falls came into view, it seemed as if there was a shaft of light from heaven shining directly on it. Even as magical as this place was, Glory knew it was simply the luck of timing. The sun was at the perfect angle, sending a bright ray through a small opening in the heavy green canopy overhead. The water looked like millions of diamonds cascading over the twenty-foot drop. An arc of rainbow colors showed in the halo mist surrounding the falls.

As waterfalls go, Blue Falls wasn't large. Although the drop was significant, the cataract was only about four feet wide where it spilled over the top and tumbled to Blue Falls Pond below. And the pond itself was an anomaly, an unusually deep bowl in the rocks and gravel that formed a perfect swimming hole before the water hurried on down the mountain. As with most mountain water, it was crystal clear and very cool.

Glory stood in a near trance watching the play of light on moving water.

Eric moved quietly away from her. She sensed his movement, but she didn't stir; grateful for his consideration of her privacy in this moment.

Before long, she felt his absence, a sensation both surprising and satisfying. She'd wanted to come here for comfort, solitude. But she'd also known the potential for a slide into depression, a reluctance to return to the hollow and reality. Eric saved her from that. She was able to draw comfort from this place, yet she yearned to have him close, too.

As these feelings settled into a sort of order, she looked around and saw him sitting on a large boulder at the water's edge. He had his feet planted with his knees drawn up and his arms resting on them. He looked as if he was deep in thought.

She went to sit beside him.

When he looked at her, his serious gaze told her he'd been buried in his own problems, using the calm here to help him find his way through them. For a moment she felt rude in her intrusion, not nearly as considerate of him as he'd been of her. But he didn't seem disturbed by her nearness. He gave her a ghost of a smile before he looked back at the falls.

His voice was hollow when he said, "There's something broken inside my son."

Glory was surprised to realize that for the past hour she'd forgotten that he was a father. And as unsuspecting as she'd been about his topic of consideration, it should not have surprised her. This was a place to draw out your most troubling thoughts for examination. What could be more worrisome than a problem with a child? Even so, Glory wasn't sure she was comfortable talking about Scott. Her own need to steer clear of the child still baffled her. But there was something in Eric's voice that touched her in a place she'd thought was dead.

"Sometimes I think the same thing about me," she said. Maybe that was the explanation for her avoidance of Scott; he mirrored her own detachment.

Suddenly she was sorry she'd said anything. Eric wanted to talk about his son; she didn't need to turn the focus on herself.

Eric gave her a sideways glance. His lids remained lowered, as if he worried he might scare her away if he looked at her too directly. "How so?"

Damn. She drew a deep breath. "I see how Scott seems so . . . disconnected. I can understand that." She folded her hands together. "That's how I felt those first weeks after the fire. I'd go through the day, do normal things, yet not feel like I actually *belonged* to what was happening." She paused, trying to decide how deeply she wanted to wade in these waters. "Has he always been like this?"

He rubbed his forehead. "It's hard for me to tell, exactly. I don't remember thinking there was anything out of the ordinary about him as an infant. But I can't tell you exactly when I noticed a change." He blew out a long breath. "It's like once something glaring happens, I can look back and see lots of little things that probably were clues. Like, hindsight, you know?"

In that instant his words teased her memory. She felt as if there was something she wanted to say, wanted to recall. But it remained just out of reach, like a word you just can't find, no matter how hard you try to recall it. *Clues and hindsight. It had to do with hindsight.*

But Eric went on, and she let it go. "Scott started saying words when he should have—maybe even earlier. Jill's mother said he was talking early, anyway. But one day I realized I hadn't heard any new words for a long while, but couldn't tell you when they stopped coming." He chewed his lip for a moment, as if debating how much to confide. "It's hard . . . with Jill and I divorced . . . I see him every week, but I don't see him every day. I don't know if that would make a difference."

"A difference in which?" she asked carefully. "His development, or your understanding of that development?"

Pain crossed his handsome features. "Jill insists it's his development; that our separation has had some sort of detrimental effect on him . . . maybe she's right."

Now they were venturing into even more dangerous territory—his marriage. Glory considered a moment before she stuck her foot in her mouth. What business was it of hers, anyway? But she hated for him to blame himself for something that most likely wasn't his fault.

She plunged ahead. "Was the divorce your idea?"

He looked at the waterfall again. "It's complicated." His shoulders sagged slightly. "We probably never should have married in the first place. But Jill got pregnant, and I thought we could make it work—I really wanted to try."

Why did it make a little flutter in her chest to hear his marriage wasn't well suited from the start? That just seemed mean-spirited.

"How long have you been apart?" As far as she knew, he'd still been with his wife when she left Dawson.

"It probably makes more sense to ask if we were ever really *together*. We lived in the same house until Scott was ten months old. We've been divorced for nearly a year."

With all this talk of divorce, Glory's mind went on the hunt again, trying to remember what seemed just beyond a paper-thin wall. The effort made her head hurt and her stomach recoil. She pulled away from her own thoughts and focused on Eric's problem. "You still didn't answer my question."

"It was Jill; she wanted the divorce. She was seeing someone else."

It was all Glory could do to keep from jumping to her feet and screaming, "Was she crazy?" But she kept her seat and closed her lips to seal her words inside.

Then she asked the logical—and much more neutral—question, "If she wanted the divorce, why is she blaming you for Scott's problems that she thinks were caused by it?"

Glory saw Eric's hands clench into fists, then relax again. After a moment he said, "Let's just say logic isn't Jill's long suit when it comes to emotional issues."

"Sometimes an unwanted pregnancy can cause irreparable damage in a relationship."

His gaze left the water and cut to her face. That sharp focus made her realize what she'd just said—and she couldn't for the life of her think why she'd said it.

He asked, "Didn't Andrew want to have a baby?"

"Why would you ask such a thing?"

"It's just you said 'unwanted pregnancy.'"

She drew away slightly from Eric's sudden intensity. "No I didn't. I said unplanned pregnancy."

"You said 'unwanted.'"

"Whatever." She didn't really want to get in an argument over semantics.

"Didn't he?" Eric pushed again.

With a dismissive smile, she said, "Of course he wanted a baby. We'd been married for six years . . . he was a little nervous, like all expectant parents." She twisted her hands in her lap, and added softly, "Of course he wanted it."

For a long moment, she could feel his eyes on her, but she concentrated her gaze on the waterfall.

"I'm sorry," he said, and some of the intensity had left his voice. "I'm sorry. That was none of my business." He swiped a hand over his face. "I didn't mean to open a painful subject. You wanted to come here alone, and I've intruded." He got up. "I'll go wait for you back on the path."

Before he turned and walked away, Glory reached up and grabbed his hand. "No." She finally dared to look at him again. "Stay. Please." She didn't want to be alone and think about where her question had come from—or why her answer to his felt like a lie.

Chapter Ten

❧

AT LEAST GRAVITY was in Glory's favor on the way home. If she'd been alone at the falls, she would have soothed her aching muscles beneath the cascading cool water before heading back. She didn't even consider it with Eric present. It wasn't that she was overly modest. Stripped down to her underwear, she'd still be showing less skin than in her swimsuit. It was more the fact that she felt herself in an emotional slide toward him, and she'd already exposed herself in ways that left her more vulnerable than their casual acquaintance should have allowed. Her desire for him to kiss her on their way up attested to that. Swimming might lead to . . . other things.

This time, Eric took the lead the entire way. The grade was steep in places, easy for feet to slide out from beneath a person. Glory moved carefully, torn between watching her footing and the movement of Eric's masculine shoulders. Occasionally her foot would slip, reminding her that she'd better be careful; she'd fallen on him once today, twice would be just too humiliating.

They hadn't said much since the moment she'd asked him not to leave her beside the pond. They sat in quiet companionable solitude until Glory had gotten up and said she was ready to leave.

Now, as they neared the church, the grade evened out some, and the path became wide enough that they could walk side by side. He slowed up and let her move alongside. As their arms brushed, he took her hand in his. He didn't say anything, just walked slowly beside her in the heat.

The contact gave her such an adolescent thrill that Glory didn't dare look at him. Really, she was twenty-eight, she was a widow; holding hands with a man shouldn't give her the shivers. But it did.

They still held hands when they reached his motorcycle at the shady edge of the cemetery. At that point, Eric drew her to a stop in front of him. He held her gaze, smiling down at her, his thumb rubbing the back of her hand.

Glory stood there like an idiot, unsure what to say.

He tipped his head toward the bike. "You want a ride home?"

Glory remembered how it felt to slide onto that machine behind him and race down the roads—at least it had felt like racing, but knowing Eric, she was certain it had been a very cautious ride. Repeating the experience was greater temptation than she cared to admit. Which is why she took a small step backward and said, "No, thanks."

Was that disappointment in his eyes?

He released her hand. "I was going to stop by and see if Tula needed anything from town before I left the hollow anyhow. It'll be a few days before anyone'll be able to drive a car out of here."

Unreasonably, Glory didn't want Granny to know Eric had been with her all afternoon at Blue Falls Pond. Guilt edged into her consciousness, not that she'd done anything to feel guilty about, she assured herself. Still . . .

"You go on and visit with Gran. I'm going to take a nice slow walk the rest of the way."

For the briefest second, she thought he was going to try to change her mind. But he finally nodded and said good-bye.

Glory stood in the churchyard until he'd started the motorcycle and disappeared down the road. Then she began her meandering stroll home.

As she turned onto the lane that led to Granny's house, Glory heard a sharp, thin chirp, like an injured bird. She paused and listened. After a second, she heard it again. Only it didn't actually sound like a bird. It was more like a yip than a chirp.

Her skin prickled. There were wildcats in this area. She'd never heard of one attacking a human. Her mind mentally judged how far it was to Granny's front porch. She couldn't see the house, but it wasn't that far away, just around the curve in the gravel lane.

Two sharp yips sounded like they came from the culvert that ran beneath the lane, sounding more pitiful than threatening. But this was wild country, not domesticated farmland of Ohio or Minnesota. Something injured and angry—and feral—was probably in that drainpipe.

Glory looked at the ditch that led to the culvert, then to the lane that led toward the house. She stood in indecision for another moment before another wild-sounding yelp made her mind up for her.

Eric had exhausted all of his excuses for hanging around Tula's house, and still Glory hadn't shown up. It was nearly three-thirty; he'd stayed so long that Tula had begun to doze on the sofa.

Even at a snail's pace, Glory should have been home by now.

He mentally took stock of the potential hazards between here and the church. The woman was proving herself to be accident-prone. She could have stubbed her toe on a root and fallen; broken a bone or hit her head. She could have been bitten by a copperhead. She could have twisted her ankle in a rabbit burrow.

He shifted in his chair.

Maybe he'd go back to the church, check the road along the way. If he didn't see her, maybe he should walk the path through the woods.

He leaned forward and rubbed his forehead.

What if he did find her and she was fine? He'd already intruded on her private time enough for one day. She was a grown woman.

He got up out of the chair, roused Tula enough to tell her good-bye, and left, still debating his course of action. He half hoped he'd see Glory appear from the path in the woods as he got on his bike.

When that didn't happen, he thought maybe he'd meet her on the lane.

He started the motorcycle and rolled it off its kick-stand.

He'd just cruise past the church. No harm in that.

He rounded the curve in the lane, looking one last time in the rearview mirror to see if Glory had appeared in the yard. When he returned his gaze to the lane in front of him he saw her.

She was sprawled facedown in the ditch that ran to the drainpipe that passed under the lane. Her legs were spread and her arms flung over her head.

His heart gave a double beat as he braked and lunged off the bike, sliding it to the ground on its side; not talking precious seconds to set it on its kickstand.

"Glory!" He threw himself onto his knees in the ditch beside her.

Her head came up, a shocked expression on her face. "Are you all right?" she shouted.

"Fine," he responded, trying to make sense of what was happening and settle his heart back in his chest.

"Your bike!" she said.

"What in the hell are you doing lying in this ditch?"

She grinned, then ducked her head close to the ground and looked into the pipe again. She whispered something that he couldn't make out.

He wrinkled his brow and asked, "What?"

"Puppies," she said softly. When he looked at her blankly, she pulled him down beside her. "Look."

Eric realized there were little squeaking sounds echoing from inside. Sounded like bats.

He squinted and looked in the pipe. At first he couldn't see more than a lump obstructing the light coming from the other end. Then he saw that the lump was moving. As his eyes adjusted he saw a dog and a pile of pups.

Glory said, "I think she's a retriever of some sort. I counted six pups—although with them wiggling around I can't be sure."

She started to reach into the pipe. Eric grabbed her wrist.

She looked at him. "We can't leave them here. What if it rains? They'll drown."

"I know," Eric said softly. "Better see if the mother's agreeable first."

Glory looked back into the pipe. "There! She's wagging her tail." She scooted forward on her belly to reach inside. "She's probably hungry and thirsty."

With a little coaxing, they lured the mother out into the open. She was dirty and thin, her tan coat matted with muck from the bottom of the drainpipe. Eric picked her up while Glory gathered the puppies and loaded them in the upturned hem of her T-shirt.

"Oh my, their little eyes are still closed." She drew in a breath as she looked at the wriggling pile in her shirt. "Oh, and their ears are so tiny."

Eric shifted the weight of the mother in his arms. "Let's get them settled somewhere. I don't think mama wants to be separated from them for long."

They started walking toward the house, leaving Eric's motorcycle where it lay at the side of the gravel lane.

Glory looked at the mother. "No collar. No tags. Do you think she's a Lab? Even with no tags, someone might be missing her."

"She's a mutt and probably a stray. There's retriever in there, but look at those ears and the shape of her nose. Those are hound. And she hasn't been groomed in what looks like forever."

Once they had the new doggie family settled in a blanket-lined box in Tula's shed, they decided they'd better wake Tula and tell her of the new boarders.

They made a game of it and led Tula out with her eyes closed.

When they told her to open them, she sucked in a breath. "Good heavens! Look at that."

She knelt beside the box, a wide grin on her face. She said to the dog, "You did a fine job, fine job, little mama. Now you can rest. You're all safe here."

Eric said, "She doesn't have tags. Do you recognize her, Tula?"

Tula shook her head. "Cain't say I do. No matter, she's welcome here 'long as she wants to stay."

Eric had been fairly certain Tula wouldn't turn away any living creature, but felt himself relaxing when she responded so happily.

Tula got to her feet and said to Glory, "Guess you'd better have Eric run you into town on that contraption of his to get some dog food. Who knows how long it's been since she's eaten."

Glory said, "Oh. I hadn't even thought of that." She looked at Eric. "Do you mind?"

He almost said she didn't need to go, he could get the food and bring it back. Instead, he bought himself more time in her company by saying, "Of course not."

For years Dawson had fought the trend to open retail shopping on Sundays. But even here in the mountains, times had finally changed. A few holdouts remained closed until noon—after church services—but most stores now had Sunday hours.

Glory held tightly to Eric as he swung the motorcycle into the parking lot at Tucker's Maxi-Mart. He stopped at the gas pump. Glory got off and went to see what they had in the way of pet supplies.

Tucker's had originally been just a gas station. Years ago it had expanded its services to a quick-stop, with milk and bread and soft drinks. Sometime later they had added canned goods, cereal, and a little deli. Then, just before Glory left town, it had been flattened by a tornado. While she had been gone it'd been rebuilt, the space redesigned to house a small-scale full-service market. The aisles were wide and brightly lit; a vast improvement to the cramped layout of the old store, where it seemed every year they managed to pile more merchandise into the already overcrowded space, making shopping there something more like a treasure hunt.

Glory found the dog food and squatted to read the labels. There were choices for senior citizen dogs, puppies, dogs with bad breath, dogs with sensitive stomachs ... nothing for dogs that had just delivered a litter of puppies. She settled on one that guaranteed maximum nutrition, pulled it off the low shelf, and stood up. When she turned around, there was a woman standing just behind her.

"Glory? I thought that was you, but I just couldn't believe it." Ovella Harrison gave Glory a quick, mechanical embrace—which was about as much warmth as the woman ever had mustered for Glory. The dog food bag prevented Glory from hugging back.

"Ovella." She couldn't think of anything else to say. After a year and a half with only the brief obligatory holiday communication, this wasn't the best way to have your mother-in-law discover you were back in town.

"Why didn't you call? How long have you been back?"

"Last Wednesday. I planned on calling ... time seemed to get away." Glory always felt like a child called on the carpet with Ovella, no matter how friendly the woman appeared outwardly. She supposed it all stemmed back to the fact that Ovella had been less than thrilled with her son's choice of a bride. She'd never treated Glory with anything less than outward affection and acceptance, but Glory had always sensed a strained undercurrent to that affection.

Ovella dismissed Glory's excuse with a wave of her hand. "No matter. Where are you living?"

"Oh, I'm staying with Granny."

"Clear out there?" A hint of the old disapproval colored her voice. For Ovella, if you lived in the hollow, you didn't really belong to Dawson at all. "What are your plans?"

"I'm sort of playing it by ear. Granny's having some problems . . . it all depends on how that goes."

"So . . . you're not back for good?"

Glory couldn't tell if Ovella sounded pleased or miffed. She told the truth, and said, "I'm just not sure."

At that moment, Eric walked up. "Hello, Mrs. Harrison."

Ovella turned to him with a smile. "Eric! Good to see you." Then she looked back to Glory. "Do you remember my daughter-in-law?"

Eric smiled so warmly at Glory that she felt the heat right to the pit of her stomach. "Yes, ma'am."

Ovella cast a curious look between Eric and Glory. Then said to Glory, "I'd better run; Walter is waiting for this cold medicine." She held up the box in her hand. "He'll be so glad to hear you're back, Glory. Promise you'll call this week."

Glory nodded. "I promise." Whereas Ovella's affection had always felt as if it had been given with reluctance, Walt had more than made up for it with his straightforward caring. Glory could actually say she'd genuinely missed her father-in-law.

Ovella gave Glory a quick brush of a kiss on her cheek. Then she said to Eric, "Tell Jill I said hello."

Then she was gone, leaving only a hint of Chanel No. 5 and a sense of being caught in some sort of misbehavior.

Eric took the bag of dog food from Glory. "Do you think she'll need anything else?"

Glory looked at him with confusion. "Ovella?"

He laughed. "The dog."

"I don't think we could carry anything else on the motorcycle." As she walked to the front of the store with Eric, Glory told herself to stop wondering why Ovella had brought Jill up. Jill's mother and she were friends, after all. And it had been clear that Ovella had no idea that Glory and Eric were together.

It had to be a manifestation of that old feeling of being brought to account for her behavior in front of Ovella. Glory really shouldn't have let Ovella discover she was back in town like this. Actually, her mother-in-law had been surprisingly gracious about the whole thing.

As they walked out, Ovella was just finishing filling her car with gas. Glory and Eric climbed on the motorcycle and settled the bag of dog food securely between them. Eric waved to Ovella as he pulled away from the pump.

Glory saw the stunned expression on Ovella's face and quickly looked away, feeling like she'd been caught cheating on her dead husband.

* * *

"Mother, is that you?" Walter called from upstairs as Ovella walked through the foyer. His words were followed by coughing.

"Yes, dear. I'll bring the medicine right up. I'm getting you some orange juice."

She took her time arranging the orange juice, the Sunday paper, a napkin, and the cold medicine on a tray. Should she tell Walter about seeing Glory? He'd been doing so well lately. Ovella didn't want him to be upset on top of his cold. He should be retired now, sitting on a sunny beach or deep-sea fishing, not grinding away every day at the paper company. He'd earned his rest.

Luckily, she'd stayed home from church today because of Walter's cold; she would have been mortified to learn through the grapevine that Glory was back. How would that look? That thought made up her mind; she couldn't let Walter find out that way.

Once at the top of the stairs, she put a bright smile on her face and entered the bedroom. "Here we are. Just what the doctor ordered."

"Honestly, Mother, you're making too much fuss. It's just a little summer cold."

"At your age, you can't be too careful."

He sputtered. "You make it sound like I've got one foot in the grave! I'm only sixty-nine."

She set down the tray and opened the cold medicine. "Plenty of sixty-nine-year-olds get pneumonia. If something happened to you . . ." Walter was the twine that held her together. Without him she'd be in a thousand fragmented pieces.

He pinched her on the butt. "Come over here and I'll show you how healthy I am."

She jumped and swatted his hand away. "Enough of that!"

He swallowed his pills with the orange juice, and she opened the paper for him. She took a deep breath and said, "Glory's back in town."

Walter lifted himself off his propping of pillows. "Our girl's back! When? Where is she?"

Ovella eased him back onto his pillows. "Settle down. She's staying out there . . . with her grandmother. I saw her at Tucker's." She wasn't about to tell him that their daughter-in-law had been on the back of Eric Wilson's motorcycle.

"Well, get her on the phone and get her over here!"

"You're sick. She said she'd call."

"She should be staying here, with us."

Ovella couldn't think of a worse idea. It was difficult enough seeing her today. To have her underfoot day in and day out, a constant reminder . . . "Her grandmother is having some health problems. She needs Glory with her."

Walter sighed in concession. "Well, she needs to come see us soon."

"I'm sure she will. Now you lie back and let that cold medicine do its work. You have meetings in New York next week."

Thank God Walter didn't know what poor Andrew had confided to her. That ugliness had died with her son and would never touch her husband.

As she closed the door to the bedroom, she almost resented the happiness on her husband's face as he closed his eyes.

* * *

As Glory lay in bed that night, thinking of puppies and Eric, her mind shifted to the question he'd asked her beside the pond: *Didn't Andrew want to have a baby?*

Her answer had been quick, a knee-jerk reaction. But it had sparked an odd feeling inside her.

Just as she was slipping into sleep, a scene played in her mind, not quite dream, but not quite memory.

Andrew had turned his back on her. He was upset. But she couldn't grasp what had upset him. She moved to him and put her hand on his back. He jerked away as if she'd delivered an electric shock with her touch.

Then he spun around and faced her, his face red with tightly reined fury. He bit out angry words, "How did this happen?"

Glory stumbled backward, coming awake before she hit the floor in her dream.

She sat straight up in bed, gasping. For a moment she was disoriented. As the room came into focus, she swallowed hard and put a hand over her hammering heart.

She remembered. They'd argued over her pregnancy.

She closed her eyes and tried to let the full memory come. It had been raining all day, she recalled. She'd made a nice dinner, laid a fire in the fireplace. She had been so certain that Andrew's reservations about parenthood would disappear once he knew there was a baby on the way.

She'd broken the news with dessert, anticipating surprise, but tenderness.

Andrew had exploded. His words rang loudly in her memory:

"I asked you how this happened. You're on the pill. It's worked for six years. You expect me to believe it just stopped working?" He was shaking with anger.

"The doctor said it was probably because of the antibiotic I was taking," Glory said, waiting for the shock to subside and Andrew to realize how wonderful this news really was. The decision had been taken out of their hands. They were having a baby.

Andrew looked sharply at her. "We'll sue. He should have told you this could happen."

Glory tried to reach out to him, but he stepped away. She stood quietly for a few seconds while Andrew paced.

"I told you I didn't want kids. We agreed."

When she found her voice, it was small and trembling. "I guess we're going to have to adapt." She didn't argue the details; he had said it, of that there was no denying. But she'd never agreed. Time and again, she'd backed off, but she'd never agreed. And when the doctor had written the prescription and told her that on rare occasion there were problems with oral contraceptives, she'd ignored it. Rare. He'd said it was rare.

She'd rolled the dice, letting fate take its course.

"Andrew," she'd said quietly, "let's give this a while to sink in before we discuss it. This happens to couples all the time and turns out to be the best thing in their lives."

He looked at her and seemed to be calming down. He touched her face. "I love you, Glory. You can tell me, did you know? Did you know this could happen?"

"No."

Tears ran down her face as she sat in the dark in Granny's lavender floral bedroom. She had deceived her husband. How could she not have remembered that?

Chapter Eleven

✿

IF GLORY LOOKED herself right square in the eye, she'd have to admit her sense of guilt had a big role in her avoiding Eric over the next two weeks. She wasn't sure if that guilt had been spurred by the look on Ovella's face in the parking lot of Tucker's—the one that made her feel she was cheating on Andrew. Or if it was Eric's keen insight, insight that had made him ask his question at Blue Falls Pond—the question that sliced through her blocked memory to the truth she'd been hiding from herself for eighteen months. What else might he see inside her, what other things might his questions shake loose?

She was a coward. Now that she'd had a glimpse of the past, she had to face the fact that there were things she *liked* about not remembering everything that happened prior to and during the fire. Coming home was painful enough without discovering unpleasant things about her own behavior.

And there were other things bothering her that made her stay away from Eric, things that had to do with Scott. She'd caught herself watching him from as much distance as she could manage without Granny coming right out and asking her what in the heck was wrong with her. In odd moments she tried to decipher two things: what exactly set Scott apart and made her agree with Eric that something was wrong with him, and why she felt so resistant to an innocent child.

She'd started making a mental list of things that were strange about Scott, tiny things that just didn't seem right, when taken as a whole signaled trouble. As for deciphering her own "strangeness," she hadn't made much headway.

So, on Thursday mornings and Friday afternoons she hid—there were a thousand ways she could phrase it in her mind that sounded less cowardly, but that was the bald truth. She was hiding. This was the second Thursday she'd stayed in her bedroom waiting for Eric to drop Scott off before she went downstairs.

At the usual time, she heard Eric's car pull up to the house. She stood back from the window so she wouldn't be easily seen from outside and watched him take Scott out of his car seat. An ache settled in the center of her chest; Eric deserved better than an unfaithful wife and a child with developmental problems. But he accepted both in his own quiet and pragmatic way. When he'd spoken of Jill, it was with none of the bitterness that most men felt toward cheating ex-wives. Briefly, Glory wondered if perhaps he still had feelings for her. But she quickly dismissed the thought, mostly because she didn't want to think it might be true.

After Eric entered the kitchen below her bedroom, she strained like the eavesdropper she'd recently become to hear what he said.

"'Morning, Tula." As always, his deep voice carried through the heating duct. Glory leaned against the window frame and let the inner warmth that his voice stirred engulf her.

Granny's response to his greeting wasn't as clear and came through only as a pleasant vibration. For one moment, the sound reminded Glory of Charlie Brown cartoons where all of the adult voices were nothing more than muted trumpets that mimicked the cadence of conversation.

"How's Glory?" This was the same question she'd heard him ask every morning. And each time, it made her heart beat just a bit faster. She realized she was in danger of falling for her rescuer. And that was a psychological cliché if she'd ever heard one. He was in the business of rescuing. It was in his nature to ask such questions.

But he came to the hospital . . . he held my hand.

God, she sounded like a teenager. He'd held her hand because he sensed she needed emotional support, no need to read more into it than that.

Granny responded to Eric's query. It was a short answer—Granny was becoming increasingly short with what she called Glory's "contrary" behavior, which included her refusal to go to church, her increasing avoidance of everyone except Granny, and her refusal to try to find a course for her own life.

"I thought maybe she'd want me to take her back into town and pick up her car. I ran into Mr. Franklin yesterday, and he said the parts finally came in from Volvo and it was ready."

Glory tensed. She'd been avoiding two-minute conversations with Eric; the last thing she wanted was a twenty-minute drive alone with him. She quickly slipped back into bed, even though she was fully dressed, turned on her side away from the door, and drew the sheet up over her shoulder. As she expected, Granny was soon knocking at her door.

Coward, coward, coward.

Granny stuck her head in when Glory didn't respond. "Glory?"

Glory rolled over, trying to appear sleepy.

"Eric wants to know if you want a ride back into town to pick up your car. It's ready."

"Oh." She yawned—which was probably overkill that Granny would see right through, she thought belatedly. "I overslept. I don't want to hold him up. I'll figure something out later. We don't really need the car right away, anyhow."

"He won't mind waiting while you throw on some clothes."

"I'll get it later." Glory's voice was more biting than she'd intended.

Granny looked at her with tight lips. "All right."

As Granny was closing the door, Glory called, "Tell him I said thanks for the offer."

She heard Granny mumble, "Oughta tell him y'rself. 'Bout time you started talking to someone other'n me."

Glory lay still and heard Granny's muffled voice in the kitchen again. Then there was a long pause. Then she heard Eric say hello to Lady—whom Granny had named and had moved, along with all six puppies, into the house. No one had come forward to claim her, even after they'd posted lost-dog posters everywhere.

"How are those pups of yours?" Eric asked. Glory could picture him, bending over, scratching Lady behind the ears. Just one more female he'd had a hand in rescuing.

Granny chuckled and said something.

Eric said, "Better go." The kitchen door opened and closed.

His car door slammed, and the engine started.

Glory didn't move until several minutes after she heard him pull away. Her own cowardice made her sick.

She forced herself to go downstairs and do at least one of the things she'd been avoiding, just to regain a bit of her self-worth. She still hadn't spoken to her in-laws. Twice she'd left messages on their answering machine, saying she was going to be in and out and would call them back. It had been easy to let days slip by between attempted calls. She dreaded the first awkward silences and missteps as they all danced around the deaths of Andrew and the baby.

These issues should have been worked out months and months ago. She was angry with herself for letting things ride; her avoidance only made it more difficult. She'd justified to herself that they didn't want to speak to her any more than she wanted to speak to them; what did they have to talk about but death and loss? Now she had to ask herself if her abandonment had hurt them. Had she deserted them when they wanted her near so they could feel close to their son and grandchild?

As Glory entered the kitchen, Granny said a cool "Good morning." Then she asked Glory to keep an eye on Scott, who was on his blanket in the corner of the kitchen, while she went out to get the newspaper from the box. As the lane to Granny's house was quite long, this usually was at least a ten-minute task.

"Sure," Glory said brightly. Her effort to lighten Granny's mood failed. She could feel a "talk" coming.

Granny put on her sunglasses and went out the door, looking like she'd eaten a sour pickle.

Well, one unpleasant task at a time, Glory thought. Granny would have to wait her turn. And, when Granny began her "talk," Glory would be able to tell her that she wasn't avoiding *everyone*—she'd just spoken to her in-laws.

She could use the wall phone in the kitchen and still watch Scott.

She paused with her hand on the phone as Lady's prancing entrance into the kitchen caught her eye. The dog's name was fitting; she had a regal bearing, as if she held some smug secret. Granny said it came from mother-hood.

Now Lady entered the kitchen as if she had something particular in mind, moving with focused purpose.

Scott had been turning his boat in the usual circles. When Lady walked in the kitchen however, he stopped. His gaze followed her as she walked to the stove and sniffed high in the air, as she moved on to the trash can and sniffed, then as she paused passing the kitchen table for one last sniff before she pranced back out of the kitchen, her mission apparently complete.

Once she was out of sight, Scott began turning the boat again, his focus concentrated as always.

For a moment, Glory almost doubted what she'd seen. Scott didn't notice when people moved around him, even when they were attempting to get his attention. She decided to keep an eye out and see if this interest in Lady was an anomaly. Eric would need to know.

She picked up the phone and dialed her in-laws, secretly hoping she'd get the answering machine again.

"Hello, Harrison residence," Ovella answered in her sophisticated Southern smoothness.

"Hi, Ovella, it's Glory." She realized her mouth was suddenly dry.

"Oh, hello, Glory," Ovella said, with a hint of expectation in her voice. But then she let the line lie silent.

Glory waited a couple of heartbeats before she said, "Sorry I've missed you. I tried to call before." It had been bad enough that her mother-in-law had discovered she was back home in the way she did. Glory didn't want to heap on more negligence.

"I know." There it was again, as if she was cautiously waiting for Glory to say something.

Racking her brain, Glory could not begin to know what Ovella could want from her, so she pressed on. "Well, how is Walt? Is his cold any better?"

"He's fine."

Glory wondered why the woman had extracted her promise to call if this was all the effort she was going to put into their exchange. But, she assured herself, although Ovella had made peace with the fact that Glory was in the family, she'd never made the road to conversation between them a particularly easy one.

"I'm glad to hear that," Glory said. "May I speak to him?" She always said "may I" with Ovella; after years of raised eyebrows over "can I," it had finally become habit.

Ovella sighed a ladylike sigh. "I'm sorry, he's not here." After a short pause she said, "He's had to come out of retirement, you know—without Andrew there to run the paper company." There seemed to be a hint of accusation in her tone, as if it were Glory's fault Walt had gone back to work.

"Oh, I didn't know." The company had been started by Walt's grandfather. Andrew had taken over the presidency three years ago. Ownership was to pass to him completely upon Walt's death.

"Of course you didn't, dear. How could you? You left so soon after Andrew's funeral . . ."

Glory swallowed. "I guess that's one of the things I need to talk to you two about, to explain why—"

"Really, Glory, there's no need to upset Walter with that kind of conversation. He's come to terms. It's best we not dredge up old pain."

"I didn't want to upset him. I just thought I should explain—"

"I know you mean well, but trust me, nothing you can say will make it any easier on Walter. You know, with Andrew an only child, Walter had counted on him to take over the business. But he's gotten past that now. We should just let things be."

"I'd like to come and see him . . . both of you." She did want to see Walt. Suddenly she needed to look into his kind brown eyes and feel the fatherly embrace of shared loss.

"He's working long hours."

"All right. Please tell him I called," Glory said, the coolness in her voice matching Ovella degree for frosty degree.

Ovella gave another sigh. "I'm sorry, I'm being rude. Things have been so hectic. Of course Walter will want to see you. Can you come by Sunday afternoon, say, three o'clock?"

"I'd like that."

As Glory hung up the phone, she glanced back at Scott. His blanket was empty except for the little plastic boat.

Panic shot through her chest.

Scott never left that blanket.

She dashed into the living room, calling his name. She glanced around and didn't see him.

She checked the front door and found it still securely latched.

She hurried into the downstairs bathroom, even pulling back the shower curtain.

No Scott.

He couldn't be far, she'd only looked away for a few seconds.

"Scott!"

She stopped in the hallway and listened for movement.

The puppies were yipping in their box in the room Granny used for a den. Glory looked toward that door and saw Scott toddle past, right behind Lady.

She sprinted into the room and, in her relief, scooped him up.

Immediately he began to scream. "Sorry. Sorry. I know you don't like to be held." She carefully set him back on his feet, but he continued to scream. "Sorry! But you scared the bejeezus out of me. Don't cry." She pointed. "Look at Lady. You don't want to scare her puppies."

Scott's eyes were squeezed shut. He rocked from side to side.

Glory took his hand and set it on Lady's back. "There's Lady. Sssshhhh. There's Lady."

His screams reduced to a thin whine, and he stopped rocking.

She whispered. "That's it. Just pet Lady. You're all right." She waited while he calmed. Lady stood patiently, as if she understood what was needed of her.

To get him back into the kitchen, Glory lured Lady with a dog treat. Scott followed right along behind. There was another oddity to put in Scott's behavior basket. Most children would be fixated on the puppies, not the quiet mother dog.

Granny came back in with the newspaper, and asked, "What happened?"

Glory tried to gloss over her previous panic. "Scott followed Lady to the back room. He didn't want to come back."

Granny looked like she'd been hit with cold water. "Really? He followed her?"

"Yes."

"Well, now, don't that beat all. He's never wandered."

"Maybe it's a new phase." Glory paused, thinking of the way Scott's gaze had followed Lady around the kitchen. "Or maybe he just likes the dog."

Lady was now lying next to Scott on his blanket. His little fist was burrowed in her fur.

"Maybe," she agreed thoughtfully as she laid the newspaper on the kitchen table. She made herself a cup of tea, but didn't touch the paper when she sat down at the table.

This would make the tenth straight day that Granny had laid the newspaper down and not picked it back up. It had been going into the trash as neatly folded as when it arrived in the mailbox.

Glory put a hand on her hip and said, "Did you reschedule the eye appointment you missed because of the washout?"

"No need. Doctor wanted to see if there was more bleedin'. There hasn't been. Things are what the doctor calls 'status quo'—means nothin's changed."

Glory picked up the newspaper. "When I first got here, you were reading the newspaper every morning. I saw it was a strain, even with your magnifying glasses, but you read it. Now you don't even open it up."

"Some days my eyes are better'n others, that's all. Seein' the doctor won't change anything."

"How are you going to make ends meet? I know you can't quilt, you haven't sewn a stitch since I got here."

"I manage. Got my social security. Got what Eric pays me."

"And how long do you think you're going to be able to babysit?"

"I told you I won't sit if I'm not fit. I'll figure out something else."

"We need to *plan*, Gran. Ignoring the inevitable won't keep it from coming!" Glory slapped the newspaper back down on the table and a piece of paper fell out.

Thinking it was an advertisement flyer, Glory grabbed it and tossed it back on the table. As it fluttered to a rest, she saw it wasn't an ad at all. It was a blown-up photocopy of the article that had been in the newspaper after the fire. There was a large picture of the burned-out shell of her house on Laurel Creek Road, dark smoke rising from the ruin, pumper truck still parked in the foreground.

In large block letters made by a wide black marker were the words "I KNOW WHAT YOU DID."

Glory went cold. She grabbed at the back of a chair to steady herself.

She heard Granny say, "Even I can read that." Her hand was on Glory's arm, guiding her to sit in the chair. "What does it mean?"

Glory shuddered as she thought of the black holes in the fabric of her memory and her recent realization that she'd deceived her husband. What *had* she done . . . and who knew about it?

Chapter Twelve

❧

IT WAS TOUCH-AND-GO, but Glory finally convinced Granny the photocopy and message had been nothing more than a teenager's prank. Probably one of those Simpson children, she'd reasoned, who were always getting their laughs at someone else's expense.

Then she'd had to defuse the resultant situation when Granny wanted to call Mrs. Simpson and give her a piece of her mind.

"If it was one of my young'uns doin' such hurtful mischief, I'd want to know," Granny said angrily.

"Well, Gran, we don't have any proof it was them. It's just a summer prank brought on by boredom. Most likely they're mimicking a movie they've seen. They don't think of how something like this could affect someone."

"That's why I need to call—it's a lesson they need to learn."

"Let's just wait and see if it happens again. No sense in making it a bigger deal—that might be what they're after, a response."

Granny didn't look overly convinced as she rinsed the dishes. Glory had to bite her tongue to keep from over-arguing and setting off Granny's lie detector.

After the kitchen was cleaned up, Granny would be taking Scott out for a walk. Glory hurried the process along as much as she dared without tipping her hand. As she cleaned, her gaze kept drifting to the hateful picture on the table. Each time she looked at the words her flesh crawled. She *wanted* it to be a practical joke—but it tripped something inside that said there was substance.

Finally, Granny put lotion on her hands, then went to kneel in front of Scott. "Walk," she said with a hand under his chin to make him look at her. "Time for our walk."

As always, Scott tensed when she tried to get him to leave his boat. Glory saw how his jaw tightened and instead of screaming, he started making a peculiar growling deep in his throat—a sound far more disturbing than angry childlike screams.

Glory, anxious for them to be on their way, suggested, "Maybe he'd like it if you took Lady."

Granny glanced up at her, "You not coming?"

Glory tried to sound nonchalant when she said, "I thought I'd make a few phone calls and clean the puppy box. You two go on."

Scott put his face down on the blanket and continued the grinding growl.

Granny looked at Glory, "You really think Lady might help?"

"It's worth a try. He seems to respond more to her than anything I've seen."

Granny called Lady, who came right away—just proving what Glory had already surmised, she was a smart dog, making a quick adjustment to her new name.

"Scottie, Lady's going with us on our walk." Granny got to her feet and moved to the door, taking Lady with her. "*Walk*, Scott."

Scott didn't move.

Glory knelt beside him. "Come here, Lady."

Lady pranced over and nosed Scott on the shoulder, as if she'd already figured out what Glory wanted her to do.

Glory took one of Scott's fists and put it on the dog. She realized it was the first time she'd touched him except in absolute necessity. And she probably wouldn't have done it if she hadn't wanted them out of the house so badly.

He raised his head. His eyes held more recognition in them than she'd previously seen.

"There, see," Glory said softly, afraid speaking too loudly would upset him again. "Lady wants to walk. She wants you to go, too." She turned to Granny. "Call her, Gran."

When Lady went to Granny, so did Scott.

Granny grinned. "Well, now. Ain't you two good friends."

They left Glory in the kitchen. She watched, wondering if she should have sent Lady on a leash, but the dog never wandered more than a few feet from Granny and Scott as they left the yard.

As soon as they were out of sight, Glory hurried into the garage and started tearing through the trash cans. She threw the contents wildly, snatching the newspapers as she came across them, unfolding them and shaking them violently until she was convinced no hidden messages had been tucked inside. Her heartbeat hammered in her ears and her palms were moist with sweat. She hated this feeling—of the pressure building inside her chest, of the nervous tension choking her. It was just like . . . a memory rushed forward in her mind, sucking air from her lungs:

Andrew slammed on the brakes after he pulled into the driveway much too fast, throwing Glory forward in the seat, making the shoulder harness jerk tight. He hadn't said a word since they'd left the party. The porch light showed his lips were pinched tight and his face nearly purple with rage.

"I don't understand what you're so upset about," she said.

"Really?" It didn't sound like a question.

"Yes, really! Everything went great. Your dad was surprised. Your mom was happy. All of the guests showed up on time. The food was wonderful. Nobody got sloppy drunk. Your toast was charming and funny. What more could you have wanted?"

He'd acted perfectly fine all evening, until they'd walked out the door of the restaurant where they'd held her father-in-law's birthday party. Then the tension descended, and Glory realized she'd been bracing herself for this all evening.

"Maybe I don't like to see my wife flirting with every swinging dick in the room. Good God, Glory, it was embarrassing. You made me look like a fool."

"I wasn't flirting, I was hosting. I mingled and made sure everyone had what they needed so your mother could enjoy the party." Glory had even been cautiously aware of how long she spent with each guest—each male guest. Experience had been a good teacher.

"Don't try to make it sound noble, 'so Mother could enjoy the party.' Do I look stupid?"

She didn't answer, but put her hand on the lever to open the door.

He erupted. "DO I? Do you think just because you were in a crowded room you could act that way and I wouldn't notice?"

"Shout all you want, I'm not going to discuss this anymore." She got quickly out of the car and went into the house, holding herself back when she felt like running. Running would only convince him she had something to hide.

Glory shivered as she remembered how she'd locked herself in the spare bedroom. She'd spent the night there, wondering just how long she was going to put up with this. It hadn't been an isolated incident.

The next morning when she'd gotten got up, her cash and credit cards had been removed from her wallet and her car keys were missing—including the spare set.

"Oh, my God," she whispered. It was as if a brilliant light had been shone into the shadows of her past. Granny had been right. She had been looking at her life with blinders on. She'd spent so much time over the past year and a half focusing on what she had lost, she had refused to see anything but the good. She'd been looking on the other side of the fence that separated her life before and after the fire and blocked out the ugly weeds growing in the green grass.

She waited with her eyes closed . . . sat immobile and barely breathing on the dirty garage floor with trash strewn around her, waiting for more memories to come. Snips and snatches of arguments popped up. Then the reality of her marriage unfolded like a bud opening into flower in the sunlight: Andrew calling home several times a day to "see how things were going." The fact that he didn't want her to drive out to the hollow alone, insisting she wait for him to go too—but never making himself available. His determination that she not work; it was his job to take care of her. The firing of the painting crew she'd hired when he'd come home and discovered they were all college boys who worked with their shirts off— Andrew had claimed it was because of their lack of experience and unprofessional appearance. That had been the last work crew Glory had been permitted to hire.

What she'd viewed as attentive and solicitous behavior in the beginning had soured and become something darker. He had been isolating her. Andrew had become more and more controlling, more and more paranoid, more and more jealous.

Andrew hadn't wanted the baby.

She had been more than unhappy. She'd been increasingly afraid.

I KNOW WHAT YOU DID

Now that these memories were free, Glory tried to see into the night of the fire. Still there was nothing. She had to ask herself why. Why had she denied the truth of her marriage?

Because the truth pointed directly to something you didn't want to see.

I KNOW WHAT YOU DID

Maybe it wasn't just the trauma that had erased her memory; maybe she was willfully blocking it out. Was the ugly truth of the state of her marriage the key? Perhaps she'd done something so hideous that she couldn't face it.

"What on earth are you doing?" Granny's surprised voice shocked Glory into a guilty flinch.

How long had she been sitting here? She realized her face was wet with tears. Luckily it was much brighter on the driveway than it was inside the garage, and Granny had on her sunglasses.

Glory turned away and wiped her face on her sleeve before saying, "I lost an earring. I thought maybe it fell in the trash."

"Oh. I'll help you look." Granny started into the garage.

"No!"

Granny stopped in midstep and looked at her. "Are you all right?"

"It's been so hot, this garbage is really nasty. You don't want Scott in here. I'm almost finished going through it anyway."

Granny looked at her for a moment, then said, "All right, then."

Ten minutes later, after Glory had confirmed no previous newspaper held hidden messages and had stuffed all of the trash back into the cans, she entered the kitchen. Granny was sitting on the floor, leaning against the wall, reading from a large-print book to Scott. Her birdlike legs stuck out of her Capri pants (Granny called them pedal pushers) and were crossed at the ankles. As usual, the boy didn't appear to be hearing a word. As usual, Granny didn't appear to notice Scott's lack of attention.

Glory listened to the comforting cadence of her grandmother's voice as she washed her hands at the kitchen sink.

Then Gran stopped reading.

Glory looked over her shoulder to see why. Granny had dropped the open book in her lap and was staring into space.

"What?" Glory's heart sped up as she moved across the room. "What's wrong, Gran?"

Granny seemed to come to herself a bit then. "I was just remembering when I used to read this to you."

Glory let go of the breath she'd been holding and sat on the floor beside her grandmother. She slipped her arm around Granny's shoulders, amazed such a slightly built woman could continually show such physical strength. Gristle and determination, that was what Pap had always said Granny was made of.

"I was too," Glory said fondly.

"Always thought I'd be readin' this to your young'uns." Granny said it in a way that made Glory feel her grandmother's loss more than her own. Then Gran said, "It's always been you and me. Strange, ain't it, no matter how big this family got—it was always you and me."

Glory hugged her tighter and kissed her thinning gray hair. It *was* strange. All of Granny's other grandchildren had grown up here in the hollow. But it was Glory—the town child, the child whose mother wanted nothing more than to wash the hollow completely from her soul—who was, and always had been, closest to Granny.

Granny sighed. "Even when you stayed away, I always felt you close."

"I'm sorry if my moving from Tennessee hurt you—it wasn't you that I was leaving behind. Never you."

Granny turned her head toward Glory. Her glasses made her eyes appear much too large for her thin face. "That's not what I meant. I meant afore. Didn't see much of you in the holler after you married." Tears pooled in her eyes, but she held them in check. Glory might not have noticed them at all if not for the glasses. "I was afraid I wouldn't get to see your baby . . . so afraid . . ."

"Gran, you know I'd never keep my baby from you." Glory's throat felt tight, and not just over the loss of her child. It wasn't like Granny to talk like this—something was wrong.

"Oh, I know *you* wouldn't have. But Andrew didn't like you comin' to the holler. Things was hard for you."

Glory closed her eyes and swallowed hard. "I know that now, Granny. I remembered."

A trembling smile came upon Granny's face. "I was hopin' you would."

Glory sighed. "But I still don't remember the fire."

"Doesn't matter. You come to see the bad with the good, that's what counts."

I KNOW WHAT YOU DID

Glory shivered and whispered, "Oh, Gran, I wish that was true."

They sat quietly for a few minutes, Glory's arm tight around her grandmother's shoulders as they both leaned against the wall.

Then Granny let out a long breath; it was a sound of resignation. "I'm afraid I cain't see, darlin'. You better drive me to the doctor."

* * *

Donna beeped Eric's office. Through the intercom she said, "Chief, your wi—um—Mrs.—Ms. Wilson is on line two."

His heart raced. Jill wasn't in the habit of calling.

"Thanks, Donna." He told himself to calm down. This was Thursday, and Scott was with Tula; Tula would call Eric first if something had happened. He drew a breath, then pressed line two and picked up the phone. "Hey, Jill."

"Hello, Eric." There was a pause. "Do you have a minute . . . I mean, am I interrupting anything important?"

There was something in Jill's voice that he hadn't heard in a long, long time—a sort of reaching out. It made the back of his neck prickle. "What's wrong?"

"Don't get worked up. Nothing's wrong. I . . . I just need to talk."

Eric glanced at the clock. "Can it keep?"

She hesitated. "I guess . . . yes, yes it can keep."

"I have a building inspection in ten minutes. I can call you after I pick Scott up this evening."

"How about you and Scottie and I go to Bongo's for pizza tonight? We can talk then."

His suspicions were back. "Are you sure nothing's wrong?"

"No. Nothing. Will you come?"

The last thing he wanted to do was fight Scott in a restaurant. The second-to-last thing he wanted was to share a meal with his ex-wife, especially in public—where all the town would see and jump to conclusions. "What about Jason?"

She gave a short sigh. "That's part of what we need to talk about."

He hesitated. Since he and Jill were divorced, it was inevitable that there was going to be another man . . . another father . . . for Scott. The most important thing was to make sure he didn't alienate whoever filled that role. The lines of communication needed to be maintained. "I see." Then he said, "But Scott doesn't like pizza."

"He doesn't like *anything*. I'll bring along his dinner."

It seemed foolish to pack up the kid's dinner so they could eat together, something he couldn't imagine Jill wanting to do any more than he did.

"Can't we discuss it on the phone?"

"Really, Eric, stop making this such a big deal. Can't you just meet me?"

He almost argued. He almost refused on the grounds that it would be too hard for Scott to sit in the busy restaurant. But something held him back. It might do some good if he and Jill witnessed a meltdown together. Maybe that would get her off the dime and get Scott some help. "Okay. Bongo's, six-thirty."

He'd have to call Tula and tell her he and Scott wouldn't be staying for the usual Thursday night dinner. Probably just as well; now Glory wouldn't have to think of some reason to be away. Her avoidance was obvious and surprisingly hurtful.

"Thanks." She sounded relieved. "See you then."

As Eric hung up the phone, he wondered what Jill had to say that she needed a face-to-face . . . and on neutral ground.

This whole eye thing was plain bad timing. Now Glory would be worse than ever; she'd start talking foolish again about how Tula was going to have to face "limitations." She never should have called Glory home. It was going to be trouble between the two of them—and it didn't seem to be doing Glory a bit of good.

The minute they'd stepped inside the doctor's office, Scott started to scream. Not that Tula could blame him; she felt near as scared herself. Poor Glory spent ten minutes trying to hold him. He bowed his back and cried harder.

"Maybe if I hold him," Tula said, putting out her hands.

"Will it make him less upset?" Glory asked.

"Cain't say. I don't take him places."

"Then let's not even try. You might do more damage to your eye if you have to struggle with him."

Glory finally gave up and laid him on the carpeted floor of the waiting room. He curled on his knees at her feet, burying his face on his arms. Within a minute he shifted from screaming to gritting his teeth and making the growling noise he'd developed recently.

Luckily the waiting room was empty of other patients.

Tula wished Eric were here. He had a way of calming people. Both Scott and Glory could use some calming.

"How's your eye?" Glory asked. Again.

"Same."

"You're sure it's not the eye with the MD?"

Tula narrowed her gaze and looked down her nose at her granddaughter. "Really, child, I can tell which eye it's in. It'll likely clear up like last time."'

"Do you think the macular degeneration is worse in the other eye?"

Tula thought of how BJ the bird dog's eyes didn't line up quite right on Sunday, and of how it had been impossible to quilt on overcast days. It probably was getting slightly worse. But there was no need giving Glory more ammunition. "I'd say 'bout the same."

Glory had had enough burdens in her young life, she didn't need to be pulled down by Tula's. She'd figure something out, make adjustments as she needed, and hopefully find another way to make a living. But first she had to get Glory straightened out and on her way to some kind of future.

Dr. Blanton's assistant appeared in the inner office door. "Tula Baker."

Glory tried to pick Scott up, but he began screaming as if she'd been stabbing him. She looked to the assistant, hoping the woman would volunteer to watch Scott while she went in with Granny.

"Maybe it'd be best if Mrs. Baker comes alone," the assistant said. "She's likely to be quite a while. You can talk to the doctor when they're finished."

Granny was already on her feet, taking very slow and careful steps toward the examination room door. Glory sprang to her feet, stepping over Scott, and took Granny's elbow.

"I can see well enough to find somethin' as big as a door, darlin'." Granny patted Glory's hand, then pulled it away from her arm and walked on alone.

Glory watched with a knot in the center of her throat. She called to the assistant, "I do want to talk with the doctor."

The door closed.

Glory went back to her chair feeling like the most useless being on earth. She couldn't help Granny. She looked down at the little boy on the floor. And she couldn't comfort Scott.

She said softly, "Come on, big guy, give me a break." She tried to distract him with toys and her keys, but he kept his face buried. The growl had become quiet and steady, like the purring of a cat. She exhaled a long breath. At least he wasn't screaming—no thanks to her; he'd found his own way to soothe.

She glanced at her watch. It was lunchtime. The poor kid was probably hungry. She didn't know how he would react to a restaurant, and she wasn't sure who in town made crustless peanut butter and banana sandwiches.

She decided she'd better call Eric.

He was out of the office. His secretary said if this was an emergency she could contact him. If not, he would be back within the hour. Glory looked at Scott. He seemed calm enough.

"No, no emergency," Glory said. "This is Glory Harrison. Just ask him to call Dr. Blanton's office when he gets in." She looked at a business card sitting on the shelf at the window where she was using the phone and gave the secretary the number.

Then she went back and sat in the chair that Scott was curled up in front of. It seemed awful to just let him lie there. But she knew anything she might do would probably set him off again. She realized he'd retreated until he found a place that didn't terrify him.

It struck her then, isn't that just what she had done? It had been too painful to stay in Dawson, so she attempted to retreat to a place that offered benign solace. Scott had very little in his own control. Maybe this was his only way to hide.

But why was the world so upsetting to him?

She watched him for a moment, wondering without answers. She wanted to pace, to move, to do something to take action. Instead, she forced herself to stay still. She picked up a magazine off the end table and absently began flipping through the pages.

After she got past the pharmaceutical ads and the jewelry ads and the replacement window ads, she saw an article that caught her attention: "Service Dogs Improve the Quality of Life." It was a broad-stroke portrayal written by a woman who trained these dogs. There were several firsthand accounts of people and their partner dogs, ranging from service dogs for the visually and physically impaired, to seizure dogs, to companion dogs for senior citizens and emotionally and developmentally impaired children.

Something inside her rose to attention as she read. She recalled the way Scott seemed to respond to Lady. Glory was only halfway through the article when the exterior door jerked open. Her startled gaze jumped from the magazine.

Eric rushed in, looking slightly wild.

At the sight of him, her spirits lifted. Surprising, since she'd been avoiding him for days on end. Although she hadn't spoken to him in almost two weeks, it felt much longer.

Some of the rigidity left Eric's shoulders when he saw Scott. Then his fearful gaze landed on Glory.

She dropped the magazine and got to her feet.

Before she could offer a word of explanation, he said, "Is Tula all right?"

"She had another bleed. I haven't heard anything since they took her back."

Eric didn't appear in the least comforted. He ran a hand through his hair and settled it on the back of his neck. "Sorry it took me so long . . . Donna should have called me."

"I told her not to. There really isn't anything for you to do here. I was just worried that Scott would be starving before we're able to leave." She glanced at the little boy, still "purring" on the floor. "We left home in a rush . . . I didn't think about bringing anything." Her gaze locked with Eric's. She tilted her head and smiled, hoping to erase a few of those lines of tension in his face. "And I didn't know where to get a peanut butter and banana sandwich in this town."

"I see. That is a tricky feat." He smiled, and it was as if someone had flipped on a heat lamp in Glory's chest.

When he looked at Scott again, his smile faded, taking with it some of the warmth inside Glory. She felt the cold gray shadow of his worry, just as strongly as she'd felt the heat of his smile.

"Has he been like this long?" he asked.

That cold gray shadow gained grave weight in her chest. "Pretty much since we got here—once the screaming stopped, that is."

Eric closed his eyes briefly. Glory stopped herself just before she reached for him. Eric was a rescuer; she somehow doubted he accepted support from others as easily as he gave it.

His eyes opened, and she saw a firm resolve replace the pain. He knelt down. Glory noticed he was careful to speak to Scott before he touched him. He picked his son up and sat in the chair next to the one Glory had been using.

Scott curled deeper into Eric's lap as Eric wrapped his arms around him. The "purring" grew quieter.

Eric kissed the top of Scott's head, holding his lips against his son's hair for a long moment. Then he said, "Thank you for taking care of him. I know it's . . . hard for you."

Oh, my God! She'd never felt so small. Had her avoidance been so obvious? Shame heated her cheeks. "I—"

He smiled at her, but this time it was humorless, defeated. "Don't. I understand."

Well, if he understood, then maybe he could clue her in. Then she realized he thought it was because Scott was different.

"I don't think you do." She licked her lips and looked for the words to explain the inexplicable. "You think it's because he's the way he is . . . but it's not him. It's me. There's something wrong with me."

He looked doubtful. She almost made another stab at dissipating his misconception, but couldn't come up with anything that sounded rational, so she let it drop, hoping he'd do the same.

After a moment, he asked, "How long to do they think Tula will be here?"

She lifted a shoulder. "They made it sound like it might be a while. That's why I called you. Maybe you could take Scott to lunch with you, then bring him back?"

Eric looked toward the closed door that led to the examining rooms. "He probably is hungry. But I don't want to leave you here alone."

Heroes. She nearly laughed out loud over his driving need to protect. "I'm fine. Really. And nothing will piss Gran off more than a waiting room full of people pacing and fretting over her. She probably would have snuck off without me if she could have seen to drive herself here."

Eric chuckled with the warmth of love and respect. "You're probably right."

"So, go feed your son. If she's finished before you get back, we'll wait."

"I don't expect Tula to watch him this afternoon. I'll figure something out." Then he added, "I'd probably better figure out something else for tomorrow afternoon, too. We don't know how she'll be feeling. I don't want her to push herself."

"Eric, you'd probably better be looking for someone else permanently," Glory said seriously.

A look that bordered on the same panic he'd shown when he rushed in the door crossed his face. "Uh, I suppose you're right. I'd just hoped this would work a while longer."

Glory stiffened. "I'm sure you did."

He looked like he was going to say something else, then closed his mouth again. He stood up with Scott in his arms. "Will you call my cell phone and let me know what the doctor says?" He fished out a business card from his pocket and handed it to her.

"I will."

She watched him walk out the door, feeling just a little colder inside. She knew he felt like the rug had been ripped out from underneath him, but he had to have known this was coming. He should have been preparing for it.

Glory had to concentrate on what was best for Granny. Eric would have to solve his own problems.

Chapter Thirteen

❀

THIRTY MINUTES LATER, Glory was still waiting for Granny to come back out of the examining room. She was glad to have the time, however. She borrowed some paper from the woman at the desk and took several notes from the article about service dogs, including the contact information of the woman who trained them. She wasn't sure what she planned to do with it. But there was a half-formed idea drifting through her mind. She wanted to have the information handy in case it gelled into something.

As she was finishing the last of her notes, the outer office door opened. Glory didn't lift her gaze; there had been several patients coming and going during the time that Granny had been back there.

Then someone cleared his throat.

She glanced up. Eric stood there with a white paper bag in one hand, Scott's hand in the other. Scott had peanut butter in his hair.

Eric said, "I thought you might be hungry." He raised the bag. "I didn't know what you liked, so I made one turkey and one ham. I'm pretty sure Tula will eat either one, so you can pick."

Glory cast a skeptical glance. "*You* made these?"

"Yeah." He held the bag out to her. "Even I can't screw up a ham sandwich."

She shook her head. "I wasn't questioning the quality. I'm not used to a man who can feed himself, let alone haul a handmade lunch to someone else."

"I already told you, all firefighters can feed themselves. Have to keep our strength up on those long shifts."

She took the bag and looked inside. She gave a long, low whistle. "Impressive . . . lettuce and everything."

He scuffed his toe in the carpet, the exaggerated action of an embarrassed child. "Well . . . I don't like to brag."

"You heroes, always so modest." She took a sandwich out of the bag. "I'm sure Gran will be snapping and snarling with hunger when she comes out." She tilted her head in consideration. "Maybe I'll just throw this at her as she comes through the door."

Eric laughed. "Tula does get a little crotchety when she's hungry."

"A *little*?" Glory rolled her eyes. Then she looked at him and held his gaze. "Thank you, Eric," she said seriously. "It was very thoughtful of you."

The intense way he was looking at her undid all of their teasing bantering. There was such caring in his eyes that it took her back to the moments at Blue Falls Pond. Her chest felt tight, and she temporarily forgot to breathe.

She tore her gaze away and forced herself to take a breath. She unwrapped the turkey sandwich and took a bite. "Umm. Well-done." It'd just be best if he went on his way, she didn't want to start examining feelings she'd been working on ignoring for nearly two weeks. "I'll give you a call after I've talked to the doctor."

Instead of leaving, Eric took the seat next to her again. Scott leaned sleepily against Eric's chest as he sat in his lap. "I took the afternoon off to stay with Scott. We'll just hang here for a bit."

Before she could argue, the inner office door opened, and Granny came out. She looked toward where Glory was sitting and said, "I have to make another appointment for tomorrow. Be just a minute. How's my little buddy holding up?"

The fact that Granny *did not* say a word to, or about, Eric ignited a panic in Glory that made her temporarily light-headed. And yet, it was good. She had confirmation of just how severe this episode was. No way could Granny talk her way around this one.

Glory got up and walked to the reception desk and stood with Granny as she made her appointment. Then she said to the receptionist, "When can I speak with the doctor?"

"There's no need—"

"Gran," Glory interrupted her. "I'm not leaving here until I speak with him. You've made it obvious I'll never get the truth out of you."

Granny gave a little gasp. "Glory! I asked you to bring me here. What makes you think—?"

"Because you just walked through that door, acting like you could see, and didn't know Eric was sitting right next to me."

"I seen him," Granny said defensively, but Glory saw the alarm on her grandmother's face in that split second before she caught herself and disguised it.

"I'm not saying you didn't see him. I'm saying you didn't see him clearly enough to identify him."

The sour-pickle lips were back. But at least Granny didn't argue—at least she didn't come out with a bald-faced lie. In fact, she crossed her arms over her chest and didn't say anything at all before Dr. Blanton stepped into the waiting room.

He looked around, seeming to take in Eric's presence, and suggested, "Perhaps you ladies would like to step inside for a moment?"

Glory said, "Sure." At the same time Granny said, "No need."

Granny faced Glory and said brusquely, "Won't hurt for Eric to hear. Affects him too."

Dr. Blanton wasn't doddering with old age, nor was he a fresh-faced youth. He was everything a person wanted to see when they looked at their doctor, tall, confident, with intelligent eyes behind rimless glasses. Glory wanted with her whole heart for him to give her hope.

He squashed that expectation with his first sentence. "Your grandmother has had a hemorrhage in the right eye—I can't tell if it's been caused by a tear in her retina or something else. We'll have to wait for it to clear before I can get a better look. A retinal tear would probably be the worst-case scenario."

"Are we looking at a permanent change?" Glory forced herself to ask.

Dr. Blanton gave a slight shake of his head. "Compounded with her MD . . . well, we'll just have to wait and see."

Glory's breath caught. The words of assurance she'd so desperately wanted were not coming.

The doctor looked at Granny and put a hand on her shoulder. "This time I want you to *show up* for that follow-up appointment."

She lowered her lashes and nodded. There was no sass about washed-out roads or the appointment not being necessary.

Glory could hardly believe her eyes; Granny cowed? This was a day to mark in history.

Once that fleeting thought passed, Glory's stomach tightened into a fearful knot. Granny not arguing was bad, bad news.

"How about her left eye? Is the MD worse?" Glory asked.

Granny cleared her throat and crossed her arms. "I ain't a horse, you know. You can ask me."

Dr. Blanton smiled and put a hand on Granny's shoulder, drawing her physically into the conversation. "Tula's had a long period of stability. I'm seeing a very slight progression over the past months. But that doesn't mean it's going to continue. Fortunately, she has the dry form, much more slow in advancement than wet."

"Is the bleeding in her right eye a sign that it's changing to the wet form?" Glory had done her homework when Granny had been diagnosed, but it had been a while.

"Not necessarily; in fact, I'd place odds against it."

Glory asked, "So will this clear up on its own like last time?"

"I can't really say, especially since I didn't get a chance to see it after her last episode."

Glory's hands were sweating. She didn't know if she was more angry with her grandmother or herself for taking the easy road and letting the last appointment slide.

But she was angry. She gestured toward Eric, who had remained seated and silent. "I should have strapped you on the back of Eric's motorcycle and made sure you made that last appointment."

Dr. Blanton raised his palms. "Now, I wouldn't recommend that. Bumping along on a motorcycle—"

"I wasn't *serious*, Doctor. But I should have made certain she rescheduled."

He patted Tula with the hand that was on her shoulder. "I'll see you *tomorrow*." Then he winked at Glory. "Until then, don't be too hard on her. I've already dragged her over the coals. I don't think she'll be missing any more appointments."

Oh, my goodness, is that a look of contrition on Granny's face?

He smiled at Granny. "Just take things easy until then. No running, jumping, rock climbing, smoking, lifting, three-legged races, headstands . . . in fact, go home and sit in one place. And elevate your head with an extra pillow tonight. Got it?"

Granny nodded. "Thank'ee, Doctor."

Eric held the door for them as they exited. Scott was asleep on his shoulder, his little arm dangling alongside Eric's muscular biceps.

When they reached the car, Eric took his free arm and wrapped Tula in a quick hug. "Don't worry. It's going to work out."

It took about a millisecond before Granny bristled. She pulled away and said, " 'Course it's gonna work out. Now put that baby in the car seat and let's get going. I'm hungry."

Now that's more like the Tula Baker we all know.
Glory saw Eric fighting a grin.

He said, "I'm taking Scott home with me."

"You ain't workin'?"

"Not this afternoon."

Granny's face grew suspicious. "Good. If'n you're not doing anything else, you can bring Glory back in to pick up her car."

This time Eric did grin. "I'd be glad to."

"Gran, we don't need two cars right now."

Granny's jaw set as stubbornly as Glory had ever seen it. If she'd thought the old gal was down, she'd been sorely mistaken.

Granny said, "I might need mine tomorrow."

"You can't drive."

"Not now. But tomorrow'll be 'nother thing."

"I won't lea—"

Her grandmother rounded on her so quickly, Glory recoiled. "Don't say it! Don't you say it!" Then she drew in a breath. "This'll be a good time to get your car."

"What if Eric has other plans?" Glory asked, lifting her chin, matching her grandmother's stubborn stance.

"I don't. I'll be happy to bring you back into town," Eric said, in a tone that held warning against argument.

Glory shot him a killing glare, tilting her head and raising her brows. He just nodded and opened the car door for Granny.

With what felt like a huge lump of ice at the base of her throat, Glory watched as Granny fumbled with fastening the seat belt. After the third time she missed the slot for the buckle, Glory moved forward to help. Eric put a hand on her shoulder and with a slow shake of his head stopped her.

The buckle finally snapped into place.

With an angry glance toward Eric, Glory set the white paper bag in her grandmother's lap. "Here, Gran. Eric made you a sandwich."

With a bright smile for Eric, Granny said, "Oh, good." She opened the bag. "I'm hungry 'nough to eat the seat of this car."

Eric sat in the Explorer with the windows rolled down, waiting for Glory to get Tula settled in the house. He'd parked in the shade and there was a light breeze moving through the car, making it easy to leave Scott dozing in his car seat. He knew there was going to be trouble when Glory came back out; he was enjoying the calm before the storm.

His mind drifted back to Blue Falls Pond. There had been a perfect moment of connection with Glory that he wished had lasted after they'd left the magic of that place. But it was clear, as Glory had been avoiding him since, that either she hadn't felt it or didn't want it. He had fought his disappointment every day, assuring himself that the last thing he needed right now was a relationship—especially with a woman who roused suspicions about the truth of a fire he'd investigated. What a tangled mess that could become.

He should let well enough alone, leave Glory to her life and concentrate on his own problems—he had plenty to fill his plate at the moment. Jill's call earlier today made him suspect that more was about to be heaped on.

It was "for the best." He'd always hated that phrase—dragged out and paraded around whenever disappointment crushed fragile dreams. But now he had to hang on to it, believe it—or he'd end up doing something foolish.

Finally, Glory came out of the house. The scowl she wore as she stomped toward the car was no doubt meant to make him shiver—and it did, just not in the way she intended.

She yanked the door open and got into the passenger seat. She probably would have slammed it closed, if she hadn't glanced in the backseat and seen that Scott was sleeping.

She hissed in a low voice, "You could have said you were busy." She glanced back at the house. "I don't like leaving her alone in this condition." She turned angry eyes on him and jabbed a finger in his direction. "*You* shouldn't want her to be alone."

God, her eyes were brilliant green when she was mad. Just looking into them made all of his resolutions of a few minutes ago flit away quickly as a hummingbird. "Did you put the cordless phone next to her?"

"Of course," she snapped.

"She's been ordered not to do anything but sit, right?"

Glory rolled her eyes as if he was the most dim-witted character she'd ever come across. "Right—which is why I need to be there to watch her. You know how she is. First it'll be, 'I'll just make myself a cup of tea.' Then, 'As long as I'm up, I'll throw in a load of laundry.' The next thing you know, she'll justify her way into washing the windows or cleaning the gutters."

As hard as he tried not to, he laughed.

Big mistake. She twisted in the seat to face him. "This is *not* funny!"

Unable to help himself, he reached out and brushed the hair away from her cheek. "I know Tula's problem isn't funny. But your reaction to it is."

"I'm just trying to take care of her." Her voice was incredulous. "I know you want to downplay it, so she can watch your kid. But things are changing, buddy, and your ignoring it won't help."

Now *he* was hot under the collar. He made himself take three deep breaths before he spoke. When he did it was between clenched teeth. "Listen. This has *nothing* to do with Scott. It has to do with what's best for Tula. Do you seriously believe she'll be happy with you hovering over her, watching her every second, cautioning her every move?"

She opened her mouth to answer, but he cut her off. "Nothing in this world means more to Tula than her independence. She *needed* to be left alone this afternoon."

"Do you understand what's happening to her? Do you know anything about this disease?"

He was getting tired of Glory talking to him as if he were an uncaring idiot. "I know that she'll never go completely blind from MD. And I know there's no successful treatment for it at the moment. I know before the central vision fails, straight lines will blur and waver. MD-affected eyes are like looking through a glasses lens with a smudge or opaque spot in the cent—"

"Okay—" Glory tried to interrupt, but he kept on talking.

"I know she'll retain peripheral vision—not much solace, but when you compare it to total blindness, she's lucky, and she knows it. Her world may lose focus, but she won't be plunged into darkness."

"All right!" Glory tried again. "You've done your research."

Eric didn't pause for a breath, but continued to recite in a rush. "With adjustments, she should be able to live her life independently for the most part. Sure, she won't be driving. She won't be quilting. She won't be reading the newspaper. But life, especially for a woman like Tula, is so much more than those things.

"And I know that if you're not careful, you're going to make her feel crippled. It does absolutely no harm to leave her alone for an hour or so while I drive you to town—but I think it'll do a world of good for her outlook." He wasn't sure he'd taken a breath in his entire speech.

Glory sat there staring at him. For a moment he thought he'd stunned her into silence. But no such luck. She said, "Let's get going. I want to get back."

Eric blew out a long breath of frustration. "All right. But think about what I said. Tula needs help in adapting, not someone to make her feel she's helpless."

Glory looked out the windshield and put on her seat belt. "She's my grandmother. You let me worry about what she needs."

Tula waited until Glory and Eric had pulled away. Then she got busy. She wanted to make a few changes without Glory around. Dr. Blanton had made some suggestions for making daily life a little more . . . accident-free. She didn't really need most of the changes yet, but who knew when she'd have some time to herself?

She moved through the house as if a contestant on a game show with only seconds to perform certain tasks. There weren't that many things to do, but she didn't want to be "caught in the act."

First, she went from room to room changing the lightbulbs, putting in higher wattage. Then she placed a dark hand towel over the edge of the bathtub to make it easier to see; she'd noticed in places of low contrast, she'd been misjudging. Then she rummaged in her purse and got the labels Dr. Blanton had given her to mark her vitamin and prescription medication bottles. Most of the time she was able to see them well enough to distinguish one from the other, but this color-coded, large-print system would prevent errors on her "bad days."

She had the last bottle in hand when the phone rang. She jumped and her hand settled over her heart. "Good gracious, Tula, calm down." It wasn't like she was doing anything wrong, for heaven's sake.

Squaring her shoulders, she took a deep breath and went to answer the phone.

"Granny? Are you all right?" Charlie asked.

"'Course I'm all right. What makes you ask?" Had he been peeking in the windows? She caught herself looking over her shoulder out the kitchen window.

"I came by around noon and nobody was home. I know you had Scott . . . it looked like y'all left in a hurry. I was worried something had happened."

Tula's chest warmed as hope sprang in her heart. Charlie might just make a good man after all. She decided to award him with a truthful account. "I had another spell with my eye. Glory drove me in to see Dr. Blanton."

"A spell? Like last time?"

"Purty much. I have to go again tomorrow, but he thinks it'll pass just like last time."

"What if it doesn't?"

"Now listen here, I been puttin' up with mother henning from Glory. I don't need you throwing in your two cents. If it don't, I figure it out from there. No need gettin' the reaction afore the disaster."

Charlie chuckled. "I can see you're good as ever. If you lost that fightin' attitude, I would be worried."

Tula huffed. She had things left to do. "Well, if that's all, then . . ."

"All right. Bye, Granny. Love you."

"You too." She hung up the phone.

Good gracious, what if Charlie caught a case of the fretfuls from Glory? Tula didn't think she could stand two of them ganging up on her.

She hurried to finish the labels. Then she tucked the spares away in her dresser drawer.

All of her hurrying had made her overheat. She grabbed a magazine and fanned her face. She had to cool down before Glory got back; she was supposed to be resting.

The ride into town had been filled with unpleasant silence. Eric didn't want to leave things that way. The last thing he wanted was for Glory to view him as the enemy. As much as he wanted to be there for Tula if her sight deteriorated, he knew Glory was going to need support too.

He put the Explorer in park in front of Franklin's Garage.

"Thanks for the ride," she said as she opened the passenger door.

Eric grabbed her arm. "Wait a second. Please."

She stopped and looked at him with anger brimming in her gaze.

He said, "I think we can both help Tula—our fighting won't serve her at all."

Glory glanced over her shoulder at Scott. "Forgive me if I think you have more than Granny's well-being influencing your judgment."

He dropped his left hand to the steering wheel and squeezed until his knuckles were white. "Do you really think I'd leave Scott with her if she wasn't capable of taking care of him? I've been watching her carefully since long before you came back here. The second I feel it's too much for her, or it's not safe for Scott, I'll act on it. But Tula is a proud woman, and her sight is plenty good to watch one child and keep him safe, but not nearly good enough for her to quilt. How is she going to make ends meet? Social security isn't enough. She won't accept charity. I've been racking my brain for months trying to figure out a way for her to sustain some sort of income."

"Oh, I see, I ran off and you had to take up the slack."

"Jesus, Glory, that's not at all what I meant. It's just I've had opportunities of observation that you haven't. And this isn't about *you*. You almost act like you want her to be impaired!"

She gasped as if he'd struck her. "How can you say that?"

"Maybe you *need* her to need you. Maybe it's the first direction you've had since the fire." He hadn't intended to lay it out quite like that, but there it was, shimmering in the air between them like a bank of hot air.

She gritted her teeth when she said, "And *you* can't save everybody. Granny is my family, my responsibility."

He lifted his hands, palms out. "Touché. Now that we have that out in the open . . .

The tense muscles in her face relaxed slightly. She ran her hand through her hair. "You have your problem. And I have mine." Her voice had softened enough to make him believe the fighting was over. "I think we both have our hands full."

He could hardly dispute that logic. Still, it took everything in him to keep from arguing further, from telling her that they could help one another, they could talk things out. Now wasn't the time. But he wasn't going to walk away from Tula just because Glory got her knickers in a twist.

He gave a silent nod, and Glory got out of the car.

She paused before she closed the door. "Thanks, Eric. Good luck finding someone to watch Scott."

She closed the door. That hadn't gone at all as he'd wanted. He should have kept his temper; it had been a very emotional day for Glory.

His father had always taught him to make sure a lady had her car safely started before he left. As he pulled out of the lot, he stopped behind her Volvo.

When Glory reappeared out of the shop office, she looked slightly puzzled as she walked past his car.

He waved her on.

She got inside the Volvo.

He waited for her car to start.

She climbed back out.

He watched in confusion. She lifted the windshield wiper and took something from underneath it. The look on her face had him out of the car and by her side in less time than it took for her to turn.

"What's wrong?" he asked.

Her face was a mixture of fear and pain as she handed him a matchbook. "This was under my windshield wiper."

Eric opened the flap of the matchbook and saw the words *I KNOW WHAT YOU DID* written in block letters across the inside.

"I don't understand," he said.

Glory was visibly shaken. "This morning there was a copy of the newspaper article about the fire stuck inside Granny's paper. It had the same words scrawled across it."

A cold fist grabbed Eric's gut. He'd never breathed a word of his suspicions to another living soul. But they were coming back to haunt him just the same.

Chapter Fourteen

❦

JILL'S AFTERNOON CREPT slowly by as she sat at her desk in the surgeon's office. She couldn't seem to hold her thoughts to her work; bits and pieces of the past kept intruding no matter how hard she tried to block them out. At what point had she lost control of her life? Where were the crossroads where she had taken the wrong turn?

At one time, she'd been happy, back in the day when boyfriends had been plentiful; when there had always been someone waiting on her doorstep—back before she'd had to choose.

After that, the fear had set in, the doubt, the idea that by doing what she was, she was missing something else—the overriding conviction that there was *more*.

Now insecurity was again getting the upper hand.

She needed to get her mind back on her work, or she'd never get out of here today. She'd had to rewind the tape with the doctor's dictation on it three times before she had the first paragraph transcribed correctly.

As much as she didn't want to admit it to herself, she was nervous about seeing Eric tonight. Which was ridiculous; she saw him at least three times a week as they transferred Scott between them. But this was different. Tonight there was something at stake.

The phone on her desk rang and she jumped, startled out of her thoughts. For the briefest moment she was certain it was Eric calling to cancel dinner, and unexpected disappointment grabbed her by the throat.

But when she looked at the caller ID, it was the Busy Bee Flower Shop.

She ripped off her headset and picked up the phone. "Hi, Mother."

"I just saw Eric with Glory Harrison again." She announced it in the tone of breaking news.

"Really." Jill worked for a neutral tone. She didn't want her mother to think her heavy-handed meddling was making any headway—she'd never get the woman off her back then.

"Yes, really," Mother said shortly.

Jill snorted. "I hardly need a minute-by-minute report of his activities."

"If you fool around long enough, it'll be too late."

"We're divorced, Mother. How much more too late do you think it can get?" No need to let her mother in on possibilities that might not come to pass.

There was a long pause where Jill could imagine her mother massaging her forehead in frustration. "I really do not think you're that dense."

Jill didn't respond.

"You need to think of your son." Mother's tone shifted to reproachful.

"I rarely think of anything else," Jill said sharply.

"Well, you don't behave as if that's the case. I cannot believe you threw away a husband like Eric to take up with that gigolo."

"Jason was afraid of commitment. He wasn't a gigolo." There *had* been a time when sex had dominated their relationship—back when they'd had to sneak around. "Is that all you called for?"

"Well, I thought you should know. Ovella said she saw them together Sunday before last"—then she added in a scandalous tone — "on his motorcycle."

"You already told me." Jill rubbed her own forehead. "I thought you said they were buying dog food. The road was washed out. He was doing a favor; hardly a romantic tryst. Glory lives with Tula; they're bound to run across one another."

"Have *you* run across Glory?"

Jill hesitated before she caught herself. Damn, that pause would speak volumes to Mother's conjecturing mind. "No. She's been out on my days to pick up Scott."

Her mother made a knowing noise deep in her throat.

The pressure to straighten up and fly right had been strong from the day Jill announced that she and Eric were divorcing. It had ratcheted up considerably since Jason had left the picture.

Mother said, "I just don't want you to make another mistake. Scottie needs his mommy and daddy together. Just look how normal Jennifer's children are."

"Scott is *not* abnormal, Mother. Jennifer's twins are only eleven months old. There's still time for her to screw them up. I have to go. The doctor is waiting for this transcript." It was a lie, but her mother would never know.

"All right. Just keep in mind he won't wait around forever for you to come to your senses."

"Thank you, Mother." Jill disconnected the call. Her stomach felt like a crumpled ball of lead. As much as she hated to admit it, she hadn't ever thought of Eric being with another woman. And now that it had been brought to mind, she didn't like the way it made her feel.

"Mr. Franklin says he didn't notice anyone around your car," Eric said as he came back out of the garage office. "It's been sitting out here since he finished it yesterday afternoon." He handed Glory a bottle of water he'd gotten from the machine sitting in front of the building. "Drink some of this."

Glory was sitting sideways in the driver's seat of her car, with her feet still on the pavement. She barely had the strength in her hands to unscrew the cap. Who was behind this . . . taunting?

She took a long swig of the water. It made her mouth feel less gummy, but her stomach immediately began to churn.

She'd never been afraid of the holes in her memory. But in light of the things that she had recently remembered about her relationship with her husband, fear of what was hiding in those holes had taken root and was growing like kudzu. Right now, she felt as if those vines were inching around her throat.

If she hadn't been so stunned, if she'd had a moment to compose herself before Eric had appeared at her side, she would never have told him about the note in this morning's paper. One instance was easy to pass off as a teen prank, but two back-to-back in two different locations carried more weight.

Of course, Eric wasn't going to let this go. He stood in the open car door, his left arm resting on the top, looking down at her with concern in his eyes. For some reason that concern made her feel guilty.

Did she have something to hide? She needed time to think—alone.

She swung her legs into the car. "I'd better be getting back to Gran." She kept her eyes forward, looking out the windshield. Eric had an uncanny way of seeing her emotions when she looked at him.

He didn't move out of the door.

She was forced to glance up at him. "I'm fine—really. You should get Scott home."

"Glory, we need to talk about this."

"What's to talk about? Some kid found a way to break summer boredom," she said dismissively.

"And what would prompt a kid to start a campaign to upset you? You've been gone for nearly two years. That's a long time for a teenager to remember something that had nothing to do with them personally."

"It's a small town. I'm sure by now people are speculating about my coming back. Any bored teenager would be curious about a fire that killed someone. You know how influenced they are by movies."

He still didn't move so she could make a getaway. "I don't think you believe that any more than I do."

"What else could it be?" She tried to sound glib but was betrayed by the slight tremor in her voice.

"I don't think you should drive back just yet. Let's go get a cup of coffee."

"No."

The windows were down and the door open on his Explorer. Scott started to fuss.

"I'm fine." She cast him a confident look. "Take your son home."

Eric's gaze cut from his car back to her again. "I don't like this."

"You're overreacting."

He gestured to the matchbook on the console. "Let me take that and turn it over to the police. If this continues, maybe they'll be able to assemble enough evidence to help figure this out."

"You're making too much of this."

"Am I?" His gaze penetrated deep. For an instant he looked at her like he suspected she was hiding something.

"I really have to go." She reached for the door. "Your son's crying."

He hesitated only a moment before he stepped out of the way and let her close the door.

In her rearview mirror, she saw him get in his Explorer and give one last, lingering look. Then he pulled out of the way so she could back out.

The matchbook still lay next to the gearshift like a coiled snake. She could almost hear it calling to her memory.

At five past six, Eric stood on the sidewalk in front Bongo's with Scott at his side. Eric hoped his son had recovered from his last restaurant experience better than he had. As Eric stood there, gathering the courage to open the glass-and-aluminum door, he could still hear Scott's terrified screams, still see his little son covering his ears and burying his face on the table. It was as if it had been *painful* for him to be in that atmosphere, as if the noises and the motion had been a physical attack on his senses.

That extreme reaction had been Eric's first real confirmation that his son was changing, that something was beginning to tilt off its axis. Scott had continued to decline and withdraw in so many other ways since then, he feared this experience would be worse than the last foray into dining out.

He knelt on the sidewalk in front of Scott. He lifted his son's chin gently and spoke softly to him, "We're going to go inside and see Mommy. She has your peanut butter and banana sandwich. Are you hungry?"

Scott's gaze roved, never making connection with Eric's, even though Eric held the child's chin firmly in place. Not a good sign.

"Okay, buddy, we're going in." Eric stood up and braced himself. "Let's go see Mommy," he said cheerfully.

The instant they stepped inside the door, Scott pressed his face against Eric's leg and began to whimper.

Eric scanned the tables. The pizza place was more crowded than he'd expected. It was oppressively warm and loud, filled with motion and laughter and the scent of warm yeast and oregano. As Eric's gaze fell upon a family seated near him, his heart ached. The parents were laughing at something the three-year-old had done, while the mother rocked a pumpkin seat with a pink-swaddled baby sleeping inside. Did those people know how lucky they were?

Scott whimpered and covered his ears. At least he wasn't screaming yet.

Jill stood up in the back and waved. She'd had the good sense to get a booth. Maybe once they had Scott a little more isolated, he'd calm down, and this wouldn't be the disaster Eric had been dreading all afternoon.

He told himself that it might be good if Scott had a full-blown fit here in front of Jill. Although she had Scott more of the time than Eric did, she swore he never behaved inappropriately. His temper tantrums were normal near-three-year-old fare. But Eric had noticed how Jill slowly and carefully organized her life so Scott was rarely in situations that prompted trouble, making it easier to reinforce her cocoon of denial. And to be honest, Eric wasn't sure she even realized that she was doing it. Like everything else about Scott, Jill's accommodations had crept forward one insidious inch at a time.

Although this might be just what Eric needed to make his point, he hated that Scott would have to suffer to accomplish it.

Instead of making Scott walk through the crowded room with everyone looming over him, Eric picked him up and walked to where Jill waited. Scott buried his face against Eric's neck; Eric heard his son's teeth grinding.

Eric laid a hand gently on the back of Scott's head, and whispered, "You're doing great, buddy. Look, here's Mommy."

He could not peel the child off him when he reached Jill, so he just slid into the booth wearing Scott like a second skin. He scooted to the far side of the tall-backed booth, away from the commotion. Scott was as isolated as he was going to get.

Jill leaned across the table. "Hey, baby." She touched Scott's back. "Scottie, are you hungry? I brought your sandwich."

Eric heard the child's teeth grind louder. A muted growl rumbled in Scott's throat, not loud, but steady, as if he was trying to block everything else out with his own soothing noise.

"Well," Jill said cheerily, "maybe you'll want to eat in a little bit." She laid the sandwich in its Ziploc baggie on the table. "I already ordered us a pitcher of beer and a pizza, so he won't have to wait too long."

Again, Jill's accommodation to Scott's behavior. But Eric hadn't come here to fight that battle. There was something on Jill's mind. He wanted to know what it was and how it was going to affect his son.

The waitress brought the beer and two frosted mugs. She set them on the table and filled Jill's mug. Eric put a hand over his glass to prevent her from filling his. "Could I have a Coke, please?"

"Sure thing." She left.

Jill eyed him suspiciously. "Are you so mad at me you won't drink a beer with me?"

"I'm not mad. I just don't want a beer." Scott was still plastered against him. It just seemed wrong to guzzle a beer over the head of a terrified child.

Jill lifted a shoulder, tilting her head just so, in the way that used to make his heart beat faster. Now he found it exceedingly annoying, mostly because it was so deliberately coy.

Jill's mother had coached her daughters well—from puberty both girls had been able to manipulate a male with remarkable skill. He might have thought it an inbred instinct, but he'd seen the quiet and disguised looks Gail Landry gave her girls; they had been more subtle than the gesturing and yelling of a football coach, but every bit as effective.

Jill took a sip of her beer, then fiddled with the cocktail napkin under the glass, carefully rolling up one corner.

Eric needed to talk to her about the babysitting problem, but he was curious enough about her reason for this little meeting to let that wait. "So, what did you need to talk about?"

Scott continued to moan softly. Eric was pretty sure Jill couldn't hear.

She moistened her lips, leaned back against the booth, and dropped her hands in her lap. "I don't know any way to say this, without just coming right out and saying it."

"That's usually the best way." Shit, she was getting married. That SOB was going to be Scott's stepfather. Eric held his son a little tighter.

She drew a deep breath. "I'm not seeing Jason anymore."

As the tension drained away from Eric's shoulders, he realized just how wound up he'd been. "Okay."

"Do you want to know why?" she asked, looking out from beneath her lashes.

"Not particularly."

"Well, I'm going to tell you anyway."

He wanted to get up and leave. No man wanted to listen to why his ex-wife broke up with the man who broke up their marriage. But he sat still.

She said, "I just think I need to concentrate on what's best for Scott right now. With working . . . well, there's only so much of me to go around."

It took everything in him to keep from shouting, *There should be* more *of you to go around than there was when we were still married and you had a job and a son, and you were banging Jason on the side. I'd say you're juggling fewer balls now . . . no pun intended.*

Instead, he just nodded, not trusting himself to open his mouth.

She went on, "I just think you and I need to work together more. Scott is still so young, still forming his personality. I think if we concentrate on it, he'll come around."

Eric stared at her, and his mouth fell open. He snapped it closed and counted to five before he responded. "First of all, I *have* been concentrating on it—twenty-four/seven. Since he drew his first breath, I haven't made a single decision that didn't consider him first. Secondly, I'm convinced it's going to take more than our 'concentration' to help him. There's something wrong, and it's getting worse by the day. My God, I can't sleep at night for thinking that every day there's less of him, every day we don't take action is a day we're not going to get back!" Talking too loud, he'd leaned forward until Scott was pressed against the table edge. Reining himself in, he sat back.

Jill blinked.

It had been a long, long time since he'd lost his temper around her. He didn't like to let her think she had that much power over him. But when it came to his son, he was vulnerable in ways that frightened him.

"Maybe we all just need to spend more time together. Look how good he's being now—"

"He's not being *good*," Eric ground out between clenched teeth. "He's terrified."

"Don't be silly. He's not screaming. You said the last time you brought him here he screamed."

"Come over here and sit by me."

"What?" Her brow wrinkled in confusion.

"Get out of that seat and come over here and sit beside me."

Slowly, as if she suspected some trick, she slid out of the booth. When she was sitting next to him, she raised a blond brow. "Okay, now what?"

"Lean over here. Put your ear close to Scott's head."

She did. And after a second she said with some surprise, "He's growling."

"He's been grinding his teeth and making that noise since we came in here." He looked his ex-wife in the eye. "Jill, this is much, much worse than screaming. He's afraid, and he's retreating deeper and deeper inside himself. He's using this noise to keep everything else out."

"Oh, for God's sake, Eric, he's just making a noise! All kids make noises. What makes you think you know so much more than Dr. Martin?"

"I'm not saying that. But I do know there's something wrong with my son. I'm making an appointment with the specialist in Knoxville. You can come with me or not; it's up to you. But I'm taking him for an evaluation."

"I'll go."

Her acquiescence took him so off guard, he didn't respond right away. It felt as if he'd been bracing himself for a huge wave that evaporated just before it crashed over him. After months and months of denial and delay, of trying to convince him that Scott's development wasn't abnormal, she'd simply said yes.

She said, "He's not *your* son. He's *our* son. I'll go." She took Eric's hand. "We'll work through this together—as a family."

Eric's elation over her agreement cooled slightly. There seemed to be something buried in her words—something much more than simply working toward a goal for their child's health. But he wouldn't risk having her turn on him now, not when he'd waited too long already. So he just nodded and held his son more tightly. *I promise you we'll bring you back, Scott. We'll find a way.*

Lingering dread distracted Glory all the way back to the hollow and dogged her steps throughout the afternoon. All of her efforts to redirect her mind by pushing her body were useless. She toiled in the garden, sweating in the sun until her muscles trembled and she felt light-headed, yet her thoughts kept circling around to unwanted topics.

There was a growing realization that her life with Andrew had not been the happily-ever-after she'd dressed it in. Their marriage had had problems. But just how big had they been? And what had those problems led to?

Around four o'clock, Granny stepped out onto the back stoop. "Didn't I teach you better'n that? Where's your sun hat?"

Glory looked up. Granny was coming down the steps, her own hat securely on her head and two tall glasses of ice water in her hands.

Glory got off her knees and brushed the dirt from her hands.

Granny handed her a glass. "You're gonna be one big freckle. You know how our colorin' does."

Both Glory and her mother shared Granny's Gaelic coloring, bright green eyes, auburn hair, and fair skin. Glory studied her grandmother's face. Her skin might have lost some of its luster, and life had washed the color from her hair, but behind those Oakleys her green eyes still sparked fire.

"Freckles are sexy. Pap always said so," Glory teased.

"Your Pap shoulda watched his mouth in front of young'uns."

Glory laughed and took a long drink.

Granny knelt, set her glass carefully on the ground, and picked up the small cultivator that Glory had just laid down.

"What do you think you're doing?" Glory snapped.

"Eye's pert-near cleared up. Don't want to waste the whole day."

Reaching down and hauling her grandmother up by the arm, Glory said, "Oh no you don't."

"I've set there all day. My butt's growin' to that couch."

"It's too hot for you out here."

Granny's gaze snapped sharply to Glory's face.

"I mean, for your eye," Glory was quick to clarify. "Dr. Blanton said to rest today." Glory saw Granny's hand tighten on the garden tool. "Let's play rummy. It's been forever since we played. That was always one of my favorite things about visiting out here." As she said it, she realized just how long it had been—since before her marriage to Andrew.

Luckily Gran loved to play cards almost as much as anything, so the diversion worked. They went to the front porch with a deck of cards and a scratch pad for keeping score.

Unfortunately, Glory's mind wasn't any more distracted by the card game than it had been by the gardening. As she stared at the cards in her hand, she kept seeing those five boldly printed words: *I KNOW WHAT YOU DID.*

Why don't I *know what I've done?* She shuddered to think. She had always considered herself an honest person, incapable of treachery and deceit. But if she'd essentially tricked her own husband into having a baby against his wishes, what else had she been capable of?

". . . What do you think?" Glory heard only the last bit of what Granny had said.

"What?" Glory asked.

Granny moved the cards around in her hand, as if planning her strategy. "I said, I thought I'd get a pet monkey and paint his butt blue."

Glory processed the words again. "I'm sorry, I thought you said—"

"Oh, for gosh sake, I *did*." She laid her cards facedown on the little table between them. Putting her bony hand on Glory's wrist, she said, "Do you want to tell me what's botherin' you?"

Glory had no intention of coming clean on this one. If Granny knew there'd been another note, she'd never rest until they figured out what was going on. And if Glory had done something . . . She closed her eyes and her stomach rolled. Granny was the last person she wanted to disappoint.

"Nothing really. I was just wondering if Eric found someone to watch Scott," Glory lied.

"He said he was staying home with him this afternoon." Granny's wrinkled forehead furrowed more deeply. "I'm a'ginning to think you need to have your memory checked."

Glory grinned and pushed Granny's accusation away with a hand in the air. "Not today. I meant for tomorrow."

"Why, Scottie'll come here like usual after school."

"Gran." Glory gathered her fortitude. "I told Eric he needs to make other arrangements—permanently."

For several seconds Granny didn't say anything. The corners of her mouth twitched, then her lips pursed momentarily. Glory was worried that she might break down and cry. It had been a very emotional day.

Glory reached out a comforting hand just as Granny jumped out of her chair. The little table between them tottered. Glory grabbed the edge and kept it from toppling over, but the cards and score pad fell to the porch floor.

Granny opened her mouth, but all that came out was a sputter. She closed it again, pressing her lips together. Glory was no longer suffering under the delusion that Gran was going to cry. From the look in her eyes, Glory would be lucky if her grandmother didn't pick up the chair she'd just vacated and break it over Glory's head.

Granny's nostrils flared. "You got no right—no say in this."

"Gran," Glory pleaded. "There's no way you can continue to sit with Scott."

"I cain't quilt. And I cain't say I'd be fit to go into town and keep books or clean offices. But I *can* do this!"

"What are you talking about?"

"I have to do somethin'. This place is paid for; Pap made sure of that. But there's the taxes and upkeep, my medical bills. Did you think money was gonna fall from the sky?"

"I'll be getting a job—"

"No! I won't have it. I'm able-bodied." She stood there shaking with fury for a moment, then she said, "It ain't just the money. I love that boy." Her gaze hardened. "Even though it's clear you cain't understand that."

Granny's words went through Glory's heart like an ice pick. Granny thought she was a woman incapable of loving a child.

Gran headed toward the front door.

"Where are you going?"

"I'm gonna call Eric and tell him to bring Scott like always tomorrow."

Jill was glad when the pizza finally arrived at their table. She returned to her seat and took a grateful drink of beer. She'd dismissed it outwardly, but that noise Scott was making chilled her to her bones. It frightened her to think there might be something really wrong with her baby. It terrified her to think of going through life dealing with it alone.

Eric didn't eat even one full slice of pizza. She nibbled with a dwindling appetite. An ache throbbed at the base of her throat. Suddenly, she wanted more than anything to reach across the table and take ahold of Eric's hand; to have him take her back to the way things used to be in the beginning, when they had clung to the hope of a happy future together. She wanted him to make everything all right.

She'd chosen Bongo's tonight because this was where she and Eric had gone on their first "adult" date. They had dated occasionally in high school, but hadn't really seen each other much after graduation. Then one day Jill had worked the sign-up table at the park, registering people for the Labor Day minimarathon. Eric had been there having a cookout with a bunch of firefighters and their families. Late in the afternoon, just as she was packing up her clipboard, Eric returned to her table. He said they needed another person to even out their flag football game and asked if she'd like to play.

She ended up catching Eric's game-winning pass.

That evening, they'd celebrated at Bongo's. Two months later, she was pregnant. It had all happened so fast, she hadn't been able to sort out her feelings. She loved Eric, but could never stop wondering if they would have been together if not for the pregnancy. That question had grown until she felt trapped, cheated out of making a free choice.

But she hadn't once wondered if Eric had felt the same way.

She looked at him now, the way he was with Scott. Maybe she'd thrown away something good.

Chapter Fifteen

❁

WALT DROVE HOME after a grueling day at the plant. He'd been delayed in New York, and since his return anything that could go wrong had. But he vowed to leave that behind him as he turned on the CD player in his BMW. He would fight those battles tomorrow. Tonight he was going home to relax with his wife.

Ovella met him at the back door with a glass of wine. "You look exhausted. Bad day?"

He kissed her on the cheek. "How could a day be bad when I end it with you?"

He'd been so worried over Ovella after Andrew had died. Her family was her life. And, as there were only three of them, one-half of her reason for living had been stripped away. Those first months had been horrible. But lately she'd begun to shine in her old way.

"Take your shoes off and we'll eat dinner on the porch. The fountain always soothes you."

He did love the sound of that fountain; the music of softly trickling water usually peeled the fatigue right off him.

As they ate, the fountain and the wine did their work. The tension began to leave his neck and shoulders.

He asked, "So, has Glory called?" He felt awful that he'd been so busy and not made an effort to get together with her.

"Yes." Ovella paused with her fork halfway to her lips. "She's coming Sunday. I thought I told you."

He leaned back in his chair and rubbed his eyes. "Maybe you did. I feel like I'm meeting myself coming and going."

Ovella got up and stood behind him. She massaged his neck and shoulders. "I wish you didn't have to work so much. This isn't the way it was supposed to be."

He closed his eyes and concentrated on her fingers working the knots out of his muscles. How had he kept up with everything for all those years and not run himself into the ground? The answer to that was simple. He was younger. And when age began to take a toll, Andrew had come on board, and the burden had begun to shift to more youthful shoulders.

How much longer could he keep this up? The company was in no shape to sell at the moment, so he guessed he'd keep it up as long as he had to. This was not the life he'd promised Ovella. Throughout their marriage, he'd worked hard and long, assuring her he'd retire when Andrew took over.

He patted her hand resting on his shoulder. "Aw, Mother, what would I do without you?"

She kissed the top of his head. "I'm not going anywhere."

Thank God for that. He'd had to live without her once. He didn't think he could do it again.

* * *

Granny was quiet through dinner, concentrating on her meal as if it might sneak off the plate if she allowed her attention to wander. After a couple of futile attempts to draw her into conversation, Glory gave up. She dealt with her food with much less dedication than Granny, mostly just fidgeting with her fork and rearranging her peas into different patterns on her plate; Lady would get most of this meal.

When Granny put down her fork and laid her napkin on the table, Glory offered to clean up. Granny didn't argue. She simply nodded and left with a terse "'Night, then."

Glory stayed at the kitchen table after Granny headed out to the front porch. After a moment, Glory heard the slow, rhythmic squeak of the swing. It wasn't unusual for Granny to use the silent treatment to show her disapproval, but this was the first time it had been directed at Glory. She'd always thought it slightly humorous in the past—watching her cousins squirm and wheedle to find a way around that barrier of quiet condemnation—but somehow it wasn't nearly as amusing when she was the object of Granny's voiceless wrath.

By the time Glory came out of the kitchen, Granny had left the porch and gone upstairs, leaving Glory completely alone with her thoughts.

For a long time, she sat on the couch in the darkened living room, trying all of the tricks the therapists had taught her to calm herself and unlock the memories hiding in her mind.

With her eyes closed, she let her consciousness ride on the rhythm of her breathing. Then she brought forth the memories that had recently come to her, one after the other, hoping that they would conjure more. She even faced the ugly recollection in which Andrew had angrily told her he didn't want the baby. She could not, however, remember anything specific that gave her more insight into the days just prior to the fire.

Maybe she was trying too hard. Sleep had released some of the memories, but Glory doubted she'd even be able to come close to falling asleep. Still, the longer she sat and tried to remember, the more desperate she became. The matches indicated someone thought she had set the fire. She felt in her soul that she wasn't capable of doing something so horrific. It was clear to her, until she remembered fully, she wouldn't be able to deny the insinuated accusation with any confidence.

The longer she sat there, the more frustration knotted her gut. It wasn't that the weeks prior to the fire were a complete blank, as was the day of the fire. It's just that everything seemed jumbled and cloudy.

But it was the night of the fire that was most important, that was what she *had* to remember. And specifics of the days prior might serve to prod memories of the hours before the fire.

She massaged her temples. Why, when she turned her mind to those hours, did she feel a cold pressure, a weighty darkness deep in her chest?

Sleep had released some memories, but Eric had been the trigger for others. She might not be able to sleep, but she could get in her car and go talk to him. Maybe he could even allay her fears that she might have done the unthinkable. After all, he'd been the investigator; he should know if there was anything questionable or suspicious.

She looked at her watch. Ten o'clock—not so late. If she left now, she could be there before ten-thirty. She should call first.

Halfway to the phone, she stopped. She hadn't left things on the best terms with him; he might discourage her from visiting if she called. And she didn't think talking to him on the telephone was going to do anything to kick-start her memory.

"To hell with it," she said. She got up, jotted a note to Granny in case she came downstairs, then found her car keys. The worst that could happen was Eric would turn her away. At least she'd have a change of scenery for an hour, and maybe that alone would help.

A short while later, she sat in front of Eric's two-story duplex having second thoughts. She'd gone as far as shutting off the engine and pulling the key out of the ignition before she got cold feet. She felt like she'd swallowed grasshoppers, and they were trying to crawl back up her esophagus. She rested her forehead on the steering wheel and closed her eyes. She didn't want to have Eric rescue her yet again. But if there was some way to put this gnawing fear to rest, she needed to do it.

A sharp rap on the driver's-side window made her jump and suck in a startled breath. She faced the window with her heart racing. Relief flooded her when she saw Eric's face on the other side of the glass.

She swallowed her doubt, gathered her courage, and opened the car door.

He stepped back and waited. "What are you doing here? Is Tula—"

"Oh, no, no." She hadn't thought how her unexpected arrival at this hour might lead him to a worried conclusion. "She's fine. In fact, her eye cleared up enough late this afternoon to play cards. She turned in early."

In the dim glow of the streetlight, she could see his square shoulders relax slightly. Instead of asking again why she was here, he motioned to the house. "Do you want to come inside? I don't like to be out here long when Scott's asleep."

The second thoughts were back. "I'm sorry, it's late." She reached for the door handle. "I should have called . . . or waited."

He touched her cheek lightly with the backs of his fingers. The gentleness stopped her as surely as if he'd wrapped one of those well-muscled arms around her waist and jerked her back. She paused and looked at him, wondering what was going on behind those caring eyes. He wore a white T-shirt and jeans and was barefooted. He looked strong and capable and . . . inviting.

"Something's on your mind," he said. "Or you wouldn't be here. Come on in—please."

She leaned slightly away, until he was no longer touching her. It was hard to think straight when he was touching her.

"Did you get another note?" There was a knife-edge to his voice.

She shook her head. "I just needed someone to talk to."

He took her hand and led her silently into the house. As she followed him, she questioned her true intentions for coming here. Did she really think he held the key to some of her memories? Or did she just want to be with the man who'd held her through her last difficult night?

She reminded herself, her problems were hers to solve. Even as she did, the feel of her hand in his told her just how easily she could let some of her burden shift to his broad shoulders.

When he stopped in the living room, she faced him and decided the first thing was to get the issue of Scott going to Granny's out in the open. "Gran called you this afternoon?"

He nodded. His eyes held none of the I-got-one-up-on-you that they easily could have. "It's important to her."

She could have kissed him for not taunting her with her unsuccessful meddling. "I know," she said softly. "She's really pissed at me."

Eric's broad grin was sympathetic, not mocking. "I can only imagine." He motioned for her to have a seat on the couch. "What can I get you to drink? I have coffee, Coke, and beer."

"You know, I think I could really use a beer." He made her feel so comfortable, she wondered why she'd hesitated coming. Even if he didn't prompt memories, she would no doubt sleep better after talking to him.

He disappeared into the kitchen, and Glory looked around. She'd been too distracted when she'd been in this room after the accident to pay much attention to detail. There really wasn't much to see. The couch. A couple of tables and a lamp that didn't produce enough light to reach into all corners of the room. A portable television sitting in the opposite corner on a discount store stand. A windup clock on the mantel flanked by two framed snapshots. Scott's pirate boat sat in the middle of the floor.

She could imagine Eric lying stretched out next to his son, while Scott spun his boat in endless circles. It made her heart hurt.

Getting up, she walked over to look at the photos more closely. The one on the left was Scott wearing a Santa hat, sitting in front of a Christmas tree. He looked to be about a year old. His eyes were bright and his expression engaged as he grinned at the camera. It struck Glory then that she'd never seen Scott smile.

The photo on the right had been taken at the hospital after Scott had been born. Jill was propped up in the bed, looking as perfect as ever, holding a swaddled, red-faced bundle in her arms. Eric was leaning down with his arm behind her, smiling a smile Glory had never seen. Both parents were flushed with pride and happiness.

She was a little taken aback that he'd kept such a photo displayed after the divorce. There was a knot in her throat as she looked at the newborn child.

"That was the happiest day of my life," Eric said. He'd come up behind her without her noticing.

She didn't turn, but kept her eyes on the photo. He handed the bottle of beer over her shoulder, and she took it without looking at him.

"He was perfect," Eric said, and there was such longing in his voice that Glory did turn. He was only inches from her, but looking at the picture. After a moment, he shifted his gaze to her face.

Her hands trembled as she gripped the cold bottle.

His thumb came to her cheek and wiped beneath her eye. "You're crying."

She didn't know she had been. She took her own hand and swiped across her cheeks and looked away. "Sorry."

He cupped her chin and lifted her gaze to meet his, much as she'd seen him do with his son. "Don't apologize. It's been a tough day."

He knew. She could tell it in his eyes; he knew she wasn't crying over Granny's eye trouble or the notes. Without her uttering a word, he knew her feelings were all tied up with the baby she had lost. And she was grateful to him for not saying it out loud, for giving her the chance to avoid the subject.

Straightening her back, she snuffed up her tears. "I'm fine." She put a little space between them and took a drink of her beer. Smiling, she said, "Just what the doctor ordered."

"Come on, put your feet up." He walked over to the couch and planted his own bare feet on the coffee table—also the assemble-yourself kind of furniture from a discount store. He then took a drink of his own beer.

Slipping off her flip-flops, she sat down and crossed her ankles with her feet propped beside his. She had headed to town without a thought to her appearance. Now she felt underdressed and a little vulnerable in loose athletic pants and a tank top with no bra. She fought the urge to cross her arms over her chest.

As Eric let her sip her beer in silence, seemingly content to do the same, she began to relax. She took a few minutes to organize her thoughts before she spoke.

"Ever since I got back, Granny's been beating around the bush about my skewed view of my life before the fire." She'd been peeling the label off her beer bottle, now she chanced a look up.

Eric's gaze was steady on her, but he wasn't looking with curiosity or judgment. He just seemed to be . . . waiting. She went on, "She thinks I'm only remembering the parts I want to."

She paused and refocused on the brown bottle in her hands. "And maybe she's right. After what you said at the falls ... about Andrew and the baby ... well, I did remember something." When she halted momentarily, he didn't prompt her to tell him, but sat quietly, all strength and caring. She had to fight the urge to crawl into his lap. "And I thought maybe if I spent some time with you, I'd be able to remember more."

He nodded slowly and waited.

"Can you tell me again what you know about the fire—all of it?" She could barely breathe for fear of what he'd reveal.

He went through an outline of his recollection of the events of that night, much as he'd done the last time she'd been in his house.

"It was the furnace, Glory. There's no need to try to remember that night." Even as he said it, she could see something shuttered in his gaze, as if he needed to put some mental space between himself and those words.

Then he asked, as if he couldn't help himself, "Did that kick anything loose?"

She shook her head. "But last time the memory came later."

"Maybe you shouldn't be alone when the memory comes," he said quietly.

She gave a sharp laugh. "I'm never alone—not since I got back here." Then what he said actually sank in. Her spine tingled, and she sharpened her gaze on him. "Why shouldn't I be alone?"

"It was the most traumatic event in your life, and you don't remember it. It's going to ... hurt." He took her hand.

She had to admit she was relieved. For the briefest second, she'd worried that he was insinuating there was something sinister hidden in that memory. She relaxed more as he rubbed his thumb across the back of her hand.

"Maybe it's the opposite," she said. "Maybe I need to be alone for everything to become clear again."

"Weren't you alone while you were away?"

"Oh, yeah, I was alone all right." Until this moment she hadn't allowed herself to realize how isolated and lonely she'd been. It felt so good to sit, holding hands and *sharing* with him. "But I now have to admit, my goal at the time was *not* to remember."

"And now you want to because of those notes." It wasn't a question, and it wasn't an accusation.

She drew a deep breath. "Well, it seems it would be good to be able to answer with something more concrete than 'I don't remember.' It's very unsettling."

"Do you think you'll be called to answer? You said it was a kid's prank." His tone said that he believed no such thing.

"Well, of course it is!" she was quick to respond. "It just made me start thinking is all. And now that I'm back here, I feel . . ." She lifted a shoulder.

"You feel what?" he asked softly.

With a slight shake of her head, she set her beer on the table and said, "I feel like I *need* to remember." She paused and lowered her voice as she twisted to face him on the couch, tucking one leg underneath her. "I feel like maybe I can stand it now." She lifted her gaze to his. "Maybe I can stand it if you help me."

Eric looked deep into those incredible green eyes and knew what that admission had cost her. Her cheeks flushed slightly. Something shifted inside his chest; she was reaching out to *him*. After two weeks without her, he clearly understood how much her nearness meant to him, how lonely he was without their budding friendship. She wanted his help. She trusted him enough for that.

Happiness warmed his soul, and he realized how long it had been since he'd felt this way—blessed with a moment of simple and pure happiness.

And he realized just how much he needed her, too.

Only the specter of past truths lay between them. But Eric wasn't sure what those truths held. It would be best for him if Glory never remembered the events of that night. Still, did he want to walk on eggshells every day with the fear that she'd remember, and his own credibility would be called into question?

Why was it that the one person he was most drawn to held the most potential for disaster? If Andrew *had* pushed her to extreme measures to protect herself, what would happen if she did remember?

She continued to look into his eyes, tempting him to act on an impulse he might regret. He didn't want to scare her off now, not after she'd found the courage to ask for help. But she sat there with the fingers of her right hand entwined with those of his left and her lips slightly parted, wearing that little tank top that left nothing to the imagination—oh yes, he was tempted. It had been so long since he'd felt the stir of desire for a woman. But Glory had come to him needing a friend, and that's what he would give her.

He set his beer beside hers, then slowly reached out with his right hand and stroked her hair, running his finger along the strands that lay upon her cheek. He'd meant it only as a comfort—at least he told himself that as she turned her head slightly and kissed his palm.

Instead of pulling his hand gently away as he should have, he closed his eyes and focused on the sensation of her lips on his skin, of the soft brush of her exhalations against his palm. A little tremor began there and coursed up the length of his arm and shot straight to his heart.

They were at a crossroads. He knew the honorable thing to do was withdraw. But damn, she had his heart racing and heat pooling uncomfortably in his loins. So he kept his hand there until the moment for retreat had passed. She covered his hand with her own, drawing it lower until it rested on her collarbone. Her skin was hot under his touch, and he felt her rapid heartbeat at the base of her throat.

As he looked into her eyes, he saw a glimmer of uncertainty, of longing and vulnerability that took his breath away. He wanted her more than he could ever remember wanting any woman.

Slowly, he lowered his lips to the fluttering pulse at the base of her throat. Gently he allowed his lips to skim, to savor the racing of her pulse.

Then she threw her head back, offering more of herself, drawing him closer with her hand behind his neck.

He kissed her throat, her cheeks, finally finding the sweetness of her mouth. And as she traced her tongue along his lower lip, he forgot all about friendship and comfort and he reached for her, swinging her around until she sat in his lap.

Her arms went around his neck, and a beautiful little moan came from deep in her throat as he engaged fully in the kiss.

One hand traveled through her hair, cupping the back of her head. He'd wanted to bury his fingers in her hair from the moment she'd collapsed in his arms that morning in Tula's kitchen. It was just as he imagined—russet silk, heavy and cool and smooth. His other hand slid around her back, finding the exposed place between her tank top and pants. Her skin was surprisingly hot and not-so-surprisingly soft. He let himself sink into the sensation of the kiss, of her nearness, of her eager response.

There was only the briefest glimmer of conscience that told him he shouldn't do this—that it was selfish. But then she pressed herself against him and opened her mouth fully, and all conscious thought vanished. There was only this beautiful, prideful, wounded woman in his arms and the knowledge he could take away all of her pain, at least for a little while.

There was a certain desperation in the way they clung to one another, even in his aroused state he was aware of it. But like a drowning man grasping a bit of flotsam, he could no more let her go than he could walk on water.

She moved her lips only a breath away as she grasped his shirt and pulled it over his head. Her hands on his chest shot new urgency through his veins. He slid his hands under her tank top, feeling the long, lean lines of her back.

Her mouth moved down his neck, trailing kisses that left a blaze of heat. As she moved lower, his hands slid into her hair once again, his fingers twisting the length, and his breath caught in his belly. He didn't breathe at all as she nipped and teased his chest. When he finally let out the breath he'd been holding, his mouth formed words the words that his mind had been holding back, "Oh God, you're so beautiful."

She lifted her head and looked from under her brows. Her dark hair fell over her face, looking wildly sexy. But it was her grin that was his undoing.

He grabbed the hem of her tank top and pulled it off. She didn't give him enough time to savor her loveliness before she pressed their bodies together and kissed him.

Leaning backward, she pulled him with her, until he was half on top of her as they lay on the couch. It was his turn to explore, and he took his time, learning her body as she had learned his. Her fingernails dug into his shoulders as he suckled her breast.

Then, her quivering whisper, "Eric, I want you inside me," brought him halfway to his senses. He raised up and looked into her eyes, now smoldering and half-closed with passion. Framing her face with his hands, he kissed her—not the kiss of hunger he wanted to give her, but one of tenderness.

"Oh, baby, you don't know how much I want it too." He rested his forehead against hers.

She grinned again. "Then we're in agreement." Her insistent fingers pressing his backside as she squirmed against him threatened to rip away his thin hold on his control.

He buried his face in the sofa. Despite his effort not to, he groaned. "Glory, you came here looking for a friend. I shou—"

He was stunned when she grabbed a fistful of hair on the back of his head and lifted his head up so she could see his face. "I came here looking for *you*. I came here wanting this . . ." Her kiss was one of driving need and desire that broke through all of the barriers he'd tried to erect.

He was lost—and yet found; rescued by the caring of a woman who needed more than he could give.

For one horrifying instant Glory thought he would refuse her. Taking the lead in asking for sex was out of her depth. She was afraid she'd ruined everything when he pulled slightly away from her kiss. Holding her breath, she looked into his eyes. He almost looked as if he were in physical pain.

Then she kissed him, pouring all of herself into that silent plea.

When his lips trailed down her neck she whispered against his ear, "Please, Eric, I need to be close. I need to be close to you."

It was as if those whispered words had held the key. She felt his resistance dissolve as his hands—those strong, capable rescuer's hands—moved fluidly over her body. Soon they'd shed the rest of their clothes.

He tempted and teased, coveted and caressed, making her feel worshiped and alive for the first time in a very long time. Her skin vibrated beneath his touch, fiery sparks springing forth wherever he trailed his fingers.

And then, just before he joined their bodies, he stopped, framing her face with his hands, and asked, "Are you sure, Glory?"

There was no doubt in her mind that he wanted her, he was trembling with need, his breath quivering in his efforts to restrain himself. She slid her hand between them and guided him home. "Yes." And her body reached for his, welcoming the feeling of fullness, of belonging.

Through clenched teeth he said her name as he carried the rest of the world away on the rhythm of their bodies.

Chapter Sixteen

❦

GLORY LAY WITH Eric curled against her back as their sweat-soaked bodies began to cool, listening to the steady thud of her heart as it slowed back to a normal rhythm. With her eyes closed she concentrated on the sound, *lub-dub, lub-dub, lub-dub*. She drifted with the primal sound, her body feeling light and relaxed. She was vaguely aware of Eric's hand wrapped around her middle.

Lub-dub. Lub-dub. Lub-dub.

The sound echoed through her sleep-hazed mind, taking her back—back to the day she first heard the heartbeat of her unborn child. She remembered how she'd strained to separate the swishing beat of umbilical blood from that of her child's tiny heart. The instant she'd heard it, she couldn't understand how she could have had trouble picking out the separate sound of the life growing within from her own life's blood.

Lub-dub. Lub-dub. Lub-dub.

Eric drew her body closer to his with a breathy sigh and wound his fingers through hers. Their entwined hands rested over her womb. She pressed Eric's hand against her belly, remembering the life that once grew there.

The feeling of comfort and security that Eric had so

unconsciously provided was what she'd longed for all of those terrible weeks with Andrew. If only he'd drawn her close in protection of the life growing within her body. But Andrew had pushed her away. Those had been the loneliest weeks of her life.

Why couldn't Andrew have been a father like Eric, a man so devoted that nothing would stop him from doing what was best for his child?

A darkness lurked in the back of Glory's mind; it wasn't much more than a sinister tingle. There was something there, something unsettling that she just couldn't bring into focus.

What could it be? She'd already remembered that Andrew had been angry about the baby. But by the time of the fire, he'd gotten past that . . . hadn't he? Of course he had. She'd been more than six months along.

Dark, slithery whispers moved in the depths of her mind, but she could not make their meaning clear. She reached out in desperation. The only thing that solidified in her mind was a sense of fear—of what, she could not say.

She shivered, and Eric responded by holding her more tightly.

Suddenly all she wanted was Eric's touch. She didn't want to see what was lurking in the dark corners of her mind. She tried to cast away thoughts of Andrew and anger and loss. This moment was a new beginning for her; she would work on the past later, when she was alone.

She roused contentedly and turned to face Eric. His eyes remained closed and his breathing steady. He slung one leg over her thigh and inched her closer. Glory kissed his chin, the ache of finding hope again after all these dark months threatening to burst her chest.

His eyes opened. A faint smile curved his lips. He snugged her closer with his leg and caressed her cheek. "You all right?"

Unable to trust her voice, she smiled and nodded.

Pulling her close, he kissed her forehead. "Liar." He wrapped his arms around her as she laid her head on his chest. "Do you want to talk about it?"

"I just have some things to sort out."

"Glory, I don't want to make things harder for you. I shouldn't have let things get so out of hand."

She shook her head, a quick, jerky motion. "It's got nothing to do with you . . . us. I wanted this; it doesn't have to make things complicated. It's just . . . this is the first time since—"

His arms tightened around her. "Shhh."

They lay in silence for a while. Glory felt herself begin to relax, comfortable in his arms, and he seemed as content in the quiet as she.

Just when she thought he'd drifted back to sleep, he said, "Jill agreed to take Scott to a specialist."

Obviously, Eric had been dealing with his own tormented thoughts. It seemed odd, they'd just shared the most intimate act two people could share, and yet they'd both been transported back to problems that had nothing to do with each other. Glory nearly silenced him with a kiss, forcing him to take her back to that place where only the two of them existed. But she knew he needed a friend as much as she did.

"That's good, isn't it?" she said.

She felt him nod, his chin bumping the top of her head. "But I think she still believes he's going to tell her what she wants to hear; that Scott's development is slow but in the range of normal."

After a moment's hesitation, where Glory weighed how far she wanted to step into Eric's relationship with his child, she said, "I don't believe he is—in the range of normal. I agree with you, something isn't right. Do you think there's anything the doctors will be able to do to help him?"

"I have to believe there is. The first step is to figure out exactly what's wrong. Whatever needs to be done"—he'd been tracing his fingers along her spine, now his hand stilled—"it's going to be important that Jill and I work together."

Something in his voice made Glory's skin prickle. "You don't think I'd interfere with that?"

"I just want to be honest with you."

She raised up and looked at him. "It's not like we're—"

He touched his finger to her lips. "Don't. I'm not sure what we are, but there's something between us. It's not something I expected, especially right now, but Glory, it's special. I know you feel it too."

She nearly told him what she feared: that she was a wreck of a woman and he—hero that he was cut out to be—couldn't help but want to save her. She did feel a special connection to him, but was it simply because she wanted to be rescued?

He shattered her doubts when he kissed her.

When he stopped, she took a deep breath, and said, "We don't have to name it. Let's just see where this goes."

He kissed her again. "Fair enough."

"I'd better be getting back to Granny's. She has an early doctor appointment in the morning." She suddenly felt shy as she sat up on the couch and gathered up the clothes that they'd scattered so heedlessly.

Eric found her tank top and turned it right side out, then slid it over her head, showing as much loving interest in dressing her as he had in removing her clothes. His hands were gentle, and he kissed her shoulder as he smoothed the straps in place. If she didn't guard her heart, she'd find herself falling into the deep end for him.

We hardly know each other. Even as she had the thought, she knew in her heart that it was wrong. They hadn't spent much time together, true, but they understood each other in ways that went beyond the few hours spent in one another's company. They knew each other's heaviest burdens. Of course, that was probably what made Eric so intensely interested in her—her burdens and her need drew him like the moon pulled the tides. It wasn't pity exactly, but it certainly wasn't a good basis for a solid relationship.

She decided to take it for what it was—comfort at the moment—and do her best to guard her heart.

After getting dressed and sliding her feet into her flip-flops, she stood, but didn't look at him. "Good night, Eric."

As she started to move away, he grasped her hand and pulled her back into his lap. He had his jeans on, but his T-shirt was still on the floor. Glory tried not to lean against his bare chest and kept her gaze on the door.

"Look at me, Glory."

Reluctantly, she did. She didn't want to be pulled back into the depths of those whiskey eyes.

He kissed her gently. "Don't lock me out again."

Her heart did a slow roll in her chest. The intensity of her reaction rocked her to the marrow of her bones. She was in much more danger of losing her heart than she'd thought. "I have to go."

There was a flicker of something in his eyes that might have been disappointment, but she got up and didn't study it too closely for fear of her own response.

Against her protests, Eric walked her to her car. Before he closed the door he leaned in and kissed her again. Then he looked at her seriously, his eyes dark in the dim glow of the car's interior lights. "Just so you know," he said softly, "this was the first time for me too . . . since . . ."

Before she could respond, he withdrew from the car and closed the door.

As she drove away, she looked in the rearview mirror and saw him as a silhouette against the wide fan of yellow light from the streetlamp behind him. He had his hands in his pockets and was making no move toward his house.

Hours later, Glory lay in bed in the lavender floral room at Granny's, drifting on contentment. She recalled the weight of Eric's warm hand over her abdomen. That time of safe intimacy had been even more precious to her than their lovemaking. Holding that feeling close to her heart, she relaxed into sleep.

Just as she released the last threads that bound her to awareness, an image exploded in her mind. Andrew's face was nose to nose with hers. His brows were drawn in anger, his lips pulled back in a grimace as he shouted at her in a wild, guttural tone. The tone was frightening enough, but it was the words that came from his mouth that slammed her back into wakefulness.

"My decision is final. You will get that abortion!"

Glory sat up in bed, gasping, every nerve in her body buzzing. It had to be real. It had to be a memory. It was too powerful even for a nightmare.

She raised a trembling hand to her throat. "Oh, my God." As the words rode out on her breath, the rest of that confrontation stepped out from behind the curtain that had been hiding it for over two years. What was revealed was so ugly, it was no wonder she had blocked it from her mind.

Closing her eyes, she let it come:

Her back was pressed against the kitchen counter. She leaned as far away from Andrew's angry aggression as physically possible. Her mind kept screaming, *This can't be. He can't possibly mean this.*

But it was blindingly clear, he meant every harsh word he spit in her face.

When he'd first mentioned an abortion, she hadn't re-acted, certain that once he came to himself he'd realize what a preposterous suggestion it was.

She found her voice. "You said you'd think it over. You can't really want this!" She'd been so sure that once the shock wore off, he'd be happy, or at the very least nervous and accepting. Never did she think he would continue on this path.

"I did think it over." His face hardened, negating any relief she might have felt with his slight retreat from looming over her. "Do you think I really believe it was an accident? You tricked me." She shook her head and tried to deny it, but he kept on talking. "You never should have gotten pregnant in the first place. It's your fault—you put us in this position. Get rid of it."

"This is a child! Your flesh and blood!" She reached for his arm, but he jerked it away. "Please, Andrew, just give it some more time. You'll get over the shock—"

"I've already made the arrangements." His voice was flat and cold, as if his anger had burned every bit of humanity from his soul.

"What!" She shook her head vehemently. "I won't go. I will not do this. If you don't want this child, I'll have it alone. But I'm not getting an abortion."

He grabbed her by both arms and hauled her against his chest. His fingers dug painfully into her flesh. "You will not ruin my life! You're my wife. You can't just walk out like I don't exist."

Glory drew her strength from the fact that the tiny life inside her depended upon her. She stopped cowering and straightened her back. "I have put up with your need to 'wear the pants in this family,' with your constant questioning of my whereabouts, with your unfounded jealousy. Every time you've asked for a compromise for the sake of our marriage, I've made it. Now I'm asking you to accept the child we created together—a part of our family."

"It's not going to happen."

"What will your parents think if I get an abortion? You're their only child—this is their grandchild!"

His steely expression softened momentarily. Glory grabbed on to the hope that she'd finally found a way to make him understand the gravity of what he was asking.

He killed that hope in his next breath. "They won't think anything because they're not going to know."

Glory swallowed dryly. "It's too late. I told your mother this afternoon."

"Glory!" Granny's voice came from the hall, accompanied by the sound of her hurrying feet. "Are you all right?"

Glory gulped in a great draft of air, trying to calm her nausea and slow her rapid breathing. It didn't help.

Just as Granny opened the bedroom door, Glory bolted from the bed and ran to the bathroom. She managed to hold back being sick until she reached the toilet.

After rinsing her mouth out and splashing her face with cold water, she slowly walked back to her bedroom, feeling drained and shaky.

Granny had switched on the bedside lamp and was sitting on the edge of the bed. She'd straightened and smoothed the tangled covers and fluffed Glory's pillow.

"Sorry, Gran. I didn't mean to wake you." Glory's voice trembled with the quaking that still rocked her insides.

Granny patted the sheets. "Come on and get back in bed." Glory did, and Granny tucked her in as if she were a small child again. "You didn't wake me. I just snapped awake, like someone doused me with a bucket of cold water, and I knew somethin' was terrible wrong."

Granny touched Glory's forehead with a cool dry hand. "No fever. Your hair's wet with sweat, though. Maybe it's passed. Summer flu's quick like that."

For a long moment, Glory was silent. Granny had been urging her to face the past—how much of that past was Granny aware of?

Granny said, "'Member how, back when you and your mama lived in that trailer in town, I always knew when you were sick? I'd just get this feelin' and call your mama—sure 'nough I'd be right."

"It's not the flu."

Granny's gaze sharpened. "Feared it wasn't. Felt too strong for just sick."

After drawing a quivering breath, Glory rested her hand on her forehead and closed her eyes again. That confession to her mother-in-law had saved her baby's life . . . at least for a while.

Just how bad had things been between her and Andrew those last months? She searched her memory for feelings as well as events. There had been a space of relative calm after that horrible day, she knew that. She'd prepared the nursery; Andrew had even gone shopping with her. Those memories had always stayed with her. Granny had been right, she'd only remembered the good.

She opened her eyes and asked the question that had to be asked. "Did you know that Andrew didn't want the baby?"

Granny's posture stiffened. "Andrew wasn't a man who wanted anyone to take your attention. You never said it to me—but I figured." She took Glory's hand in hers. "You remembered then?"

Unable to speak, not wanting to explain, Glory just nodded.

Squeezing her hand, Granny said, "Maybe you can let the past go now there ain't secrets left buried in your mind. You're too young to spend the rest of your life hidin'." After a moment she asked, "You been to his grave?"

The question seemed odd, odd enough that it took Glory a few seconds to process whose grave Granny meant. Then, with a listless shake of her head, she whispered, "No."

"Might do you some good—now that you remember. Make peace. Let go."

"Maybe." She didn't tell Granny that there were still things that were a mystery to her, things that had to be settled before she could begin to let go.

Chapter Seventeen

❧

"MRS. McELROY SAW Glory Harrison leaving Eric's house late last night." Gail Landry paused; Jill held the phone tightly and could just see the I-told-you-so expression on her mother's face. Gail's voice dropped to a scandalously low tone when she added, "He didn't have a shirt on."

The words not only set Jill's teeth on edge—her normal reaction to her mother's meddling—but twisted her gut with anxiety. She'd never actually considered there would be another woman in the picture. Eric had behaved like a monk since the divorce; she didn't have a doubt that her mother and her cronies wouldn't have missed a single liaison, especially considering their vigilant efforts in tracking his activities with Glory.

"Mom, I really don't have time for this. I'm going to be late for work." Jill's impatience had nothing to do with her job. Even after the divorce, she'd been the one in charge—she'd been the one to leave, the one to end the marriage. But suddenly she felt as if she were trying to catch sifting sand with her bare hands.

"You'd better make time, or that woman'll have her hooks in him. Maybe you should have a little chat with Glory when you pick Scott up tonight."

"Honestly, Mother! What do you expect me to say?"

"Just that you're trying to work things out with your husband and you'd appreciate her keeping in mind that you and Eric have a child that needs a family. She lost a baby; she'll get it."

"Maybe I should just pee all over him and mark my territory." It was obvious she was going to have to do something, but her mother's constant coaching was really getting under her skin.

"Really, Jill! Must you be so vulgar?"

"Eric and Scott are *mine* to worry about. I don't need these phone calls, nor do I need you adding to the gossip around this town by taking reports from everyone who lays eyes on Eric." Before her mother could respond, she said, "I have to go. Bye."

She glanced at the clock. Eric didn't go in to work until after he dropped Scott off at school on Friday mornings. She picked up the phone and dialed his number.

He answered on the first ring. "Glory?"

An electric shock shot through Jill from head to toe. She forced a smile into her voice when she said, "No, Eric, it's Jill."

"Oh, sorry." There was obviously disappointment in his tone. Then he went on, "I just called out to Tula's and got the machine."

"Is there a problem?" She hoped he interpreted the near panic in her voice as concern.

"No. I just needed to talk to Glory . . ." There was a long pause. "You know, see how Tula's doing today with her eye."

God, the man was a horrible liar. Clearly she had to do something. "I was calling to tell you I can pick Scott up from school at lunchtime and run him to Tula's. I know how much time you've had to spend away from the station lately. This way you can have an uninterrupted day at work." At this stage of the game, the less incidental contact between Eric and Glory, the better.

"There's no need," he said. "I want to talk to Tula anyway."

"Well, I'm sure you'll be able to get ahold of her by phone sometime in the next few hours. There's no need for you to take a chunk out of the middle of your day to run Scott all the way out there. I'm free at lunch today."

"You're going to have Scott all weekend; why don't you take the time to run your errands? I've already planned my day around taking him."

Jill's chest tightened with frustration. She forced herself to say, in a cheery voice, "Good idea." After a carefully timed pause, she said, "Tomorrow's Saturday, why don't we take Scott to the park in the afternoon. I'll pack a picnic and we can talk about which doctor we should schedule him with . . . you know, make a game plan."

There was just enough hesitation in Eric's response to tell her he had other plans for tomorrow. She held her breath. Eric *always* put Scott first; that's one thing she'd always been able to count on.

"Okay," he said. "What time?"

"Pick us up at twelve-thirty."

"I thought maybe we'd just meet there."

"I suppose we could . . ." She let it hang there.

"Never mind. I'll be there at noon."

"Great. See you tomorrow," she said, in her most upbeat tone. Then she hung up the phone and chewed on her thumbnail for a few seconds. This might be more difficult than she'd thought.

Eric decided to stop trying to reach Glory by phone. Once he'd thought about it, he realized that it might be awkward for her to discuss anything about last night—and that was the subject he most needed to discuss—with her grandmother within earshot.

As he sat at his desk ignoring work he should be doing, he couldn't explain why he felt so nervous. It was almost as if he were waiting for first-date feedback: *Did she enjoy it as much as I did? Would there be a second date?*

But he and Glory weren't teenagers with a blank and unscripted future before them; they were mature adults with very complicated lives and other people who depended upon them. If they embarked on a relationship, it wasn't going to be a smooth road. Challenges would come from both in and outside their relationship, from both the living and the dead.

Even as he realized how dangerously potholed it would probably be, deep in his gut he knew he wanted to try traveling that road with Glory. Trouble was, after the way she left last night, he didn't think Glory felt the same.

Hence the nerves.

He was too old for nerves when it came to a woman.

"So knock it off," he mumbled, and picked up a report he needed to review before he met with the mayor this afternoon.

The morning moved with unnatural slowness. The antsy feel reminded him of when he was a kid and had to wait thirty torturously long minutes after he ate to go swimming. The only time in his adult life that he could re-call feeling like this was when Jill had been in labor.

Finally, the hands on the clock begrudgingly moved to twelve-thirty, time to go pick Scott up from school. As he drove to the church, he couldn't help but wonder about Jill's unprecedented offer to drive Scott out to Tula's. Jill really seemed to be coming around. As amicable as their shared custody had always been, recently it had become strained. Today's offer was the signal of better things to come, he just knew it.

When he entered the preschool, Mrs. Parks was sitting on the floor next to Scott. As unexpected relief washed over Eric, and he realized how tense he always was when he walked through this door, never knowing if he'd find his son in a total meltdown or in heartbreaking isolation while other children colored or sang songs.

Mrs. Parks looked up at Eric with a smile. "He had a good day today."

Scott was playing with little wooden blocks, adjusting the line into precise order. He hadn't shown interest in any toy except his pirate boat for weeks. He wasn't allowed to bring the boat to school, but he'd never filled his time there with other toys.

Maybe this was a phase, as Jill insisted, and Scott was finding his way through it. Eric's heart grabbed on to that hope.

With a knot of emotion in his throat, he knelt in front of his son. "Scott."

Scott continued to straighten the blocks.

Mrs. Parks said cheerily, "I think it's a good sign. He's finally using some of our toys. And he hasn't cried once all morning."

Eric smiled as he picked up his son. "Tell Mrs. Parks good-bye," he prompted, irrationally hoping that some recently closed door in Scott's mind had reopened, and he'd smile and speak.

Scott laid his head on Eric's shoulder and clung tightly.

"Good-bye, Scott. See you next week," Mrs. Parks responded, as if Scott had actually told her good-bye.

When Eric buckled Scott in his car seat, he kissed his forehead and asked, "You hungry?" The kids had lunch at eleven-thirty as part of their social activities, but Eric always asked the question, hoping for some spark of response in his son's eyes. And this time, there was one. Scott looked directly at him and gave an almost imperceptible shake of his head.

A giddy laugh bubbled from Eric's chest. "Already had lunch, did you?" He ruffled Scott's fine blond hair.

As he drove to Tula's he thought just maybe the dark cloud had passed. Scott showed signs of improvement. Jill was cooperative. And Glory . . . ah, Glory. He wanted to leave the past in the past and look to the future.

He was whistling when he entered Tula's kitchen.

"My, my, ain't we in a chipper mood?" Tula teased with a smile.

He kissed her playfully on the cheek. "It's a good day."

"Ev'r day the good Lord gives us is a good day." She shook a bony finger at him.

"How's your eye today? What did the doctor say?"

"Said it don't have nothin' to do with the macular degeneration. Was just one of those fluky things. Clearin' up nice now—he calls it 'quiet'; my eye's 'quiet.' "

"So you can see all right?"

"Saw fine by bedtime last night. Glory makes too much of things. I'm old. Got to expect some wear and tear."

He couldn't help but wrap his free arm around her. "We should all grow old like you."

Tula shrugged away. "Stop talkin' nonsense." She put her hands out toward Scott. "Give me my boy."

Scott shifted to Tula's arms without complaint. Eric watched him with a careful eye for any other outward signs of improvement, but Scott behaved as always with Tula—compliant but not interactive.

"Guess I'd better get back to the station." Then he said, as if he'd just had the thought, "Maybe I'll say hi to Glory before I go."

Tula was settling Scott on his blanket. She straightened and looked at him. There was something that sparked in her eye, and Eric shifted uncomfortably.

"She ain't here. Went into town."

"Oh. Well, tell her I said hello."

"Sure." Her tone bordered on suspicious. The old gal didn't miss a trick. He'd wanted to ask what Glory was doing in town, but Tula's antennae were already picking up more than he thought was prudent at this point in time.

Movement behind Tula caught Eric's eye. He was surprised to see Scott getting up from his pirate boat, moving toward Lady standing in the doorway. His little face was more animated than Eric had seen it for months. He put a hand on the dog's back.

Eric whispered, "Look at that."

Tula put a hand over her heart. "Land's sake. I never seen him do that before."

When Lady turned around and walked out of the kitchen, Scott followed.

Tula and Eric inched along behind. In a low voice, Eric said, "He had a good day at school. And he shook his head no when I asked if he was hungry. Maybe he's coming out of his shell."

Tula's green eyes, eyes so much like Glory's, looked up at him. They sparkled with gathered tears. "I pray to Jesus ever' night. Maybe He sees it's time."

The thought of Tula praying faithfully for his son squeezed his heart with love. He could barely get the words out to agree, "Maybe so."

When Lady lay down next to the box with her puppies, Scott plopped down next to her and put a chubby fist on her back again. They both seemed content.

Eric said, "I'll call later and see how it's going. It's Jill's weekend, so she'll be picking him up."

"All right."

He started down the hall toward the kitchen.

Tula stopped him by saying, "Been forgettin' to tell you, we're havin' a family reunion of sorts on Sunday— Glory bein' back and all. There'll be lots of young'uns. Might be good for Scott."

In his mind, Eric could see Scott playing in Tula's yard with a group of children. He was running and laughing, interacting like a healthy little boy. Oh, how Eric wanted that picture to come to life.

"It *is* Jill's weekend." He rubbed his chin, thinking of the tiny markers of progress he'd seen today. "But it probably would be good for him. I'll see if Jill will let me steal him away for a few hours," he said as he left.

Just as he reached his Explorer, Glory's cousin Charlie pulled up in his gray-and-red Suburban.

"Hey, Eric." Charlie stepped around his truck to shake Eric's hand. "How's she doing today?" He gestured with a lift of his chin toward the kitchen.

Eric didn't know which surprised him more, that Charlie was in tune with a problem that didn't sit at the end of his own nose or by the fact he was here without his five kids to dump on Tula. Eric was amazed that such a lazy-ass could have a single one of Tula Baker's genes floating in his blood.

"She says she's better; she saw her eye doctor again this morning." He added, with just a hint of sarcasm, "Nice of you to stop by to see how she's faring."

The sarcasm was lost on Charlie. He grinned affably and shrugged. "Ran into Glory in town. She said she might be gone a long while and asked if I'd check in."

"Must take a burden off your shoulders with Glory here now to keep a watch on Tula."

Charlie laughed, the ridicule in Eric's tone again whizzing right past his head. "Gran don't need anyone to 'keep watch.'" He shook his head. "Better hope she doesn't hear you say such a thing."

Eric waved as Charlie headed toward the house. Then he called, "Did Glory happen to say what she was doing in town?"

"Said she was going to the cemetery. She had flowers. Reckon they were for Andrew."

"Oh. Thanks." Eric got in his Explorer.

With his optimistic mood now dampened slightly, he turned around and drove back toward the road. Even though there was no traffic, he sat at the end of the lane for a long moment before he pulled out. Glory visiting her husband's grave the day after she and Eric had sex for the first time didn't bode well, not well at all.

When he returned to town, he cruised past the cemetery. The Harrisons had a special section near the entrance that was surrounded by an antique wrought-iron fence, the Harrison Garden. Eric saw Glory's Volvo parked there. Then he saw her, on her knees with her head bowed.

With a stomach that ratcheted another notch tighter, he made himself drive on past and not intrude upon her privacy.

It had taken nearly an hour to gather her courage before she entered the cemetery. As Glory placed a bouquet of white daisies bound together with a pink satin ribbon beside the small marker on her daughter's grave, her hands trembled and her chest felt too tight to draw a breath. This was the first time she'd seen the engraved stone; she had been too cowardly to return here after the day of the funeral. It shamed her that almost two years had passed, and she had not laid a single flower as an offering to the spirit of her child.

There was a harsh cruelty in the very smallness of the grave that Glory hadn't been able to bring herself to face. Now it had been long enough that the outline of disturbed earth and mismatched new grass wasn't a glaring indication of just how tiny that casket had been. She didn't think she could have stood that, even today.

But there was something beyond her cowardice for not coming here. She never really felt her child was contained in this earth, but was still somehow bound to her heart, following wherever she went.

For a long time she just stared at the headstone. She and Andrew hadn't settled on a name, so Glory had named her stillborn child alone; Clarice Ovella Harrison. It seemed only right that the child who was never held in the loving arms of either one of her grandmothers had something of theirs.

Glory recalled how oddly Andrew's mother had reacted when Glory had told her—with cold eyes and mouth sourly drawn. But then, Glory asked herself, how should one behave when your only child had died tragically and your grandchild had been born dead? It had been an impossible time; no one had had the slightest control of their emotions.

She reached out and touched a shaky hand to the small granite stone. Closing her eyes, she traced the letters as a blind woman would read Braille. Then she waited for the calm, the rush of warmth and connection that Granny said she always experienced at Pap's grave. But the only thing Glory felt was alone and cold to her core. Maybe Granny had such a positive reaction because she had shared most of a lifetime with Pap; Glory hadn't even had a moment to see the color of her daughter's eyes.

After a while she gave up hoping for a shift in her emotional state and opened her eyes. The bouquet blurred; summer-grass green smearing deeply into the pure white of the delicate petals, round yellow centers now irregular smudges of color, ribbon an indistinct slash of pink. She felt as if she'd tried to swallow a watermelon whole and it was stuck halfway down. Only when she let herself sob did the pressure begin to lessen. And when she began to cry, it was as if a dam had burst.

The movement of the sun registered as its heat traveled from the back of Glory's neck to the side of her face. She cried until she was as wrung out as an old sponge, with no hint of resiliency left, ready to shred into brittle chunks.

Only then, when her grief for her daughter had turned her inside out and left nothing, did she turn to her husband's grave.

In contrast to the small marker Glory had chosen for Clarice's grave, Andrew's seemed almost garish in its pretension. Glory had been appalled when Ovella had selected it from the brochure and insisted nothing else would do. But Glory hadn't had the heart to deny a grieving mother what she felt was a fitting tribute to her son. Glory had left town before it had been erected; it was even gaudier in person than it had appeared in the photograph.

The marker had two large built-in urns that were filled with fresh-cut flowers. She wondered who would have left such lavish arrangements. It couldn't have been Ovella; she would have left flowers on her grandchild's grave too.

Glory brushed insignificant things like flowers and monuments away and tried to focus on what Granny had said was important: Make peace, let go. Glory couldn't deny the soul-cleansing effect of crying over her daughter's grave.

She drew a deep breath and let it out slowly. "Granny says you and I have unfinished business." Glancing around, Glory made sure she was alone. She felt a little nuts talking to a grave. But that was how Granny did it, and she was Glory's only guide in this. "I suppose she's right."

She cast about in her mind for a place to begin and realized how difficult it had been for her to speak freely to her husband in life.

"I've been away from here for nearly two years. And for all of that time, I ignored the truth of our relationship. But I'm remembering things clearly now. Maybe it was my shame at failing in this marriage that made me mourn for things that never were—or at least hadn't been for a very long time. Our marriage was rotting deep inside. If I had stayed in Dawson, I might have faced the truth sooner. But that's neither here nor there now."

Taking a moment to fortify herself, she plunged into the heart of the matter. "I can never forgive you for telling me to abort our baby. Never. It makes me physically ill to think what might have happened if I hadn't already told your mother. I want to believe you couldn't have forced me to have an abortion—but then, I know I allowed you to manipulate me into lots of things that I never thought possible.

"We were still together in the end, but I can't for the life of me understand how. There must have been a turning point, an understanding; I remember you helping get ready for the baby's birth . . ."

Her words trailed into the past, she remembered what they had been doing prior to the fire—painting and decorating the baby's room. They had been nearly finished. The project had dragged on because the smell of the paint had made Glory queasy.

On the day of the fire, she'd hung the curtains—soft moss green with tiny ivory dots. She could remember how rich the fabric felt in her fingers. Andrew had refused any infantile patterns in the décor. Glory hadn't fought over it, it didn't matter to her. What mattered was there was a bright, sunny room with a comfortable rocking chair where she could hold her baby, sing to her, to show her how it felt to be loved. She remembered thinking, *This is why I'm here in this world, to love this child.*

That day, Andrew had come home just as she was arranging the folds of the new curtains:

"What do you think?" she had asked without stopping her work when she heard him enter the room behind her.

Andrew didn't answer, so she turned around ready to repeat the question. That was when she saw the thunderous expression on his face. Her stomach dropped to her toes.

"What's wrong? What's happened?"

He stayed in the doorway, his hands fisted at his sides. "I saw you."

There was no sense in acting like she didn't understand what he meant. "What did you see me doing this time?" She quickly reran her day in her mind, trying to remember when she'd been in the company of a man Andrew might consider capable of having an affair with a woman nearly seven months pregnant.

"You were getting in your car in front of Cam Wilkes's house. Cam was all over you."

"His wife made these curtains. I was picking them up. As for his being all over me, I can't imagine what you think you saw." She spoke dispassionately; she'd learned early on that the more emotional she appeared, the stronger Andrew's suspicions became. She was tired to her core of these scenes. She supposed she'd find her car keys missing again tomorrow.

"His wife wasn't home," he said in a tone that indicated he'd caught her in a lie.

"How do you know that?" Glory's skin turned clammy. Had he followed her around all day?

"Because I saw her going into the hair salon on the square."

"Then you drove all the way out to River Road to see what was going on at her house? Or were you following me?" She was losing her battle to keep the emotion out of her voice.

"What was Cam doing home in the middle of the morning?"

"Honestly, Andrew! How do you jump to such conclusions?" She was tempted not to explain, but for some reason she didn't think this was the time to push him. He'd been irrational before, but there was something in his eyes this evening that frightened her. So she told him the truth that he most likely would not believe. "Cam is on vacation this week. I needed to pick up the curtains. Sandy said she had an appointment but that he'd be home all morning, so I could stop by anytime."

"So you chose the time when you knew she was going to be gone."

"For God's sake, I didn't know what time her appointment was!" It took everything in her not to shake her fist at him. "I don't know why I put up with these ridiculous accusations! I'm as big as a cow, what makes you think any man would even think of me in that way?"

"Certain men would."

She furrowed her brow and gave her head a slight shake. "What are you talking about?"

His aggressive stance relaxed slightly, but she could see the tension still humming in his muscles. "Never mind." He ran a hand through his hair. "Just watch yourself. You've got no business being in a house alone with a man. People will talk. Or do you want to make a fool out of me?"

"Most people wouldn't give it a second thought! As for being made a fool, you're doing a fine job of that yourself."

He stepped toward her, and for the briefest moment she braced herself for a blow. He'd never hit her. But he was getting much more volatile.

Instead of hitting her, he loomed over her and shook a finger in her face. "One of these days, you're going to push me too far."

She made herself look him in the eye. No more would she back down for the sake of peace. "I honestly don't know how much longer I can take this, Andrew."

"What's that supposed to mean?"

She looked squarely at him and said the words she'd been contemplating for months. "I'm seriously thinking about leaving you. I can't live like this. I don't want my child to grow up in this kind of environment."

That dangerous look was back in his eye. But his words were far from what she expected. "Why did you call it your child?"

"Andrew, I'm exhausted. I cannot go another argument over semantics. I'm tired of watching every word that comes out of my mouth. I've been faithful to you since our first date, but you obviously want something I can't give you."

"You're not leaving me."

And just like that it became blindingly clear. She'd

been ignoring the obvious for too long. She had to leave him. For her sake—for her child's. "I'm sorry, Andrew. We need some time apart. Maybe in a few months . . ."

He reached for her with a swiftness that made her flinch. But the violence she anticipated did not come. He wrapped her in his arms and said, "You're my wife. You promised yourself to me. You can't break that promise."

"People break promises all the time. Sometimes it's for the best."

He pushed her an arm's length away from him, his fingers digging into her arms. "How can you even think about walking away?"

"I've been thinking about it for a long time."

"Well, it's news to me!"

"Really, Andrew? Can you honestly say you're happy? You come home angry more days than not. How can you want to live this way?"

He thrust her away and paced in a tight little circle. Then he rounded on her and shouted, "I give you everything! You don't have to lift a goddamn finger! What do you want?"

Her fear of him vanished. Now that she'd made up her mind, the power he'd held over her diminished. There was nothing left to lose. "I don't have the most important thing in a marriage. I don't have your trust."

"And whose fault is that?" he asked accusingly.

"Apparently you think it's mine—which is why this is never going to work."

He took a swing at the door as he stormed out of the room. It slammed against the wall, the doorknob knocking a hole in the drywall before it bounced back and half closed.

She waited several minutes before she went after him.

As she left the nursery, she felt a pang of regret. She'd never sit in here and rock her baby.

Andrew was in the kitchen. His hands were braced on the casing of one of the windows that looked onto the swimming pool. But he wasn't looking out the window; his head was bowed between his shoulders.

She stopped just inside the kitchen and waited. The baby seemed to be upset by the argument; tumbling and twisting inside her, sticking little feet and elbows painfully under ribs and into kidneys. She couldn't help but question her conviction, this was her child's future—she couldn't afford to make the wrong decision.

At that moment, when her resolve was most vulnerable, Andrew turned to her. Tears tracked down his cheeks. "I can't believe you're doing this to me."

When she opened her mouth to speak, he held up a hand to silence her.

"Just don't do it today," he said. "Don't leave like this. Sleep on it—that's all I ask."

She hesitated. What harm could waiting until tomorrow morning do? It would give Andrew a little while to come to terms. No matter what happened between them, they would always be linked by their child. She had to do what was best for the baby; had to keep the lines of communication open. It wasn't too much to concede.

"All right. But I won't change my mind. We need some time apart—to think about what we really want."

"I *know* what I want. You and I are meant to be together forever." There was a chilling finality in his tone.

The last thing Glory remembered of that night was Andrew moving into the guest room and her going to bed alone.

Chapter Eighteen

❧

AFTER LEAVING THE cemetery, Glory drove out Laurel Creek Road for the first time since her return to Dawson. The road was narrow and curvy, as were most roads in the area. It dead-ended not too far beyond where her house once stood. She slowed as she neared her old driveway. Butterflies fluttered in her stomach. *I have to do this,* she told herself. What she'd remembered so far was horrible, but was there something else? Had she done something even more horrible in her desperation to be free of Andrew?

Those notes . . . had there been truth in them? She couldn't believe it of herself, and yet if there was nothing ugly lurking there, why couldn't she remember? She had almost everything back—except those last hours.

A heavy chain was strung across the driveway entrance between two metal posts. A NO TRESPASSING sign was suspended in the middle. Weeds had sprung up between the bricks in the drive. What once had been meticulously maintained was now abandoned.

She pulled off the edge of the road and parked. After shutting off the engine, she clung to the steering wheel. She couldn't seem to pry her hands loose and get out of the car. Eric had suggested she shouldn't be alone when her memory returned fully—did he suspect she'd had something to do with the fire, too?

Maybe she should leave this for another day, perhaps bring Granny with her.

No, she wouldn't drag Granny into this. It wasn't a burden to be shared; it was Glory's past, her choices, her actions.

She got out of the car before she could chicken out. The yard was so overgrown that she decided to step over the chain instead of fighting her way through the weeds.

Once over the chain, she approached the site where the house had once stood. There was nothing but a rough patch of ground where the basement had been filled in. The swimming pool gaped drily beyond that. The carriage house remained untouched by tragedy, but not by time. The paint was mildewed, tiny trees sprouted in the clogged gutters, and vines had begun to snake up the walls. The weather vane on the cupola sat tilted as if swatted askew by a giant hand.

Her heart raced and felt as if it sat at the base of her throat. Slowly, she began to walk around the old footprint of the house. Memories rushed over her—garden parties and birthdays, holiday dinners and lazy Sunday mornings—not the ones she was seeking. She came full circle and stood where the steps to her front porch had once been.

Her knees trembled and suddenly felt weak. A buzzing started in her ears and she became light-headed. She crumpled where she stood, sitting hard on the ground.

Drawing on her newly recovered memory of the last evening in her house, she sat very still, waiting for the picture to complete itself. A fierce ache centered in her chest, but she refused to cry. Over and over again she relived those last hours.

Andrew had been surprisingly considerate that evening. It had been his idea that he take the spare bedroom. He'd spoken to her gently, telling her how much she meant to him and how important it was to him for them to stay together. She recounted every minute, yet she could not remember getting out of bed.

She remembered she'd turned in early, physically exhausted by emotional stress. She'd fought not to be swayed by Andrew's surprisingly nonvolatile temperament throughout the evening. His behavior had been increasingly irrational. More than once, she'd feared that erratic behavior would explode into violence. There was no way she could bring her baby into such a household.

But, she'd thought, Andrew came from a powerful family. Power was hard to fight in a small town, especially when the powerful want certain things kept in the dark. Outwardly, Andrew could be very charming and persuasive. Beneath that veneer was a man obsessed. What might he truly be capable of? It wasn't beyond comprehension that he would convince everyone she was the unstable one; she might lose custody of her child.

Her troubled thoughts had kept her awake for hours, but, sometime after midnight, she'd fallen asleep. The next thing she recalled was opening her eyes and seeing Eric's smoke-stained face in the rain.

Sitting there before the ghost of her home, Glory closed her eyes. Eric said she'd been near the back door— so clearly she'd gotten up at some point.

Stop trying so hard. Relax. Let go. Breathe.

Beginning at the top of her head, she went through the exercise of relaxing each muscle, moving down her body until she reached her toes. She kept her mind free of thought, drifting on a sensation of near weightlessness.

A hand fell on her shoulder.

With a scream, she jerked away and shot to her feet, turning quickly.

Eric stood with his hands before him and an apologetic look in his eyes. "It's okay. It's me."

Adrenaline buzzed through her veins, and her knees felt rubbery. "Why in the hell did you sneak up on me?" Hand on her chest, she dragged in a breath.

"I didn't. I called your name twice. I was beginning to worry that you weren't conscious."

Now that she'd had a moment to gather herself, she asked, "What are you doing here?"

"I was driving by and saw your car."

She tilted her head in doubt. What purpose would Eric possibly have to be here in the middle of the day?

He sighed roughly and ran a hand through his hair. "All right. I'd seen your car at the cemetery earlier and thought you might come out here. It's so isolated, I didn't want you to be alone."

Crossing her arms over her chest, she said, "What if I want to be alone?"

He glanced at the place where her house used to stand, then toward the carriage house. "Sorry. I didn't think . . . I just want to help you, Glory."

"I know." She made herself put words to her most unsettling suspicion about his interest in her. "But you can't save me. It's not your job to fix me. I know you feel it's your duty to keep everyone safe—"

"Is that what you think? That I'm feeling somehow responsible for you—you're an obligation? You think I made love to you just to make you feel better? Jesus, Glory! I thought we knew each other better than that."

"Do we?" She searched his face. "I've seen something in your eyes when we talk about my remembering the fire. You're hiding something from me."

In the second of hesitation that followed, Glory saw it again.

He said, "You've asked me more than once about that night, and I've always answered you."

"Yes. Yes, you have. But I'm sensing there's something more."

Eric held her gaze for a long moment, as if he wanted to make sure she understood the depth of his sincerity. "I care about you. I don't want to see you hurt. I have a feeling you suffered enough at Andrew's hands."

She was startled by the boldness of his statement. "What makes you say that?"

"I knew Andrew better than most people think. He required unquestioning loyalty and had some pretty serious control issues in high school—I saw things that told me he hadn't changed."

"What kinds of things?"

"I saw the way he was with you . . . dominating, suspicious of your every move."

She was stunned to realize Eric had even been aware of her relationship with her husband. "How could you know that?"

"Because I looked in his eyes the day you and I were talking in the drugstore after Scott was born. Because he was still the same as when we were younger. Andrew required total, 100 percent devotion—and no one dismissed him without repercussions."

A shiver of confirmation slithered down her spine. Andrew had said he wouldn't let her go—and in her deepest heart she had understood there would be no way out. With a dry mouth, she asked, "What do you mean, 'repercussions'?"

"Things seemed to happen to people who slighted him . . . or left him."

"What kinds of things?"

"Listen, I've got no business saying all of this to you—"

"It's too damn late now! Tell me!"

He looked around, then said, "We need someplace to sit down. Let's go sit in the car."

"All right." She followed him with a mixed sense of dread and validation; she didn't want to believe she'd been married to a bad person. And yet . . . For years she'd been convinced she had been doing something to make such trouble in their marriage. Everyone—their friends, his business associates, the whole damn community—had such high regard for Andrew.

It was nearly four o'clock, but still warm even in the shade where the Explorer was parked. Eric put all of the windows down, then got out and opened the rear hatch, returning with two bottles of water.

"Here." He handed one to her and opened the other himself. "It was hot this afternoon, and you're starting to look a little dehydrated."

There he was, trying to save her again. Still, she took the water without comment. He was right; she'd dumped most of her body's moisture into her tears at the cemetery. After taking a drink, she said, "You think Andrew was a monster?" She couldn't believe such words had left her lips.

He huffed. "That's not what I said at all. Andrew had his good points. He just had one serious . . . character flaw in my opinion.

"We were friends in high school."

"I remember," Glory said, not wanting to feel like she didn't know anything at all about the man she'd married. Eric and Andrew had been several years ahead of her, but everyone knew them—every girl who'd passed through puberty dreamed of dating them. "But you two seemed, I don't know, strained over the past years."

Eric nodded. "Andrew needed to be in control of every relationship—romantic and otherwise. It wasn't hard for him to do because everyone looked up to him, everyone wanted to be his friend."

"So what happened to make you see?"

"There were a lot of little things. None alone would mean much, but over the years, when you put them all together . . . well, it became pretty clear to me."

"Such as?"

He looked uncomfortable, as if he didn't want to go into detail. He rested his elbow on the car door and rubbed the back of his neck. "Such as, everything had to be Andrew's idea . . . socially. If someone else brought something up, Andrew managed to change things around enough that he could claim it was his idea. He was actually so good at it that no one seemed to notice or care."

"You said there were things about his romantic relationships . . ."

Eric shifted uncomfortably. There were things that he'd rather not reveal to anyone, least of all Glory.

He said, "More of the same; he had to be in control. Sometimes when he dated a girl, I got the feeling that she didn't actually *want* to be with him. At first I thought they stayed because he was the most popular guy in school, but sometimes it seemed like something . . . I don't know . . . *darker* was going on."

Glory made a little sound in the back of her throat that told him she knew exactly what he was talking about.

He went on, "And sometimes he was . . . paranoid. There really wasn't a better way to describe it. He'd get an idea in his head that a girl was cheating, or that some guy was gunning for his position as team captain in football or basketball, and nothing, I mean nothing, would convince him otherwise."

Eric wanted Glory to know he understood her difficulties in her marital relationship. He *didn't* want to tell her the worst, the most damning of his suspicions. If he told her about Emily MacRady, he'd have to admit his own contribution to Andrew's being able to get away with a very dangerous act of revenge.

Glory was quiet for a long while. When she spoke, her voice was so soft that he had to strain to hear. "There were days when I thought I was crazy. Everyone thought Andrew was perfect, that we had the perfect marriage. I thought there had to be something wrong with me—I wasn't trying hard enough, you know?"

"That was another thing Andrew was good at, making other people think problems were their fault." He wanted to reach out and touch her, to tell her Andrew was a bastard, and she was just one of his silent victims. But that wasn't what she needed. She needed time to think.

He was about to suggest he follow her to Tula's to make sure she got home safely, when she said, in a voice so distant he wasn't sure if she was talking to herself or speaking to him, "I was going to leave him." She continued to stare out the windshield. "I'd told him the day of the fire."

Eric's gut turned over. That was *not* what he wanted to hear. It opened up a whole realm of nasty possibilities—possibilities he should have dealt with eighteen months ago.

Glory had declined Eric's offer to drive her home. He'd been a true friend this afternoon, something she valued as much as his intimacy as a lover. He'd instinctively known that while she needed the comfort of his nearness, she also needed to deal with her thoughts and feelings privately.

Bits and pieces of the past had filtered into her consciousness all afternoon. Now she'd pieced together most of what happened the day of the fire. Even her time in the hospital afterward was becoming clearer.

After Eric put her in her own car and kissed her cheek good-bye, she knew there was one more stop that she had to make before going back to the hollow.

Several minutes later, she pulled up in the circular drive at the elder Harrisons' spacious home. Ovella wouldn't welcome an unannounced visit—especially since they had planned a specific time on Sunday. But it wasn't Ovella she needed to see.

While Ovella had had severe reservations about Andrew's marriage to Glory, Walt had been the polar opposite. He'd welcomed her as a daughter; in fact, he willingly filled in for the father she'd lost as a young child—he even walked her down the aisle.

It wasn't quite five o'clock, and Walt's car wasn't in the drive. Glory got out of the car with a prayer that Walt's car was in the garage and he was home.

She owed him. That had become especially clear this afternoon as she'd remembered that he had been the first person to show up at the hospital emergency room. It had been Walt who had held her hand and grieved with her when the doctor told her that the baby had no heartbeat. Even after Granny had arrived, he'd stayed. Even after he'd heard his own child was dead, he'd stayed. He'd stayed with Glory until the grandchild he'd been so anxious to have was delivered, stillborn.

And Glory had never thanked him. She couldn't let another day go by without telling him what it meant to her—and apologize for being so weak that she hadn't recalled his extraordinary strength and kindness until now.

At the thick oak front door her stomach flipped. It had been a long time since she'd stood on this threshold. She squared her shoulders and rang the bell.

When Ovella opened the door and looked Glory up and down with surprised concern, she realized what a mess she must be. She hadn't even taken a look in the rearview mirror before she came here.

"I'm sorry to barge in like this . . . I . . . I was hoping Walt was home."

Ovella, ever the consummate hostess, recovered quickly from her surprise. "He isn't home yet, but should be soon." She stepped back and opened the door wider. "Please, come in."

Ovella guided her into the living room. Glory was somewhat disappointed they hadn't gone to the back of the house, to the comfortable kitchen and family room. The message was clear; she was a guest in this house, not family.

They sat down, Ovella in the wing chair and Glory on the pristine white sofa.

Ovella said, "I have to admit, I'm surprised to see you. I thought we'd agreed on Sunday afternoon."

As always, Ovella made Glory feel like a bumpkin with no manners. "Yes, we did. And I'm sorry for just showing up like this, but I have some things on my mind and really need to talk to Walt."

"I see."

"Not that I didn't want to see you, too," Glory added, much too late from the look in Ovella's eyes. "But I would have waited as we'd planned . . ."

"Of course. Would you like something to drink? Iced tea, perhaps? You look dreadfully wrung out, dear."

"Tea would be very nice, thank you." Glory felt as uncomfortable if she were in an audience with the president.

Ovella smoothed her hands over the knees of her linen slacks. "I'll be right back."

Glory offered her a smile as she got up and left the room. What Glory had felt like saying was, *Don't hurry.*

While Ovella was gone, Glory got up and looked at the collection of photographs arranged on the grand piano, a new addition since she'd last been here. It was nothing short of a shrine to Andrew; all that was missing were little lighted votive candles.

The photos ranged from Andrew's birth, documenting every stage of his life up until an awards banquet a week before his death. There were shots of Andrew and his parents, Andrew and his football team, Andrew and his prom date, Andrew on a fishing trip, Andrew with his buddies at college graduation, Andrew and the mayor of Dawson, Andrew seated at his desk in the president's office at the paper mill, Andrew and a U.S. senator, Andrew toasting his parent's thirty-fifth wedding anniversary—but not a single photo of Andrew and Glory.

She'd known Ovella had little love for her, but until this very moment, Glory hadn't realized she'd held no place in this family—or in Andrew's life—as far as her mother-in-law was concerned. Glory had thought herself beyond being hurt by rejection from Ovella Harrison. She was wrong.

She turned her back on the display, determined not to allow negative feelings to interfere with her visit with Walt. As she moved back toward the sofa, she caught a glimpse of herself in the mirror over the fireplace mantel. It was worse then she'd imagined. Much worse. She had puffy, bloodshot, raccoon eyes from crying without the benefit of waterproof mascara. Her hair was limp from the heat and humidity. Her skin was pale enough that it looked translucent. Stepping closer to the mirror, she swiped a finger under her eyes trying to get rid of some of the mascara. It didn't help.

She didn't want to greet Walt this way. She picked up her purse and made her way to the powder room. If Ovella was offended that she didn't ask, tough.

As Glory stepped into the half bath, she thought she heard the back door open and close. She hurried to get her face washed, thinking Walt had come home.

After scrubbing with scented hand soap and mopping her smeared mascara with a tissue, Glory looked like Plain Jane but at least no longer like local wildlife. She applied ChapStick—the only thing even close to a cosmetic in her purse, and stepped back out into the hall.

She listened for voices, to see if Ovella and Walt were still in the kitchen, or in the living room. She didn't hear anything except the ticking of the antique grandfather clock in the entry hall and the purr of the central air-conditioning. Upon returning to the living room, she saw Ovella and two glasses of iced tea, but no Walt.

"There you are, dear," Ovella said. "I was getting worried. But I see you look much better."

Glory tucked a strand of hair self-consciously behind her ear. "I didn't realize what a mess I was. It's been a rough day."

"I can see that."

"I thought I heard Walt come in," Glory said.

Ovella cocked her head slightly and said, "No. He hasn't come home yet." She got up and handed Glory a glass of tea. "Here, have something to drink. You'll feel better."

Disappointed that Walt hadn't arrived to save her from one-on-one conversation with Ovella, Glory took the glass and sat back on the sofa.

A few strained seconds passed while they both sipped their tea.

When Glory couldn't stand it anymore, she broke the silence. "I don't know if you know why I came back."

Ovella set her tea on a coaster and raised a brow. "I did hear that Tula was having some health problems. I assumed that was what brought you back after all this time."

Glory looked at the glass in her hands for a moment. Then she said, "Yes. It's her eyesight."

Ovella nodded sympathetically. Then she said in a neutral tone, "I understand you're seeing Eric Wilson."

Glory's head snapped up. "Not exactly. We've run into one another because Gran watches his son, that's all."

"Oh."

Glory wanted to get this conversation steered in another direction. "I came by to explain why I spent so long away; I'd like to wait until Walt comes ho—"

"Do I see Glory's car in the drive?" Walt nearly shouted as he entered the house through the kitchen door.

Glory set down her glass on the coaster Ovella had placed next to her and jumped off the sofa. When Walt appeared in the living room door, grinning from ear to ear with his arms spread wide, she hurried into his embrace.

He wrapped his arms around her tightly. "How's my girl?"

She pulled slightly away so she could look into his eyes. "With a welcome like that, how could I be anything but great?" She kissed his cheek.

He wrapped an arm around Glory's shoulders and escorted her back into the living room. "Mother, isn't it good to have our girl home?"

Ovella smiled. "Glory was just about to explain why she's stayed away so long."

Walt eyed the iced-tea glasses. "I could use one of those, Mother."

"Of course. I'll be right back." She looked at Glory. "Don't start your story without me."

As soon as she was out of the room, Glory said, "While Ovella's in the kitchen, I want to tell you how much it meant to me to have you with me at the hospital that night. I know it's taken me far too long to thank you. It had to be a horrible night for you too, but you made me feel like I was the only thing that mattered."

He glanced toward the door, then looked back at Glory. "It's very considerate of you not to bring this up in front of Ovella. She's still having such a hard time. She's practically keeping the Dixie Bee in business single-handedly; she takes fresh flowers to the cemetery every other day." He shook his head, as if wishing things were different. Then he took Glory's hand and smiled. "And there's absolutely no reason to thank me. I was right where I wanted to be. You're family—and family sticks together when things get rough."

"Still—"

"Here you are, dear." Ovella swept into the room as gently as a breeze.

Walt took the glass from her with an appreciative smile, then took a long drink. "Now that's what a man needs after a long, hot day at the plant."

As Ovella sat down, she said to Glory, "I did tell you that Walt had to come out of retirement, didn't I?"

Glory nodded.

"Eh, retirement is for old folks," Walt said with a grin. "I was getting so bored, I thought I'd dry up. It's been good for me."

Ovella agreed, "Of course it has. Just look at that healthy glow." She reached across the small space and patted his knee.

Glory smiled at the genuine affection that passed between her in-laws; it showed in their smiles and glittered in their eyes. It was hard to believe that a couple who showed such respect for one another had raised a son who turned out to be a husband like Andrew.

"I know I've just dropped in, so I won't keep you," Glory said. "I just wanted you both to know that I'm sorry if my staying away for so long hurt either one of you. I was an emotional wreck when I left. The longer I stayed away, the harder it was to think about coming back." She looked at her hands in her lap. "I probably should have stayed and faced the . . . changes in my life."

"So you're staying now?" Walt said hopefully.

"I'm not sure. I think I might. Granny's eyesight is failing . . . I guess I'm trying to take stock and actually plan a future instead of blowing on the wind."

"That's a very wise idea," Ovella said.

Walt added, with a wink and a smile, "As long as that plan involves staying in Dawson. There's probably a position in my office, if you're looking for good, steady work."

"Now, Walter, don't push," Ovella said softly.

Glory stood. "I'll keep that in mind," she said, with a little laugh. Walt, bless his heart, had to know she wasn't qualified for any type of corporate work. But she had no doubt he was sincere in his offer. After all, Walt was the one who tried to get Andrew's will overturned to make her the beneficiary. Glory had put a stop to that immediately. Since then, he'd been making discreet offers of financial assistance.

"Do you have to rush off?" Walt asked. "Stay for dinner."

"Yes," Ovella chimed in. "Please. We'll eat on the screened porch."

"Thank you, but I should be getting home. I've been gone for hours, and Granny has just had another episode with her eye. I shouldn't have left her this long."

Walt and Ovella walked her to the front door. Walt gave her a solid hug and Ovella air-kissed her cheek.

Glory said, as she opened the door, "Now that I've barged in this evening, I won't bother you on Sunday."

"Don't be silly. You're welcome anytime." Ovella sounded entirely sincere. "Sunday will be no problem. You might like to bring a suit and swim."

"Thank you. I appreciate that. But Granny has arranged a family dinner after church. I was going to have to duck out on the cleanup detail to come. Can we make it another time?"

"We understand," Walt said. "Let's get together some-time next week for dinner."

"Oh, yes, that'd be lovely," Ovella agreed.

"Sure. Give me a call."

Glory got in her car and an innocent comment Walt made suddenly rang clearly in her mind, " . . . *she takes fresh flowers to the cemetery every other day.*"

As Glory drove away, she wondered why there hadn't been any on the baby's grave.

Chapter Nineteen

❀

As GLORY TURNED onto the lane that led to Granny's house, she was glad it was six-thirty; the last thing she wanted was to finish this day by running into Eric's ex, especially since she'd managed not to cross paths with Jill so far. It was silly to feel guilty for sleeping with Eric; he and Jill were divorced. But after all of the emotional unbalance of the day, Glory didn't think she was prepared to throw those feelings into the mix.

As she rounded the curve, her heart sank when she saw an unfamiliar car parked in front of Granny's house.

To be safe, Glory decided to turn around, head back to the road, and take a little drive. Even if it wasn't Jill inside with Granny, Glory wasn't in a social mood.

Just as she slowed to a stop so she could make a U-turn, Jill came out of the house leading Scott by the hand. She looked directly at Glory's car. *Crap.*

Jill didn't get in her car; she just stood there, looking expectantly in Glory's direction. There was nothing to do but drive on up to the house.

Before Glory got out of the car, she took one quick glance in the rearview mirror, knowing full well what a mess she was. She squelched the groan her reflection prompted. There hadn't been a miracle makeover while she'd driven to the hollow.

Feeling like the ugly stepsister to Jill's Cinderella, Glory got out.

Jill smiled her brilliant cheerleader smile. Glory responded with what she was certain appeared to be a washed-out, haggard one of her own.

Jill said, "Hello, Glory. It's been a long time."

"It has—a very long time." In fact, Glory couldn't remember Jill ever speaking to her—certainly not when they'd been Jill Landry and Glory Johnston. It seemed that Jill had given her a cordial hello or two after she'd become Glory Harrison.

"Are you glad to be home again?" Jill asked amiably. "I know living out here is probably much more comfortable for you than the Harrisons' mansion in town."

Although the pleasantly cloaked dig rankled, Glory said smoothly, "I came home for Granny. It wouldn't make sense to be staying in town."

"Of course, I just meant . . . well, you know, Mother and Ovella are such dear friends . . . the Harrisons were devastated when Andrew was killed. It would be a daily reminder if you were in the house. And I know you and Ovella aren't exactly cut from the same cloth."

"You mean she doesn't like me." *How about a "Sorry about your husband and baby"?*

"Now I didn't say that. I just meant the Harrisons are from a different world than the rest of us. And it has to be especially awkward for you—without Andrew as a buffer."

At least Jill included herself in the great unwashed masses, Glory thought. "We get along all right. In fact, I was just there for a visit."

Jill's eyes widened before she caught herself and schooled her features. "You came straight from there?"

Glory touched her hair and decided to keep this from dragging into an even more cumbersome discussion. "Yep. I was quite a contrast to Ovella's Estée Lauder finish."

Jill burst out laughing, a genuine laugh, not one manufactured for politeness. Which caused her to go up a notch on Glory's scale in likability.

Jill said, "Oh, I can just see it now! Did she actually allow you to sit on the furniture?"

"The white sofa in the living room, actually. I have to admit, I didn't exactly give her the opportunity to stop me—or get a garbage bag for me to sit on." Glory was laughing, too. It felt good, like a warm spring rain after a long, bitter winter.

When their laughter died down, Glory made a point of speaking to Scott, who was standing like a statue holding his mother's hand. "Hi, Scott. Did you have a good afternoon with Lady?"

At mention of the dog's name, Glory could swear she saw a flicker in the little boy's eyes. But just as quickly as it came, it was gone.

Jill said, "Those puppies are just darling. If I didn't have to be at work all day, I'd think about taking one."

"You know, it might not be a bad idea to think about a dog for Scott. I was just reading an article about companion dogs for children with special needs."

Instantly, Glory could see she'd said the wrong thing.

Jill said, "Scott isn't a child 'with special needs.'"

"I didn't mean . . . it's just that he seems to enjoy being with Lady. He's more—animated around her."

"All little boys like dogs."

Glory thought most three-year-olds preferred active, playful, yipping puppies to a sedate older dog like Lady, but she kept that thought to herself. "He does seem to like Lady. He's started following her around the house."

"Really, there's nothing wrong with Scott. Obviously, Eric has said something to color your thinking." Before Glory could say anything, Jill went on, "I'm glad I agreed to take him to a specialist, just to have all this nonsense put to rest." Jill's gaze sharpened. "If you had children, you'd understand."

She didn't seem to notice Glory flinch.

Jill continued, "They're all so unique and develop at their own pace. Scott's life has been upset by the divorce. I think we made a serious mistake in thinking he was too young for it to affect him. It would probably be best for Scott if Eric and I reconcile; in fact, we're talking about it." Her blue eyes showed neither malice nor calculation.

Eric and Jill were talking about getting back together? It felt as if Jill had given Glory a slap across the face followed by a backhanded return; a one-two punch. Eric had said they were coming to an agreement on what to do for Scott—but reconciliation?

It took Glory a second to recover. "I'm sure you'll do whatever needs to be done for your son." Her voice sounded wooden, but she couldn't help it.

"Well," Jill said cheerily, "I shouldn't keep you. Tula had dinner ready to put on the table when I came out." She led Scott to the driver's side and opened the rear passenger door.

Glory studied her, trying to put this conversation in some perspective. Outwardly Jill had been pleasant enough. Had there been spiteful undercurrents? Or was that just Glory's guilt and fatigue coloring Jill's statements?

Glory supposed it really didn't matter. The fact was, Jill and Eric were considering reconciliation and Glory felt as though the last prop holding her upright had just been knocked out from under her. She'd made a huge mistake in allowing herself to rely on someone else. She'd told him he couldn't save her; but suddenly she realized just how much she'd grown to count on him to do just that.

"Good night, then," Glory managed. "Have a nice weekend."

Jill's head popped back up and she looked across the top of the car. "Oh, we're going to have a great weekend! Eric and I are taking Scott on a picnic tomorrow afternoon."

With a grimace that she hoped appeared to be a smile, Glory waved and went inside. A few minutes later she heard Jill's car start and roll slowly away from the house.

"Why, child, you look like the wrong side of a bad Saturday night," Gran said when Glory entered the kitchen.

"It's been a long afternoon. I'll tell you about it later. Right now I need a shower. You go ahead and eat." As she passed through the kitchen, she kissed Gran's cheek and asked, "Did Charlie stop by this afternoon?"

Granny stiffened. "Yes, and you got no business sendin' people to check up on me."

"He wasn't checking up on you. He was supposed to be asking what he could do to help set up for the reunion on Sunday."

"He asked—and I weren't born yesterday, missy. I seen what you were up to."

"Oh, Gran," Glory said with a chuckle. "Stop being so prickly."

As she went up the stairs, she heard her grandmother still sputtering in the kitchen.

After a shower that left her feeling more wrung out than refreshed, Glory found Granny on the porch swing. The air was thick and heavy, the promise of a storm ripe in the air.

"Your dinner's on a plate in the refrigerator," Gran said when Glory stepped onto the porch.

"I'm too tired to eat. I'll save it for tomorrow." Glory went and sat beside her grandmother on the swing.

"Don't do nobody any good to starve yourself. Bet you didn't eat no lunch either."

Glory put an arm around Gran's shoulders. "I don't have the strength to chew and swallow. And I did eat. At Brewster's Coffee Shop when I was running errands in town."

Granny cast a skeptical glance her way.

"Really, I did. A club sandwich. You can call them and ask."

They swung gently in silence for a few minutes. Then Granny said, "Did you go see Andrew?"

Glory nodded.

"And did it help?"

Glory lifted a shoulder. "In some ways. I told him some things that needed to be said." The depths to which she'd allowed her marriage to deteriorate shamed her. She looked out across the yard, soft in the folds of twilight, and said softly, "I was going to leave him, Gran."

Granny gave a short, quick nod. "Don't believe in breakin' vows given in God's church."

Glory's heart sank even lower.

She was feeling very bleak until Granny added, "But sometimes it's got to be done." Granny took Glory's hand and squeezed tightly. "There was somethin' dark inside that boy, down beneath all the shine he put on for ever'body to see. I seen it the first time I laid eyes on him."

Glory turned her surprised gaze on Granny. "Why didn't you say something back then?"

"You was in love. Sayin' something like that would only have made you mad at me—made you more set on him than ever."

Glory nearly denied it, but the truth of the matter was, Granny was right. She'd been barely seventeen when she started dating Andrew. He'd been home for summer break from college. She'd been charmed and infatuated with him from the start. She would no more have heeded Granny's warning than if she'd warned Glory of alien abductions.

"Well, let's make a pact," Glory said. "If you see me about to do something so foolish again in the future, promise me you'll speak up—and I promise I'll listen."

Granny chuckled. "You say that now." Then she patted Glory's leg. "I'm perty sure you've learned a lot since you was seventeen."

"Good God, let's hope."

"Don't use the Lord's name in vain, missy."

Glory smiled inwardly and leaned her head against Granny's. "Yes, ma'am."

Heat lightning blinked in the sky. A tiny, humid breeze ruffled the leaves.

"Gonna be a storm tonight," Granny said as she got up. "Don't forget to close your car windas afore you come up to bed."

Glory nodded. "Good night, Gran. And thank you."

Granny stopped at the front door. "What for?"

"For being here for me. For letting me come to grips with things at my own pace. I don't think I could have come back here if it weren't for you."

Granny waved a hand in the air. "Your questions woulda brought you back sooner or later. That's the thing about unfinished business—always nags 'til it's done." She opened the screen. "Don't forget them windas."

Glory listened to Granny climb the creaky stairs, then close the door to her bedroom. It was full dark; Gran, no matter how tired she was, refused to go to bed before full dark. She used to stay up reading. But Glory noticed there were no books piled on Gran's nightstand; her eyesight had grown too poor for small print. How would Granny make a living? For that matter, how would she?

As Glory sat rocking in the swing, the article she'd read in the doctor's office teased her mind. She'd worked with animals. Granny had lived in the hills her entire life. There was a wealth of practical experience there. Maybe they could find some venture to go into together.

The idea of service and companion dogs began to catch fire. There was such need. Just look at the difference in Scott when he was with Lady. Of course, Glory would require additional training. Perhaps there were grants available to subsidize funding for such a project. Maybe they could even breed the dogs for optimum temperament and adaptability. And when the time came, Granny might benefit from a companion dog; if she was already in the business, she'd be much less resistant to the idea.

In spite of Glory's fatigue, a little humming ball of excitement began to vibrate in her chest. She'd have to do a little legwork next week and see how feasible it would be.

Thunder rumbled in the distance. Tired to the marrow of her bones, Glory went inside to get her car keys so she could close the car windows. She'd also left her purse in the car, having put it on the floor of the backseat—just like Andrew had always told her to do to prevent someone from snatching it off the seat.

She walked barefoot across the dewy grass, then gingerly across the crushed stone that made up Granny's drive. Approaching the car from the passenger side, she opened the back door to pick up her purse before she went to the other side to close the windows.

In the illumination of the dome light, she picked up her purse and saw something white under it. Having lived with Andrew for years, she had learned never to leave clutter in her car.

Alarm bells sounded in her head as she reached down and picked it up.

It was a T-shirt with a large fire department logo on the back. Beneath that it read, NATIONAL FIRE PREVENTION WEEK.

The Dawson Fire Department had handed these out a few years ago. Almost everyone in town had one. How had it gotten in her car?

When she turned the shirt over and held it beneath the light, she saw what she knew she would, a printed picture of the Dawson firefighters with the caption, "We protect our families with smoke detectors. Do you?"

But there was an addition. To the side of the picture there were words scribbled in black marker. She squinted to make out what they said. When she figured it out, she also saw the other alteration to the shirt.

She dropped it as if it had burst into flames in her hands. She stepped back from the car, her heart taking startled flight.

A burned hole showed where Eric's face should have been; and to the side the handwritten note: *Are you going to kill him too?*

Eric roamed his empty duplex, as tense as the approaching storm front. The day of the fire, Glory had told Andrew she was leaving him. Had Eric known that at the time, it certainly would have made him look at things differently.

Even so, that didn't change the facts of the fire. And would he have pushed Glory harder to remember considering her condition and the available evidence? Andrew's body had been burned in his bed—after the carbon monoxide had killed him. Glory had been beside the back door. It didn't take a fire investigator to see what that indicated. If Glory knew he suspected something other than an accidental fire, would she make the same conjecture? What would that do to her?

Why couldn't she just let the past go and move toward the future? Nothing was going to undo the tragic outcome of that night. It wasn't going to serve any good purpose to drag all of the hurt and suspicion back out into the light when, short of a confession by an arsonist, there could be no other ruling on the cause.

He thought of the two accusatory messages Glory had received. Someone else out there had similar thoughts and wanted Glory . . . what, upset? To leave Dawson? To confess to arson and murder?

Or was there something more dangerous lurking in someone's mind. Was there someone out there who wanted to cause Glory physical harm? He shook his head. Then why all of the warnings? That didn't make sense. This was a psychological battle being waged.

How much pain could one woman take without breaking? When he'd seen her today at the ruins of her old home, he'd wanted to take her in his arms and protect her from all of the pain of the past. But there was no way to block that from her. He knew Glory was a strong woman, stronger than even she suspected. She didn't really *need* his protection, no matter how much he wanted her to.

He didn't want to wait until Sunday to see her again. He wished he hadn't agreed to the picnic with Jill tomorrow; Scott probably wouldn't like all of the commotion of the park on a busy Saturday afternoon. But Eric didn't want to set Jill at odds with him again. Scott needed to get to a doctor who could help him—the sooner the better. And it was going to take her full cooperation to ensure that a treatment plan was followed through. If that meant a semimiserable afternoon in the park, so be it.

He'd like to drive out to the hollow right now. But Glory didn't need Tula asking if there was something going on between him and Glory. So instead of taking Glory on a long sultry walk before the storm, he paced.

He meant what he'd told her; he didn't want to make her life more complicated. But it appeared the only way he could be *in* her life was going to cause serious complications.

Like an irresponsible child, he wanted all of this just to go away and leave him and Glory alone to discover each other fully. He could love her; it would be so easy—if only the rest of the world would stop erecting roadblocks.

Glory stuffed the T-shirt in the trunk of her car, fearing Granny might find it. Then she went inside and locked all of the doors and closed the first-floor windows. She shut off all of the downstairs lights and turned on both the front and back porch lights. For several minutes she prowled from window to window, trying to see if there was anything moving near the house.

Once she felt sure there weren't immediate dangers lurking in the bushes, she fought the urge to call Eric. In fact, she had the phone in her hand more than once. But she told herself that she had to stop expecting him to hold her hand every time she suffered a fresh blow.

She made the rounds of all the windows again. Nothing stirred in the shadowy yard.

Maybe she'd call Eric just to hear his voice. She wouldn't tell him about her visit with Walt and Ovella, or her unsettling conversation with Jill, or this latest message. It would calm her just to speak with him.

Who was she kidding? The second she heard his voice her emotions would shine through.

That's it. She was going to bed—as far away from Granny's kitchen telephone as possible.

Before she went upstairs, she checked on Lady and the puppies. When Glory entered the room, Lady lifted her head but didn't get up from where her pups slept jumbled together, pressed close to her body. The little ones were indistinguishable, just one mass of lumpy tan fur. All except for the dark one, the runt, a male Glory had taken a particular liking to. He always stuck out in the pile.

She whispered, "It's all right, girl. Just checking."

Lady laid her head back on her paws and closed her eyes, issuing a sigh that clearly said motherhood was exhausting.

Glory got quietly ready for bed by the glow of the night-light in the bathroom. She was too spooked to turn on lights; unable to shake the feeling of being watched.

She lay there in the sticky heat, watching the ceiling flash bright white in the intermittent lightning, hearing the storm inch slowly eastward, with her thoughts in a turmoil.

Who had put that shirt in her car? Someone who knew she had a . . . connection . . . with Eric. Rumors did fly in a small town. She and Eric had been seen together plenty; on his motorcycle, at the hospital, at the body shop, even at the doctor's office. She supposed someone might have seen her car parked in front of his house night before last. Too bad there were so many varied opportunities that it didn't really narrow the field of suspects.

Three. Now there had been three taunting messages, each one becoming more specific, more hateful.

"Glory?" Granny called from down the hallway.

She got up and hurried to Granny's room. Gran met her at the doorway.

They both said at the same time, "You all right?"

Then they both answered, "Yes."

This brought a chuckle from both women. Then Granny said, "I just got this peculiar feelin'."

"It's the storm coming, Gran. You always said it had an effect on you."

"Reckon it could be. It's hotter'n Hades, ain't it?"

"It'll be cooler by morning. The storm can't be that far off now."

"Count between the flash and the thunder like I taught you, and you'll know for sure." Granny smiled and headed back to her bed.

Glory watched her for a moment from the doorway, realizing just how much of her life had been influenced by this extraordinary woman. "'Night, Gran."

"If'n you get scairt when the storm hits, you can come and get in bed with me," Granny said lightly. Many a summer night when sleeping over at Granny's, Glory had come running into this room and climbed into bed between Granny and Pap.

How could she tell her grandmother that she was scared, but not of the storm? And Glory didn't think hiding in bed next to her 110-pound grandmother was going to save her this time.

"Okay, thanks." With effort, she matched Granny's tone. "'Night, Gran. Love you."

"Love you, too, Mornin' Glory."

When Glory got back in bed, she was nearly afraid to allow her thoughts to return to her problems; Granny was so sensitive to Glory's moods and all. But if she didn't try to figure out where the notes were coming from, she'd think about Eric. And she wasn't prepared to delve into that particular dilemma right now.

So she thought about the exposure her car had had today; where and when that shirt could have been put inside it. She had the only recent-model Volvo in town, so it was easy for anyone to spot. She'd never locked her car doors in Dawson, even when Andrew had been alive to chastise her. Besides, it had been so hot today that she'd also left the windows partially open.

The car had been parked on the square for over an hour.

She'd stopped at the gas station at the edge of town before she'd gone to the cemetery. They didn't have pay-at-the-pump, so she'd had to go inside.

At the cemetery her car had always been within her sight. Then it had been safely in the Harrisons' drive. After that on the dead-end road where she used to live.

It boiled down to the fact that anyone could have put the shirt in there, at almost any time. It could even have been put there the night she'd gone to Eric's. She normally just reached behind the seat to drop or retrieve her purse. It was a fluke that she opened the back door tonight.

Could someone have slipped it inside while the car was parked here?

That thought made the creepy feeling that she was being watched come back.

The heat in the house served to make her frustration worse. If only that storm would hit and stir up the air. Glory flopped her damp body from one side to the other, kicking off the sheet.

She was just going to have to be ultra-aware of everything around her from now on. Be vigilant. That was the only way she'd ever be able to narrow down who was doing this to her. The question of why would have to wait until she found out who.

You know why. You started that fire.

"No." She pulled her pillow over her ears, even though the accusing voice came from inside her head.

At some point she finally began to relax. She hung in that place between true sleep and awareness, the place where the body is quiet but the mind as active as a beehive. Where near dreams mix with reality in odd and sometimes uncanny ways.

She was back at the cemetery. Suddenly hundreds and hundreds of flowers began to fall from the sky, a blizzard of color and fragrance. Glory had to bat them away in order to see. When she looked down to where they were accumulating on the ground, she saw they'd been drawn like a magnet to Andrew's grave, mounding nearly waist high. But not a single petal rested on baby Clarice's grave.

Eric arrived at Jill's at twelve on the nose. In his pocket he had several typed pages of information on doctors and clinics they needed to discuss. As he approached the door, he had such a dichotomy of feelings that he was nearly ashamed of himself. On one hand, this was the opportunity he'd been seeking for weeks; they were finally going to take steps to discover what their son needed. Yet, he couldn't help but feel slightly resentful of Jill's manipulation. They had never taken Scott to the park; they rarely did more together with him than hand him from one to the other. That realization made him feel even guiltier. Maybe Jill had a point; Scott needed more of a sense of security and family than they were giving him.

He rang the doorbell.

She opened the door with a smile. "Hi, come on in. We're not quite ready."

He wanted to tell her to hurry the hell up. The longer it took them to get to the park, the later it would be when they got back. Although it was Saturday, he had hoped to make a few inquiries and phone calls after they decided which doctor they were going to start with. It seemed each day of delay was a day that they would have to overcome later.

Jill disappeared into the kitchen. "I just have a couple of things to finish up, then we can go. Scottie's been such a good boy this morning. He's been playing and watching cartoons, letting Mommy get things ready."

Eric didn't respond.

Scott sat in front of the television, which was tuned to Bugs Bunny. Jill was deluding herself thinking he was actually watching it. It was as clear as day to Eric that Scott was focused on circling his pirate boat, not even looking up when there was a boom or a crash on the TV.

Eric knelt beside his son, hoping to see that little glimmer of response he'd experienced yesterday. "Hi, buddy."

Scott just spun the boat.

Autism. Eric finally put a name to his fear. There were so many signs; still, he hoped against hope that the ultimate diagnosis would be different.

He picked up his son. Scott kept the boat in his hand and nestled his face in the curve of Eric's neck. Eric's thoughts moved away from denial; there were new treatments and therapies, so much more hope than ever before for children with autism.

"We're gonna get you some help, buddy. Things are going to be better."

It was nearly twenty minutes later when they got to the park and began to unload all of the paraphernalia Jill insisted they needed for their picnic. What Eric had thought would be a quick brown-bag lunch at one of the park tables was turning out to be an "event," complete with linen napkins, real silverware, flowers, and enough chilled drinks in the cooler to last all afternoon. When she pulled the food out of the picnic hamper, it wasn't ham sandwiches and chips; Jill had prepared an elegant meal, complete with shrimp cocktail.

"I just thought we should do something nice," she said when Eric eyed the spread. "This should be a new beginning for the three of us."

A warning shimmered beneath Eric's skin. Taken with her announcement that she wasn't seeing Jason any longer, that comment worried him. But it made no sense at all that Jill was insinuating they get back together—she'd shot down every attempt he'd made to save their marriage. It was far too late.

He pulled out his paper with the list of doctors. "I've done some research. This is the list of doctors that I think would be best for evaluating Scott. I'll just tell you a little about what I know of each of them, then we can decide where to begin. Of course, some of these evaluations take several days, so you might need to arrange time away from wo—"

She brushed the paper away, pushing it back toward him. "Let's just have a nice lunch first. Scottie's PBB sandwich is in that Tupperware." She pointed toward the basket. "Can you get it out for him? He's probably getting hungry."

Eric wanted to say, *The fact that our near three-year-old son can't tell us he's hungry tells me we don't have time to waste eating grapes and fancy cheese and shrimp cocktail.* But he held his tongue.

"Here's your sandwich, buddy." Scott didn't pick it up. "Aren't you hungry?" Eric prompted.

"He'll eat in a few minutes. I'm sure he's excited," Jill said cheerily. "This is our first picnic in the park, after all."

Again, Eric bit his tongue and just put a comforting hand on his son's back.

She laid out the food in what must have been an attractive display. Eric was too preoccupied watching Scott for signs of distress to enjoy the taste of anything—or join in the small talk Jill was attempting.

After twenty minutes, Scott still hadn't touched his food. When Eric leaned closer, that growling purr was coming from deep in his son's throat.

Eric was about to comment on it and segue into the topic that had brought him here when Jill said, "I finally saw Glory out at Tula's last night." She popped a grape into her mouth. "She was a total mess."

Eric sat up straighter. "What do you mean?"

Jill looked at him for a second. "Well, it was obvious she'd been crying. Tula said she'd been to the cemetery. You would think after all this time she'd have cried herself out. She looked old and tired."

"She's younger than you." The words were out before Eric thought. But it was her other comment that ignited his anger. "Just how long do you think a mother should grieve for her child? Tell me, Jill, what's the socially acceptable limit?"

"No need to get nasty. I was just making an observation." Then her gaze sharpened on him. "What makes you so sure she was crying over the baby? Her husband is dead, too. And she didn't even know that baby."

It astounded him that Jill, after delivering a child from her own body, could speak so callously. "We didn't love Scott any less before he was born."

"Of course we didn't! But Glory's . . . situation was much different."

"What do you mean?" he asked, now wary of the uneven ground on which he was treading. There was a look in Jill's eye that bordered on jealousy—he hoped he was misreading her.

"I shouldn't gossip. It's over and done. There's no baby and no husband, so it shouldn't matter anymore."

Eric was torn between asking her to explain and punching her in the mouth.

Jill sighed. "You know Mother and Ovella are the dearest of friends. And poor Ovella, she's lived with the truth so long in silence . . . she's an amazingly strong woman."

It was clear there would be no avoiding finishing this conversation. "Yes. It's terrible that she lost her only child."

Jill glanced around, as if to make sure no one was within listening range, and lowered her voice. "It's not just that—though that would certainly be enough to break most women. Ovella hinted to Mother that the baby wasn't Andrew's."

Eric's blood felt like molten lava. First of all, he didn't want to believe it. Second . . . "You sitting there telling me that is a bit like the pot calling the kettle black, don't you think?"

She stiffened. "I *did not* try to foist another man's baby on you!"

He looked her in the eye and raised a brow. "Well, now we're just quibbling over details, aren't we?"

"I didn't ask you here to fight about Glory Harrison. Where is that list of doctors?"

Jill had to admit, even she'd had doubts about that claim. Her mother had said that Ovella *hinted* concern about Andrew's marriage. Her mother had "felt certain" it had been about Glory, knowing "the stock she came from." Andrew had been such a perfect husband. Planting the seed in Eric's mind might just scare him away from the woman.

She sat closer to Eric as he shared the information about several specialists and clinics with her, wishing she'd never agreed to this. The more he talked, the more frightened she got. In the end, she picked Duke University, mainly because it was far enough away that it would require an overnight stay. They could live like a family, and Eric would see how much they all needed to be together.

As she packed up the picnic, Eric asked, "Can I have Scott on Sunday?"

Her hands stilled. "Why?"

"Tula invited us to a family reunion at her place."

"I could never get you to go to *my* family reunion!"

Eric shifted impatiently. "Your family reunion was in Michigan. You asked *once*, and I couldn't get away from work." Before she could respond, he added, "I thought it might be good for Scott to be around other kids."

"He's around other kids at school."

Eric put his hands on his hips. "What's the big deal? You normally ask me to take him one of the days on your weekend anyway."

It was hard to come up with a counter to that one. She did, but it was because she had things to do that Scott wouldn't enjoy. Eric always seemed thrilled with the extra time. "Okay. What time?"

She feared his sudden interest in the Baker family reunion had more to do with Glory than Scott. So much for a rumor scaring him off.

Chapter Twenty

❦

As Eric drove out to Tula's Sunday morning, Jill's accusation buzzed in his brain. Could it be true? Could Glory's baby have been fathered by someone else? Not that he would blame her for seeking comfort in the arms of another man, married as she was to such a controlling bastard.

Still, it didn't ring true of the Glory he knew.

However, he thought, the Glory he knew had been out from under Andrew's mental abuse for a year and a half.

A man like Andrew would not have taken a wife's betrayal sitting down. Had Glory been so desperate that she'd been driven to extreme measures to protect herself?

No matter how he looked at it, he couldn't believe Glory had cheated on her husband. Ovella, had she suspected such a thing as her daughter-in-law's carrying another man's child, would never have breathed a word of it to anyone—even her closest friend. People like Ovella worried more about social image than they did about putting food on the table.

He was going to put this out of his mind.

Turning onto Cold Springs Hollow Road, he studied the sky; deep blue with occasional white puffy clouds.

The storm that had passed on Friday night had lifted the heavy humidity. Even the contours of the mountains showed in rare clarity. The sun was hot, but it was pleasant in the shade; a perfect day for a family reunion. A perfect day with Glory. And that was *all* this day was going to be about. No rumors. No doubts.

He'd come early, before Tula would be home from church. As he approached the house, he saw Glory in the yard, setting up a volleyball net—or at least trying to. From where he was, it looked like a battle at fever pitch—and the net was winning.

She looked adorable, in a white T-shirt that showed just a glimpse of skin above her denim shorts. She was bent over, her thick hair completely blocking her face as she tried to set one of the poles in the ground. She was wrestling the thing so intently, he was nearly to the house before she noticed his car.

When she did, she stopped, put her hands on her hips, and blew the hair off her face. The pole beside her fell over. She gave it a dirty look that made Eric laugh out loud.

She met him at his car door when he got out. There was an awkward moment where Eric didn't know exactly what to do. Kiss her? Were there other Bakers lurking around somewhere that she didn't want to know about them?

She touched his cheek and cleared up his confusion. "Hey, you," she said sweetly.

He put his hands on her waist and kissed her gently.

"You're just in time." She gestured toward the net, stakes, string, and poles lying in a jumble in the grass. "I was about to turn that pole into a pretzel."

"Just let me get Scott, then we'll beat it into submission." He opened the back door and lifted Scott from his car seat, then set his little feet on the ground. Scott clutched his pirate boat in one hand and the quilt Tula had made in the other.

"I've put the puppies in their playpen," Glory said. "Maybe Scott would like to sit in there with them while we get this thing put together." She pointed to the ten-foot circle of two-foot-high rabbit fencing. Lady was lounging in the grass just outside the enclosure.

"How about it, big guy?" Eric asked, giving Scott a playful jiggle. "Want to play with the puppies?"

They walked over to the playpen. Eric picked Scott up and stepped over the fence. Then he knelt and the puppies migrated as one bouncy, tumbling mass in their direction. When they started to lick Scott's face, he began to cry.

Eric tried to calm the puppies as he whispered encouraging words in Scott's ear, but Scott grew more tense by the moment.

Just as Eric was ready to give up and get back out, Lady jumped over the fence and put herself between Scott and the puppies.

Scott stopped crying.

Lady nudged her nose under his forearm, getting him to put his hand on her head.

Eric laughed. "Maybe you'd rather sit outside the fence with Lady?"

"Isn't that amazing," Glory said. "I've seen him respond to her like that more than once."

Eric put his hands on his hips and smiled as he watched his son sit contentedly with the dog. "It is something, isn't it? It seems like Lady knows just what she's doing, too."

While Scott and Lady sat beside the playpen safe from puppy attacks, Eric and Glory put up the volleyball net. When it was up and strung tight, Eric said, "There, now that wasn't so hard."

Glory picked up the volleyball and threw it at him, hitting him squarely in the stomach.

He ran and grabbed her around the waist before she could get away. "Watch it, girl, or you'll be blowing up that inflatable jumping thing by yourself."

"And what kind of attitude is that for a hero to take?" She turned in his arms and faced him, sliding her arms around his neck.

The sound of her laugh lightened something inside him. He kissed her again—a serious "I've missed you" kiss, unlike their tentative "hello" kiss. As their lips touched and their bodies pressed closer, he realized just how much he *had* missed her. It had begun the minute she'd driven away from his house on Thursday night. When he'd returned to his living room it had felt as if she had taken all of the warmth and vitality with her when she left.

But, he realized, his joy in her presence, his need to be near her, had started long before that. On the morning after her car accident, she had been the first thing he'd seen when he opened his eyes. He liked that feeling. And, even though there had been no sexual intimacy that night, he liked the feel of her sleeping snuggled against his body, of his arms wrapped around her.

Their relationship seemed so fragile that on Thursday, as he'd watched her drive off into the night, he'd wondered if he dared hope he'd experience waking with her beside him again.

Looking in her eyes now, he believed there was hope.

As he looked closely, he also saw that she looked tired, as if she hadn't been sleeping well.

"Ahem."

Glory jumped guiltily out of Eric's arms.

Charlie stood there with a wily grin on his face. "Am I interrupting?"

"Did you learn to walk on those cat's paws when you were sneaking out of women's bedrooms in the middle of the night?" Glory asked, apparently deciding to fight fire with fire.

Charlie gave a low whistle. "All that piss and vinegar must come from Granny."

With a satisfied-looking smile, Glory said, "Granny hears you talk like that, and you'll see she didn't pass it all on—she saved some to use on foulmouthed grandsons."

Charlie walked over and kissed Glory on the cheek. "No need to get prickly. I won't tell anyone you were making out with the fire chief."

"Did you come to make yourself useful, or just to see if you could get under my skin?" Glory asked.

"Do I have to choose?" Charlie offered a cocky grin.

"Go get the folding tables out of the basement." Glory gave him a playful shove toward the house.

As he walked away, he muttered, "Just as bossy as Granny, too."

When Charlie was out of earshot, Eric asked, "You two always that way with each other?"

"No. Sometimes we're mean." Glory winked and started toward the garage. "I'll get the heavy-duty extension cord. You drag that blower over to the moonwalk."

* * *

By the time they had the turrets to the castle-shaped moonwalk inflated, people were beginning to arrive with covered dishes, lawn chairs, and children.

Granny had come home right after Glory got the extension cord and had taken Scott and Lady into the house with her. She came out now, leading Scott by the hand.

Eric came up to the stoop and lifted Scott into his arms. "Look at all of the kids. Should we go see what they're doing?"

Glory watched, admiring his devotion to his child. He took Scott over to several preschoolers who were playing a very loose version of soccer.

Granny drew her attention when she nearly shouted, "Good gracious! There's your aunt Helen, Glory, come all the way from Chattanooga." Granny hurried to give her daughter a hug. "I thought you weren't coming."

The two women eased out of their embrace and Helen moved toward Glory. "And miss all this fun! I traded shifts at the hospital. Have to do a twelve-hour on Monday, but it'll be worth it. Nobody has reunions like the Bakers." She hugged Glory and whispered into her ear, "How's my favorite niece?"

Glory rarely saw Helen—she was one of the few who'd left the hollow. But she always loved the time they spent together. Being around Helen was like having her mother without the rules and restrictions and the overriding pressure to rise above their roots.

"I'm good, Aunt Helen." As Glory said it, she realized it was true. She *was* good; she felt stronger than she had in years. "Where's Uncle Kenny?"

Helen laughed and hooked a thumb over her shoulder. "Comin' along."

Glory looked beyond her aunt. Uncle Kenny, a short, stocky man with iron-gray hair, was headed their way. He had a blanket thrown over one shoulder, a soft-pack cooler on a shoulder strap on the other, two folding lawn chairs in one hand, and a huge picnic hamper in the other. He was staggering under the weight.

Helen said, "He said he didn't need any help. I've decided to start taking him at his word. Dang man never says what he means. Time he learns."

"Well, if it doesn't break his back, maybe it'll teach him." Glory laughed. She started toward her uncle to give a hand.

Aunt Helen stopped her. "How's he going to learn if you don't let him face the consequences?"

Uncle Kenny huffed past, red-faced, but not making a peep to ask for help. This appeared to be a test to see which half of the couple was more stubborn. Glory put her money on Aunt Helen; she had the Baker-gene edge.

As the family assembled, Glory reacquainted herself with her extensive web of cousins. Eric fit right in; of course, he did know most everyone at least in passing. Glory had to chuckle when she saw him lay his contribution of peanut butter and banana sandwiches on the food table.

Granny called everyone to prayer before the meal. It was the only time Glory ever saw this crowd silent and still. It didn't last long. Almost at the same time as they chorused, "Amen," the chaos began again.

Glory, Eric, Scott, and Lady shared a blanket under a sassafras tree. Scott offered Lady some of his sandwich and grinned when she took it.

Glory said, "Lady has to be good for him. He seems to trust her more than he does the rest of us."

"I've noticed." Eric went on to tell her how responsive Scott had been on Friday. "I hope, once we get this figured out, that he'll have more good days than bad. It's been sliding the other direction for so long, I'd almost worried it was too late. But Friday—that was encouraging."

It nearly broke Glory's heart to think such a small thing could give him such elation—and he was elated, there was no other word for it. It showed in his eyes, in the animation of his features when he described what had happened, in the excitement in his voice.

As her gaze moved to Scott, Glory felt the pinch of shame once again. Why was she so closed to this child? A child who needed so much; a little boy hiding from the world, who felt comfortable only in the company of a sweet brown dog.

Eric continued to tell her of the different programs and clinics he'd been reading about that assisted children with delayed developmental disorders. Glory tried to focus her attention on the details, ready to offer her opinion if he were to ask for it. Of course, she wouldn't presume to comment otherwise.

After he exhausted his list, he did ask. She carefully offered her immediate impression of the different approaches—certain to prefix her opinion with the fact that she had absolutely no experience in this area.

"But," she admitted aloud for the first time, "I have been considering learning a whole lot more." She stretched her legs out in front of her, crossing her ankles. She hadn't yet mentioned her idea to Granny. "I read an article about trained companion and service dogs the other day. After seeing firsthand how calmed Scott is by Lady"—she glanced at the two sitting side by side, Scott's hand running back and forth over Lady's back—"I think there could be a real need. I'm considering taking whatever instruction is required, then starting a training program for the dogs. I worked with animals in my last couple of jobs."

Eric's first question wasn't at all what she expected. "Here? You'll set up your program here?" He leaned slightly forward as he waited for her answer.

The intensity in his eyes made her hesitate. Did he want her to stay? Or to get out of Dodge so she didn't complicate things with Jill and Scott?

Glory decided not to answer straightaway. Instead, she gathered her courage and marched into territory filled with emotional land mines. "I saw Jill on Friday. She said you three were going on a picnic yesterday afternoon." She let the comment lie and waited for Eric's response. If it had been an insignificant occurrence, why hadn't he mentioned it?

"Yeah," Eric said. "We were talking about Scott's doctors."

She studied him for a moment. A long afternoon in the park seemed like an unlikely place for a divorced couple to discuss their child's future—unless it was a case of mixing business with pleasure. Would he be honest with her and tell her they were considering reconciliation?

Then he added, almost defensively, "I told you we were going to work together to find help for Scott."

"I know. Is there something else you want to tell me?"

He looked genuinely perplexed. "Such as?"

In that instant, Glory wanted to back away from the entire conversation. How could she question him about his intentions with his ex, when he'd made absolutely no promises to Glory? In fact, he'd been very clear that he would do whatever was necessary for the welfare of his son.

She lifted a shoulder and busied her hands with her paper napkin. "It's just—"

A couple of ATVs started up and were unloaded from a trailer, revving engines drowning out her words. She turned toward the commotion until the four-wheelers sped away and the noise subsided. When she glanced back at Eric, she saw he hadn't been distracted in the least. His sharp brown gaze remained as focused on her.

When she didn't repeat herself, he said, "Why don't you tell me what's bothering you? And while you're at it, you can answer my question—are you staying?"

She licked her lips, stalling. It was so complicated. One thing hinged on another, and that one on the next— Eric, Granny, Scott, Jill, Ovella and Walt, Glory's past, her plans for a business.

"Hey, you two!" Charlie came up and sat down on the edge of the blanket. He had two cold bottles of beer in his hands. He offered one to Eric.

Eric gave Glory a quick look that said this conversation wasn't over. Then said to Charlie, "No, thanks. With all of the equipment showing up,"—he motioned toward the four-wheelers—"I'd better stay sharp."

Charlie laughed. "Granny always threatened to get an ambulance to stand by when we all get together. Maybe that's why she invited you; less conspicuous than a big white truck with a red cross on the side and ambulance written backward on the windshield. Did you bring your first-aid kit?"

"Built right into the Explorer; never go anywhere without it."

Charlie then held the beer out to Glory. "How 'bout you?"

She raised a brow. "Aren't you supposed to offer to the lady first? What if he'd taken it—would I get yours?" For once she was thankful that cousin Charlie was about as perceptive of what was going on around him as a dog on scent. Anyone else might have picked up on the vibe that they'd interrupted a serious conversation.

"No way, man." Charlie hugged his beer to his chest. "And as far as being a lady . . ."

Glory slapped him lightly on the back of his head.

"Hey!" He ducked and rubbed his head as if she'd really clobbered him. "I was just getting ready to say Eric is company. Don't you have any manners, girl?"

Just then Charlie's middle son, Curtis, came running up. "Daddy! Daddy! Jared won't let me have a turn on the dirt bike."

Glory blinked. Curtis was only eight; he didn't belong on a dirt bike.

"Curtis, say hello to Mr. Wilson, cousin Glory, and Scott."

Curtis scrunched his freckled face and managed a "Hello" to Glory and Eric. His face relaxed when he added, "Hi, Scott." His accent was so strong that it sounded more like *Haah*; the fact that Glory noticed it said she had been gone too long. It was amazing how quickly the ear changed to accommodate the location. Upon her return she had realized she'd taken up the northern way of pronouncing her home state, with the accent on the last syllable. Down here it was Tenn'essee.

Curtis asked, "Scott, want to come see the dirt bike?"

Scott did shift his gaze from the dog to Curtis at least briefly.

Eric looked tempted to take a chance and see if Scott would actually go with Curtis. In the end he said, "Maybe later, Curtis. Thanks for asking."

"Okay." Curtis's gaze returned to his father. "*Now* can we go make Jared let me have a turn?"

"Gotta go referee," Charlie said as he got up and walked off with his hand on Curtis's skinny shoulder.

Glory called, "I hope they're at least wearing helmets!"

Charlie gave a noncommittal wave without turning around.

She looked at Eric. "I hope you really do have an emergency kit in there. You have no idea how wild things will get before the day is out. It's sort of a 'who has the best toys and can outdaredevil the next guy' kind of competition."

Seventy feet away, a go-kart kicked up a rooster tail of dust and grass clods as it made a sharp turn.

"Oh, I think I'm getting a pretty clear picture," Eric said drily.

Glory cringed when a minimotorcycle fashioned after a Harley-Davidson roared past, driven by a girl who looked to be no older than five. Eric's gaze followed the girl, too. Glory didn't have to ask what he was thinking; it was all over his face. *Will Scott ever have fun doing regular kid things?*

She wanted to reach out and assure him that he would, that with a little speech therapy and the passage of a few more months, Scott would work his way to a normal level. But she wanted to be truthful. And the truth was, as much as she wanted to hope it would be so, she wasn't sure that Scott would ever function at a normal level.

Before Eric could bring back their unfinished conversation, Charlie's oldest, Jared, came up wearing a bright orange T-shirt and khaki shorts covered with dust. "Dad said I should see if Scott wants to come and see the dirt bike." He rushed on before Eric answered, "We won't let him on it or anything, and I'll watch him."

Glory saw the indecision in Eric's eyes—and the overwhelming desire to have his son eager to do adventurous things like investigate another kid's dirt bike.

"Maybe you could take Lady, too. Scott likes to go where Lady goes," Glory suggested.

"Scott, you and Lady want to walk with Jared to see a bike?" Eric asked.

At the mention of Lady's name, Scott looked at his dad.

Eric got to his feet and held out a hand to his son. "Come on, I'll go too."

Jared patted his thigh and called Lady.

They started away, Scott happily following the dog, with his quilt balled in one arm. Eric stopped and said to Glory, "You can come, too."

She waved them on. "Go on. I'll clean up the plates. Maybe take a little nap 'til you guys get back."

Eric left with a bright smile and a light step. Glory hoped these little changes in Scott truly indicated progress and that Scott's increased awareness over the past couple of days wasn't just an aberration.

Glory lay back, lingering under the tree, enjoying the contentment of being in the family fold. Eric fit so well with this family, it was almost as if he belonged. And that thought made her glow from the inside.

"You look like the cat that got the cream," Granny said.

Glory opened her eyes.

"Don't frown at me. It's a good thing. Ain't seen you this relaxed since you got home."

"Didn't know I was frowning."

"You was. It's all right to be happy, darlin'." Granny sat on the ground next to her.

Unwilling to delve into her deepest feelings, Glory diverted the conversation. "Have you noticed how Scott is with Lady? He just followed her off to see the dirt bike."

With a slow nod and a smile, Granny said, "It's somethin', ain't it?"

"I read an article in the doctor's office the other day about how dogs are being used in therapies for all kinds of things. I always thought dogs were just used for physical handicaps. There's a growing demand. I'm thinking that might be something for me to look into."

"Well, you got experience with animals. Might be a good idea."

"I'll have to do a lot more research. And I'll probably need some help." It was true; a partner would be a valuable asset. And handling dogs wouldn't require sharp, detailed eyesight, but patience and understanding. Granny would be well equipped for the task.

But Granny didn't bite at the hint.

Glory had to move carefully; she didn't want Granny's cast-iron pride to cause her to dig in her heels before Glory had even begun. "This could be an incredible opportunity. But I'll need a place with lots of space."

"Reckon you could set up here, if'n you wanted. Got plenty of acreage."

Glory sat up quickly. "Really?"

"Don't see why not."

"I'm sure the income at first will be slow. But after we've been set up a while, you should be—"

Granny's gaze sharpened, and her lips took on that firm line that signaled trouble. "I said you could set up here. I got my own work."

Glory knew when to back off. "All right. I'm still exploring the idea. This would be a great location."

Granny patted Glory's leg. "You let me know when you decide."

"Sure will, Gran." Step one, introduction to idea. Step two, figure out a way to draw Granny in without making her feel like a charity case.

Step two was going to be the problem.

Scott stood between Eric and Lady, looking at the dog, not the dirt bike. But at least he wasn't crying or covering his ears to shut out the high-pitched whine of the engine as it approached.

Jared knelt by Scott and said, pointing, "Look, here he comes!"

The kids had worn a track with the bike. It was a big loop that circled into the woods, dipped into a couple of shallow ravines, cut around a giant stump near the edge of the yard, and bumped over a rise just high enough that the older kids could get the wheels to leave the ground.

Curtis was the current rider, having successfully accomplished his coup with the help of his dad. When he saw Scott standing there, he pulled the bike to a stop in front of them. "You want to take Scott for a ride, Mr. Wilson?"

Eric was impressed with the boy's generosity. "Thanks, Curtis. I think we'll just watch this year. Maybe when he's older."

Curtis grinned and gunned the engine. The bike took off with such a jerk, Eric thought the boy was going to be bucked off. But Curtis held on and disappeared on the track into the woods.

Jared said, "Curtis thinks he's gonna do motocross." He made a *pffing* sound. "Like that's ever gonna happen."

Eric smiled at the twelve-year-old. "You never know, Jared. It could—if he wants it badly enough." *Wouldn't it be great if someday I could help Scott work toward greater things than verbalizing when he was hungry and not having a meltdown every other day at school?*

Jared smirked. "Yeah. And I might be the next Hulk Hogan."

A laugh popped out of Eric's mouth before he could stop it. Jared was the stringiest kid he'd ever seen. Short for his age, he was nothing but bone and sinew—no fat, no bulk, no muscle.

"You haven't hit your growth spurt yet," Eric said encouragingly, trying to make up for his initial response. "In a couple of years, you'll probably be bench-pressing two hundred."

Jared cast him a skeptical look. Then he said, "Don't matter. I want to be a swimmer. Olympic gold." Confidence now shone in his smile.

"Are you on the team at sch—"

"Eric!" Glory yelled, running their way. "Eric, we need you! There's been an accident!"

Eric reached to scoop Scott up.

"Go. I got him," Jared said.

With one last look at his son, he ran toward Glory.

She shouted, "One of the ATVs flipped. Connie's eleven-year-old was on it. I've told them not to move him." She fell into a run next to him.

As Eric approached the child lying on the ground, everything else faded into an indistinct blur. He began to assess injuries before he even got down on his knees beside the boy. *Large laceration on the forehead. Could be a concussion. Copious bleeding from the mouth. Angle of left shoulder indicates break or dislocation. Boy's cries indicate severe pain. Both legs moving. Position of four-wheeler suggests it probably rolled over him. Check for spinal trauma.*

Connie and Tula were on the boy's other side, trying calm him and keep him still.

"What's your name, son?" Eric asked and gave the mother a look that told her he wanted the child to answer.

"T-t-trevor." He was beginning to shake.

"Okay, Trevor, we're gonna get you to a hospital. But until then I'm going to help you." Eric glanced over his shoulder at Glory.

She answered his unasked question. "The ambulance is on its way. You want me to get the kit from the Explorer?"

He nodded. Then he began to examine the child more closely. "I want you to hold as still as you can, Trevor. It's important until we know if you've hurt your neck."

"'K-k-k-kay," he said, without moving unnecessarily. The trust in his eyes—the same as Eric saw in most accident victims—sparked a pang of guilt in him; those injured held such faith that Eric could help them, when in reality, he didn't have much more to work with than a pressure bandage, a neck brace, and educated determination.

He spoke with calm assurance. "All right. You're doing great. I know your shoulder and head hurt. Anyplace else—just tell me, don't show me and don't shake your head."

Trevor's crying died to a whimper, and Eric could see him mentally checking all of his parts. "My mouf."

"I see." Eric looked at the boy's mouth. "Anyplace else?"

After a short pause. "No."

Eric saw the amount of blood coming from Trevor's mouth was just about to send his mother into orbit, so he gently moved the boy's lips to ensure that the front teeth were all still in place.

"Can you stick your tongue out at me?"

Trevor's gaze cut toward his mom. Then, slowly, he stuck out his tongue.

"Looks like you bit it." Then Eric looked at Connie and said quietly, "Always looks much worse than it actually is. Might not even need a stitch."

Glory returned with the emergency case and set it on the ground.

"I'm going to put a collar around your neck, Trevor, just in case you hurt it. But I want you to hold still and let me do all the work. Okay?"

"Uh-huh."

Eric had the cervical collar in place and a pressure bandage on the forehead gash by the time the ambulance arrived. As soon as the paramedics reached the boy, he stepped back.

Trevor's eyes widened, and he cried, "Wait. Stay."

"I'm not going anyplace. I'm just letting these guys get you ready to go. I'm right here." He glanced around the concerned faces gathered around them. He didn't see Jared or Scott. He turned to Glory and said, "Jared is watching Scott. See if you can find them." He couldn't believe a kid Jared's age would miss seeing a bloody accident.

"Sure." She disappeared beyond the crowd.

Glory hurried toward where the kids had been riding the dirt bike. When she got there, the bike was on the ground and no one was around. She turned, scanning in all directions, looking for some sign of Jared's orange shirt. She didn't see him.

"Jared! Scott!" She walked to the edge of the woods and listened for a reply. She doubted that Jared would take Scott into the woods, so she turned her efforts to more likely spots.

She'd seen Charlie and Curtis up on Granny's porch as she'd passed. She ran back to the house. "Charlie," she called as she neared. "Where are Jared and Scott?"

Charlie looked up from where he was holding a bag of ice on Curtis's leg. "They were still by the dirt bike a minute ago. Curtis burned his leg on the exhaust, and we came to get ice."

"They're not there now." Panic inched up her throat.

"They probably went to see about Trevor."

Even as she ran back toward the accident, she didn't really think she'd missed seeing that orange shirt in the crowd.

Chapter Twenty-one

❀

As TREVOR WAS loaded into the ambulance, everyone began to drift away from the accident. Glory canvassed to see if anyone had seen Jared in the last few minutes. None had.

Eric followed the stretcher to the ambulance, talking to Trevor and Connie. Glory spied Granny headed back toward the house.

"Gran!" She ran to catch up with her grandmother. "Have you seen Jared and Scott?"

Granny's eyes immediately registered Glory's panic. "No. Did you check the garage? Jared likes to tinker with Pap's tools."

Glory sprinted in that direction, calling, "Go tell Eric—tell everyone! We need to find Scott."

The garage was empty. She headed to the last place she knew Jared and Scott had been. On her way she passed the porch and called to Charlie, "I can't find Jared and Scott."

"I'm sure they're around somewhere," Charlie said, but he did get to his feet and follow her.

A few kids had returned to the dirt bike. She questioned them all, but no one had seen Jared since before the accident.

Eric sprinted up just as Glory was debating on which direction to try next. "You can't find them?"

"No. No one's seen them," Glory said, trying to keep the panic from her voice. "I haven't seen Lady either."

"Shit." Hands on his hips, Eric looked around, as if hoping Glory had just overlooked them.

Tula was breathless when she caught up. "Jared's used to watchin' young'uns. He's real good with his little brothers. Maybe they just took a walk."

Eric looked doubtful. "And didn't even check out the accident?"

"We should get everyone to fan out in different directions. We could be missing them just because they're moving," Glory suggested.

Eric looked toward the woods. "I'm starting there. You organize everyone else."

"Wait," Glory said. "Here comes Jared."

They all turned to see him sprinting out of the woods. His face was a mask of fear. "Mr. Wilson! I just turned around for a second, I swear. When I looked back, he and Lady were gone. I thought they followed the track, but I can't find them." As he got closer, Glory saw tears running down his cheeks. "Scott never runs off. I didn't think . . ."

Fury flickered across Eric's face, but was quickly banished. "Which way were you looking when they disappeared?"

Jared pointed toward Trevor's accident. "Curtis burned his leg and was screaming bloody murder. I looked at his leg, then Dad came and took him to get ice. I looked over there to see what was happening, then when I looked back—"

"Okay, that pretty much rules out the direction of the house. Jared, run over to my car and get the set of walkie-talkies from the back." While Jared was gone, Eric said, "I'm starting straight into the woods from where the track cuts in. I'll take one of the walkie-talkies—cell phones are no good here. Glory, you organize everyone else. Find out if anyone has walkie-talkies; they'll work a short distance and give us some communication. I don't want to wait any longer to start."

Charlie stepped forward. "Glory, you go with him. Take Jared, too. You'll be able to cover a wider piece of ground. Granny and I'll get everyone else organized and moving; won't do much good if everyone runs every which way."

Jared dashed up, breathless, and handed the walkie-talkies to Eric.

"Okay. Let's go. Jared, you're with us." He turned on the walkie-talkies and handed one to Charlie.

Glory and Jared hurried alongside Eric as they entered the woods. It was going to be like finding a needle in a haystack. They were only guessing that Scott had gone this direction.

"We should call Lady," Glory said. "Scott won't answer, but maybe Lady will."

"Good idea," Eric said.

The three of them, with Jared in the middle, spread far enough apart that they could still see one another and worked deeper and deeper into the woods, calling Lady as they went.

After about fifteen minutes, Glory yelled to Eric, "Do you really think they could be this far?"

"I'm just hoping the dog is still with him."

Eric's words sent a fresh shaft of alarm through her. Scott would be calm if Lady was with him. He wouldn't understand the danger. But if he was alone . . . She couldn't stand the thought of him lost and frightened; he understood so little of what went on around him already.

"Keep going forward," Eric called. "The others can start another direction." Glory saw him say something into the walkie-talkie. Then he yelled to her, "Charlie has people fanning out. We should keep going."

Glory waved her agreement, then called Lady again.

A minute later, Jared called, "I found something!"

Glory's heart sped up.

She and Eric, reached Jared at the same moment. The boy held up Scott's quilt. It was filthy, and the binding had been torn loose on one side.

At least there was no blood. Still, Glory felt like throwing up.

Brittle fear flashed across Eric's face, but his tone was encouraging when he said, "We're on the right track, then. Keep a sharp eye out; he could be hiding or hurt."

. . . or hurt. God, how could he get those words out without choking?

Eric focused like a trained rescuer, looking carefully at the ground and at the vegetation surrounding where they stood. "Paw prints. Lady's still with him." He concentrated on the ground as he began to move. "This way. Spread out again."

He called Charlie on the walkie-talkie and told him where they were and that everyone should concentrate in this direction.

Glory looked at her watch. It had been nearly an hour since the last time anyone had seen Scott. A lot could happen to a little boy in an hour.

They called the dog with renewed vigor, careful to listen for a bark or a rustle in the brush in response. They headed into a ravine through which a rapid-flowing stream passed. It sounded like heavy rain as it tumbled over rocks and hurried downhill, making it less likely to be able to hear a small boy's cries.

Glory knew from experience that those wet rocks could be very slick. If Scott had fallen and hit his head, he could drown in only a few inches of water.

As she hurried down the steep slope of the ravine, her feet slipped out from under her. She slid on her backside a good twenty feet before she was able to stop and get back up.

Eric called, "You all right?"

"Yes." She rubbed her abraded palms together to reduce the stinging, but kept going.

They all three reached the creek at the same time, Glory downstream of the other two. She called Lady again.

"There!" Glory's heart leaped with relief. The dog barked off to her left, farther down the sloping ravine. "This way!" She hurried—there was no running on this rocky and uneven slope—in the direction of Lady's bark.

"Lady!"

The dog barked again.

Oh, God, please let him be all right.

Glory moved faster. If something dreadful had happened to Scott, she didn't want Eric to be the first one to get there.

Lady barked again without being called. Why wasn't she moving this way?

Glory nearly ran straight over the edge of a drop-off. She skidded to a stop, pinwheeling her arms to regain balance. She heard several stones tumble over the edge.

Lady barked again. Right beneath her.

When Glory looked over the edge, she was relieved to see it was only about a four-foot drop. "Scott?" She was ready to lower herself over the edge when she saw the ground sloped down about five feet to her right.

Lady barked again.

"I'm coming! Scott, I'm coming!"

She scrambled down and around the outcropping.

Scott, whole and apparently unhurt, sat next to the rushing stream with his gaze fixed on the moving water. Lady was circling around him.

Glory scooped him up, clutching him to her chest. "Here!" she yelled. "He's okay! He's okay!"

Scott stiffened in her arms, but she couldn't let him go. She kissed his sweaty head and squeezed him tighter. "Thank God. Thank God."

Eric jumped from the overhang, landing right beside her. Jared scurried down the way Glory had come.

Glory handed Eric his son. And for the first time since all this began, she saw Eric begin to crumble. She put a hand on his back and murmured, "He's all right," over and over again, as tears ran down her cheeks.

"And Lady stayed right with him," Glory said to Granny late that afternoon, after the excitement of the day had died down and all of the Bakers had packed up their toys and headed home. The two of them sat on the porch swing while Eric was upstairs giving Scott a bath. "She didn't leave him to come and get us. She just barked until we found them. She was circling around him—I think she was trying to keep him out of the water. It was amazing. And she hasn't even had any training."

Gran nodded. "Some creatures are just born to protect."

"Yes." Glory's mind immediately turned to Eric; that was the best way she knew to describe him, *born to protect*. Maybe there was truth to Jill's insinuation that they were getting back together for Scott. Perhaps he'd discovered Scott needed rescuing more than Glory did, and returning to Jill was the best way to accomplish that goal.

Granny interrupted her thoughts. "I wonder which one of them led the other into the woods."

Glory shrugged. She had wondered the same thing. She doubted they'd ever know. But, she wondered, as disconnected as Scott appeared most of the time, what were his memories going to be like?

She'd begun to wonder a lot of things about Scott's world these past days. She'd attributed it to her burgeoning interest in service dogs, but the reality was it had much more to do with her growing feelings for Eric. To help Scott was to help Eric.

"After this, I'm thinking even more strongly about the dog training idea," Glory said.

"I think you should do it."

It was rare for Granny to take a side in someone else's decision making. "You do?"

"Seems a good Christian effort—helpin' others."

Glory laughed. "A good Christian effort would be doing it for free. I need to make a living."

"God don't ask people to starve for their good deeds."

Glory wrapped an arm around Granny's shoulders. "I love you, Gran."

"You, too, Mornin' Glory."

After a moment, Granny said, "Today we more'n made up for all them Baker reunions without splints or stitches. Always knew we was on borrowed time."

"Could have been worse," Glory assured her. "Trevor escaped a spinal injury—" Connie had called a half hour ago with that report. "Scott returned unscathed from his adventure. We've been pretty lucky." She got up. "I'm going to check the dryer." She'd washed Scott's clothes and thrown them in the dryer just before Eric took Scott upstairs for a bath.

When she came back to the porch, she was carrying Scott's freshly washed quilt. "Do you think we can fix this?"

She handed it to Granny.

"'Course. Just needs new binding."

"Can you do it? I mean, with your eyes—you haven't sewn anything since I've been back."

Granny handed the quilt back to Glory. "No, I cain't. But you can."

"Gran, you know I can't hand sew."

"Cain't never did anythin'. Go get my sewing box, and I'll talk you through. It ain't brain surgery."

Glory looked at the quilt. The stitches were fine and even, hard to believe a human hand could be so consistently precise. She was sure to screw it up. "Maybe one of your friends—"

"Shush, girl! I ain't never seen anybody so afraid of a needle and thread. Just go get the box."

The sound of Eric's footsteps coming down the stairs echoed though the screen door.

"Maybe we should put it away 'til later," Glory said. "If Scott sees it, he's going to want it."

"Good idea."

Eric stepped out on the porch just as Glory stuffed the quilt behind her. Scott was in his arms, wrapped in a bath towel. His hair was wet and stuck to his head, and one little fist was knotted in Eric's not-so-clean shirt.

Glory was surprised by the urge she had to get up and put a kiss on Scott's bath-rosy cheek. "His clothes are folded on the dryer."

Granny had spare clothes here for Scott, but Eric wanted to take him home in the same outfit he had come in. Glory wondered if Eric would tell Jill about today's incident.

"Thanks."

As Eric went back inside the house, Glory noticed he was holding his son just a little more tightly than usual. And for the first time, she felt compelled to do the same. And that reaction frightened her just a little bit—she couldn't explain why. For weeks she'd been thinking her reaction to Scott indicated she was broken in some way. Shouldn't she be relieved finally to feel something normal?

A few minutes later, Eric returned with Scott dressed and his hair combed. He hesitated before he went down the front steps. "Want to walk me to my car, Glory?"

The tone of his voice said he had something more to say than good-bye. She nearly shook her head no; if she didn't hear the words, she could hang on to the idea that there might be a future for the two of them. But, of course, she didn't do anything so childish. She got up and walked to where he stood.

He said, "'Evenin', Tula."

Granny smiled as she continued to swing. "'Evenin', Eric." She blew a kiss to Scott. "Night-night, little 'un."

Eric was quiet as they walked across the yard. The sun was behind the trees, casting near-vertical fingers of golden light through the breaks in the leaves. The dew had yet to fall and the locusts droned.

Normally, this was Glory's favorite time of day, especially in the summer. It was calm, the bridge between busy day and relaxed night. She wished it could be prolonged. But it always slipped away long before she was ready to let it go.

And she feared Eric was about to do the same.

He fastened Scott into his car seat before he said anything to her. After he'd closed the back door of the Explorer, he said, "I wish I could stay longer. But Jill's expecting Scott home."

"I understand. I was going to try to repair his quilt, but if you think he'll need it to sleep . . ."

He looked surprised. "*You're* going to fix it?"

"I said I'm going to *try*. Gran seems to have faith that I can do it."

He smiled and touched her cheek. "So do I."

Glory broke eye contact before she said something she shouldn't.

Eric said, "He shouldn't miss it. He has another one he sleeps with at Jill's."

Glory lifted her gaze and tilted her head to one side. "Are you going to tell her about what happened today?"

Eric's mouth twisted with indecision as he looked toward the woods. Then he looked at Glory. "Yes. I couldn't keep something like this from her."

Oooh, honesty. One of the building blocks of a serious relationship.

Eric glanced over Glory's shoulder, as if to make sure Tula wasn't looking this way. Then he leaned down and kissed her quickly, but there was an undercurrent of urgency to it. "Can you come by my house later? I'd come back here, but . . . what I have to say I want to say in private."

Glory couldn't find her voice, so she nodded.

"It might take a while at Jill's. I should be home no later than nine-thirty."

She managed to squeeze out an "Okay."

She watched him drive out the long lane, feeling like she was watching him exit her life. Of course he would want to remain friends, would want to help her as one friend helps another. But she'd recently come to understand that was not at all what she wanted from Eric Wilson.

Glory took a shower and changed her outfit three times in her indecision about how to approach this evening: Did she want to dress for seduction? Let Eric know just what he'd be missing if he let her go? Once she had the low-cut dress on, she nearly laughed at herself—she was no seductress.

Then she tried the sophisticated, self-assured, I-really-don't-give-a-rat's-ass-what-you-do linen slacks and prim sweater twin set. Of course, Eric wasn't a man to play those kinds of chase-me-if-you-really-want-me games.

In the end, she put on a comfortable pair of jeans and a gauzy white shirt; a might-as-well-be-comfortable-when-he-dumps-me outfit.

Then she went downstairs and decided to forget trying to fool Granny about her reason for heading into town at nine o'clock on a Sunday evening.

"I'm going to see Eric," she said simply.

Granny was reading the large-print book that Glory had picked up at the library on Friday morning. She pulled her glasses off and looked up. "All right." Then she put her glasses back on and her nose back into the book.

Glory stood there for a second. She'd prepared a long explanation about why she and Eric needed to talk. "Don't you want to know why?"

Granny didn't look up. "Not partic'arly."

Glory shifted her weight from one sandaled foot to another, biting her lip. "There are a few things he and I—"

Granny's gaze snapped up and her mouth puckered with impatience. "Really, Glory. You're a grown woman." She took off the glasses again and pinched the bridge of her nose. "I don't need no explanation about why you're going to see Eric—or anyone else for that matter."

"Oh."

"And I'll 'ppreciate the same consideration from you when it comes to my affair—ah, activities."

Glory sat on the couch next to her grandmother as carefully as if she were sitting next to a bottle of nitroglycerine. "Have I done something to upset you?"

"Not yet."

"Then why the throwing down of the gauntlet?"

"'Cause I can see it comin', just as sure as the sun comes up in the east. You're gonna try to take care of me.

And I'll tell you right now, if that's the case, you're gonna have to find someplace else to live."

"Hey! All I did was drive you to the doctor."

"You think I don't know that dog business is 'cause of me? You think I need you here—I need you to support me. That ain't the case."

"Honestly, Gran, I'll be doing the service dogs, here or someplace else. I just thought you might enjoy helping."

"I ain't a charity case."

"I said 'helping'—not having money shoveled to you for nothing in return. It's called a job."

Granny's mouth pinched closed. Glory hoped the comment would make her begin to think differently.

But Granny wasn't finished. "'Sides that, I seen the little things you're doin'. You been readin' those booklets from Dr. Blanton's office. First it was the throw rug in the hallway disappeared, then the one in front of the kitchen sink. Next you'll be marking the edges of the steps with bright orange tape."

"And what's wrong with that? It's to keep you safe."

"It's too soon! I don't need none of that yet. And believe you me, when the time comes, I'll take care of it!" She took Glory's hand. "So let's just get things straight right now. I won't treat you like a teenager and you won't treat me like I need to be in a nursing home, and we'll abide just fine. Otherwise . . ."

"Otherwise, you're kicking me out."

"We're growed women. We can share a house—but we each got to respect the other. That's all I'm sayin'." She paused. "Otherwise, I'm kickin' you out." She grinned and patted Glory's hand. "Now get on."

Glory drove into town, mentally preparing for what Eric needed to "say in private," fighting the self-pitying feeling that everyone she cared about was trying to shut her out.

Glory arrived at Eric's shortly after nine-thirty. His porch light was on and his front door open. She climbed the steps and looked through the screen into the living room as she knocked.

He wasn't in sight.

She heard his feet thumping down the stairs as he called, "Come on in."

He met her at the bottom of the stairs as she entered. His hair was wet, he had on a T-shirt and shorts and was barefooted. He kissed her cheek, "Sorry, I just got back and took a quick shower." He led her back toward the kitchen, not to the couch where they'd made love. "How about something to drink?"

He'd been at Jill's for a very long time. Glory's stomach was feeling pretty rocky at the moment. "Do you have Sprite?"

"Sure. Have a seat." He motioned her to the table. Then he poured a can of Sprite over ice for her and opened a can of Coke for himself.

When he sat down at the table, he said, "I checked with Connie after I got home. Trevor's been released. The dislocated shoulder was the worst of it. He was a lucky kid."

"That makes two very lucky kids today." She took a sip of Sprite and noticed her hands weren't too steady.

Eric slumped back in his chair and propped his feet on another one. He rubbed his eyes with the heels of his hands, and Glory saw just how much today's scare had taken out of him. "Don't I know it."

"Jared was still very upset when Charlie took the boys home."

Eric sat a little straighter. "I told him not to beat himself up. The important thing was that Scott was all right, and the best thing to do was take a lesson from this; little kids can get into trouble faster than a frog can grab a fly."

"I know, he told me. Still, he nearly had himself hyperventilating at one point, worrying over what *could* have happened."

"He shouldn't. Useless worry like that can make a person crazy."

"Tell me about it," Glory said drily.

Eric looked intently at her. "Yes, I guess that *what-if* gate swings both ways—the bad and the good that didn't happen. But working rescue, I've come to understand you deal with what *is*, not what might have been. Anything else is a waste of valuable energy."

Glory tilted her head. "You don't ever think how different it could be for Scott?"

He looked as if she'd caught him in a lie. His voice was grave when he admitted, "I try not to—but sometimes, it's just *there*, you know? It flashes in my mind at unexpected moments—like when that little girl rode by on the mini-Harley today . . ." He paused. "I guess my point is not to allow it to consume you, not to let it have a place in your daily life."

"Like I have?" Glory might have gotten defensive if he didn't look so miserable at the moment.

"I wasn't thinking of you, actually."

"Jill?" Her mouth went dry as she forced herself to face the conversation that had to be—made herself deal with what *is*.

He closed his eyes briefly and sighed. He appeared more exhausted than he had the morning after her accident when he'd stayed awake most of the night.

She took pity and said the words for him: "You're going back to her."

Chapter Twenty-two

❀

FOR A LONG MOMENT Glory sat holding her breath. Her heart felt about to burst in her chest. She'd known that this moment would be difficult, but until now she hadn't understood exactly how deep her feelings for Eric were. After months and months of being alone, isolated from all emotional risk, she'd soaked up his friendship, his support, his caring intimacy as drought-cracked land drinks in the first precious drops of rain. In an unbelievably short time, he'd become dear to her, a partner, a lover.

He didn't say anything, just stared at her with an unreadable expression on his face.

Glory finally overcame the vapor lock in her lungs. "That's what you wanted to tell me in private, isn't it?"

His expression lost its ambiguity and took on angry definition. "What gave you the idea I'm considering going back to Jill?"

Of all things, she didn't think she'd find herself on the defensive in this discussion. "I saw Jill on Friday when she picked Scott up."

"She said we were getting back together?" His voice held a razor edge.

"Not directly, I suppose, but I certainly got the message." She rushed on, "And I understand. Really, I do. If it's best for Scott . . ."

Eric looked as if he was about to explode. His breathing was rapid and rough. He said tightly, "Do you really think I would have made love to you if I was considering going back to my ex-wife—for any reason? Is that what kind of man you think I am?"

"When you put it that way . . ." Of course that wasn't the kind of man he was. And this conversation wasn't at all what she'd prepared herself for. "You aren't?"

He stood and hauled her out of her chair so quickly, she was crushed against his chest before she could begin to react.

"Jesus, do you really think I could hurt you that way? After all you've already been through?" He eased back and framed her face with his hands and kissed her roughly, with an intensity that left her knees trembling and her insides a mass of quivering heat. "I think I'm falling in love with you, Glory. I never imagined I could feel like this . . . I want you—your body, your heart, all of you."

When he kissed her again, the lead weight Glory had been carrying around in her chest melted and slid away from her heart as if converted to liquid mercury. Her arms went around his neck, and she met his passion with her own.

Locked in an embrace, he moved them until her back was against the kitchen wall. He put his palms on the wall on either side of her head, keeping his body pressed against hers. His mouth caressed her ear, then moved to her throat, sending shivers down her neck and stirring the embers of heat in her most intimate places.

She lifted her chin and ran her hands into his hair as his lips found the hollow at the base of her throat.

He whispered against her skin, "You're the woman in my heart . . . only you."

Glory clung to him as if her life depended upon it. She could hardly believe his words; it was too much to hope for—and yet, he'd said them.

His hands moved to her breasts; even through her clothes, his touch ignited fire. His hands caressing her, his warm, moist breath on her flesh, the feel of his hair against her fingers, all made every inch of her beg for more.

His mouth returned to hers, his kiss an expression of where he wanted to take their bodies.

She burned for him in a way she'd never experienced.

Running her hands under his shirt, she felt the solid muscle of his back. Such strength . . . if only he could protect her with that strength. But she knew there were things about herself that no one could protect her from. And until she resolved just how treacherous those things were, she had to maintain some emotional distance.

She wanted nothing more than to give herself to him completely, but batted away her carnal fog. She had to think; there was too much at stake here to screw this up.

When she pulled away from his kiss, her mouth throbbed from the force of their passion. She licked her lips, savoring the taste of him.

He looked deeply into her eyes, keeping her pressed against the wall. His breathing was as ragged as her own, his body as fully aroused.

It would be so easy to let this moment ride on its own momentum to the natural conclusion. So very easy. She throbbed with need. But that need went deeper than the flesh. And she didn't want to risk fulfillment of that soul-searing emotional need by succumbing to physical desire now.

She removed her hands from the inside of his shirt, held his gaze and tried to draw a steady breath. "You haven't told me your reason for asking me here."

He caressed her cheek with such gentleness it stirred an ache in her soul, an ache that would undoubtedly be eased if she allowed him to make love to her.

With his forehead resting against hers, he said, "At the moment, I'd rather do this than talk." He dipped his head and nipped her lower lip.

Closing her eyes, she gathered her resolve. "Me, too. But . . . there was something on your mind; that needs to come first."

He groaned and said, "Oh, yeah."

She realized what she'd just said, *needs to come*. "You know that's not what I meant!"

With a gruff laugh, he said, "You're right." He stepped away but kept a hand on her arm. "There are things we need to talk about."

She sat back down in the chair he'd plucked her from minutes ago. He paced restlessly about the kitchen. She wasn't sure if it was physical discomfort from unfulfilled passion or mental unrest that kept him moving.

"I guess there are two things we need to get out in the air. First," he said, "I should tell you why I spent so long at Jill's this evening."

A confession? Or an explanation? Glory tried to keep herself from jumping to conclusions.

He said, "I don't want there to be secrets between us, Glory. I want total honesty or nothing at all."

She nodded slowly, never taking her eyes off him. "So do I."

"I learned the hard way that communication is the key to making a relationship work—communication and honesty."

That heavy coating of lead was accumulating around her heart again. Honesty might be more painful than she'd ever realized.

"Jill does have it in her head that she and I need to get back together for Scott—that he'll benefit from living in a house with both his parents."

"And do you share that opinion?" She was proud of the steadiness in her voice—a brave woman, facing honesty in all of its harshness.

"Hell, no. There is no way a child is better living in an environment with two parents who can't trust one another. That poison is bound to leak out and hurt him." He looked directly at Glory when he said, "And I could *never* trust Jill again. Scott's problems don't change that reality." He circled the kitchen again before he leaned against the counter. "I had no idea she'd said something to you."

A thought hit Glory like a stiff, cold wind. "Why did she?"

"What? Say something to you?"

Glory nodded. "She was clearly warning me away from you."

Eric said, "No one knows that you and I . . ."

"That's what I thought, too. But Ovella asked me about you the other day. Obviously, we're out there more than we thought."

Glory wondered if Jill could be the one sending her the messages. It made as much sense as anything. If Jill wanted Eric back, what better way to get Glory to leave town than to threaten her with exposure of her darkest secret? And the more Glory remembered, the more she feared that there *was* a secret.

Jill had had the opportunity to put the T-shirt in the Volvo. That brought up another question. At some point during Eric's investigation, could he have insinuated to Jill that he thought the fire might be arson? It was all too possible.

Glory's fingers and toes went numb.

Eric cut a hand through the air and spoke again. "It's not important who knows about us. I made it clear to Jill tonight that there is no chance of us getting back together. I can't believe she really wants it anyway—not for the long haul."

Glory wished she could be so certain.

He crossed his arms. "Now for that second issue, the reason I asked you here. I have a question for you, but I don't want you to answer it tonight. I want you to really think it through."

Glory sat silent, waiting, worrying, her mind trying to unravel several mysteries at once.

Eric went on, "I care too much for you to treat this as a casual affair—I don't have casual affairs." He gazed deeply into her eyes for a moment, then swallowed as if the words were difficult to deliver. "My question is, do you think you'll be able to accept Scott—as he is? He's a part of me. And I understand if you can't; it's a lot to ask of any woman. But he's the center of my life; I can't allow myself to follow my heart freely as if he didn't exist."

He wanted more than a casual affair. Did *she* want more? Her heart answered yes. But her mind said it might not be the best idea—and Scott wasn't the only reason. If there was even a shadow of a doubt about her involvement in that fire, how could she have a lasting relationship with Eric?

Still, the question he posed was serious enough to unravel their relationship without any other issues. Apparently her aversion to Scott had been ill concealed. Eric was a father first. That was part of what she admired about him, his devotion to those he cared for. It was such a different thing from what she'd experienced with Andrew. Andrew demonstrated his love through control, albeit in the sheep's clothing of protection.

She knew Eric thought her reluctance to interact with Scott stemmed from his unique problems. But it wasn't that, never had been. And although she still could not name the reason she held herself apart from him, something had changed today. There had been a shift inside her when she'd held him beside that rushing creek, a tiny crack in the wall that seemed to have separated her and Scott from the first day.

Could she overcome her own shortcomings and love this little boy freely?

As if he saw the workings of her mind, Eric said, "I mean it. I don't want you to answer now. I want you to take your time. It's too important to answer impulsively, on the heels of"—he pointed to where he'd had her pinned against the wall—"that."

She nodded slowly. "All right."

There didn't seem to be anything to say after that. She'd come here expecting to lose Eric forever. But he wanted more from her, not less. And that was nearly as frightening.

Was she the woman he thought her to be?

If Eric had at one time entertained the notion that the fire that killed Andrew had been intentionally set—who did he think had set it?

The comments he had made about Andrew had been critical; but arson? Eric hadn't gone that far.

Besides, it didn't fit. Why would Andrew set a fire and not escape himself? Even more perplexing, why set the fire at all? If he'd wanted to be rid of Glory, all he had to do was let her walk out the door.

No, if that fire had been intentionally set, the one most likely responsible (to any logical-thinking person) was Glory. The one found trying to escape the burning house. The one with no money, no job, no way out of a destructive relationship—and no memory of that night.

She needed air. She got up and headed out of the kitchen. "Don't walk me out." Hurrying through the house, she went straight to the front door without looking back. Once she was in her car, she glanced up and saw his shadowed form standing in his front door.

As she started to pull away, she realized the car was listing slightly to the left and the steering was sluggish. She stopped and got out. The front driver's-side tire was flat.

Eric called through the screen door, "What's wrong?"

"Flat tire." She felt close to tears. She didn't want to talk anymore. She wanted to be alone, to drive fast with her window down and her thoughts uncensored.

He came down the porch steps, across the sidewalk, and knelt beside the tire. "Not just flat—slashed."

"No." She looked more closely. He ran his finger along a two-inch gash in the sidewall. "I'll be . . ."

He stood up and looked up and down the dark street.

"Teenagers! You'd think they'd find better things to do—"

"Save it. You and I both know better." He started toward the back of the car. "I assume there's a spare in the trunk."

"Yeah. I'll pop it." Of course, he was right. The street was lined with vehicles and Glory's car was parked directly under the streetlight. This wasn't a random act.

After she popped the trunk, she knelt to look at the ruined tire. As much as she'd wanted to think this the act of a jealous ex-wife, it was unlikely that Jill would load up her son this late at night and drive past Eric's house on the off chance that Glory would be there.

Or was it? How badly did she want Eric back?

She called to Eric, "Did you tell Jill I was coming here tonight?"

He didn't respond. Was he pissed that she would insinuate Jill could have done this?

She started toward him, no need to shout for the entire neighborhood to hear. He stepped out from behind the car holding the defaced T-shirt that she'd forgotten she'd hidden from Granny in her trunk.

Her heart froze in midbeat.

"No secrets. That's what you said." His voice was tight, angry. "Is this your idea of honesty?" The muscles in his arms were tense, near trembling, as he gripped the shirt. "What else aren't you telling me, Glory?"

Chapter Twenty-three

❧

GLORY TRIED TO snatch the shirt from his hand. "I told you, I'm not your responsibility. You don't need to protect me. These are just pranks to upset me and don't concern you."

He didn't release the shirt but used Glory's grip on it to pull her closer. "You said you wanted honesty. Is this how you begin?"

When she just stared at him, he added, "And what do you mean, it doesn't concern me? It's my face that's been burned out of this photo. I'd say that's personal. And what is being insinuated here definitely concerns me professionally." He drew her a little closer and looked down at her. "Have there been others?"

Glory ignored his question and wrenched the shirt from him. "Go inside. I'll change my own damn tire."

"Have there been others?" He grabbed her arm when she tried to walk away.

His intensity drew an automatic response from her. "Just the two you've already seen."

"I don't think you understand how dangerous this could be."

"I doubt she'd go as far as actually hurting me."

"You know who's doing this?" He sounded stunned.

"I think you do, too." The instant she said it, she wished she could take it back. She had no proof that Jill was behind all this. There just wasn't anyone else who made any sense.

"How would I know?" he asked, the tension in his voice ratcheting up another notch. "You think I know and am keeping it a secret so you'll be more frightened?"

"No," she said. "I think you're keeping it a secret because it'll open up a whole can of worms you'd rather not touch."

"Jill? You think it's Jill?" he asked, sounding surprised.

She just stared at him, her arms crossed over her chest. Was he playing her, or had it really not crossed his mind?

"Jill wouldn't do this," he said with certainty.

Glory bristled. It seemed all but written in the sky to her; how could he not see? "How can you be so blind? She wants you back . . ."

"I told you, that's not happening. Jill's not perfect. And I admit her comments to you were misguided, but this . . ." He shook his head. "No way."

"Jealousy makes people do things you never thought they would."

"I guess you'd know that firsthand." There was a heavy innuendo in his voice.

"What are you getting at?" She felt the tide of this conversation turning on her. And she didn't like it.

"Jealousy changes people—and not just the one who's jealous."

She shook her head and threw a hand in the air. "You've completely lost me."

He looked straight in her eyes and asked, "Was there some reason for Andrew to think the baby wasn't his?"

She felt as if he'd clubbed her in the head. Her ears even rang for a moment. "I knew there was something about the fire that you've kept bottled up. If you suspect I set that fire to get rid of Andrew, then just say it!"

A porch light came on at the neighbor's house.

Eric slammed the trunk closed and said, "Let's go back inside. This is going to be complicated."

There were other issues that needed to be put on the table, and Glory had a feeling he was about to lay one of them down. She tried to calm her temper and walked ahead of him up the steps.

The few seconds it took to walk back into the house had given her time to absorb the illogicality of his question. What would make him ask about the paternity of her child?

Since the couch was the only place to sit in his living room, Glory pressed herself deep into one corner in order to sit as far away from him as possible. Eric foiled her attempt to increase the physical distance between them by sitting on the coffee table directly in front of her. He leaned forward and rested his elbows on his thighs, lacing his fingers between his knees.

His presumption that she wanted to be close to him after he'd asked such a hurtful question made her even angrier.

"First off," she said coldly, "I don't know where you got the idea that someone other than my husband fathered my baby. But just for the *honesty record*; yes, Andrew was Clarice's father. I've never been with anyone else— *ever*. Until last Thursday night, that is."

Eric recoiled slightly as if stung, his relaxed posture stiffening. Then he sat stock-still for a long moment, staring just beyond her. His jaw worked as if he was clenching and unclenching teeth. His breathing became noticeably louder.

The truth dawned as bright as the morning sun in Glory's mind. "*Jill* gave you that idea."

He ignored her assumption and said, "No matter what happened between you and Andrew, I don't think you started the fire." The tone of his voice said this was the beginning of a much longer declaration.

Glory wanted to make him admit Jill's scheming, but the look on his face had been confirmation enough. There was a deeper question that needed to be answered. "Do you think it was intentionally set? You've told me again and again that it was the furnace—an accident."

Eric moved slightly closer to her. "All of the evidence at the scene tells me that the fire was a faulty furnace. The fact that you and Andrew suffered carbon monoxide poisoning backs up that theory. After a thorough investigation, accidental fire was the right ruling."

"But?" she said, fearing his speculation, yet needing to hear it.

"There are a few things that raised questions in my mind—not enough to change the ruling." After a pause, he said, "You said you'd told Andrew you wanted a separation that day. Can you remember anything else that happened that evening?"

Glory explained how Andrew had come home in a mood, accusing her of sneaking around with Cam Wilkes and that was what pushed her into a decision she'd been inching toward for months. She told Eric that Andrew had convinced her to sleep on it and that he'd moved his things into the spare bedroom. The last thing she could recall was going to bed alone.

"He reacted with hostility at first?" Eric asked. "Then calmed?"

"Yes. At first I thought he was finally going to explode into real violence. But when I didn't back down, he left the room and seemed to regroup. He was really making an effort to convince me we could work things out. That's why I felt I owed it to him at least to sleep on it, as he asked."

"And he moved into the spare room. You went to bed in the master."

"Yes."

"And you said Andrew was a fanatic about the smoke and CO detectors. Testing, replacing batteries."

"Yes. He replaced them four times a year, the same day he sent in our quarterly income-tax payments."

There was something in Eric's eyes that said something had clicked into place for him.

"Glory, what I'm about to tell you—it's not going to change anything. And I have nothing to back it up but my own intuition and what I personally know—or suspect, is more accurate—about Andrew."

In spite of the warm night, Glory was chilled to the marrow of her bones. "You think Andrew started the fire?"

"If all I had was the evidence that presented itself, I'd say no. But knowing what I know . . . I just can't convince myself 100 percent that he didn't."

With a tilt of her head, Glory prompted him to elaborate.

He went on, "When Andrew and I were seniors in high school, he dated Emily MacRady almost the entire school year."

Glory remembered the prom photo on Ovella's piano. Emily had been Andrew's date.

Eric said, "Just after prom, Emily broke up with Andrew and started dating someone else. Within a week, MacRady's barn burned to the ground."

"What would make you think Andrew did it? Was it ruled arson?"

"No. Accidental fire. It was Andrew's attitude afterward that made me wonder. He seemed so . . . satisfied. I even asked him outright if he'd had anything to do with it."

"And?"

"He gave a smug shrug and walked away. It was creepy really. I'd never been afraid of Andrew's occasional eruptions of temper. That emotion was out there where you could deal with it. But this subdued reaction, the veiled treachery in his eye, was very disturbing." Eric swallowed drily. "The worst part of it was, I gave him the tools to do it."

"What do you mean? How could you have—?"

"Not purposefully. And I don't know if I was milked for information and our conversation was the beginning of his plan, or if it was just a case of unfortunate timing."

Eric rubbed his eyes with the forefinger and thumb of one hand. Then he went on, "I'd been interested in firefighting since eighth grade. I read anything I could get my hands on about it—it was the investigation that really intrigued me. We'd talk about it sometimes, Andrew and me. Just a few days before the MacRadys' barn burned, we'd had one of those conversations. I can't remember which one of us started it. But it was basically about how a person could set a fire and not have it detected as arson."

"That doesn't mean Andrew burned that barn. It was probably coincidence."

"I know that's what everyone would believe. That's why I never said anything. It wouldn't have done any good. Maybe if I had . . ." His gaze slid to the floor, and he rubbed the back of his neck.

"Oh, come on! Even if something like that did happen way back then, it doesn't have any bearing on what happened on Laurel Creek Road. Andrew had no reason to set our house on fire. And he *died* in it, for Christ's sake! It doesn't even begin to make sense."

She thought for a moment, then went on. "Besides, I was the one by the door. If anyone set it, maybe it was me. Everything you've said about Andrew's paranoia and possessiveness was true. Maybe I was so afraid I'd never be able to get away from him—afraid he'd hurt the baby if I didn't . . ."

Eric slid off the table onto his knees before her and took her hands in his. "Look at me."

Slowly, she did. She could hardly believe she'd said the words that she'd been terrified of for days. *Maybe it was me.*

"No matter what he made you think of yourself, there is absolutely no way that you could have committed such a horrible act. No way in hell!"

"Then why was I by the door and not in bed—the last place I can remember being?" Now that it was out, her need to know what she'd done was greater than all else.

"Pregnancy can reduce the effect of carbon monoxide poisoning." He squeezed her hands. "Maybe you woke and tried to find your way out after he fell unconscious."

"I don't remember waking."

"And you won't. You probably wouldn't remember that even if you hadn't experienced all of the other memory blocks. You were confused, near losing consciousness yourself."

"But if Andrew set it, why wouldn't he just leave? Get out right away?" she asked.

"Glory, do you know where we found him?"

"In bed. No one would set a fire, then go get in bed!"

"He was in the *master* bedroom, not the guest room where you said he was going to sleep. He'd been lying beside you."

It seemed too bizarre a concept to grasp. Andrew had been controlling, jealous, and even paranoid—but what Eric was implying was plain crazy.

As she thought over the facts of what she did know for certain, several things took on clearer meaning: his uncharacteristic calm after his initial anger. His insistence that she sleep on her decision before she packed up and left. His words: *I know what I want. You and I are meant to be together forever.* Forever.

He had lain down in bed next to her and waited for them both to die, together. Forever.

Could it have been like that?

Glory closed her eyes and fought nausea. Had she been living with a man so totally on the edge?

Eric said the words that she was thinking, "Andrew didn't plan on getting out of that fire. He probably blocked the flue from the furnace to increase the CO level so you were both unconscious before the fire actually started."

She made herself ask, "Why fire? If he planned on dying too, why go to the trouble of making it look like an accident?"

Eric gave a half shake of his head. "Could be a couple of reasons. He obviously wasn't thinking rationally. But he was a businessman—a shrewd businessman; Andrew always wanted to make sure he got his due. Accidental fire; insurance pays. Even so, my guess is the stronger reason would be that he wanted to protect his parents from scandal."

"This is all just speculation." *Speculation that rang disturbingly true.*

"Yes," he said. "No way to prove any of it."

"Could Andrew have been that . . . crazy?" She'd become increasingly frightened of him, but even in her most far-fetched fears she'd never come up with such a strange and tragic scenario.

"I don't know. He was paranoid and possessive. But who can tell what really goes on in a mind like that?"

Glory started to tremble. "He wanted me dead . . . wanted our baby dead."

Eric moved onto the couch beside her and pulled her into his arms. He felt warm and solid next to her frigid, shaking body.

He said, "I don't want you to think about that anymore." He kissed the top of her head. "That's one of the reasons I didn't want this conversation ever to have to take place. But I couldn't allow you to think that you'd had anything to do with that fire." He rubbed her back.

"And we can't *know* that's what truly happened. It was an accident. A horrible, tragic accident."

"What did I do to make him hate me so?" Her voice was muffled against his shirt.

"He didn't hate you, Glory. He loved you. Andrew loved you in his own tormented, confused way."

Eric returned to the living room with a steaming mug with a tea-bag tag dangling over the rim. He pressed it into Glory's hands and sat down beside her.

"I called Tula and told her you were staying here tonight."

Glory's startled gaze snapped from her tea to his face. "You what?"

"There's no way you're driving back out to the hollow in this condition—even if there wasn't someone circling you like a vulture leaving threatening notes."

"What did you tell Gran?"

"The truth."

"Now she'll be worried."

He grinned. "Maybe, but she won't be lecturing you for spending the night with me."

She threw him a glare.

"Really," he said more seriously, "I thought it was best. Lies just get all tangled and end up doing more damage in the long run. She already knew about the first note anyhow. Besides, she should probably be on alert too—just in case."

"In case what?" Glory's throat tightened, and her heart skittered through an erratic beat.

"In case someone delivers more messages; maybe she'll see them."

Glory gave a bark of bitter laughter. "Eric, the woman is losing her sight."

"Her right eye is fine. She said it had cleared up completely." He blew out a breath. "That's beside the point. The more people we have paying attention, the more likely we'll find out who's doing this."

Glory pursed her lips for a moment, then said, "You really don't think it's Jill?"

With a shake of his head, he said, "I really don't. She might be manipulative, but she's not a stalker."

"Eeww. I hadn't thought of it as a stalker. That sounds so . . . serious."

"It is serious. Whoever it is, is persistent with this theme; and they keep making it more personal. I don't think they're just going to disappear. I think you should turn in the notes and the shirt to the sheriff tomorrow."

If she hadn't been convinced that Eric truly believed Jill was innocent of these pranks, his suggestion to bring in the law sealed it.

"What can the sheriff do?" she asked.

"Nothing if he doesn't know about it."

Now she was getting spooked. "I should go home. If you're right, Granny shouldn't be out there alone."

"You're not going anywhere. I called Charlie, and he's going to stay at Tula's tonight."

"Did you tell him why?"

"Didn't I just say the more eyes we have working for us the better?"

"Yeah, but Charlie . . . he'll take it as a joke. Lady'll probably do a better job of watching after Gran."

"Maybe Charlie never comes through because no one expects it of him. He knows what I expect. I made it perfectly clear."

There was some truth in what Eric said. No one had expected anything from Charlie but charm and good times—he'd been a champion at delivering both.

"At least Lady's there, too," Glory said wryly.

Eric sighed and shook his head. "Drink your tea. Then you're going to bed."

She sipped dutifully for a few moments. Then she set her cup on the coffee table and leaned back against him. His arms came around her, holding her back tight against his chest.

They sat that way for several minutes. Glory was content to remain there for the rest of the night. But he finally kissed the crown of her head and said, "Time for bed."

"You're not going to make me go alone, are you?" she said quietly.

"Nothing would make me happier than crawling into bed with you."

She turned with a smile, and he kissed her lips.

He said, "You've had a lot thrown at you tonight. And I don't think either of us is making the soundest of decisions at the moment. We need to take a step back—at least for a while."

"Oh, I see, sort of like a *we-haven't-slept-together-yet* do-over?" she said. "Really, Eric, that bridge has already been crossed. There is no uncrossing it." She turned in his arms and kissed him on the mouth. "And I want you to come to bed with me."

A weak moan came from deep in his throat. His hands framed her face, and his mouth sought hers. The passion that burned in his kiss confirmed that he wanted what she wanted. She pressed herself against him, opening her mouth to his, and began to feel herself slide into the place where nothing mattered except the sensation of Eric's body next to hers.

She said against his lips, "Come on." She attempted to get up off the couch and pull him with her.

He pulled back, drawing her onto his lap. Looking steadily into her eyes in a way that caused a hitch in her breath, he said, "When we make love again, I want it to be a pledge toward the future, a beginning."

She wanted him to make love to her, needed it. And maybe that's just what he was afraid of . . . that she needed the comfort of the moment; that she wasn't making a conscious decision to commit herself fully to this relationship.

"I don't believe either of us will know with any certainty until we actually travel that road. I'm not asking you to rescue me, Eric. You're not responsible for my choices. And right now, I'm choosing to be with you. If we decide there are things that we can't overcome, I won't break."

For a long while he studied her face, as if memorizing her features before a long separation. "But I might."

His unguarded confession tightened the bond that, she now could see, had been forming since the day he'd pulled her from the fire. The thickness in her throat told her she was close to tears—and the last thing she wanted to do was cry. All of the tears she'd ever shed in front of him had been tears of loss, pain, and fear. What threatened to fall now were tears of hope, trust, and affection. But he might not be able to tell the difference.

Instead of crying, she concentrated on showing him just how much she cared for him. She turned herself on his lap until she was straddling him. His eyes were filled with anticipation, with passion restrained, but he held completely still.

Sliding gentle hands behind his neck, resting her thumbs against his jaw, she began to kiss him—not fierce, ardent kisses, but soft kisses of reverence, of promise. From the corner of his lips, along his jaw, on his beard-stubbled cheek, across his brow, and finally coming full circle to his mouth.

She could feel his entire body trembling, as her own did in response.

Leaning only slightly away from his face, she whispered, "I've never trusted anyone like I trust you."

He finally moved. A slight tremor shook his hand as he trailed the back of his fingers along the side of her neck. They came to rest against the crest of her collarbone. "I don't want to abuse that trust."

Glory's body was electrified, every sensation heightened. She knew there was no going back for her; she'd been his since the stormy night he'd held her bruised body and asked nothing in return.

She put her hand on his and moved it between her breasts, over her heart. Flattening his palm against her chest, she held it firmly against her. "I trust you with my heart. Can you trust me with yours?"

With his other hand, he took hers and pressed it on his own chest. "I do. I trust you with my heart. But—"

She kissed him quickly. "No buts, not tonight. I understand your life—your responsibilities. But tonight, it's just about us. You and me and what our hearts want."

This time when she pulled him off the couch, he followed her. He closed and locked the front door on their way to the stairs.

At the base of the steps, his passion finally broke through his restraint. He grabbed her and spun her around, drawing her into his arms. His lips took hers with a rough force that sent a thrill through her entire body. She'd never wanted a man like she wanted him. She wanted to draw him inside her, completely envelop his soul with her own.

His hands cupped her backside, drawing her more firmly against him.

She needed no more invitation.

They didn't make it upstairs. They were both too impatient, too desperate in their need. He took her right there against the wall next to his front door.

Leaving their clothes where they landed on the floor, Eric carried her to his bed. As he laid her down, he smiled. "Now I'm going to do this right."

More than once throughout the night, Glory saw just what a perfectionist he was.

Chapter Twenty-four

❧

AFTER CHANGING THE TIRE on Glory's Volvo, Eric followed her to the sheriff's office. She rather reluctantly filled out a report and gave a detailed accounting of when and where she'd received the notes.

"Really," she said for the hundredth time, "I'm sure this is all just a prank. I feel a little silly making such a big deal about it. I really don't think the slashed tire is related."

This time Eric stood behind the chair where Glory was sitting and kept his mouth shut. He let the sheriff, a laid-back father figure, do the convincing.

With a tap of his pen on the report form, Sheriff Cooper said, "Could be. Could be more. Never hurts to have something on file, just in case. And we'll increase patrols past the Baker property. No harm in showing a presence—usually that's enough to stop pranksters."

Glory stood up. "Thank you, Sheriff."

Sheriff Cooper stood, too. "Now you call me right away if you get any more of these."

"I will."

"And bring those other notes by next time you're in town. I'd like to have them on file, too."

Glory nodded, looking embarrassed and uncomfortable.

Eric walked her to her car, kissed her good-bye, and watched her drive away. Then he went back inside.

He knocked on the open door of the sheriff's private office as he stepped in. "Could you check with city police to see if they've had any reports of property damage last night?"

"Just hung up from there." He nodded toward the phone on his desk. "And so far, no reports. But it's early; some folks might not have discovered that they were victims of mischief makers just yet."

"What do you think of this?" Eric asked.

The sheriff rolled in his lips and shook his head. "Not sure. First reaction, I'd say prankster—but it seems too personal. It's for sure someone who wants the lady upset. You did the right thing in making her report it." He seemed to think for a moment, then asked, "Was there something suspicious about that fire that didn't find its way into your report?"

"What makes you ask that?"

The sheriff rubbed his chin. "All the notes make it pretty clear someone thinks Ms. Harrison is guilty of arson—and murder. Any possibility they're right? You know, inconclusive evidence and the like."

"No. It was the furnace . . . *conclusively*. No evidence to the contrary."

Sheriff Cooper gave a nod of acceptance. "Well, probably just someone out to get Ms. Harrison riled up. There are some sick and twisted minds out there. Never know what some people will do for entertainment."

Eric left the sheriff's office as convinced as ever that this was a personal attack; it went after Glory's most vulnerable point. For what purpose? Was it meant to frighten Glory into . . . what? Breaking down and admitting guilt? Leaving town again? There had to be a motive; until he figured out the why, he'd be hard-pressed to discover the *who*.

When Glory got home, Granny was doing laundry, her usual Monday chore.

" 'Mornin', Glory," she called from the utility room. "Got some sweet tea in the fridge. Why don't you pour us a glass? I'll be out in a minute."

"All right." Glory poured the tea over ice and set the glasses on the kitchen table. "Did Charlie come and stay last night?"

"Oh, yes. We played cards—then he played guard dog, lockin' doors, sleepin' on the couch so's he could hear better if'n someone was up to mischief."

Glory wondered exactly what Eric had said to Charlie to induce such uncharacteristic diligence.

Granny stepped into the kitchen, wiping her brow with a paper towel. "It's hotter'n Hades today. Let's take this out to the front porch."

"Sounds good." Glory picked up both glasses and headed toward the front of the house.

"I just need to grab something, and I'll be right along," Granny said.

When Granny stepped out onto the porch, she held her sewing basket in one hand. "Might as well work while we talk." She set the basket next to Glory's chair.

Glory eyed it suspiciously while Granny opened it and pulled out Scott's quilt. When she handed it to Glory, Glory said, "You know I can't sew."

"That's why I'm gonna teach you." She spread the quilt neatly over Glory's lap, then pulled out a long, narrow strip of fabric that matched one of those in the quilt pattern. It had been folded lengthwise and pressed crisply. "This here will be the new binding. Now for a child's quilt, such as this, it won't take no time 'tall. First take off the old binding—those little scissors with the blue handle will be just right for ripping out the stitches."

"Don't you want to talk about last night?" Glory picked up the scissors and began picking out Granny's perfect, even stitches.

"Rather not hear the p'ticulars. Thought I made that clear yesterday."

Glory rolled her eyes. "I was talking about the tire slashing and the T-shirt with the . . . message on it."

"Oh, that. I figured we'd get round to it."

"Eric seems to think it's serious; made me file a report with the sheriff. But I'm still not convinced the tire was associated with the notes."

The look on Granny's face said she had an opinion about that but wouldn't offer it unless asked. She was a stickler for standing behind her bargains; she'd said if they were to continue living together, she'd stay out of Glory's business, and Glory should stay out of hers.

"Really, Gran, I think you're taking this privacy thing too far. Just tell me what you're thinking."

Gran gave a half nod, as if to acquiesce now that Glory had made the request. "Well, seems that if somebody wanted to really put you in a pickle, they'd cut all four tires—or at least two. Maybe whoever did it wanted you to be able to drive away—not be stuck at Eric's overnight."

Glory shook her head. "I still think it was just a random thing. You're right; if someone wanted to punish me, they'd take out more than one tire." She thought for a moment. "Whoever sent those notes just wants me upset; probably not someone willing to do something illegal like vandalizing property.

"I can't figure who would be so nasty."

Granny picked up her tea glass and leaned back in the chair across from Glory. "Who indeed?"

"You say that like it's obvious."

"No. Not obvious. Just gotta ask the question to get to the answer."

"Who would want to hurt me like that?"

"What makes one person strike out at 'nother? Love. Hate. Jealousy. Greed."

"Well, at least we know it can't be greed." Glory gave a half chuckle. "I don't have anything."

"You might have something someone wants—don't have to be money," Granny said.

"I don't have—" Glory stopped midsentence. "Eric? I'm not at all sure our relationship is going anywhere."

"Prob'ly won't if some folks have their way."

"You're suggesting Jill?" Glory set the sewing in her lap. "I had that thought already. Eric's convinced otherwise; I guess he should know her better than we do."

Granny pursed her lips for a moment before she said, "Could be Jill. Or someone who wants Jill to have him. Or could be somethin' else entirely. Don't reckon we'll know until they make a mistake and get caught. 'Course maybe they'll just stop, and we'll *never* know. Be fine by me. Don't like all this ugliness."

Glory picked up the quilt and began working again. She didn't want to tell her grandmother what she was really thinking; if it meant she'd never know who was sending those notes, she'd just as soon have them keep coming until they had it figured out.

"I know I can undo stitches," Glory said finally. "It's the putting back in I'm not so sure about."

"It'll be a fine thing when you get done. Best way to show you care is by doin' something special like this." Granny touched the quilt, and there was a look of longing on her face.

Glory knew how much it had meant to Granny to give the labor of her hands to those she loved.

Laying her hand on top of Granny's, Glory noticed the similarities in them. But Granny's showed the years. How could such work-worn hands create such fine and delicate stitches?

Granny sighed roughly. "Now that you got them stitches out, let's get this binding on, and you can take it to Scott."

Glory's head snapped up. "I'm not taking it to him. He'll be here on Thursday."

"He'll miss it. 'Sides, it'll be nice for him to know you were the one who fixed it."

Glory sat in silence.

"It's no disrespect toward your little Clarice if you do a kindness for Scott." Granny's voice was soft, so soft Glory nearly missed what she said.

Quietly stated, those words nevertheless echoed in her mind. But unlike a dwindling echo, they gained strength with each repetition.

Glory closed her eyes and thought of Eric's question; could she accept Scott as he was?

Suddenly she realized Granny had hit the bull's-eye; opening her heart to Scott *did* feel like a betrayal to Clarice.

But it went deeper. Much deeper. The thing that caused fear to clutch Glory's gut and made her want to run in the opposite direction wasn't Scott's disability—it was his need, his great, cavernous need, his total vulnerability. She'd failed her own child, how could she give to someone else's? Worse yet, what if she failed again?

She clutched the quilt to her breast and felt the tears well in her eyes.

Granny stood in front of her, her figure blurred in Glory's vision.

"I knowed you'd understand, in your own time." She kissed Glory's forehead, then knelt before her. "It's time for your heart to move on. Little Clarice is with Jesus and happy as a spring lamb, safe and secure in his embrace."

Glory leaned forward and threw her arms around her grandmother. She still clutched Scott's quilt tightly in one fist. As she slid to the porch floor, Granny's arms encircled her.

With her head on Granny's shoulder, Glory wept; at last the cleansing tears of letting go.

"Glory! Eric's on the phone!" Granny called out the back door.

Glory set the garden hoe aside and went in, hoping he wasn't going to rag her about taking those notes to the sheriff. It hadn't even been a full day yet, for Pete's sake.

"Hello."

"Hey, Glory. Listen, I hate to leave you alone right now, but the clinic at Duke University called and they have a cancellation for Scott. If we don't take it, it'll be weeks before they can get him in. We're on our way right now."

We, as in he and Jill. Jealousy nearly edged out concern. "That's great. I'll be thinking good thoughts. And don't worry about me, I'm not alone."

She heard him exhale. "I know. But I'd feel better if I was there."

"Just look after your son. How long do you think you'll be gone?" She hoped her voice didn't sound too needy.

"A couple of days. Our appointment is in the morning. They said to plan on a day and a half of testing."

Glory wanted to ask if they were sharing a hotel room, but managed to squelch the urge. She heard Jill say something in the background.

Eric's muffled voice responded, "We'll discuss it later."

Glory didn't like the fact that Jill was listening to Eric's conversation with her. "Call me when you get back. And be careful."

"You, too."

"Okay."

"I mean it, Glory. Keep your eyes open—in fact, why don't you just stay home until I get back." His tone said he knew what her reception to that would be.

"Watch it, hero. I'm a big girl."

He laughed.

She said, "Good luck. See you in a few days."

When she set the phone back in its cradle, Glory wondered, when exactly had a couple of days begun to feel like an eternity?

To pass the time and try to keep her mind from playing scenes of Eric and Jill living like a family for two days, Glory attacked the garden with renewed vigor. Once it was weed-free, she washed all of Granny's windows. Then she tore into repairing Scott's quilt.

By the next afternoon, she'd taken out nearly as many stitches as she'd put in, striving to match the fine needlework of her grandmother. Finally, Granny told her just to get it finished, or she was going to have the dang thing worn threadbare before Scott got it back.

But Glory wasn't ready to be finished. She was improving as she went. Something about the near-endless repetition of stitches and the steady motion of her hands was soothing. Plus, she used the time to analyze her feelings about becoming a part of Scott's life as well as Eric's. And for the first time, she didn't experience an overwhelming sense of disloyalty.

She'd come to accept the past enough that she no longer felt the urge to run, to hide from everything that had happened here. The new memories she'd begun to build with Granny and Eric now acted as a counterbalance to tragedy.

She would stay in Dawson. The rest—Eric and Scott— she still didn't know. She supposed the ball wasn't really in her court anymore. So much of what Eric would do hinged upon Scott's diagnosis. She could only make choices for herself and her new life. And that's what it finally felt like; a new life, one of promise and possibility.

She tied off the last thread. Scott's quilt was done. She held it up in front of her for inspection. Not bad. Maybe she'd try her hand at another quilting project.

She put the quilt aside, still unsure about delivering it. Then she went inside and pulled out the notes she'd taken from the magazine article on service dogs. She called two of the organizations referenced in the article, requesting information. There were endless things to be considered—funding and her own training not the least of them. But it was a beginning.

After that, while she and Granny had sweet tea on the porch, Glory explained the skeleton of a plan she had thus far.

"You ain't thinkin' I need one of them dogs, are you?" Granny asked.

Glory decided to be honest. "Not like a Seeing Eye dog, but if you decide to throw me out, it might be nice to have a dog around here. They can be trained to call 911, you know."

"In case I stub my toe and crack my head open?" Granny said, her dander obviously rising.

"Yeah, Gran, in case of that."

Glory put enough challenge in her tone that Granny's expression shifted. A slight smile came to her lips.

"Reckon lots of folks could use a dog that can dial 911."

"And that's just the tip of the iceberg," Glory said.

"Seems to me," Granny said, "we could start with them pups we got right under our own roof."

Glory could see the wheels of enthusiasm beginning to turn, the brightness come alive in Granny's eyes. At her core, Granny was a giver. And training the dogs would allow her to give to others in a new way.

A good portion of the "observation" done by the Duke team evaluating Scott had to be done without Eric and Jill in the room. During those times, Eric had felt like he'd crawl out of his skin. But that was nothing compared to the way he felt as they waited to go in and hear the results of those observations from Dr. Brandenburg.

He held Scott tightly on his lap. Jill had reached over and clasped his hand. Over the past hours, even her determined optimism had begun to slip.

There was one other couple with a child in the waiting room. Even so, it was silent enough that Eric could hear everyone breathing.

"Mr. and Mrs. Wilson." The secretary called them in.

Eric wasn't sure his knees would hold out when he stood up. But they did. Jill's didn't. She faltered, then sat back down.

He shifted Scott to his left hip, then extended his hand toward her. "Come on. We'll get through this." God, he wished he felt as confident as he sounded.

Slowly she put her hand in his, that same trust brimming in her eyes that haunted Eric from accident victims; as if he had the power to save. Right now, he felt like he could use the saving.

Suddenly, he wanted Glory—*needed* her to stand beside him, to hold his hand while he faced the news that would shape his son's future.

They were seated in front of the doctor's broad desk. It was clean and organized, evoking confidence that the man knew what he was about.

Dr. Brandenburg folded his hands on top of a thick folder, filled, Eric supposed, with all of those observations. "I think our team has enough evidence to say that without a doubt, your son is suffering from several of the symptoms of autism."

Eric felt as if he'd stepped into a snare that whipped him off his feet and had him suddenly dangling upside down thirty feet above the ground.

Why couldn't the man beat around the bush a little bit? Ease them in.

Jill made a squeaking noise.

When Eric glanced at her, she was pale. Her lips were moving, but nothing but that thin squeak came out. She had been in denial for so long, he supposed this had to be more of a shock to her than it was to him—and *he* felt as if he'd been gutted.

Dr. Brandenburg got up and retrieved a glass of water, giving it to Jill and telling her to take a sip.

Each breath Eric took while that happened brought him layer upon layer of steely calm. Now they could *do* something.

The doctor sat back behind his desk—an objective distance from the emotional upheaval his words had just caused. "This is not the end. It's the beginning for Scott. It might be a long road, but we can help."

Eric asked, "What's our first step? Where do we start?"

Jill led Scott to the front door, while Eric followed along with the suitcase. She'd convinced him to spend last night in North Carolina when he'd wanted to drive back immediately after their appointment with Dr. Brandenburg.

Eric set down the suitcases, kissed Scott's head, and moved back toward the door.

"You're not just leaving, are you?" Jill asked.

He stopped and turned around. "What were you expecting?"

"You can't just leave me with him! He has autism." That panic she'd first felt in Dr. Brandenburg's office was back in full roil.

Eric rubbed his forehead. He looked tired, but Jesus, she was tired too!

He took her by the arm and led her to the couch. Scott sat on the floor with his pirate boat. Suddenly, what she'd viewed as play now seemed ominous, dangerous even. That ceaseless spinning had condemned her child.

"Jill, Scott isn't any different than he was two days ago when we left here. We're going to get a good night's rest, then we'll make the arrangements the doctor suggested for therapies."

"But"—she glanced at her baby—"what if—"

"There's nothing different about tonight. Just do what you normally do. We'll worry about changes and modifications tomorrow."

She could hardly whisper, "What if they don't help?"

"We have to believe they will. If one fails, we'll find another. Remember the doctor said it might be trial and error until we hit on the right combination."

She shot to her feet. "That's easy for him to say! It's not his little boy."

"Do you want me to take him?"

"What?"

"Do you want me to take Scott with me?"

Anger bubbled in her chest. "No. I want you to stay here and behave like his father! We have to do this together."

When Eric stood in front of her and put his hands on her shoulders, she wanted to lean into him, make him wrap his arms around her so she could feel safe. But he held her firmly away.

"Jill, you know that's not going to work. We tried to build a marriage on the wrong things before; let's not make the same mistake twice. I'll be here. I'll always be here for Scott."

"But not for me?" She felt like crying.

"I'll support you, help you in any way I can. But my moving back here would be wrong. We'd both be miserable, and that can't be good for Scott."

. . . *both be miserable?* She wondered if he'd be so sure of that if he didn't have Glory Harrison sitting out in the hollow waiting for him.

Exhausted as he was, Eric didn't want to go face his empty house. So when he left Jill's, he went by the fire station. He checked in with the guys on duty and discovered nothing had happened in his absence except two fender benders.

He stopped in the garage to look over the equipment. It was just another stalling tactic; he knew his guys kept everything in top shape.

As he stood there, staring at but not focusing on the gauges of one of the trucks, he warred with himself. The first thing he'd wanted to do when he left Jill's was call Glory. So, why hadn't he done it?

Because I'm afraid when I tell her, it'll be the end. I asked her if she could accept Scott as he was . . . now there's a clear uphill battle ahead. What if she won't fight it with me?

Behind him someone cleared a throat.

It was Glory; his heart accelerated.

She held up Scott's quilt and approached with a little uncertainty. "I was in town and wanted to drop this off. It's all fixed."

He didn't miss the hint of pride in her voice. "*You* fixed it?"

She lifted her chin. "Yes, I did. And I'll take no criticism on my work. I'm a beginner."

He took ahold of the quilt and reeled her closer to him. "You won't hear criticism from my lips." He ducked close and kissed her.

She pulled back and looked around guiltily.

He laughed. "We're not in eighth grade. Besides, I'm the boss, remember?"

"So you can do whatever you want?"

"Pretty much," he said as he took the quilt from her hands. For the first time in weeks, he felt awkward with her.

"I've been waiting for you to call," she said softly.

"We just got back a little while ago."

"As tired as you look, it can't be good news."

"I need some comfort food. Can I buy you an ice-cream sundae?"

For a brief second there was fear in her eyes. Then she smiled and said, "Hot fudge with whipped cream and extra nuts."

They walked at an easy pace to Swisher's Ice Cream Shop. He liked walking down the streets of this town with her at his side. They both had deep roots here, had eaten sundaes at Swisher's as children and burgers and fries at Wimpy's as teenagers.

He had been alone a long time; although he'd never thought of himself that way until recently. He knew he was ready for a partner, a love to share his everyday life. And he wanted Glory to be that person. But she hadn't yet answered if she could accept his son. It was a package deal . . . and that deal had just gotten a whole lot more one-sided.

They sat in a booth at the back of the shop and ordered sundaes. They managed to avoid the subject at hand until after their ice cream was served.

Eric watched Glory fiddle, sculpting her whipped cream with her spoon. He recalled how much he'd wanted her with him when he received the diagnosis.

He decided it was only fair to lay it all out. "You were right. It wasn't good news. In their words, Scott is 'exhibiting several symptoms of autism.'"

"Autism," she echoed.

Eric nodded. "It wasn't a surprise . . . I fully expected it—" He couldn't continue.

Glory got up from her side of the booth and slid in beside him. She took his hand in hers.

He took a deep breath. "There are several things they suggested as far as therapies . . . speech to begin with, some possible modification of his diet . . . we won't know what will help until we try."

The ice cream was melting in both of their dishes; a thick, sticky drip slipped from the rim of his to the table.

Glory cleared her throat. "Yes. Well." She licked her lips. "At least you have a place to begin. Now you can take some positive steps."

"Yes. But I hadn't thought about what it might mean to you . . . to us."

"Scott is the same boy he was three days ago. Nothing has changed that would affect my decision."

He smiled slightly at her use of the same argument he'd used on Jill.

She went on, "I've been thinking, as you asked me to. I have a lot to say, and I'd like to say it all at once."

He nodded and grasped her fingers more tightly; his stomach felt like a boulder in his midsection.

"While I was working on the quilt, several things became clear. I finally think I understand my reticence toward Scott. It was something that never made any sense to me. I love children—and I'm not so shallow as to pick and choose only those who are perfect.

"I told you all along that the problem was me. Every time I thought of opening up, helping Scott, something inside me shut down. I guess I felt like I was betraying Clarice—helping another child when I couldn't help her. Letting another child into my heart when I'd lost her. I know it's crazy, but that's the truth of it. For a long time, something inside me was broken. And in that way, Scott and I are much alike. I understand how he feels—isolated, detached, insulated from emotions. And I want to help him in any way that I can. That said, I don't want to be the cause of more difficulty. I know you and Jill have to do whatever is best for your son; I don't want to interfere."

"I thought we understood each other on that point. It will never be best for Scott. It's not happening."

Glory nodded. "I do understand you won't be moving back in with her. But my . . . presence . . . could lead to more difficulties."

"Jill will have to under—"

"It's not just Jill's attitude that I'm talking about.

"My relationship with Andrew wasn't always the mess it was in the end. Somehow I allowed it to veer off course so far that it became destructive." She held up a hand when he opened his mouth to argue that it had been Andrew's doing. She went on, "Maybe there's something inside me that fueled that destruction. Had I been different, the outcome might have been different. And until I know myself better, I'm not ready to risk all of our futures." She paused and looked into his eyes. "Not yet."

He sat waiting.

She said, "Okay, you can talk now."

"I think that's a load of bullshit."

Her eyes widened, and she sat up straighter.

"There is no way in hell that you were responsible for the darkness inside Andrew. It was there long before you entered his life. The fact that you even think our relationship could take such a turn—"

"That's not what I said! All I'm asking for is some time. I care for you, Eric. I think we can be really good together, but I won't rush into something. Especially since it's not just you and me that will be hurt if things don't work out. You asked if I could accept Scott. I'm answering you as honestly as I can. I'm a work in progress."

"Aren't we all?" he said tersely.

"Does it have to be all or nothing? Is that what you want?"

He looked directly into her eyes. "If I say yes?"

Her green eyes took on the same steadfast resolve that he'd seen so often in Tula's. "Don't."

In his mind, when she came to him with her answer, he'd planned on telling her he loved her—no matter what her response. Of course, in his imaginings he'd envisioned a positive reply, followed by declarations of love on both sides. Still, he'd prepared himself for the alternative; if she couldn't accept Scott, he wanted her to know how he felt. He'd tell her and then he'd let her go. But he hadn't planned on this half-in, half-out scenario. He was surprised by how much it hurt. Her feelings didn't begin to touch the depths of his. Telling her he loved her now would be plain bad timing.

He bit the inside of his cheek as he tried to decide the best course. He wanted to say yes, all or nothing, now or never—he wanted her that badly. But when now or never would definitely be never . . .

He drew in a deep breath, knowing he was taking the risk of his life. "I've been doing some thinking too," he said, gravely. "And I want more."

Chapter Twenty-five

❀

THE GRAY LIGHT OF dawn was squeezing out the inky darkness of night in the hollow. Glory tossed and turned in the warm bedroom. Her head throbbed, and her eyes were dry and itchy. She'd tried to relax, tried to think of the nights that she'd lain in this bed listening to Granny and Pap talking on the front porch right below her window; remembered cool rain showers that wet the windowsill during spring nights; spread herself out so none of her limbs were touching her torso. But even her old tricks for overcoming the sticky heat failed her.

She hadn't been able to get Eric's words out of her head: *I want more.*

Eric didn't have casual affairs. He wanted more. And God help her, she did too. But it scared her senseless to think she might screw this up.

No matter how she looked at it, it boiled down to the same question: Did she want him enough, did she love him enough, to take the risk?

When they'd parted in town yesterday afternoon, she and Eric had decided to give each other a few days without contact to dig really deep and think things through.

Can I live like this for a few days?

She rolled onto her back and ran her fingers from her forehead back through her hair. The pressure as she pulled against her scalp eased some of the throbbing in her head.

She was on an emotional bungee jump. One minute falling so fast and frightened that she nearly called Eric and told him to forget it; she couldn't take the emotional risk so there was no sense in prolonging her suffering. The next moment, she'd bounce back, leaving her stomach behind, her love making her feel as light as a feather, and she'd almost have to tie herself to the bed to keep from calling him and telling him that she loved him beyond reason, and everything else—everyone else— could be damned.

Lying still hadn't seemed to cultivate a clear decision. Maybe sweating and exertion would be a better inducer. She heaved herself out of bed and got dressed. After loading a backpack with water and some fruit and a peanut butter sandwich, she wrote a note to Gran, telling her that she was hiking to Blue Falls Pond and would be back by late afternoon.

Checking quickly on Lady and her brood, she saw the puppies in a pile, fat bellies, curled tails, and tiny paws all jumbled, oblivious to the heat. Lady lifted her head and gave a sleepy wag when Glory entered. She stooped and petted the dog. "Take care of Gran while I'm out," she whispered, then left the room.

Stretching her neck and shoulders, she was looking forward to the long hike and spending time at Blue Falls Pond. She felt confident everything would become clear, as it always had when she sat on the bank of the pond and watched the glittering falls and the halo of a rainbow overhead.

She took a deep breath and went to the front door. Just the thought of being there made her feel like a new woman.

She made it only as far as the front porch. Scrawled across the porch floor in black spray paint were the words: *LEAVE NOW.*

"I don't know how I missed hearing someone out here. I was awake all night," Glory told Sheriff Cooper as he took photos of the porch floor.

"It happens. I swear some of these kids are part cat."

She crossed her arms over her chest. "So you think it was kids?"

"Maybe. Spray paint is normally their weapon of choice." Then he asked, "Anything else disturbed?"

She spared a look at Granny, standing just inside the screen door with her hands on her hips. Then Glory shook her head, and said, "I took a good look around. Everything's fine."

He nodded toward Lady. "Dog didn't bark?"

"No. She doesn't know a stranger."

"Nothin' wrong with that." He knelt and scratched Lady behind the ears. She danced from paw to paw, tail wagging, tongue lolling—showing herself for the watchdog she wasn't.

When he stood, he said, "I'll have a deputy come all the way up the lane here on his patrols. Just 'til we get this figured out."

"Thank you, Sheriff. I'd appreciate that."

He tipped his hat to Tula and headed back to his cruiser.

Glory called, "Sheriff!" She hurried down the steps. When she caught up with him she said softly, so Granny wouldn't hear, "I'd like to keep this quiet. Please don't mention this to Chief Wilson if you happen to see him."

"Yes, ma'am."

When Glory returned to the porch, Granny said, "I reckon this person never heard of 'sticks and stones.' What a pitiful waste of time and energy." She started away from the door. "Prob'ly have to paint over it. I'll get the brushes."

"Do you still think it could be Jill? Would she drive all the way out here in the middle of the night with her son just to do this?"

"I'd like to think not—Eric's got his hands full without shenanigans like this." She disappeared from the doorway.

Glory looked at the words painted on the floor and a chill ran down her spine. Each threat moved physically closer. Where would it stop?

The next afternoon, while Glory dozed in the hammock after being vigilant all night long, she heard a car coming up the lane. Sheriff Cooper had been true to his word; a deputy had driven right up to the house every two hours like clockwork. Granny had busied herself making cookies to give to him on his next pass. The heavenly smell had been teasing Glory's senses for thirty minutes.

She heard Granny come out of the kitchen and down the back steps.

The car stopped and shut off its engine.

Glory forced her eyes open and lifted her head.

It wasn't the deputy at all. It was Eric and Scott.

She threw her legs over the side of the hammock and hurried over, trying to reach them before Granny told Eric about the little message on their doorstep.

Granny was just taking Scott into her arms. "Eric called a bit ago," she said to Glory. "Looks like we're havin' overnight comp'ny."

Eric shifted and looked at Glory. "Sorry. Jill's down with the stomach flu, and Gail wasn't home. Half the night shift's out with the same virus, so I'm going to have to cover a shift."

Granny didn't act like she noticed the excuse was directed at Glory. She smiled and jostled Scott. "Oh, we don't mind, do we? I made cookies, and Lady's been lookin' for Scott all day. Let's go see if we can find her." She headed back into the house.

Eric handed Glory a small duffel. "Everything he needs is in there."

She took it. There were so many things she wanted to say, yet nothing would come out of her mouth.

He started to get in his car, then hesitated. "I'll be here to pick him up for school at eight-thirty. Maybe we could go to breakfast after? I know I said I'd wait, but I don't like things being left like this."

Glory bit her lip and nodded.

Eric got in the Explorer and turned around. Glory watched him drive away, knowing her heart would break if he was actually driving out of her life.

Tomorrow. Will I be any braver tomorrow than I am today?

That night, Glory dreamed of the fire. She was fumbling in a smoke-filled room, feeling blindly for the way out.

The smell of the smoke grew so strong, it was difficult to breathe. She heard the crackling flames. Lady was barking.

Lady?

Glory sat straight up in bed. Lady's frantic barks were coming from the hall. The choking smoke was real. The crackle of fire, real.

A tingle of stark terror shot through her body, and she froze.

This can't be happening! Not again!

The image of funeral markers rose in her mind.

Death. Fire was death.

Granny and Scott!

Glory's heart slammed into overdrive and she sucked in a gulp of air that made her cough.

She tried to shout a warning, but only sucked in more breath-stealing smoke. She sputtered and gasped.

Think. Stop panicking and think!

The smoke was thick at the ceiling. She rolled off the bed, taking her pillow with her. She ripped off the pillow-case and held it over her mouth and nose, then crawled toward the bedroom door.

Lady ran up and down the stairs, barking her heart out.

Granny's bedroom was near the top of the stairs, toward the back of the house; Scott was with her.

The tiny night-light at the top of the steps was some-how working. Smoke rolled in waves up the staircase ceiling.

Glory still didn't see flames. She crawled faster.

Granny's door was closed.

Glory banged on it hard before she opened it. "Gran!" The single word set off a coughing fit.

She covered her mouth again and crawled toward Gran's bed.

The smoke wasn't quite as thick in here. Was the fire at the front of the house? If so, they'd have to get out fast; the bottom of the stairs was near the front door.

Reaching up she grabbed her grandmother's arm at the same moment that Granny sat up, gasping.

Glory pulled her grandmother to the floor beside her. Then she urged her to move toward the door. "Go, Gran." Glory coughed. "Stay low," she rasped. "I'll get Scott."

Last night Granny had pushed her full-size bed against the wall and put Scott on the wall side. Glory reached for him, but grabbed only empty air.

She got on the bed, feeling under the covers in case he'd hidden near the foot. Nothing. She ran her hand in the small space between wall and mattress and still no Scott.

Fear got a fresh hold on her.

Frantically, she searched under the bed. Panic shook her good sense when he wasn't there. When she pulled herself out from under the bed, Granny was still there.

"Go! Follow Lady." She pressed the pillowcase against Granny's face.

"Scott?" Granny was wheezing.

"I'll find him. The door was closed—he has to be in here. Go. I can't carry you."

Just then, she heard a man calling from downstairs.

"Up here!" Glory helped Granny toward the top of the stairs.

Lady raced up and down, howling.

Glory saw the dark shape of man heading up the steps. "Deputy Hawkins." He identified himself. "Help's on the way."

"Take Gran!"

He scooped Granny into his arms. "Follow me, ma'am," he said to Glory as he started down the stairs.

Glory headed back into Granny's bedroom.

Calling Scott's name was a waste of precious breath, so she crawled around the perimeter of the room; feeling more than looking for the little boy.

She'd made it about halfway around when Lady shot past.

Glory hurried along after the dog.

Lady stuck her head behind an upholstered chair in the corner.

Glory grabbed her and pulled her back out, shoving her toward the door, dived behind the chair.

Scott was curled deep in the corner, holding his quilt over his face.

Glory pulled him to her. "It's okay." She coughed and made sure that the quilt stayed over Scott's mouth and nose.

There was no way she could crawl and carry Scott too. She stood in a low crouch. Even so, the smoke was more dense than it had been on the floor.

Scott began to cry, which made him cough. He bowed his back, making his body stiff and difficult to handle.

"It's okay." She patted his back and moved faster.

The night-light was out. Glory felt along the wall for the stair opening.

"Almost there."

Her knees nearly buckled when she saw the base of the staircase was in flames.

She could hear the deputy calling from somewhere downstairs.

She shouted, "Get out! Going out the window! The window!"

Please let him get out of here! Don't let him get hurt trying to get up here.

Scott was choking. She tried to cover his mouth and nose, but he jerked his head away.

She ran back to Granny's bedroom and slammed the door on the billowing smoke.

The window over the kitchen roof was open. Glory didn't want to take a chance of putting Scott down to take out the screen, fearing he'd bolt and run.

She held him tight in one arm, braced herself on the upholstered chair, and kicked at the screen. It ripped from the frame. She immediately stuck their heads out for a gulp of air.

How was she going to get out on the roof with him? What if she couldn't hold him and he fell?

She glanced back toward the bedroom door.

There was no other way.

She drew their heads back inside and sat on the floor. Scott's stiff legs kept him upright, his face even with hers. He'd choked enough that he'd thrown up on the front of his pjs and the quilt.

"It's okay, baby."

She wrenched the quilt from his grasp.

He screamed.

At least while he was screaming he was stick-straight. Glory wrapped the quilt around her back and brought the ends around front and tied them behind Scott's back.

Then she stood, held him steady with one hand, and balanced them as she crawled through the window onto the shingled roof. It was only one story, but steeply pitched. She scooted along on her backside until she reached the guttered edge.

"Help! Back here! Help!" She paid for her shouts with a lung-tugging coughing fit.

The deputy appeared below. "Is there a ladder in the garage?"

"Just take the baby!" The knot in the quilt had drawn so tight she couldn't get it untied. She wriggled it lower on Scott's body until she could get him free. "I'll lower him by the arms. You catch him."

The deputy stepped closer and raised his hands.

"Don't drop him!" she shouted.

The slant of the roof prevented her from finding any leverage to prevent toppling over as she lowered Scott.

She put one knee in the gutter, grabbed Scott by the forearms, leaned back, and eased him over the edge.

He wailed louder.

"A little more!" the deputy shouted.

Glory heard a siren in the distance.

She leaned closer to the gutter.

Something snapped. The gutter fell away from under her knee. She let go of Scott before she tumbled off the roof, hoping the deputy would catch him.

Her back hit a giant lilac bush, scraping her skin and tilting her to the side. She landed hard on the ground on her shoulder. White-hot pain shot across her shoulders and up her neck.

She rolled onto her back, trying to regain the breath that had been knocked out of her lungs.

Scott was screaming. Pain or fear?

As soon as she could squeak, she rasped, "Scott? Scott?"

The deputy knelt beside her, Scott in his arms. "He's fine, ma'am. I caught him. Don't move. Where are you hurt?"

The sirens blared closer.

"Can't tell yet," she wheezed.

"Stay still," he said, and put a hand on her shoulder to keep her down. "Help's here."

Revolving red lights reflected in the trees overhead. "Gran?"

"She's a little woozy. I have her lying down in the back of my cruiser."

"Lady? Is she out?"

"The dog? Haven't seen her out here, but I'm sure she got out."

The puppies!

There were shouts in front of the house. Booted feet pounded the ground and stopped behind the deputy, who immediately said, "Your son's fine."

Eric, thank God. She wanted to shout to him, but all that came out was a raspy squeak.

She heard Eric say something soft and calming to Scott. Then he told the deputy, "Take him around for some oxygen." Then he was by her side.

"Glory!" His hands were on the back of her neck, feeling the alignment of the bones.

The image of him hovering over her in his fire gear transported her, ever so briefly, back to the night on Laurel Creek Road.

But this time, she thought, almost giddy with relief, she had saved the child. God in Heaven, she hadn't failed Scott. An incredible lightness bloomed in a place that had been dark and heavy for so long.

She wanted to grab onto Eric, tell him the answer to his question, the question that had threatened to keep them apart; Scott had found a place in her heart, a special place that only he could fill.

But now wasn't the time.

"I think I'm okay," she said. "Is someone taking care of Gran?"

"Paramedic."

Eric continued to check Glory, before he put an arm around her shoulders and eased her to a sitting position. "Take it slow. Are you dizzy at all?"

"No." She looked toward the house. "The puppies!" The back room appeared dark, no flames.

He spoke into his radio. "Bring a hose around back." Then he stood. "I'll get them."

Glory forced herself to her feet. Her shoulder hurt like a son of a bitch, but she was whole. By the time she was upright, Eric was gone.

A few seconds later, the window opened in the back room. Glory hurried to the sill.

"It's gonna suck the fire this way. We don't have much time," Eric said as he handed puppies out two at a time. Smoke was already drafting through the open window.

"Lady?" Glory asked when he reappeared with the last two.

"Right here biting my boot. Had to take the last pup out of her mouth. She's next." He disappeared momentarily, then lifted the dog through the window.

Glory wasn't sure her shoulder could take Lady's forty pounds, but she braced herself and lowered the dog to the ground.

"Now you!" Glory said.

"I'm going back the way I came. Brady's bringing a hose through the back."

"No!"

He paused for a split second. "I know what I'm doing. Take care of Scott." He pulled on his mask and was gone.

Chapter Twenty-six

❀

"ERIC!" GLORY STARED at the smoke that filled the window he had just left, wanting to crawl in after him. There was a cold knot of fear in her chest. She stared at the window as the black smoke boiled out into the night.

Men shouted over the macabre background music created by the rumble of the pumper truck and the roar of the fire. The steady drone was punctuated by the squawk and crackle of communication devices. She moved toward the kitchen door, where the fire hose snaked into the dark house.

A deep groan of timber preceded a crash. Orange embers rode the updraft into the dark sky.

Glory tried to go in the kitchen door, but the choking smoke held her back. "Eric!" She ran to the front of the house.

The porch roof had collapsed, along with the front wall of the house. The firemen in front battled the flames from the outside.

She ran up to one of them. "Eric's still inside!"

The man put a hand on her shoulder and moved her out of the way as he shifted position with his hose.

There was no way Eric was coming out the front. She

ran to the rear again. Just as she rounded the corner, she saw two men stumble out the kitchen door. A third firefighter stood just outside, pulling the hose out of the house.

Glory ran faster.

The two men staggered a few feet away from the house, sat hard on the ground and pulled off their masks. The back of the coat nearest her said *Wilson*.

She came to a sliding stop on her knees beside Eric, her hands immediately going to his sooty, sweat-soaked face.

He coughed and put a hand on her shoulder. "I'm okay." He started to get up, motioning to the man with the hose toward the front of the house.

"Where are you going?" Panic rose in her voice.

"Back to work." Eric got up and followed the firefighter with the hose around the house.

The other man got to his unsteady feet and was right behind Eric.

Glory's legs were shaking too much to move.

The sun was coming up by the time the flames were out. Nothing remained of Granny's house except the chimneys and the shell of the kitchen. The rest had collapsed into the basement. Charred black timbers jutted at odd angles out of the smoking rubble.

Scott had finally fallen into an exhausted sleep in the backseat of the police cruiser. Glory sat next to her grandmother on the ground, arm wrapped tightly around Granny's shoulders, watching the sooty smoke curl lazily into the awakening sky. It almost seemed peaceful after the power of the raging blaze.

"Oh, Gran. I'm so sorry." She squeezed tighter. "I know you and Pap lived here your entire marriage."

Granny patted a bony hand on Glory's knee. "I still got what's important. House ain't nothin' without family. House can be rebuilt."

"But your photos . . ."

"Got 'em all in here." Granny touched her chest. And although the words were strong, Glory saw the tears glistening in Granny's eyes.

As the rest of the firefighters reeled in the hoses and stowed equipment, Eric came and stood before them. He was filthy and sweaty and was the most beautiful sight Glory had ever laid eyes on.

Then Glory saw the five-gallon gas can he held in his hand.

"I don't think it's going to be difficult to determine the cause of this fire," he said grimly.

Glory's stomach rolled, and she closed her eyes for a second. "Oh, my God . . ." She shuddered; Gran and Scott could have died. And it was all because of her.

Eric said, "Whoever it was didn't know a thing about disguising arson. This was sloppy beyond belief."

Glory looked directly at him. "Did Jill know Scott was out here?"

Anger shadowed his tired features. "She *could not* have done this."

"You didn't answer my question."

She saw his jaw flex as he gritted his teeth. "No. She didn't know." He drew a deep breath. "It wasn't her. First of all, she's not capable of such a sociopathic act. Second, she was sick as a dog. And third, she lived with a firefighter long enough to learn a few things. She's much too smart to have left such a careless trail of evidence."

When Glory didn't respond, he said, "There's plenty here to point the finger at who did this. It's just going to take a few days." He gave Glory a pointed look. "And it won't be Jill."

"I hope you're right, Eric," Glory said. "I hope you're right."

Without a word, Eric left them and returned to his crew.

"He's right, you know," Granny said. "Ain't Jill behind this."

Glory looked at her. "How can you be sure?"

"It ain't in her. I can tell 'bout what's inside people once I'm with 'em for a spell."

"Like you saw inside Andrew?"

"Like that." Granny nodded.

"You weren't so sure it wasn't her when we were talking about the notes," Glory said.

"Notes is differ'nt. Even a good woman jealous enough might send notes. But this is differ'nt."

"Let's hope so, Gran."

Eric didn't have to wait for lab results to point the finger at the arsonist. Later that day he was alone at the scene, as he liked to be when conducting his investigation (Deputy Hawkins had taken Glory and Tula to Eric's duplex and Scott to Jill's). One of the day-shift firefighters had delivered Eric's Explorer, so he had everything he needed to collect evidence.

As he walked in a slowly increasing spiral around the house, he saw a small shiny disk at the edge of the gravel lane.

He knelt to check it out.

Leaning close, he couldn't believe what was staring him in the face. Dear God, Glory was going to be shattered. He was glad she wasn't here. How would he soften the blow of this betrayal?

He used his pocket knife to slide the small BMW key fob emblem into an evidence baggie. It was clean and shiny; it hadn't been lying there long.

Then he went by his duplex. He had only one question for Glory. When he asked it, she was angrier than he'd ever seen her.

"Come on!" she shouted. "Are you so desperate to protect Jill that you'd jump to such an illogical conclusion?"

"All I asked was if Walt Harrison had any opportunity to put that T-shirt in your car."

"Yes, I suppose he did. But so did the rest of the population of Dawson. That key fob could have been dropped by one of the kids at the reunion. They've all got stuff like that."

"Seriously, BMW?"

"He *could not* have done this."

"When I said that about Jill, you didn't believe me."

"And you don't believe me."

"I believe you want to believe it." He turned around and walked out, angry with himself for even coming here first. It had been the wrong thing to do.

When he got in his Explorer, he radioed the sheriff to meet him at Walt Harrison's house.

* * *

Are you sure?" Sheriff Cooper asked as they got out of their cars in the Harrisons' drive.

"As sure as I can be without questioning him. You know as well as I do there's only one BMW in Dawson." Eric's blood simmered; he could have lost both Glory and his son. He had to get ahold of himself before he met the man face-to-face, or who knew what he'd do.

"All right, then," Cooper said. "Let's get this over with."

Eric nodded.

They waited for several minutes after ringing the bell. Then they rang again.

Finally, the door opened. Walt Harrison didn't appear surprised to see them on his doorstep. He did look like a man on the brink of collapse, however. With a look of resignation, he stepped back and motioned them inside. "Is everyone all right?" he asked in a tortured voice.

"You know why we're here, then?" Sheriff Cooper asked.

Walt's nod was almost imperceptible. "Glory? Tula? Are they all right?"

Eric wanted to grab Harrison by the shirtfront and slam him against the wall. This man nearly killed the people Eric loved most in this world.

Cooper said, "Everyone made it out."

Walt's entire body slumped as if the tension that had been holding him together had been released. "I was going to come in. I just needed a little time. How did you know?"

Eric snapped. He advanced on Harrison, his hands fisted, stopping just short of touching him. "You bastard! My son was in that house! I thought you loved Glory!"

Harrison looked him right in the eye. "I love Glory like she's my own daughter."

Eric spun away and paced around the foyer. Then he pulled out the baggie with the BMW emblem in it and waved it in front of Harrison's face. "Stop playing these games!" He shook the baggie.

Sheriff Cooper put a hand on Eric's shoulder. "Maybe you'd like to tell us what happened, Mr. Harrison."

"Please understand—"

A car door slammed outside, then the front door burst open. Glory rushed in out of breath.

"The flowers!" she said. "There were no flowers!"

Walt grasped her by the shoulders and hugged her close. "I'm so sorry—"

She glanced wild-eyed around the foyer. "Where's Ovella?"

The deputy who drove Glory there hung back in the doorway. "Sheriff, she said it was an emergency that she get here."

Cooper nodded to his deputy. "It's fine. Wait outside."

Eric stepped closer to Glory and asked, "What about flowers?"

"Clarice's grave. There were no flowers." She turned to Harrison. "You said she took flowers every other day. But there weren't any on the baby's grave." She looked back at Eric. "It wasn't Walt. It was Ovella."

Harrison shook his head and said again, "I'm so sorry." Then he looked at the sheriff. "My wife isn't well."

Eric asked, "Where is Ovella?"

"In a stress center, where she belongs. I just got back from taking her there. She's getting the help she needs."

Eric said, "You're telling me your wife set that fire?"

Walt Harrison's chin quivered momentarily before he regained his composure. "Yes, she told me she did."

"She just came in here and told you she set fire to Tula's house?" Eric said with disbelief.

"Not quite like that. I found her at the cemetery.

"I awakened around four and found her gone. She sometimes goes to the cemetery early in the morning, but never that early. I got worried. My car was gone—it had been parked behind hers." He swallowed drily. "When I got in hers, I found these." He went to the desk in the corner of the room and picked up several sheets of copy paper and handed them to Eric.

"Copies of the newspaper articles about the fire." He handed them to the sheriff. Then he said to Glory, "Like the one you found in your newspaper."

Glory dipped her chin in understanding. Was it any easier for her to think that her mother-in-law tried to kill her instead of her father-in-law?

Harrison continued. "Those were my first hint that something was really wrong."

"Why? Why did she attack Glory like that?" Eric asked, unable to keep the anger out of his voice.

Harrison's shoulders slumped even more with his sigh. The man looked as if he'd aged overnight. "Ovella never fully recovered from our son's death." Harrison hesitated, rubbed his hand across his mouth, then said, "My wife had some health problems—psychological problems—early in our marriage. She received treatment in Knoxville, and we managed to keep it to ourselves. For years she'd been fine. But after Andrew died . . . she started making some startling accusations about Glory. That's why when Glory decided to leave town, I didn't try to stop her. Ovella improved—I thought it was just grief—she was getting past it. I had no idea . . ."

"What kind of accusations?" Eric asked.

"She told me that Andrew told her the baby wasn't his." He shook his head. "I know that's ridiculous."

"Do you think Andrew really told her that?" Eric wondered if Harrison had any suspicions that his son had inherited his mother's disorders.

Harrison rolled his lips inward and drew a deep breath. "I really don't know. Sometimes I worried that Andrew had the tendency toward paranoia . . . but there wasn't ever anything concrete . . ."

"So she thought the baby wasn't Andrew's. Hardly reason to set fire to Tula's house nearly two years later," Eric said, moving closer to Glory and putting a supportive hand on her arm.

"Don't you see, logic had no part in this. My wife is *ill*. She was convinced Glory had set the fire that killed our son. When I found her this morning, she was crying over Andrew's grave, saying justice had been done."

"If she thought Glory had done it, why didn't she go to the authorities and report it?" Eric asked.

Harrison shook his head slowly. "Mother would never let Andrew's name be sullied by such scandal. She never even said it to me before today."

"Did you know she had been threatening Glory before she set the fire?" the sheriff asked.

"If I had suspected at all, you can believe I would have taken her to get treatment immediately, and this never would have happened." He paused. "The awful thing is, I don't think she *wanted* to do it. She kept asking why Glory didn't just leave."

"My presence drove her to avenge Andrew?" Glory said softly.

"Oh, Glory, who knows what went on in her mind. She was a proud woman . . . ," Harrison said.

Eric tried not to feel sympathy for the man who could have prevented all this. If there had been any hint of Mrs. Harrison's problem around town before this, Eric would have known where to start looking the minute that first note showed up. As it was, one tragedy just heaped on top of another.

Sheriff Cooper said to Eric, "If you want to go check on your boy, I'll finish up here." He turned to Harrison. "We'll need to know where Mrs. Harrison is receiving treatment and such."

Eric took Glory by the arm and started to lead her out. At the door to the foyer, she pulled away and ran into Walt's arms.

Eric watched them cry together. Tragedy heaped on tragedy, pain upon pain. At least this would be the end of the cycle.

Outside the Harrison house, Glory turned to Eric and said, "I'll have the deputy take me back to your place. You'll want to check on Scott, and I need to get back to Gran."

"I don't want to leave you. Not now." Eric pulled her against his chest. After a few seconds, he said, "I guess I owe you an apology about not trusting your judgment about Walt."

She leaned back and looked up at him. "And I owe you one about your judgment about Jill—so let's call that one even."

He sighed. "Ovella."

"Yeah. Ovella," she said sadly. She kissed his chin. "I'll see you later." She didn't want to talk about it now. Everything had come so quickly, she needed some time to sort out her thoughts.

As she rode next to the deputy in silence, she looked at the past with a new perspective. Ovella had always seemed so rigid . . . brittle. Glory had assumed it was because she thought herself above everyone else. But maybe it was the outward sign of holding herself together by a slender thread.

Had Andrew's controlling nature been a symptom of a similar dysfunction? She would never know. But it hurt her to think that maybe, just maybe, he could have been helped before all of this began.

Eric drove to Jill's. When he went in, he found Scott spinning his pirate boat and Jill lying on the couch in her bathrobe. She looked wiped out.

"Feeling any better?" he asked.

"The worst has passed. I even ate a cracker."

"I'll take Scott with me so you can rest."

"I want to keep him here—close—but thanks for offering."

Eric smiled and nodded. He knew how she felt. After coming close to losing him, he wanted to keep his son close, too.

"Do you know any more about the fire?" she asked.

He sighed. "It's ongoing; you know I can't discuss—"

"For Christ's sake, Eric, Scott almost died! Stop with the protocol."

"It's still my job, Jill." He started toward the door, then

turned. "Something like this certainly puts a different perspective on things, doesn't it?"

"Like there are worse things than your child having autism?" she said quietly.

"Like that."

When Eric pulled up in front of his duplex, the front door was open to the screen and the windows were open. He decided he liked the feeling of coming home to a house with Glory inside.

He opened the door quietly and was glad he had; Glory lay curled on her side, sleeping on the couch. The pile of used tissues on the floor next to her said she'd cried herself to sleep.

He tried to tiptoe to the kitchen, but she stirred.

"Scott okay?"

"Good as ever." Eric went to sit on the floor next to the couch. "Got a couple of scrapes from the shingles, that's all." He took Glory's hands in his, even though his fingernails and the creases in his skin were still outlined in soot. "And I have you to thank for that."

"You have me to thank for his being in danger in the first place." She inched to the edge of the couch. "Eric, if I had had any idea that something like this would happen, I wouldn't have stayed there; I would have found a place by myself." Her bloodshot eyes pooled with tears. "I am so sorry I put your child at risk."

"It wasn't your fault."

"You know, when I was in that burning house, the only thing that mattered was getting him out, keeping him safe."

"And you did." He kissed her forehead. "You were the hero this time."

She laughed softly. "At least you didn't have to rescue me, for a change."

"Hey, I like rescuing you."

She smiled and looked at his stained hands. "Here I am talking, and you probably want food and a shower."

He was still in the clothes he'd worn under his fire gear. He had managed to clean his face with the disposable wipes he had in the Explorer, but he was dirty and smelled of house fire. "I'll get one in a bit. How's Tula?"

Glory sat up and swung her legs over the edge of the couch. "Stubborn as ever. Even though Deputy Hawkins and I both ragged her all the way into town, she still refused to go to the ER and get checked." She pushed her silky hair away from her face. "Paramedics said she's okay, and I really do think she is. She's up in your bed."

"We'll keep an eye on her."

Needing to be close, he pulled Glory down into his lap. They sat quietly for a few moments, Eric thankful to the core of his being for the good fortune that saved those he loved. And he did love Glory.

As if she read his mind, she said, "You know, things become brilliantly clear when you think you've reached the end of the road. When I thought I might never see you again . . . I swore if I made it out alive, I wouldn't be afraid of anything. Life *is* chances, and it's a sin not to take them."

His heart took flight, but she spoke before he could say anything. "Eric, when I couldn't find Scott in that fire . . . I can't tell you what that did to me." A tear slid down her cheek.

"Shhhh." He hugged her close. "I know exactly what it did to you, because that's the way I felt when we got the alarm. Scott, you, Tula; I'd have died if anything had happened."

She nuzzled the side of his neck and placed a soft kiss on his throat.

He didn't want to ruin this moment; would have been happy to sit there for the rest of the day. But there was more that needed to be said.

"Ovella probably won't stand trial," he said.

"What good would it do if she did? She's sick. She's where she can get help. There's no way Walt will be able to keep this quiet. Everyone will know."

"You don't sound angry."

"Oh, I'm angry. I'm angry that she made some people think I could have done some awful things. I'm angry that she burned Gran's house. I'm angry that Scott and Gran could have been hurt. But I understand what losing a child can do to you"—she nodded slowly. "Oh, yes, *that* I understand."

"Don't you think Walt should have seen it coming?"

Glory sighed, then coughed. That cough was enough to make his anger rise again.

Then she said, "Ovella was very, very good at making people see only what she wanted them to see. Her husband included. Plus, Walt was dealing with his own grief." She paused. "I can't blame Walt—you don't know how wonderful he was when I was in the hospital—in spite of his own loss."

Eric looked at her for a long moment. "You're an amazing woman. How do you find the strength?"

She looked into his eyes. "From you. I get my strength from loving you."

Eric lay back on the floor, taking her with him. He

rolled her onto her back and looked into green eyes that reminded him of a cool evening in the forest. "I've been waiting to hear you say that." He kissed her, softly, gently. "I love you, Glory."

She pulled him closer, drawing him into a kiss that could quickly lead to other things. He slid his hand under her shirt and let himself go; wrapped himself in her love— a love he'd waited a lifetime for.

"Well, for Heaven's sake!"

At the sound of Tula's voice, Eric jerked himself to a sitting position as quickly as any teenager caught going for second base.

Tula continued down the steps, wearing an old robe Eric didn't even remember he had. "I took the bed upstairs just so there wouldn't be this sort of hanky-panky!" She fluttered a hand over her heart. "It ain't good for an old woman to see such things."

Glory tugged the hem of the shirt down and giggled.

Tula's bony bare feet padded across the hardwood floor toward the kitchen. Her eyes remained dramatically averted. "I'll just go make myself some tea to calm my nerves. When you two get y'rselves calmed down, you can come join me."

Glory's giggling got worse when Tula left the room.

Eric whispered, "Hey, we're in trouble here. I think you must be delirious from lack of sleep."

She reached up and pulled him back down on top of her. "I'm deliriously in love." She touched his cheek. "And don't worry about Granny, we have an agreement. I won't treat her like an old lady, and she won't scold me for doing this."

She kissed him until he could swear the floor vibrated beneath them.

Epilogue

❀

Glory sat on a boulder in the sun with her feet dangling in Blue Falls Pond. Eric was sprawled on his back beside her, dozing off the picnic lunch they'd just eaten. Lady bounced from here to there chasing a dragonfly. Glory looked around the most beloved spot on earth and thought this was a perfect Labor Day. She was glad she and Eric had decided on a quiet afternoon instead of the raucous activities the Baker clan had planned.

Scott and Jill were spending the day with a man Jill had met in Knoxville. He worked for an organization that served children with autism and acted as a liaison between all of the parties involved in the child's treatment, parents, doctors, therapists. Luckily, the guy seemed to genuinely care for Scott, too.

As for Scott, the speech therapist was doing wonders helping him develop his communication skills. Already, he had begun to say a few words.

Glory pulled her sewing out of her backpack and threaded a needle.

"Do you really think you're going to have that thing finished before he's a teenager?" Eric asked, opening one eye.

Glory dipped her foot deeper in the pond and flipped water at him. "I'm getting faster." She spread the section of quilt she was working on across her thighs. "Gran says I'll have it finished by Thanksgiving."

"My bet is the house will be rebuilt and kennel finished long before Scott sleeps with that quilt."

It was a teasing argument that never died between them. Glory wondered what they'd spar about once the quilt was done.

"So you admit, he *will* sleep with it!" she said triumphantly. "That's all that counts."

"That's what I love about you, your grace in victory."

"You'll miss me next month when Lady and I are off getting trained."

He sat up. "I miss you already." He kissed the tip of her nose.

"Probably not as much as Scott will miss Lady."

"Yeah, well, once she gets back, she'll be his forever."

"And I can start on those mischievous puppies of hers. Do you think there's a prayer I'll get one good service dog out of that litter?"

Eric laughed. "Tula says she's keeping Roscoe no matter what."

"Yeah, well, he's the last one I'd expect to qualify as an assistance animal, so Gran's not going to get a fight from me."

After a moment, Eric grew more serious. "I really admire what you're doing."

She put down her sewing. "Thanks. I love it so far—and it's going to be good for Granny, too."

"Have you and Tula decided on a name?"

"Cold Springs Canine Helpers. Says where we are, what we do. Can't get much simpler than that."

Eric shifted, dragging his backpack from where he'd been using it as a pillow. He slid his hand inside, but didn't pull it back out.

"What are you up to?" Glory asked.

"I was wondering, with your busy life and all, if you'd have room for one more thing?"

"What?" she said, suspiciously.

He drew his hand out of the backpack. "Me." He held out a beautiful diamond set in platinum. "On a permanent basis."

She tilted her head and smiled, her heart afire. "Oh, I think I can squeeze you in—if you're willing to relocate."

He leaned close and whispered against her lips, "I've always wanted to live in the hollow." Then he kissed her.

"It's going to be a houseful; you, me, Gran, Scott, various pooches."

"I won't take up much space. We can even bunk together if it'll help."

"Oh," she said, as he slipped the ring on her finger, "it'll definitely help."

About the Author

Susan's first book, *Back Roads*, won a RITA for Best First Book and two National Reader's Choice Awards in 2004. She lives in her native Indiana hometown with her husband, two college-age children, a menagerie of critters, and a rock band in the basement.

Visit her Web site at: www.susancrandall.net, or contact her at P.O. Box 1092, Noblesville, IN 46061, or susan@susancrandall.net.

The car engine idled and the windows began to fog in the
cold Kentucky night. Caroline Rogers switched off the ignition and allowed the stillness to envelop her. The air was
crisp and the snow fresh, lending an expectant hush to the
surrounding pastures and fields. The only sound was her
sister Macie's unsteady breathing from the passenger
seat. Caroline could sympathize; she suddenly felt a little
unsteady herself.

It was one a.m. and Caroline had done her reconnais-
sance. Ms. Stockton was in the habit of going to bed before
midnight, with all of the downstairs lights still on—including those on the Christmas tree in the living room window.

Christmas. She couldn't believe it was almost Christmas. Although she'd tried to deny its approach by averting
her eyes from the decorations on the town square and ignoring the endless gift ads on the television, Christmas was
still coming—an unwelcome and unwanted reminder of
how things used to be. Even her younger brother and sister
hadn't begun their annual campaign of not-so-subtle hints.

Since the winter she'd turned seven, the winter she'd
come to live with the Rogers's, the holiday had held a
sense of rebirth, of life, and love, and second chances.

This year it just held grief.

I'm too young to feel this old.

Caroline stared at the blue-white snow, feeling just a little sorry for herself. She rarely allowed self-pity to get a toehold, but tonight there was no fending it off. According to her life plan—her carefully constructed life plan—at twenty, she should be halfway to her degree in fine arts. If all had gone well, she'd be interning for National Geographic over the holidays instead of sneaking around, freezing her ass off, taking a photograph she had no business taking.

But she'd buried that life plan along with her parents.

Moonlight glistened on the rolling ground between her car and the solid red-brick two-story farmhouse on the hill, casting the swales in gray-purple shadow. The scene was dear to her heart, even though it no longer belonged to her.

"I don't think we should do this," twelve-year-old Macie said, looking out the window with wide, apprehensive eyes.

"Really, Mace! Stop being such a goody-two shoes." Caroline's frustration over her own self-pity, added to the fact that Macie was right, made Caroline uncharacteristically short-tempered.

Macie's chin dropped to her chest. "Sorry."

Shame heated Caroline's face. Macie was a good kid, which had made Caroline's own life immeasurably easier for the past ten months. She knew this to be a concrete fact because their thirteen-year-old brother, Sam, was the polar opposite, constantly tempting the devil himself.

She put a hand on Macie's leg. "No, I'm sorry. I didn't mean to snap."

Macie lifted her chin and gave Caroline a gentle smile.

hat was Macie, gentle and giving and always willing to
ke the blame. She was bound to be trampled on. Caro-
ne wished she could help Macie find a way to curb her
epidation without losing her innate goodness.

A part of Caroline understood Macie's need to please;
eing abandoned by two sets of parents before your
velfth birthday had a way of making a conscientious girl
ok inside herself for reasons for so much misfortune: If
ily I'd been less trouble, or made better grades, or
idn't made Mom worry so. Still, the girl needed to de-
elop some self confidence.

Caroline's conscience chided, Self confidence, not the
ass balls to break the law. And they were breaking the
w. Shiny new, reflective no trespassing signs were
osted along all boundaries of the five-hundred-acre
operty that until recently had been the Rogers Farm.

"But we don't have permission." Macie apparently
asn't ready to take the big plunge into lawlessness—
en to please her big sister.

"It's just a picture, for goodness sake."

"What are you going to do with it, anyway? We have
ns of pictures of the house."

"Not since we had to sell it. It's different now. Just get
t and we'll be back home before you know it."

"We should ask."

"Honestly, Mace!" Caroline threw her car door open,
abbed her camera, and got out. However, she was care-
l to close the door softly. Her last encounter with the
oman who had bought their house and surrounding
rmland hadn't gone at all well. Caroline didn't want
acie to know they'd been virtually forbidden to return
their old home.

True to Ms. Stockton's habit, the lights on the first floor were blazing. For a woman who said she'd bought this land for seclusion, she seemed mighty afraid of the dark.

Macie got out of the car, walked to Caroline's side, and whispered, "She'll see our footprints in the snow."

A wicked little part of Caroline thought, serves her right. Maybe she'll think she's got a reason to be scared of the dark. But she said, "It's supposed to snow again before dawn."

"What if it doesn't?" Panic strangled Macie's whisper.

"It's not like they're going to track us down by our footprints for taking a picture." Caroline just wanted to take the photo and head home to her darkroom. The image had been formed so solidly in her mind that she feared the actual photograph wouldn't capture all of the emotion she'd envisioned.

Macie looked up the long lane, toward the house. After a moment, she said, "Maybe we should make a snowman in the front yard, just so she knows it wasn't a serial killer or something."

Caroline shifted her camera and wrapped an arm around her sister. "You really are a good person. Snowman might take too long. But if it'll make you feel better, we'll tramp out a smiley face in the front yard."

Macie smiled, then fell in step with Caroline as they headed up the lane. They moved in the shadow of the solid line of Norway spruce their father had planted along the west side as a wind break.

When they reached the house, they skirted to the side yard. The six-pane double-sash window that faced them spilled warm golden light onto the snow. From just the right angle, Caroline could see the Christmas tree that

vas centered in the window facing the front porch. She
ositioned herself so the camera lens framed the image
he'd formed in her mind weeks ago. Then she motioned
Macie toward the window.

The girl moved with all of the assurance of a rabbit ap-
roaching an open field.

"Hurry up," Caroline whispered.

Macie shot her a pinched look, but moved marginally
aster. She stopped within an arm's reach of the side of the
ouse, just as she'd been told.

"Put your hand on the glass."

Macie's gaze cut to Caroline. "Fingerprints."

Caroline made a hissing sound and a mental note to
mit the number of hours Macie watched CSI on televi-
ion. "You're wearing gloves."

Slowly, Macie reached for the glass.

The second her palm settled against the lighted pane,
aroline's breath caught in her chest. Perfect. "Raise your
hin a little," she coached.

She focused the camera.

"Hold your breath."

"Why?" Macie started to move.

"Hold still!" Caroline lined up the shot. "I can see your
reath. Now hold it."

As the shutter gave its reassuring click, Caroline's
eart skipped a beat and her entire body hummed with
ectric energy. She knew this was going to be a remark-
le photograph.

What she didn't know was that it was destined to
ange her life forever.

THE EDITOR'S DIARY

Dear Reader,

Love has a funny way of catching up with you . . . even if you're running as fast as you can in the opposite direction. So stop sprinting, kick off those sneakers, and pick up these two irresistible Warner Forever titles.

Romantic Times BOOKclub Magazine raves "Susan Crandall brings a strong new voice to the genre" and they couldn't be more right. Pick up a copy of her latest, IN BLUE FALLS POND, and try not to cry. I double dare you. For nearly two years, Glory Harrison has been trying to outrun the tragedy that drove her from home. But when her ailing Gran needs her, Glory knows she can't run anymore. She must return to Tennessee and face the memories of the fire that took the life of her husband and unborn child. Her one saving grace is fire chief and an old friend Eric Williams. His kindness and strength give her the courage to face her demons . . . and slowly break the walls around her heart down. But there are dark truths lingering in the shadows of Glory's past, truths that threaten her future with this real-life hero who saved her life the night of the fire and every night since. Can their fledgling love survive it?

And Thierry de Bennicoeur from **Michelle Rowen's** BITTEN & SMITTEN knows all about dark truths lingering in the shadows. It's not easy being a six-hundred-year-old vampire with a death wish and a sun-intolerance. And just when he's about to throw himself off a bridge, the most beautiful woman he's ever seen stops him. Well, interrupts him is more like it. Sarah Dearly has had a *really* bad date. She was buried alive . . . before dessert! And her creepy date bit her neck. Not to mention the guys with stakes and the way her date disappeared into dust. Thierry says Sarah is the newest vamp in town and that they have to stay one step ahead of the vampire hunters. But her . . . a vampire? Sure, she's got a hankering for blood lately, but she doesn't feel any different. She's still the same unemployed girl looking for love. But now she's got her heart set on a much older—and much paler—man.

To find out more about Warner Forever, these titles and the authors, visit us at www.warnerforever.com.

With warmest wishes,

Karen Kosztolnyik

Karen Kosztolnyik, Senior Editor

P.S. Next month we're thrilled to kick off a brand new feature called Authors' Corner. We're devoting these two pages to the masterminds behind the books—the authors! All of your favorite Warner Forever authors will be here, chatting about everything from what inspires them to what motivates their characters. So pull up a chair and join us in the Authors' Corner. We'll kick it off with **Marliss Melton** and **Paula Quinn** talking about their latest books **TIME TO RUN** and **LORD OF TEMPTATION**.